L.J. HAYWARD

Why the Devil Stalks Death
Copyright © L.J. Hayward

Cover Art: L.C. Chase, lcchase.com
Editor: One Love Editing, oneloveediting.com
Layout: L.C. Chase, lcchase.com

ISBN: 978-0-9944571-9-6

First Edition
December 2018

Also available in ebook, ISBN: 978-0-9944571-8-9

L.J. HAYWARD

TABLE OF CONTENTS

ONE AFTER

Déjà fucking vu.

Okay. So it wasn't a torture shack, but that didn't mean it was pleasant in comparison. Sure, the intimidation technics were subtler—dull, uniform colour to the walls, floor, ceiling; sparse furniture; no clock; soundproof; temperature on the just-about-uncomfortable side of cool. And the psychological ramifications weren't going to be as traumatic—it was a generic space, not one targeted directly at him—but Jack Reardon wished he wasn't here. Wished harder than he'd wished for anything in his life—including when he'd wished to *not* be in the torture shack—to be back at home, before everything went haywire. Before all the shit happened that had led to here.

Here. A police interview room. Table, two chairs. Cuffs locked to the table. Bland. One size fits all.

Arrested for suspicion of murder.

Jack laughed and it sounded a little scary. Unhinged. He shut up and tried not to think too hard about where he was. How he'd ended up here. Where the others might be. Steph and Adam. Ethan.

Oh God. The expression on his face the last time Jack saw him, standing in the hotel suite doorway—shock, confusion, hurt. Then nothing. Just . . . nothing. And his words. Christ, they were still sawing through Jack's chest, blunt and painful.

The chain between his cuffs rattled, unexpectedly loud and angry in the silent room. Jack startled, realising only after that he'd been tugging on the lock securing him to the table.

"God fuck it," he growled and gave in to his anger for a glorious minute, pulling and twisting against the cuffs.

Who gave a shit if those sanctimonious pricks undoubtedly watching him thought they'd broken him? It just felt good to let the worry and fear show for a moment. Not worry or fear for himself, but for Ethan and what he might do. Was he okay? Where was he now? How much had he seen? Heard? "Enough" was the answer Jack feared. Enough to send him back to his old ways. Would anyone survive his deadly anger? Would Jack?

He couldn't afford to think along those lines. He had to concentrate on getting out of here and finding out what the fuck was going on. And he wasn't getting out of here if he lost his calm and began abusing the furniture.

Sitting back in the uncomfortable chair, Jack settled his manacled wrists on the table. Closed his eyes. A few deep breaths later and his hands unclenched, fingers spreading over the smooth, cool surface. He worked his way up his arms, consciously releasing the tension from his muscles. Up into his shoulders, feeling the strain ease, the weight of worry and fear fade. Then down his spine, loosening his core so he slumped a little. Thighs spreading. Calves tightening, then relaxing. Toes curling inside his shoes, then stretching and finally stilling.

Another deep breath and Jack went *sideways*.

There had been occasions—usually troubling, panicking ones— when he'd managed a trance state with no preparation to access the implant. This wasn't one of those. The cops were giving him plenty of time to think and worry and work himself into a mindset where he'd be more likely to say something he didn't want to reveal. Time alone, in a featureless room, to wear down his patience and give the illusion of being confined for longer than actuality.

He had wished for some time alone, but for fuck's sake, not like this.

The overlay from his neural implant appeared before his inner eyes. A remnant from his days in the SAS, the technology—equivalent to a smartphone grafted onto his right temporal lobe—was highly classified. No one in domestic law enforcement knew about it. They wouldn't know to block it. His dummy phone, part of his cover, had been taken off him, so they believed him isolated. Yet, he was wary of calling anyone. What if they did know? What if they were monitoring any signals coming from the room?

Rather than make the one call he was desperate to, Jack collated all the data they'd discovered on the Judge into a single file and, after a long hesitation, added Ethan's vague offering as well.

Recalling the assassin's words sparked off that burning anger again.

How could Ethan have done it? Kept it to himself while Jack worked at the deadly puzzle and, ignoring protocol, used Ethan as a sounding board? He'd listened to all of Jack's frustrations and hadn't said anything, not until . . .

Forcing aside that memory, Jack ensured the pertinent information was in the file. He'd worry about it after he was out of here and the Judge neutralised. After Jack's secrets were exposed.

Peripherally, he heard the door opening and footsteps entering the room.

Swiftly, he slid *sideways* again and opened his eyes. "You wanted something, Detective Connors?"

The man leading the team investigating the Judge had come personally to Jack's home to arrest him. He'd cited "suspicion of murder," but Jack wondered if that was just an excuse to get him here. Jack hadn't killed anyone. Lately.

Connors was dressed in police detective *de rigueur*—basic suit, black leather shoes, white button-down, unimaginative tie. Not especially tall, rather compact, but powerfully built. He didn't bother hiding his feelings—anger, grief, grim determination.

It began to make sense. Suspicion of murder. The fact Jack hadn't seen either of the Strike Force Infinity members since being brought in. One look from Connors undid all of Jack's relaxation and twisted his gut into a tight, painful knot.

Honesty, more so than any number of lies, was a sharp weapon.

"What's happened?" Jack asked.

More silence from Connors, and then he reached into a pocket and pulled out a phone. He flicked through a couple of pages, settled on one, read for a moment, and then came to the table, gaze never leaving the screen.

"Lieutenant Jack Reardon." His voice was low and rough, like he'd smoked a pack a day for the past twenty years.

"Mister, not lieutenant. I was discharged eight years ago. What's happened, Detective Connors?"

Connors sat, still perusing whatever information he had on his phone, probably a file detailing Jack's life. What they knew of it, at least.

"SAS." A hint of approval in his tone. "Tough unit to get into."

"Tougher to survive. Care to tell me why I'm here, detective?"

He glanced up then, eyes still showing all of those dark emotions directed at Jack. "Medical discharge."

Two small words that cut into Jack like a shard of ice. Eight years on and he was still tender about the whole situation. Sure, when he'd been discharged, he'd been injured and suffering PTSD. But that hadn't been why they got rid of him.

There was no way in hell Connors knew that, though, so the man was fishing. Jack knew the game. Now he knew it was being played, he also suspected the transparency of Connors's expression when he walked in. It had been a mask, one aimed to inspire something in Jack he could use.

"Yeah," he said, tone neutral.

"And now you're a . . ." Connors consulted his phone again. "A security guard with the International Security Office."

Oh, yeah, they were playing a game. Connors hadn't actually asked a question and yet Jack was answering them. The detective knew full well Jack was a specialist security advisor, not just a grunt. He was baiting Jack with little bits of misinformation, prompting him to correct them, generating a precedent for Jack telling Connors things he wanted to know.

Two could play that game.

"Specialist security advisor," Jack said, setting up his own precedent.

"Sorry. Yes, it specifies that on the next page. ISO. That's in Canberra, yet you live in Sydney."

"That's right." Time to give a little more than prompted, show Connors his game was working. "It's a mobile job. I work out of an office here, mostly."

Connors nodded thoughtfully. "ISO would keep you busy."

"Busy enough."

"Get to travel a lot."

Where the fuck was this going? "Fair bit."

Connors looked up at him for more than a moment, and one mask fell away, only to be replaced with another one. He smiled. "Always wanted to go to Bangkok, myself. I hear it's quite beautiful."

Oh. Fuck.

"That's what I've heard, too." *Please, don't let the cops know about Bangkok.*

"You've never been?"

The first question and it was barbed six ways to Sunday. Even before the phone was turned around and pushed towards him, Jack knew what he would see.

"Then someone who looks awfully like you, Mr. Reardon, was in Bangkok a month ago. Recognise him at all?"

Shit fuck damn.

Sure enough, that was a picture of Jack in Bangkok, trotting down the stairs at their hotel, adjusting the jacket of his dinner suit. He was scowling, black brows pinching together, the ambient light of the building behind him making his Indian-Caucasian skin into something like polished copper. Nothing about the picture pinpointed Bangkok.

Then Connors swiped to the next picture.

A wider shot, getting in the name of the hotel—Millennium Hilton Bangkok.

At least he was on his own in the picture.

"That's me," Jack admitted. Goddamn, this was going south rapidly.

"Really? Did you just say you hadn't been to Bangkok?"

"Actually, I didn't. All I said was I'd heard people say it was beautiful." Jack shrugged. "It is, if you like the heat and ignore the pollution and political instability. Bloody lovely in that case."

"Obviously you didn't enjoy your stay." Connors pulled the phone back and flipped through a couple more screens.

Thankful they hadn't seemed to get a shot of his companion, Jack smirked. "Had worse trips. Had better ones, as well."

Connors settled on a new page and frowned at it. "You see, what confuses me is that there was no ISO operation in Bangkok on the dates you were there, Mr. Reardon."

He didn't give Jack time to answer the non-question this time, just going directly for the killing thrust.

"And your . . . *companion* for the evening. Not an ISO employee as far as we can ascertain."

Detective Connors shoved the screen back at Jack. It displayed a new picture—Jack on the street outside the hotel, still scowling, this time directly at the man next to him, who looked pretty damn fine in his own dinner suit. Connors flicked through a series of photos of them on the steps of the hotel, then in a taxi. Jack's expression in the photos went between a scowl and forced neutrality and back again. His companion was always smiling, mostly at Jack's uncomfortableness, his glee teasing and annoying.

The last shot, of them at their destination, reversed their expressions—Jack snickering, the other man grumbling. Over their head was a recognisable sign, and a slender, smiling Thai man beckoned them into a shadowed entrance.

"So, Mr. Reardon, why were you in Bangkok? Business? Or pleasure?"

Jesus fucking shit.

TWO
BEFORE

"**A**h, Bangkok," Lewis Thomas said, throwing his arms wide as he sang the opening lines to "One Night in Bangkok."

"No!" Jack snapped. "I've warned you how many times?"

Unrepentant, Lewis grinned and fixed the drape of his suit jacket. "Come on. It's Bangkok! How can you resist?"

Jack scowled. "Very easily. Anyone would think you'd never been outside of Australia before."

Before Lewis could respond, their taxi arrived outside the Millennium Hilton. Giving his friend and colleague a warning glare, Jack stalked over and got into the back seat. Lewis followed him, making lip-zipping motions that would have worked better to soothe Jack's grumbles if the man hadn't been smirking at the same time.

Thankfully, Lewis made good on his promise and shut up while the taxi pulled out and, discreetly informed by the concierge, headed for their destination.

At first blush, Bangkok was much like any other capital city. Roads teeming with traffic and bordered by tall buildings of steel and glass. But then suddenly there would be a temple or an old villa, ancient stone and gold and peaked roofs. Or an ultramodern, climate-controlled megamall, and one street over, a bustling, vibrant street market with more history than Jack's whole family. On the Chao Phraya River, there were wooden longtail boats alongside sleek motorboats.

As fascinating as the contrasts were, Jack was over it. They'd been in Bangkok for three weeks, about two weeks longer than even the most excited tourist. Three weeks of *not* taking in the sights in a river cruise, or taste testing his way through every street-side food cart, or gaping in awe at the lavish temples. Instead, he'd been swimming through the seedy, dark underside that could be found in any city around the world.

He was ready to go home, and hopefully, after tonight, that would be possible. Job done, subject secured, he could go home and . . . what? Hope like hell Ethan had shown up? It had been nearly four months since they'd last been together in Vietnam, after the fiasco in Canberra. Granted, Jack had been away from home for the last three weeks, but Ethan had proven proficient at tracking Jack down if he wasn't in Sydney when Ethan wanted him. What if he'd run into trouble getting into Australia? What if he was hurt?

What if he'd changed his mind?

Jack shrugged off the thought and concentrated on the here and now. If everything went to plan, he'd have something to smile about. Maybe.

Lewis gazed out the window at the rolling scenery, unconsciously fidgeting in his suit. Unprepared for this turn of events, they'd had the suits tailored that morning and, unable to stand still long enough for the snappy Thai woman to take exact measurements, Lewis's dark blue, slim-fitting suit wasn't quite as *roomy* in certain areas as it should be.

"I still don't understand why you need me for this part," Lewis muttered. "I'm not a field asset."

How about that? Jack had something to smile at already. "And yet, you are entirely . . . *suitable* for this bit."

Lewis eyed him suspiciously. "Is that a jab at the *suit*?"

"Of course not." Jack kept a completely straight face.

"This is payback for the costume in Melbourne, isn't it?"

With a wounded gasp and hand pressed to his chest, Jack said, "As if I would."

"Right." Lewis shifted again, tugging at the tight crotch of his suit pants. After a moment, he began singing *that* song again—until Jack jabbed him in the ribs. "Hey, watch the suit!"

"Then don't sing that song."

"You know, you'd be much nicer to work with if you just stopped screwing your face up all the time."

"I'm not screwing my face up." Jack scowled, then forced his expression to smooth out.

"Hah. You've been frowning almost constantly for the past couple of months."

"Have not."

"Seriously," Lewis harped on. "Is something wrong? You've been snapping like a dingo with rabies lately. I mean, you nearly reduced Claudia to tears last month."

Jack grimaced. He and Claudia Sterne had sat back-to-back at work for five years and still could barely manage a civil conversation. But then, Claudia didn't like *anyone*. She was abrasive and condescending and a snob. No one had managed to dint her hoity armour in all the time Jack had known her. Who would have guessed reminding her to lube up her broom before she rode it home would have done the trick? The entirely provoked comment had earned Jack another round of lectures from the human resources counsellor.

"Did your boyfriend leave you?"

Jack didn't get a chance to wallop Lewis because they'd arrived.

Silom was one of the more popular nightlife areas of Bangkok, and there were several strips of brightly lit, extravagant go-go bars bustling with locals and tourists wishing to partake in one of Bangkok's more infamous treats. However, the street they'd stopped on was quieter, darker, less blatant about what it was offering.

The taxi driver told Jack the fare in well-practiced English, and Jack pulled the notes from his clip, handing them over with a much less graceful thanks in Thai. Lewis climbed out of the car and tried to shift his goods into a more comfortable position. His efforts, however, broke off when he got a look at the sign hanging over the door of the building in front of him.

"This is where you're taking me?" he demanded as Jack joined him.

A doorman stood in an alcove, deep enough he was only a vague, darker shape in the shadows. Similarly, the building's façade was nondescript brick and tinted windows. The only mark of the business inside was a wrought-iron circle hanging over the door. A single, short arrow came off the circle, pointing slightly east of the circle's north.

The symbol of Mars—the god, not the planet—or more commonly, male.

Jack couldn't help the nasty grin he shot over his shoulder. "This is what you get for singing that damn song all the time."

"No, this is what I get for letting you talk me into shit like this."

Noting their interest, the doorman sidled forwards. He asked something in Thai, eyeing them both up and down.

"Don't speak much Thai, but I do have these." Jack produced two poker chips, both showing the same symbol as the club.

With a knowing smile, they were ushered to the door, which opened promptly at the doorman's knock, and Jack and Lewis went in.

The entrance was outfitted like an old gentlemen's club, with thick rugs and several sets of leather chairs next to small tables displaying newspapers from around the world. The walls were polished panels of oak on the lower half, lushly stylised brown wallpaper above, dotted with oils of landscapes, and portraits of old men Jack had no hope of recognising. There was a fireplace, merrily burning within its black marble mantelpiece, brass urns, silver snuff pots and small figurines of stalking tigers arrayed across it. Soft lighting heightened the sense of exclusivity.

Lewis leaned in close. "Posh den of iniquity."

Jack shushed him with a hard stare.

From behind a screen, the host appeared. He was an older man, thin and distinguished in his expensive tuxedo, streaks of grey running through his black hair. With a keen eye he took in their dinner suits, stance, and expressions. Coming to the correct conclusion, he faced Jack.

"Sir, it is a pleasure to have you with us tonight," he said in accented but perfect English. "How may we serve you?"

Jack revealed the two poker chips again. "I was told this is a place a man can relax and find some entertainment."

Smoothly, the host took the chips and they vanished into his tux. "Indeed it is. What would you and your associate be interested in?"

Hearing Lewis shift uncomfortably, Jack decided against making him suffer too much. The unit leader was here against his wishes, giving in to Jack's insistence he couldn't do this part alone. Besides, he didn't want to risk the hard work of the past three weeks just because watching straight-as-a-plumbline Lewis Thomas try to seduce a male prostitute would make a hilarious story back at the Office.

"Nothing too specific," Jack said. "Just a bit of a taste of what's on offer."

The host glanced at Lewis, then nodded. Lewis huffed but didn't object.

"Thirty thousand, each," the host said politely.

Jack took the baht notes from the clip and held them up. "And if we like what we see?"

Another knowing nod. The host flashed a couple of black cards, the club logo embossed on their surface. "Fifty thousand. Each."

Feeling Lewis's disapproving glare on the back of his neck, Jack counted out more notes. He exchanged the lot for the two cards.

"A moment, please, gentlemen." The host disappeared behind the screen again.

"Really?" Lewis muttered as Jack held out one of the cards. "He already pegged me as not interested."

"No. He pegged you as curious. Come on, you don't have to use it."

Lewis snatched up the card and shoved it in a pocket. "This is the last time I let you organise anything."

A moment turned into several, then five minutes, and Lewis started pacing.

"Stop it," Jack murmured.

Lewis stopped but started fidgeting. "I just want this finished. We've been here too long as it is."

He wasn't talking about the awkwardness of waiting to be sent into a high-end gay brothel. Their original job had been to find out if the intelligence coming out of Bangkok about one of their highest-priority subjects was valid. As part of the secret Meta-State Agreement, Thailand operations were under the purview of Internal Threat Assessment. Normally, it would have been handled by the Singapore branch, but since their teams hadn't been making much headway, they'd asked Sydney for help. Jack's South Asian heritage had seemed to do the trick. He wasn't Southeast Asian or Caucasian, so the locals weren't quite so wary of him. As a result, what had started as a weeklong op turned into a full-on hunt for Theta Subject. Three weeks hunting their subject through underground gambling dens, some of the less savoury brothels and high-stakes poker games where the buy-in was ludicrous but getting out with all your blood was the real prize.

It wasn't all thanks to Jack's skills, though.

In the eleven months since Director Harraway had been exposed as a traitor, arrested, and packaged off for a lifetime sentence in an ultrasecure prison, the Office of Counterterrorism and Intelligence had felt the change. With the flow of intelligence no longer strangled by Harraway, both Internal and External Threat Assessment investigations had exploded with forward momentum. The Office had a vitality it hadn't experienced for years.

All thanks to the assassin Ethan Blade. Or more precisely, the mysterious person who'd contracted Ethan Blade to take out the organised-crime-boss and terrorist-wannabe Samuel Valadian—thereby exposing Jack's long-term undercover operation and thrusting him into an uneasy alliance with the assassin—and ultimately, revealing Harraway as a traitor. It hadn't helped that Ethan had been exactly Jack's type—lithe, lean, beautifully sculpted out of muscle and taut flesh, possessed of an occasionally wicked humour, and incisive intelligence.

"So?" Lewis drew Jack back to the present. "Did he?"

Jack played dumb. "Did who what?"

"Did your boyfriend leave you?"

"I don't have a boyfriend to be left by." He could feel the scowl approaching and tried to stop it, but his brows prickled in angry frustration.

The rote "I don't have a boyfriend" answer was more of a lie and less of a cover, now. He and Ethan had finally talked about it and agreed they were committed. Ethan had said he would move in with Jack, albeit four months ago—and he hadn't communicated since. So did Jack have a boyfriend or not? Ethan had definitely said "see you soon" when they parted, but apparently they had very different definitions of "soon."

"Well, something definitely changed," Lewis continued, showing a remarkable lack of self-preservation. "For a while there, after the Harraway thing, you were, and I hesitate to use this word in conjunction with you, *happy*. But now? Sheesh. Claudia was the worst, but not the only casualty. I figured you were getting it regular, then it stopped. Was I right?"

Yes. "No. I don't have a boyfriend, then or now. Nothing's changed."

Lewis eyed him with a shrewd expression but dropped the topic. Jack couldn't help but feel there might be a "for now" clause on the look, but he was willing to let it go, too. Right now, they had a job to finish.

The host reappeared and Jack and Lewis were shown into the inner sanctum.

THREE / **AFTER**

"**W**ell?" Connors asked after a short silence.

Jack sat back in his chair, restraints clinking. "Pleasure, obviously."

"Obviously. I *hear* it's a nice establishment."

"Decent. Had a bit of fun. Left. Nothing that memorable."

"A bit of fun," Connors mused. "Wasn't there a disturbance while you were there?"

Jack cocked an eyebrow. "Something with another patron. My friend didn't like the commotion, so we left pretty quick." This was getting ridiculous. Time to move things along. "What's this got to do with anything? Why do you have pictures of me on holiday in Bangkok?"

Flicking away the photos of Jack and Lewis, Connors matched his expression. "Oh, don't worry, we haven't been spying on you. That's not what the New South Wales police does."

Intentional jab? There had been rumours for years that the ISO was a cover for a covert organisation of spies. The fact it was true didn't mean Jack had to let Connors know he was on the right track. "Then how did you get those photos?"

"A mere curiosity. They popped up while I was looking into your involvement with the strike force. I wouldn't have bothered you with them except for the fact I've worked with Lewis Thomas in the past, when he was with ASIO. He left, um, about eight years ago now. Works as an investigator with some financial group, I think. The thing is, back then, Thomas would never have gone to a gay brothel."

"Nothing wrong with being a bit curious." Lewis wouldn't enjoy Jack using him like that, but that was a fight they could have when Jack wasn't under arrest, everyone was safe, and the Judge taken care of.

Connors agreed with a nod. "Is that how you met him? Picked him up in a bar?"

Another exploratory question, or just coincidence?

"We met on a job. One of his clients did some work for the ISO in PNG. It was a contested area, so we put a security team on them. Look, we both know this has nothing to do with Lewis or Bangkok. It's something about the Judge, or Infinity. Just tell me so we can get this sorted and I can get out of here and back to work."

His speech had zero visible impact on Connors. The man was good, or he didn't really care. He just looked at his screen again, flicked, then looked up. "Somewhere to be, Mr. Reardon?"

Jack barely suppressed the eye roll. "It's the Judge, isn't it? He's struck again."

Connors's gaze flinched.

If Jack hadn't been staring him down, he would have missed the flash of that grief and anger from the start of their meeting. Oh fuck.

The strike force. Infinity. Their tiny little team. None of them here now. It made a cold, horrible sense all of a sudden.

"Who was it?" Jack asked, ice coating his guts. Ethan would pay for this. Fucking pay.

The detective pulled on a new mask, one of pure wrath. "You tell me." Connors's eyes were crosshairs, and Jack was caught.

Before either of them could react, the door buzzed open and another cop came in. A woman, older than Connors, petite, dark-haired and brown-eyed, in a grey pantsuit. Her expression was fixed.

"Connors, we need to talk."

Connors held Jack's gaze for a burning second longer, then picked up his phone, stood, and walked out. The woman gave Jack a quick, hard look, then left as well, closing the door behind her.

"Fuck." Jack tugged furiously on his restraints.

No fucking way was he going to let them make that accusation. The cops thought he was the Judge. The Goddamn fucking psycho Judge.

Oh Christ. Jack leaned over his knees as far as he could, trying to take some deep breaths, to calm down.

Someone from Infinity was dead. Who? There were only two candidates. Stephanie or Adam.

No matter who it was, there was one thought flitting at the edges of Jack's mind. A thought he knew he'd have to think sooner rather than later, but one he really didn't want to. With a sigh, he gave up the fight and let it come.

Ethan.

There was a vague outside chance it hadn't been the Judge. That it had been Ethan.

That last look he'd given Jack—hurt, swiftly and completely morphing into dead-eyed nothing. A blank canvas, capable and willing to become anything required to get the job done. Whether that job was exposing a Meta-State traitor, killing a presidential candidate in South America, seducing Jack across a hostile desert, or hiding knowledge of a psychotic killer, the job always came first.

Except when Ethan claimed Jack came first.

It wasn't a comforting thought right then.

Jack glanced around the interview room again, looking for an escape route. That, or how to ensure a cold-blooded assassin hell-bent on personal vengeance didn't get *in*.

It didn't matter, though. Here or somewhere else, if Ethan wanted Jack, he would get him. The perils of falling into the sights of one of the most successful assassins in the world.

They left him alone with these terrible thoughts for a couple of hours. Jack went through the entire grief process in that time.

Denial. It was all a lie. No one was dead. Connors was just fucking with him.

Anger. Goddamn the fucking Judge. This was all his fault. Jack would kill him. Hunt him down and strangle the fucked-up life out of him. And fuck Ethan, too. He'd lied through his bloody teeth. Jack had *trusted* him.

Bargaining. If it was the Judge, he'd gone too far this time. Made a big enough mistake he'd be caught. If they got him, then anything else would be okay. If they got that sick fuck off the streets, Jack didn't care what else happened. Please, God, whatever happened to him, just let them catch the Judge.

Depression. Nothing was going to happen while Jack was locked up. He was stuck here, and as long they thought he was the killer, then they weren't hunting down the true guilty party. What if it was Ethan?

What if they caught him? What if Jack was released just to watch Ethan be locked away? Christ, when did it all get so messed up? Why couldn't they just go back to how it had been? Ethan's surprise visits. Nights of wild sex and firm denials of feeling anything other than lust for this strange, enticing man. Back before the moment Jack knew it was something intense and no longer deniable.

Acceptance. Jack was here. He wasn't getting out until they were satisfied he wasn't the killer, or until the Office came for him. No matter his personal crises, the Office wouldn't leave one of their assets high and dry. Whoever may have died wouldn't go unavenged, not when the Office decided to move. And Ethan . . . well, Jack would fight, either against Ethan or for him, no matter what, and there was peace in accepting that as well.

The door opened just as Jack was starting to calm down again. Connors stepped in, this time with the woman.

"Mr. Reardon, sorry to keep you waiting," Connors said, smoothly back in control. "This is Superintendent Dumay."

Dumay nodded to him. "Nice to meet you, Mr. Reardon."

Jack matched her nod. She'd been overseeing the strike force. While Jack had neither seen nor spoken to her, he'd witnessed enough aftermaths of Stephanie's reports to Dumay to be wary of her.

"Some new information has come to light, Mr. Reardon," she said, taking the lead. "And it's suitably distressing enough to make me willing to do anything to cut to the chase."

Connors leaned back against the wall, the very personification of couldn't-give-a-shit, which only made Dumay's statement that much more chilling.

"What information?"

Dumay's dark eyes regarded him for a long, assessing moment. She reminded him of his director, Donna McIntosh. McIntosh was this woman's physical opposite—tall, blonde, and blue-eyed—but underneath the superficial coating, both were tough and uncompromising. McIntosh's eyes could go Arctic cold in an instant, and Jack didn't doubt that Dumay's could go burning hot just as quick.

"Are you aware of the John Smith List?"

Jack's hard-won calm wavered. "Yes."

The John Smith List ranked every known assassin and was updated by all intelligence and security agencies in the world as new information came to light. Above thirteen were the small operators, two or three confirmed kills, nothing too flashy or risky. Below five were the heavy hitters, the sensation-makers, daring and dangerous. Between those two groups were the solid middle, the hardworking assassins quietly going about their jobs with ruthless efficiency and little to no fuss.

If he wasn't highly sensitive to it through his work with the Office, his cover as an SSA with the ISO required a working knowledge of the list. On a personal note, it helped to understand what it meant when the man he was fucking was number seven on that list. Though, after getting to know Ethan and how he operated, Jack suspected if anyone ever discovered just how many jobs he'd really pulled off, five, even four, would be a conservative estimate of his true rank. Seven, Jack had long since decided, was just another layer of protection. Not too high to risk the notice of one through four, but not so low he looked like easy pickings to those coming up behind.

And they were back to Ethan. Was he why Dumay brought up the JSL?

Dumay nodded approvingly. "So you would have heard the name Eve Garrote before?"

Jack gaped. Not Ethan, then. On one hand, good. On the other, what fresh hell was this? Jack struggled to remember the latest rankings.

Taking pity on him, Dumay said, "She's currently sitting at five."

On the brink of becoming one of the big ones. If she was ambitious enough, she'd probably be after the next big target, to give her a boost into the very top levels. No one on the strike force would do that for her, so she was an unlikely option for the killer.

"What's she have to do with all this?" The lack of information was beginning to morph back into anger.

"Tell us something first, Mr. Reardon. You weren't in Bangkok for pleasure, were you. You were on a job."

With the introduction of a new, heretofore unsuspected player, Jack was officially out of his depth. Too much shit he didn't know, too many hostiles in his territory. It was time to get out of here.

There was no way the Office didn't know where he was or what the cops had accused him of. They should have been here by now. Still, he decided to give them a little nudge.

"I'd like to call my supervisor, Officer in Charge John Axworthy. He's at the ISO HQ in Canberra."

"I'm well aware of the ISO's location," Dumay said. "Mr. Axworthy has been contacted and has yet to get back to us to either confirm or deny whether you were working for the ISO in Bangkok. It would really help us, and yourself, if you were just honest with us, Mr. Reardon. What were you doing in Bangkok?"

His last tether getting thinner and weaker, Jack couldn't help but grin. "You really want to know? It's simple. Fucking with a man."

FOUR

BEFORE

Unlike the entrance, the room they came into was more familiar to Jack's gay club sensibilities. Not that he'd ever bothered with the places much. More often when he was younger and his main criteria for a random pickup was young, hot, and wild.

The room was big, with a bar along one wall, a stage along a second, and a third was mirrored, reflecting back the images of blatant sensuality on display. The stage was currently curtained with thick red velvet, but there were scattered daises with dancers in scanty costumes to suit just about every taste. Cowboys, leather, police, soldiers, right up to corporate suits and bewigged judges, as well as all the way down to dummy-sucking boys in nappies. Tables and chairs were clustered around each dais, occupied by the men who were drawn to whatever fetish was on display.

The music was a pleasant thrum against Jack's senses, not too loud but definitely there as the dancers gyrated in perfect rhythm. The atmosphere was thick with the scent of musk and the oil rubbed into the gleaming, male bodies on display, along with an underlying tang of sweat, alcohol, and overworked cologne. Soft light haloed the dancers but left the rest of the place in a shroud of shadows that gave the illusion of privacy.

"Right," Lewis whispered to Jack, "this is more like it." He watched a leggy young woman sashay past, a tray of drinks balanced on one hand. Masses of black curls framed an exquisitely beautiful face, large, almond-shaped eyes outlined in incredibly long lashes, mouth painted a luscious red. She saw Lewis watching her and winked, throwing an extra swing into her hips, which were barely covered by a French maid outfit, the line of her fishnets precisely set down the back of her toned legs.

Jack smirked at Lewis and indicated a table on the far side of the room. Unlike those around the daises, this table *was* a dance platform, complete with pole in the middle. Entranced by the vision of the waitresses, Lewis didn't protest the choice, sinking into a chair at the table and waving over another of the unbelievably gorgeous girls.

Settling back, Jack eyed the dancer contemplatively. The youth was, at most, twenty and all long limbs and lean torso shown off perfectly by an outfit that was, basically, a leather harness to hang a series of thin chains off and a considerably generous thong of black satin. There was strength in his slender body, lifting him effortlessly off the table to twirl around the pole in tight formation. His legs curled in a suggestive manner as he spiralled down and landed on the table, legs on either side of Jack, back arched. He looked at him with half-lidded, challenging eyes.

Admitting the artfulness of the display, Jack leaned forwards and tucked a baht note into the dancer's harness. With a wink, the dancer spun around and rolled so he ended on his back in front of Lewis, head dangling off the table and all but in the man's lap. He smiled up at Lewis invitingly.

"Jesus," Lewis hissed.

Jack handed over a note. "Just tuck it somewhere safe and he'll leave you alone."

Wincing, Lewis shoved the money under a strap of leather and sat back hastily. The dancer's smile widened, and he blew him a kiss. Then, with a sinuous little wiggle, he was back on his feet, dancing around the pole and dispensing some well-paid-for attention on the couple of other men at the table.

"I swear," Lewis said when they were alone. "Last time you *ever* organise something like this."

Jack shrugged as the waitress came over. "Can I get you gentlemen something?"

"Scotch, straight up." Lewis stared fixedly at her as if he could banish every other man in the room.

"Bourbon," Jack said when she turned to him.

"I won't be long, gentlemen." Then she walked away, with Lewis's gaze glued to her back.

When their drinks arrived, both made a show of sipping the liquor, but neither let more than a discreet trickle pass their lips.

As the dancer sashayed past them with a hip thrust and welcoming smile, Lewis leaned in close. "How long?"

"As long as it takes," Jack murmured back. "Just try to look not so uncomfortable."

"I'm not uncomfortable." Lewis sounded about as convincing as Jack had when claiming there was no boyfriend.

"For what it's worth, I didn't *pick* it. Is it my fault Theta Subject likes these sorts of places?"

Lewis grumbled but let it go.

Their dancer was tireless, slinking and spinning for their entertainment, always with a smile and wink for the men ogling him. By the time Jack caught sight of Theta Subject entering the club, he'd tucked a thousand baht into the young man's outfit while Lewis silently objected to each tip.

With a small nod, Jack indicated their prey to Lewis. Between them, they kept an eye on Theta Subject as he made his way across the room and to a table like their own. He immediately tucked money into the thong of the dancer and sat down, waving for a drink without having to tell the waitress what he wanted. Clearly a popular regular, Theta Subject became the object of the dancer's attention. The young man in a barely there police uniform all but ignored the other patrons at his table and gyrated for Theta Subject alone. A drink was delivered with a lingering caress along the man's shoulders from the waitress.

It had to be the tips, Jack reasoned as he watched Theta Subject absorb all the attention from the staff on that side of the room. There wasn't a lot else to recommend him, on the surface at least. Middle-aged, portly around the middle, stick thin legs, balding, sweaty-pale. It was conceivable he had a winning personality, but considering who he was and what he'd done to get on the Office's hit list, Jack doubted it.

"Got to be the money, right?" Lewis whispered, mimicking Jack's thoughts.

Jack snorted and feigned another sip of bourbon.

Theta Subject held out longer than Jack guessed he would, downing three drinks before producing one of the black cards. It was scarcely clear of his pocket before the dancer was off the table and hauling Theta Subject towards the back of the room. There, a bouncer took the card and opened a door for them. The amorous couple disappeared through it post-haste.

"Now?" Lewis asked.

Jack shook his head. "Give the man some time."

Lewis groused but kept his mouth shut. Jack waited nearly ten minutes, then, catching the eye of their dancer, produced his own card.

Eyes lighting up, the dancer slid off the table and right into Jack's lap. He kept dancing, rocking on Jack in time to the music. If Jack hadn't been working, it probably would have been enticing. As it was, Jack gently pushed the young man to his feet, standing as well.

"Won't be long," he said to Lewis with a leer.

The dancer, snuggling into Jack's side with a determined wiggle, pouted. "I'll treat you good, sir."

"Or maybe longer." Jack winked as he turned away. "Behave yourself."

As with Theta Subject, the bouncer took Jack's black card and let them through. Beyond the door was a spiral staircase, which the dancer dragged him up rapidly. On the next floor they emerged into a long, dimly lit corridor. There were doors along it, each marked with a Thai word and a small sliding panel.

Jack's dancer directed him to a room halfway along, pulling him in and closing the door behind them.

"Can we lock the door?" Jack asked as the dancer wound his strong arms around his neck and rubbed against him.

"No need, sir. My room. No one else will come in."

Feigning annoyance, Jack shoved the youth away. "Fine. I don't like being interrupted, though."

"Oh no, sir, no one will come but us." He plastered himself on Jack once more. Head tilting, he aimed for a kiss.

Jack got a hand over the boy's mouth before it could connect with any part of his skin. "No kissing."

Under his fingers, the dancer pouted.

Putting space between them, Jack looked him over and gave a satisfied nod. "Get undressed."

Disappointment seemingly forgotten, the boy began a sexy striptease, which would have been better served by starting with more clothing.

Jack surveyed the room. It had just enough space for the decently sized bed, a dancing pole in one corner, and a shelf holding an impressive collection of toys. The boy used the available space well, and Jack pretended interest in the show, leaning back against the door. One eye on the dancer, he listened to traffic in the corridor. In the time it took the dancer to divest himself of his harness and thong, there was no traffic in the corridor and no opening or closing doors.

"You like?" The dancer sprawled back on the bed, naked and perfectly on display.

Jack schooled his expression into something appropriate and unbuttoned the front of his dinner jacket. The young man on the bed smiled and wiggled in anticipation.

It was, objectively, an enticing view and yet nothing. It wasn't just that this was work. He was in a four-month dry spell. Any willing, naked male form—within respectable reason—should have held some sort of appeal. However, all he felt right now was a faint frustration that this subterfuge was required at all.

Jacket open, Jack undid his pants, but instead of pushing them down, simply slid a hand in. Retrieving the slender tube from its hiding place, Jack concealed it in his hand as he removed it from his pants. He rubbed that hand up over his belly, in slow circles and approached the bed. The dancer's gaze locked on that motion, lower lip caught between his teeth as he watched Jack caress himself. Jack's other hand went into his hair, raking it out of his eyes and finding a small, plastic cartridge, matt black to match his colouring. He snapped the thin tether of hair tied around it, masking the wince of pain as a moan of pleasure.

"Roll over," he said, and the young man complied without hesitation. "Keep your head down."

Thanking management for instilling obedience in their prostitutes, Jack quickly assembled the mini-injector. The cartridge from his hair slid into the narrow tube and clicked into place. He knelt one knee on the bed next to the dancer and gently coaxed his thighs apart. Obeying, the dancer moaned and gyrated his hips invitingly. Sliding the injector up the inside of his leg, Jack distracted the dancer with a slow caress down his spine. Just as the young man was arching up into the touch, groaning wantonly, Jack jabbed in with the injector.

At the sting of the needle, the dancer gasped and rocked forwards. Jack pressed the plunger fast, leaning on the young man's lower back with his other hand, holding him down.

A startled string of Thai erupted from the dancer as he struggled, but the drug was fast acting. The words faded away into a soft sigh, and his body relaxed under Jack's restraining hold. The placement of the injection would hide it from suspicious minds long enough for Jack to be well away.

Letting the dancer go, Jack fixed his clothes. He removed the spent cartridge from the injector, put it in a pocket, and replaced it with a different one. Ready, he leaned against the door, listening for movement in the corridor. Hearing none, he opened the door and slid out.

Moving swiftly and quietly, Jack checked each door along the corridor. He'd only seen Theta Subject enter this section, but he wasn't the first. Peering through the peep-slots, Jack caught a few sights he'd rather do without before finding the room he wanted.

All he could make out through the slot was a naked, white arse and a pair of slender, brown legs waving about on either side of it. The sounds coming from the pair of them were more than enough to cover Jack's entrance. Placement was not vital on Theta Subject, and Jack shoved the needle into the most prominent exposed body part.

By the time Theta Subject noticed the sting amongst the pleasure, Jack was out of the room and walking away.

Making a show of adjusting himself as he left the private section, Jack nodded to the bouncer and made his way back to Lewis. A new dancer had taken over the table, a nubile young thing in a cowboy get-up who kept tipping his hat at Lewis.

"Have fun?" Lewis asked as Jack sat back down beside him.

"Tolerably."

Lewis snorted. "Then pay this kid. He keeps bugging me."

Jack peeled off several notes and tucked them into a pocket on the dancer's vest.

"How much longer?" Lewis asked quietly as they were left alone.

Checking his watch, Jack said, "Any second—"

FIVE AFTER

Nicely belligerent, sweetly ambiguous, and totally honest, Jack was proud of his answer. Theta Subject certainly was fucked after that. All the symptoms of a major cardiac event, carted away by an ambulance, who took him to a small secluded airfield instead of a hospital.

Theta Subject, known as the Messiah, a digital terrorist with a God complex, was currently cooling his heels in the basement of the Office's Sydney branch.

Dumay eyed Jack steadily. "You aren't helping yourself."

"You're not giving me much reason to." Jack flicked a glance at Connors. His nonchalant pose had tensed, ready to defend his superior. That raging pain was back in his eyes, as well. The longer Jack dissembled, the longer the detective felt his work associate's murderer was on the loose—or at least, not confessing.

Dumay was silent for several minutes, then she tried a different approach.

"Jack, you know something that could help us find the Judge before he can kill again. I've already lost one of my people. If I lose another one because you wouldn't talk, then I won't care who you work for. You will never see the light of day again."

Jack had been threatened quite a few times in his life. Had believed a couple of times that it would actually happen, and Dumay's quiet, deliberate words sent a shiver down his spine. Not because he feared her threat would ever come true, but because she *believed* she would do it if necessary.

Jack could respect her conviction, but that didn't mean he had to give in to it. "I'd like to talk to my supervisor, OIC John—"

"Fuck you!" Connors leaped forwards, fists slamming down on the table. "This isn't some pathetic little game, Reardon. That sick bastard walked right into this building and killed one of ours. It's on record that you circumvented our security. You did it again, didn't you. You got in without anyone knowing, and you went up there and you slaughtered—"

"Connors!" Dumay surged out of her chair and threw her shoulder into the taller man's chest, shoving him bodily backwards. "That's enough. Get out!"

Wild-eyed and trembling violently, Connors kept up his tirade. "It's him, ma'am. I know it is. He fits the profile. He's on record as being discharged from the army because of questionable mental health. He flipped and now he's taking it out on—"

The door slammed open and two uniforms raced in.

"Get him out of here," Dumay ordered as they wrestled the raging man off their senior sergeant. "Calm him down. Send him home with someone to watch him."

With a final, token lunge at Jack, Connors was dragged out of the interview room. Only when the door was closed, leaving him alone with Dumay, did Jack realise he'd knocked his chair over and was standing as tall as he could with his hands shackled to the table.

"I'm sorry about Detective Connors," Dumay said when she'd caught her breath. "He's a very passionate man. The death has upset him terribly."

Jack shook his head. "Then he should never have been in here."

Dumay gave him a direct look. "We would be hard-pressed to find anyone in this building who isn't upset by this turn of events."

"You seem to be doing okay."

"Yes, well. I am older than Connors." She came around the table and straightened his chair.

Once they were both seated again, Jack said, "You think I'm the Judge?"

"We suspected. Connors is right. You do fit the profile. Ex-military. Disgruntled. An expert in circumventing security measures. You have the capability."

"Then why would I help you try to find him? If I was the Judge, why would I reveal my methods like that?"

She shrugged. "Part of the profile described an overabundance of arrogance. Serial murderers have been known to help the police in their investigations. They get a thrill at seeing how close the authorities can get."

Jack snorted. "You sound like Adam." God, if he was dead . . .

"He knew his work."

Past tense. Jack swallowed a sudden burst of fear. Hoping like hell it didn't translate to his voice, he said, "You're the ones who contacted me."

"Hmm, very serendipitous." Dumay gave him an expression that bore only a superficial resemblance to a smile. "However, we have redirected our thoughts regarding the Judge's identity. You fit the profile, but so do a lot of other people."

"No. Something else happened, while I've been here. The Judge made another move. Something I couldn't do from in here." Another killing?

It was Dumay's turn to be reticent. "Tell me about Bangkok, Mr. Reardon. What were you really doing there?"

She left him no other recourse.

"I'd like to talk to my supervisor, please."

The calm façade cracked, just a millimetre, and only for a second, but Jack saw it. Dumay was right. There was no one in this building willing to show Jack any sympathy.

"As I said, we've tried to contact him." Her tone turned grim. "In the meantime, *help us*, Jack."

Someone knocked on the door, saving Jack from another request to talk to Axworthy. Dumay fixed him with a glare, then stood and went to the door. Opening it, she leaned out, listened for a moment, then turned back to Jack.

"We'll take this up where we left off very shortly, Mr. Reardon."

"I'm sure we will." But she was already gone.

And it was back to waiting. To chewing over the small morsels of information he had gathered, finding very little of any substance. The Judge in this building. Adam, probably dead. Ethan was still an unknown quantity. The other largely confusing bit was Eve Garrote. She had to mean something to all of this for Dumay to have mentioned her. Try as he might, Jack couldn't fit her puzzle piece in with the others.

When he began to wonder if Ethan knew her, if they met for drinks at an assassin bar and discussed the killer-for-hire topics of the day, he knew he'd been too long alone with his thoughts.

By his shaky estimation, he'd been in this room for nearly eight hours. Most of the day gone and he knew little more than he had at the start of it. Lucky he'd missed his morning coffee otherwise the pressure in his bladder would be more than it currently was. It also meant he'd been awake for a solid thirty-six hours. He felt the fatigue dragging at his shoulders, hated the ache in his bones. His arse hurt from sitting on the hard chair for so long. The chafing on his wrists had rubbed the top layers of skin away, leaving red marks. He'd broken the time limit on his deodorant about twelve hours ago. His clothes were starting to feel grimy with multiple applications of sweat—angry sweat, exertion sweat, panicked sweat.

When the door opened again, he had his mouth open to demand a visit to the toilet, but it died on his lips when he recognised his next visitor.

"Ma'am." He'd never been so fucking happy to see Donna McIntosh in his entire life.

"Uncuff him," she commanded one of the cops escorting her.

"But—"

"You heard your superintendent," McIntosh said patiently. "Mr. Reardon is being released into my custody. Uncuff him."

Finally, the Office had come for him. He'd never thought McIntosh would come for him personally, though.

Jack was released without any more fuss, and he followed his director out of the interrogation room, his legs tingling after so much inactivity.

Thankfully, their first port of call was a toilet. As Jack dashed in, he heard McIntosh berating the cops for not showing him any common decency. Smiling, Jack unleashed his bladder, feeling more than just physical relief. He was getting out of here. It was only a matter of an hour, tops, before he could get out there and start hunting down Ethan.

"Jack."

Startled, the last piss splattered across the floor as Jack jerked at McIntosh's voice. "Ma'am!"

"Are you blushing?"

Stuffing his dick away, Jack glared at her. "Of course I am. Jesus."

McIntosh waved aside his affront. "It's the closest thing we have to a secure room at the moment. Wash your hands. Leave the tap on."

"Christ." Jack did as he was told. "What the hell is going on out there?"

"The Judge got inside—"

"Here and killed someone," Jack said hastily. "They told me that much, while accusing me of doing it. Who died?"

"We don't know. They've kept the lid on it very tightly. It was one of your strike force members, though."

"Yeah. Got that." He hesitated, then said, "I think it was Adam."

Blue eyes regarded him for a moment, and then she nodded. "We'll keep prying, don't worry."

She knew about him and Adam. He'd suspected the Office did. They always kept a very close watch on their assets when undercover.

"We haven't been able to find either of the Infinity members," she continued, soft so the water covered their conversation. "Whoever wasn't killed has gone missing. Whether they ran or were taken, we don't know."

That answered the question of what had happened to deflect suspicion off Jack, at least. Which was the only positive he could find right then. "Shit. The Judge?"

"Possibly. We're not ruling anything out. And neither are the cops. Everything's been locked down. They're working nothing else right now. I had to call in the minister just to get you out."

Jack gripped the sink for support. There seemed to be so little air right then. "Is that why it took you so long to come for me?"

"Not exactly." McIntosh moved closer, lowered her voice further. "We could have had you out six hours ago, but it was decided here was the safest place for you for the time being."

This place was safe for him? A building the Judge could get into undetected? That Jack could get into undetected?

"What the hell does that mean?"

"Jack, I'm sorry." And she really looked it. It had to be bad. "You've picked up a ticket."

Fuck. He'd been working with the Office for nearly eight years now. Worked several high-profile cases, involving some of the deadliest criminals in the world. He'd foiled at least a half-dozen assassination attempts. Taken out a group of terrorists in Canberra. And never once in that time had he ever picked up a ticket. He'd escaped unscathed.

Until now, apparently.

"What for?" He searched furiously through his catalogue of jobs, looking for where he might have slipped up, to get exposed so they knew who to put the ticket on. He was coming to a conclusion as McIntosh spoke.

"The buyer is unknown, but we can make a guess. It's for the Messiah. His self-stylised Disciples bought the ticket. Most likely."

"Great. Catching him was pure chance. Fuck." Knowing the answer, he needed it confirmed all the same. "Garrote picked it up, didn't she?"

"Half an hour after it was put out." McIntosh smiled icily. "You should be flattered. She's number five."

Jack closed his eyes. "Not exactly a good thing."

"No, I suppose not."

He gave his director a bland look. "Remember when you put me on this op? Remember what you said?"

She nodded. "Best-laid plans, Jack. But I am sorry."

SIX BEFORE

The debrief for the Bangkok job held no surprises. The Messiah, denoted as Theta Subject, had been running rampant across the internet for several years, hacking highly secure systems and releasing very sensitive information to the public. The latest secret to be broadcast, which the Chinese government was still strenuously denying, was that the "tragic and accidental deaths" of forty-seven Burmese during a Chinese military exercise on the border between their countries had in fact been a sanctioned operation. The brutal attack, according to the leaked documents, had been in retaliation for a death sentence handed down on a Chinese national in Myanmar for murdering a representative of the People's Assembly. All of which had been covered up, until the Messiah spilled it across the internet.

Of course, just having the man locked up didn't alleviate the threat of his stolen information being leaked. There were, at last estimation, over a million Disciples across the world, those who followed the Messiah's mad ramblings and defended his acts of terrorism as a protest against government conspiracies. It was entirely likely the information had been spread amongst the Disciples, and if word got out that the Messiah had been caught, the shit wouldn't just hit the ceiling, but explode through it. Making sure the world didn't know the Messiah was in government custody was paramount.

Jack met up with Lewis on the stairs as they were heading home.

"You never answered my question," Lewis said.

"Which question?"

"About the boyfriend. Leaving you."

He should have known Lewis wouldn't let this go. Of course, it might all be moot now. Ethan hadn't left Jack hanging for this long since they'd made plans to hook up regularly.

Still, Lewis was his closest friend and had been for long enough now that if anyone would understand, or at least not turn his back on Jack, it would be him.

Letting out a long breath, Jack gave in. "He's not a boyfriend. Just a . . . regular partner. And I haven't heard from him in four months, so . . ."

They went down a flight in silence before Lewis said, "Shit, man. I'm sorry. I was sort of just joking, you know. You all right?"

"Yeah." His voice was rough. "Sorry for being a bastard lately."

"You don't have to apologise." Lewis skipped down several steps. "To me. Claudia, on the other hand . . ."

Forcing aside thoughts of Ethan, Jack decided it was time for a topic change. "You know Tan's going to make a play for the Messiah."

"Yeah," Lewis said. "But you know what? I'm not sure I want to fight him when he does. I'm happy being covered in glory for just catching the bastard. Someone else can wade through the sleaze for all his secrets."

Before Jack could do anything more than grunt in agreement, Lewis's phone beeped a message and Jack's implant *ping*ed. Exchanging grimaces, they checked their messages and, together, headed back up to the tenth floor to McIntosh's office, where Miller asked them to wait.

"Any clue what it's about?" Jack glared at the closed door between him and answers. "Theta Subject can't have escaped this quickly."

"I don't know," Miller drawled from behind his desk. "Can you account for your whereabouts for the past hour, Reardon?"

"Why don't you ask your mother?" Jack couldn't wait for the next big drama to happen—to someone else—so everyone could stop poking him about breaking Ethan out of a cell.

While Lewis snickered and Miller rolled his eyes, the office door opened and McIntosh looked over the tops of her glasses at them like they were misbehaving twelve-year-olds. Instantly, they all got serious.

"Gentlemen." Their director's tone was dry. "Thank you for being prompt. Miller, start calling up Lewis's team. I'd like everyone ready to go when I'm done with this pair."

Jack barely suppressed a groan. This clearly wasn't a "thanks for catching the bad guy, here, have a week off" chat. Lewis, too, couldn't quite hide a grimace. Though it was looking likely he wouldn't have to worry about Theta Subject for too much longer.

McIntosh waved them into her office, closing the door behind them. "I know you were both heading home, but I'm afraid this can't wait."

As they sat, Lewis asked, "Theta Subject?"

"Being reassigned to an ETA team for now." She raised her eyebrows as she took her seat, waiting for the protests. When she didn't get any, she smiled. "As I thought. Don't worry, I won't let your parts in his capture be forgotten."

Both of them murmured variations of "it was nothing, just our jobs."

"All the same. I realise you've both just come off an intense operation, but this new objective can't be ignored."

"We're at your disposal, ma'am," Jack said dryly.

McIntosh looked at Lewis. "As unit leader, you of course have your choice of any extra assets required for the job. However, I am assigning Jack as the UC operative, no arguments." She gave them a stern look. "From either of you."

Jack internalised a wince. He'd been avoiding undercover roles since the muddle in the desert with Valadian. Fifteen months in deep cover with a paramilitary group had messed with his head in so many ways, it had taken a year to get over it all.

"Don't give me that look, Jack," McIntosh said firmly. "This won't be a long op or a difficult one. It's not even a deep cover. You will, in fact, be going in as yourself."

"As myself?" Jack demanded.

It wasn't as reassuring as McIntosh thought it should be. Undercover usually meant an assumed identity he could hide behind, a barrier against whatever dirty deeds he might have to do to get the job done. In the desert he'd been Jaidev Reed, an Australian-born Indian working as an all-purpose thug for Samuel Valadian. Fifteen months of despicable acts piling up, one on top of the other. Towards the end, even Jaidev hadn't been able to hold it back, and Jack had begun to lose his distance and perspective. He'd started to enjoy Valadian's company. If Ethan hadn't come along to tip it all arse over tit, Jack would have either started to believe in Jaidev's work or gone on a killing spree amongst Valadian's forces.

Shoved into an operation as Jack Reardon wouldn't give him the chance to keep it at bay. Whatever it was he would be asked to do would be right there, sitting against his skin without a cushioning layer of someone else's clothes.

"Yes. Are either of you aware of a serial killer called the Judge?" McIntosh asked.

Both shook their heads.

"I hadn't expected you to be, actually." McIntosh handed a file to Lewis. "Two murders, seven months apart, were identified by the National Homicide Monitoring Program as being indicative of a serial murderer three years ago. Both victims were killed in their homes in Melbourne and displayed in similar poses."

Lewis shared the photos of the scenes with Jack. One was a woman, middle-aged, naked, on a bed, legs out straight and together, arms stretched out to either side, like she'd been crucified. Her body showed multiple stab wounds, though the sheets around her weren't stained with enough blood to be the site of the actual murder. The second was an older man, posed exactly the same, but on a dining table, also not the place he was stabbed repeatedly.

"They were moved post-mortem," Lewis said.

"Yes. Both were killed in the bathroom, most of the physical evidence washed away in the shower. The killer then posed them." McIntosh waved for them to move to the next set of photos. "At both scenes, they found a printed passage from the Bible."

Pictures showed the notes found with each victim. It had been a very long time since Jack had read the Bible, and he didn't recognise either passage. Lewis, too, shook his head in incomprehension.

"I don't see anything here about how they relate to the victims," Jack said.

"We haven't had time to source complete files," McIntosh explained. "This job was only approved two minutes before you walked into my office."

Jack and Lewis raised eyebrows at that. Both of them, Jack especially, remembered how the last hastily organised operation went down. Jack may have found Ethan through it, but it had taken a year of hell to find peace with it all.

Ignoring their silent questions, McIntosh continued. "Two more recent murders have been flagged as part of the same serial. Both here in Sydney. The current consensus is that the killer was picked up on an unrelated charge, and when he got out of prison, he relocated and has been driven to kill again."

Lewis flipped to the newer case photos. One was a young man, early to mid-twenties, slightly overweight, cheeks roughened with pimples and a failed attempt at designer scruff. He was posed on the floor of what appeared to be a computer room. On the edges of the photo, Jack could make out several wide-screens and keyboards.

The fourth victim was another man, perhaps early thirties, very fit and tanned and clean-shaven. He was lying on an unremarkable bed in an unremarkable room.

"Apart from all being Caucasian, there's no apparent link between them," Lewis mused.

"Part of why this case is causing so many problems," McIntosh confirmed.

"So why is it our problem?" Jack asked. "Don't they have a Behavioural Analysis Unit in Melbourne to deal with these things?"

"They do. With the advent of the two new killings, the police and BAU has initiated a new strike force, called Infinity. They're operating out of the Local Area Command in Surry Hills. ADFIS also has an investigation running."

Jack's head snapped up. The Australian Defence Force Investigation Service was the military's special policing unit. "Why is ADFIS looking into this?"

"The last victim is Captain Shane Morrissey of the Intelligence Corps."

Jack whistled. "It's a wonder ADFIS has allowed the BAU to keep their investigation. With a victim in a position like Morrissey's, they normally wouldn't risk a civilian agency getting too close to it."

"Precisely," McIntosh said. "ADFIS has been trying to shut down Infinity, but the police commissioner is standing firm. They claim the first three victims as civilians. Officially, Infinity isn't looking into Captain Morrissey's death." Her "officially" couldn't have been any drier even if it'd been left in the desert for a month.

"Is Morrissey our interest?" Jack took the file from Lewis and began flipping quickly through the admittedly sparse papers. "Are they worried he may have spilled military secrets?"

"I'm certain they are," McIntosh replied. "But he's not our in on this. We have, in roundabout terms, been invited in by the BAU." She slid a new piece of paper across the table, in Jack's direction.

Curiously, Jack picked it up and, with Lewis reading over his shoulder, scanned it.

It was a request from the strike force leader, one Senior Sergeant Stephanie Phelps, for a consultant from the ISO. Specifically, for Specialist Security Advisor Jack Reardon.

"They asked for me specifically."

"Usually, I would have drafted some excuse for why SSA Jack Reardon was unavailable, but this time, I'm intrigued enough to put you in play. You'll go in as yourself, Jack, or at least, as your ISO cover."

"What's my goal for this operation?"

"Exactly as the BAU request states. Advise them in your capacity as a security specialist and, presumably, as a military expert since their requests for a military liaison have been rejected. Find out why these particular victims were chosen." McIntosh smiled grimly. "In other words, Jack, help them find this killer. All the information we have is in the file. I suggest you both get intimately familiar with it ASAP."

Stomach sinking, Jack asked, "Why?"

"You're scheduled to meet with Senior Sergeant Phelps tomorrow morning at the Surry Hills LAC at 9:00 a.m."

Jack gaped at her. "I just got back from Thailand this morning. I've spent the past three weeks scouring the dregs of Bangkok for a self-proclaimed god of sleaze. I have barely washed the slime off, and you want me to go back in tomorrow?"

Levelling her best Arctic look on him, McIntosh said, "Required prep time is minimal. A couple of hours to read the files and make some initial strategies with the team. Just be thankful I didn't say you'd be there at 6:00 a.m." With a request for a preliminary job outline submitted within two hours, she sent them on their way.

On the eighth floor, Lydia had already assembled the team in an operations room. Despite the dearth of solid information, it still took them the entire two hours to have something ready to go. Prelim outline submitted, jobs assigned for the early-morning start, they left the building at eight thirty and headed for the pub.

SEVEN

AFTER

Leaving the bathroom, McIntosh said, "When we get out of here, we'll head straight for the Office."

Jack nodded. Finally, he was going to get started on *really* hunting this bastard down.

The Judge had penetrated the LAC building and killed someone on site. It meant he was not only highly intelligent, as Adam had speculated, or extremely proficient, as Jack had shown, but also that he was very much aware of being tracked, and by whom. His profile outlined a meticulous planner, a need to finely control things to the nth degree and an ability to adapt to any environment. Knowing Ethan as well as he did only emphasised those points for Jack. Which is why he knew, without a doubt, that the Judge wouldn't only know all about Steph and Adam, but about Jack as well. He would know that Jack would be after him physically now, not just following a paper trail. That should make the Judge keep looking over his shoulder.

Their police escort led Jack and McIntosh through the narrow corridors of the building. The director's heels clicked on the hard floor in an imperial manner, making police and support staff jump out of their way as they headed for a lift. Just as they reached it, the doors swished open and Dumay stepped out.

"I know I have to abide by the commissioner's decision, Ms. McIntosh," Dumay said, tone cool, "but perhaps I could appeal to *your* sensibilities. Mr. Reardon is our best lead on finding the Judge. If you take him out of here, you're leaving us blind and deaf."

McIntosh didn't exactly look down her nose at the senior detective, but it was hard not to when she had several inches of height on the other woman. "I perfectly understand, Julia. However, the fact remains, you've had over two months to find this killer, and you're still grasping at straws. I think it's our turn to have a go."

Dumay, as Jack suspected, went red-hot. Coals flared in her eyes as her shoulders went back and her chin came up. "What, precisely, does the ISO think it can do in this situation, *Donna*? You're just a security detail. You have no jurisdiction on this."

"If you'd care to read the commissioner's orders again, you'll find that Minister Simmons has granted the ISO provisional authority to pursue this case. When one of our own is *wrongly* accused of being a serial murderer, then we have every right to correct that." Then she swept past Dumay and into the lift.

Resisting the urge to fist-pump in victory, Jack followed his director.

McIntosh turned to face the other woman, and while her tone hadn't warmed any, she did offer a small gracious smile. "Thank you for your cooperation, Julia. I'll be sure to make note of it in my next chat with Minister Simmons and the police commissioner."

Before Dumay could get out a response, the doors swished shut. Jack let out an explosive breath.

"Don't relax, Jack," McIntosh murmured as they descended. "We're not out of here yet. Don't forget about Garrote."

"Yes, ma'am." Jack repressed a shiver at the reminder of his life marked with a dollar sign.

McIntosh gave his arm a sympathetic pat. "We're watching for Garrote, don't worry."

"She's number five. We won't see her coming."

"We won't need to. You'll stay at home base until the ticket is cleared and the Judge dealt with."

Jack gave a few grumbly protests because it was expected. Building confinement was nothing new, and when Jack decided he needed to leave, he would. McIntosh knew it as well, but the motions had to be made.

When Jack had worked here, he'd parked in the visitor carpark, above ground. Instead of stopping on ground level, the lift kept going down to the garage under the building. The cavernous space was well lit and populated by patrol cars and unmarked vehicles. Probably by McIntosh's design, there were currently no people.

"This way." She guided Jack across the garage, her heels suddenly silent on the cement.

"The cops know about the ticket," Jack told her as they went. "Dumay dropped Garrote's name while trying to get me to talk about Bangkok."

Mentioning the city got the expected reaction. McIntosh's eyes went so frosty Jack's balls actually retreated into his body.

"What do they know about Bangkok?"

"Nothing much. Just that Lewis and I were there. They had photos. CCTV images, by the look of them. Lewis got made as well. Detective Connors knew him from ASIO."

"This is not good. We'll have to get straight on to containment. And External Monitoring has some explaining to do."

Jack felt a surge of pity for the poor techs down on the fourth floor. External Monitoring, part of Intelligence, were responsible for covering the activities of the Office assets and spinning anything they couldn't make disappear. Which included making sure any images of assets that appeared on the internet were dealt with speedily to keep covers intact and jobs a secret.

"Leave Ex Mon to me," McIntosh said, her voice warming a bit. "And don't worry about the police knowing about Garrote. She made no secret of picking up your ticket, but why it was bought in the first place isn't free knowledge. Don't worry, they won't discover it. They couldn't even find one local killer."

That was true, but if Dumay had relaxed the shackles placed on Adam, he probably could have found the Judge by now. And would still be alive.

"Don't," McIntosh warned him in a serious tone. "What's happened, happened. You can't change it, no matter how much you might want to rile and rage against Dumay. All we can do now is catch the killer."

Knowing she was right didn't appease the anger and frustration. How far had the Judge managed to get while Connors pissed around with him in the interview room? Had he taken Stephanie? Or had she run? Where would she go? Despite all the time they'd spent together, Jack didn't really know her. Didn't really know Adam, either, but maybe he'd have had a better chance of finding him. If Adam were the one on the run . . .

McIntosh led him to a dark-coloured, unmarked idling car with a lightly armoured field asset behind the wheel.

"Anything suspicious?" McIntosh asked the driver as she settled into the front passenger seat.

"Nothing here and nothing along our route, ma'am. It appears to be all clear."

"Good. Jack, I left you a gift on the back seat."

Jack had already found it and was surreptitiously checking the Heckler and Koch USP, finding one full magazine already in it and another two on the seat. "Thanks." He pocketed the spare mags and held the gun close to his thigh.

Up front, McIntosh leaned over and retrieved another weapon from the foot well. Her French manicure tapped against the FN P90 as she swiftly checked the compact firearm and then settled it familiarly in her arms.

The driver checked his watch and then eased the car towards the exit. "Ten seconds," he said as he slowed on approach to the boom gate. "Starting . . . now."

"Let's go, Jack." McIntosh was already opening her door and, as the car creeped forwards, she slid out and within a couple of steps, disappeared into a dark alcove behind the gate mechanism.

Jack followed without question. Someone in the Office had to be diverting the LAC's cameras to give them this tiny window to get out of the car unseen. Apparently they weren't taking any risks with getting him back to the Office.

In the shadowed alcove, McIntosh opened a door marked "High Voltage Within, Building Maintenance Only" and made sure the space beyond it was clear with the business end of the P90. When Jack joined her, she nodded and waved him through.

Once the door was closed behind them, soft lighting panels lit up, showing a steel-framed spiral staircase leading down. Jack aimed the USP down it, checking for strays. When he was certain it was clear, he started down, McIntosh behind him.

Every time a new building was put up in Sydney, tunnels were built into the foundations, linking into a complex network of secret passages that could get a person from one side of the city to the other with minimum time above ground. The network was patrolled twice a day for intruders and unauthorised technology. Still Jack kept at the ready, not willing to take any risks with not only his own life, but that of his director as well.

His senses were on high alert, his body reacting as it had been trained to by the SAS. Every sound seemed magnified, every flicker at the corner of his eye processed and analysed in a heartbeat, his body tightening with the potential to duck, jump, or weave at a split second's notice. His world condensed to his immediate surroundings, to this immediate time. While they were here, he couldn't waste time worrying about Ethan or Stephanie or where the Judge might be. Jack locked on his target—getting them safely to the Office—and that was all that mattered.

It took two hours to reach Bondi Junction. Walking above ground would have taken half that time, but their lives were worth the delay. They came up into another hidden room, this time in a secluded corner of a shopping centre carpark. Another car was waiting here, this time driven by a strike team member, a second one in the back seat. Jack got into the back, while McIntosh took the front passenger seat again.

They could have taken the tunnels right to the Neville Crawley Building and emerged into their own garage, but it never hurt to be too cautious when dealing with someone of Garrote's reputation.

Knowing the car was bulletproof, Jack still slouched down so he was less visible. Tinted windows would mean nothing to some of the equipment Ethan, and Garrote, could undoubtedly get their hands on.

Where was Ethan now? Was he somewhere, brooding, snapping together his ridiculously frail-looking but effective, Assassin X sniper rifle, just waiting for Jack to reappear? Did he know Garrote? Were they collaborating on hunting him? Jack almost wished one of them—the Judge, Garrote, or even Ethan—would come at him right now. He was feeling the need to punch something, hard.

Adam . . . *Fuck*. He was going to make someone pay. Even if it was Ethan.

It wasn't quite peak hour, but the traffic was thick and had slowed the roads down to crawls. What should have taken less than thirty minutes stretched out into nearly an hour, every second of which Jack was hyperaware of each car around them, of pedestrians and the darkened windows of buildings when they were halted at red lights.

Once they were behind the armoured door to the garage of the Neville Crawley Building, Jack let out a little frustrated sigh. McIntosh twisted in her seat to give him a slight frown. Sure, he was as safe as he could be, but at the same time, he had effectively exchanged one cell for another. McIntosh didn't want him going out to hunt down anyone, but that was what Jack did. The Office was already stocked with enough assets who could track *anyone* through digital records and third-hand anecdotes, but Jack wasn't one of them. He was a field asset. Out there was where he needed to be.

"Patience, Jack," his director said as the strike team guys got out of the car. As usual, she seemed more aware of Jack's mental state than he would prefer her to be.

"Yes, ma'am."

McIntosh's gaze remained steady against his dry tone, then she sighed and nodded. A silent acknowledgement that at some point, she would agree to do things his way.

Still, as they got out of the car, she put a hand on his arm and held him back from rushing up the stairs. McIntosh turned to him with a pointed expression. "Are you going to be able to think and act objectively on this, Jack?"

There was a whole painful discussion behind the single question. A reminder of Jack's stupid admission after the Valadian operation about coming to like the man he was spying on. The whole Ethan Blade situation. His connection to Adam.

"Yes, ma'am," he answered promptly because she would expect nothing less.

"I hope so." Her voice was firm and her gaze cool. "Do you recall that conversation we had, about a year ago, in my office? When you told me you were 'back'?"

"Yes," Jack said warily.

Quite apart from his actions getting the all clear from the DIC and minister, that speech to McIntosh had been the most important step in proving he was still loyal. He'd meant it, too. After so long of feeling detached and aimless, fighting alongside Ethan for the benefit of the Office and the Meta-State had fixed him in the one spot. It had given him his purpose back, shown him the right path to take. A path he'd kept to for the past year, despite a couple of attempts to push him off it.

Christ, if McIntosh was starting to question him again, he didn't know what he'd do.

"Don't take this the wrong way, Jack, but for a while there, you had started to drift away again."

Here it came. She was going to take him off the job. Tell him he had to get his shit together before she'd let him out of the building.

"Canberra was a terrible blow to you," McIntosh said gently. "Losing your partner like that isn't an easy thing to deal with. The Office can give you as much counselling and support as there is, and still it won't heal every wound."

Already on an edge, Jack considered walking away from the conversation. He had come to grips with the fallout of what had happened with the terrorist incursion in the country's capitol, and his own culpability in Harry's death. He was able to live with the guilt, but that didn't mean it still didn't hurt.

She touched his arm. If the quivering tension in his muscles didn't scare her off, nothing would, so he didn't pull away. "I have my suspicions, but for whatever reason, you're back again. I just don't want *this* job to be the one that pushes you away once more. You're one of the best assets we have, Jack. I don't want to lose you."

All Jack could do was nod, but after a couple of swallows, managed, "You won't lose me, ma'am."

"Good. Because I fear this is going to get a lot more deadly before it's over. Deadly *and* personal." On that grim note, McIntosh walked towards the lifts.

Jack followed slowly, chewing over her words. It wasn't hard to guess what suspicions she was talking about.

It had been so long since he'd thought of his own life in terms of what it meant to someone else. Not to McIntosh or his handler or even the person pointing their gun at his face. But to someone who was at home waiting for him so they could have dinner together, or watch the latest episode of whichever show they were binging, or so they could unleash their own hellish day on sympathetic shoulders.

That, he'd come to realise over the past couple of weeks, was what he really needed to keep him *here*. And damn it, he was going to get it back.

If Ethan didn't kill him for fucking someone else.

EIGHT

BEFORE

The No Ones Inn was a pokey little pub down the road from the Neville Crawley Building and a regular for the Office staff. While Lewis and Lydia joined a table of fellow ITA assets, Jack headed to the bar to get a drink and slotted in between a woman on her phone and a suited man with his back turned. "Bourbon, straight," he said to the bartender and surveyed the pub while he waited.

Normally after a trip away, this was exactly what he needed to shift him out of whatever mindset work had forced on him and back into his life. Something familiar to plant him firmly back in Sydney, to convince every sense he was home again. The sound of Australian accents all around him, the familiar taste of a local brew, the sight of brands and logos he'd grown up with. Though this new case wasn't demanding a different persona from him and wasn't shipping him off to somewhere possibly unfamiliar, he didn't want to fall too far back into his real life. He might be going in as Jack Reardon, but he wasn't exactly going in as himself, regardless of what McIntosh said. SSA Reardon was as fake as Jaidev had been.

"Well, hello again."

Jack turned to the voice and found the man in the suit facing him. Under the generic suit, his lean, long body was promising, but it was the sweep of blond hair across a high brow, sparkling blue eyes and mischievously smiling mouth that caught Jack's attention. Recognition hit him a second later.

"Quinn?"

Well before Jack had realised just how far he'd fallen for Ethan, he'd hooked up with this man a couple of times between two of Ethan's visits. He'd first met Quinn right here, under much the same conditions. Freshly back in country after a job in Singapore, picking someone up for sex had been the last thing on his mind. However, Quinn had been determined, and after two more "chance" meetings, Jack had succumbed. Quinn was a committed top, and Jack had enjoyed getting fucked the few times they'd hooked up. Hadn't minded, either, that Quinn proved to love sucking dick as much as Jack loved being sucked. His brief fling with Quinn had ended naturally when the man returned home to Melbourne.

Quinn grinned. "It's so nice to be remembered. I was hoping I'd run into you again, Nishant."

Jack used his Hindi middle name in most social settings these days. It was easier—and safer—to be Nishant with people who didn't really know him.

Returning the grin, Jack said, "It hasn't been that long."

"It's been a while. Eight months or so. How's things?"

Along with his first name, Jack didn't talk about his career with just anyone. "Same as always. You?" Likewise, Quinn had never offered up his job, but the man gave off a professional air mixed with an incisive intelligence. Jack figured doctor or corporate CEO.

Quinn gave him a grimace. "Back in Sydney, for work, *again*. Though it would be nice to mix in some pleasure." His gaze dropped down Jack's body with obvious intent. "*Again*. I've been in town for a week, coming here most nights, wondering if you'd ever show up."

Jesus. It was tempting.

He'd had a lot of fun with Quinn. When they'd chatted here, and sometimes between fucks in Quinn's hotel room, he'd even liked the man. Smart, a little arrogant, occasionally goofy, but with a sense of humour that tended towards self-deprecating, when he wasn't being bitingly insightful. The first time they'd gotten naked, Quinn had pretty much summed up Jack's scars exactly for what they were. Thankfully, the man hadn't had the time to work out what Jack's tattoo meant. It was, literally, Jack's cross to bear. Only Ethan had ever worked out what it meant to him.

And where the hell was Ethan, anyway? That last embrace in Vietnam, when Ethan had whispered, *"I'll see you soon,"* had felt so promising. So committed. Four fucking months later and nothing. It wasn't the first time Ethan had gone silent and invisible. This time, though, he'd actually requested radio silence, promising to get back in touch when he was ready. Jack had wanted to give him the space he obviously required. Didn't want to be needy or clingy, but *Christ!*

Quinn's hand landed on Jack's hip. The No Ones Inn wasn't a gay bar, but it wasn't overly hostile, either. Still Quinn shifted so his gesture wasn't easily observable, which put him close enough for Jack to smell him over the general odour of clashing colognes, perfumes, and alcohol. The crisp, spicy scent sparked a few warm waves in his abdomen—a recalled sense of feeling this man against him, inside him, of fucking his mouth until Jack came down his throat.

"I'm here indefinitely at this stage," Quinn continued, quiet and husky. "I couldn't stop thinking about you after last time, and when I decided to come back, all I could think about was finding you again." His hand slid to the small of Jack's back, warm and mildly possessive. And promising.

So bloody tempting, but . . .

Jack discreetly removed Quinn's hand. "Sorry, not this time."

Quinn didn't fight. He was a talker, a negotiator. So, rejected hand curling around his tumbler of scotch, he just nodded. "Okay. Can't say I'm not disappointed, though. I really like you, Nishant. Thought perhaps you might have liked me, too."

Taking a fortifying sip of bourbon, Jack shrugged. "I did. I do. But the timing's not right at the moment."

Even if, for some reason, Ethan had decided to ditch him, Jack wasn't ready to give up just yet. In that moment, Jack decided he would call Ethan, his request for silence be damned. Four months was long enough to wait, even if he did come across as needy. Maybe being needed was what Ethan was waiting for.

"Is there another guy?" Quinn's tone was neutral, but with a hint of bitterness.

Opening up to Lewis was one thing. To a past casual hook-up? Jack wasn't quite messed up enough to do that. Besides, right then, he had no idea if there *was* another guy.

"I have a new work project," Jack replied. "Starting tomorrow, and I can't afford any distractions."

Quinn gave a slow nod to his drink. "Wow. Rejected in favour of work. I feel so appreciated."

The sour grapes almost made Jack wish for those times when Quinn's expression had become intent and his questions sharp-edged. Not offensive, just unwelcomingly penetrative. As uncomfortable as those moments had been, at least they hadn't been this awkward.

Before Jack could get out a growling defence, Quinn's expression smoothed out and, in a much more even tone, said, "Sorry. I don't take rejection that well."

Jack wondered if he could trust the contriteness, but grunted the all clear, anyway.

"And hey," Quinn said, his voice lowered for Jack alone to hear, "if you ever need any stress relief, I know how much you like fucking my mouth."

Jack swallowed his bourbon the wrong way. He had forgotten just how blunt Quinn could be. Coughing, he reached for a napkin, hastily mopping his chin and chest while Quinn patted him on the back.

"Bib here!" Quinn called jokingly to the bartender while a couple of people on either side of them chuckled. "You okay now, mate?" he asked Jack, his usual mocking smile in place. "Don't need mouth to mouth?"

Jack scowled at him, only making the man laugh.

In the low, private voice Quinn said, "Don't worry, I haven't forgotten that you don't like kissing. But I mean it. I've been thinking about you a lot since February. I like you, and even if we have to squeeze time together in between our jobs, I'm willing to work at it."

And there was the above-average persistence, right on cue.

"I don't have a lot of free time." Jack trotted out the old line he used when a hook-up wanted more than one night.

"Me neither. I'm not asking for a set schedule or anything. Just drinks every now and then."

"Just *drinks*?" Jack asked wryly. "Drinks" was how Quinn had insinuated himself into Jack's space last time.

Quinn laughed. "Yeah. *Just* drinks, I promise. But so we're clear, I won't say no if you change your mind about us, either. Until such a time, I'm offering friendship."

If Jack hadn't been about to start another undercover job the next day, he might have taken Quinn up on the offer. As it was, he said, "I'd like that, but I'm going to be really busy for a while. Several weeks, probably." Citing an early start in the morning, Jack said goodbye with an actual pang of disappointment. Quinn wasn't one to argue, but his gracious nod of defeat wasn't as smooth as he'd probably intended it, either.

Feeling like shit, Jack stopped by the table with his colleagues, said his goodbyes there as well, and walked the short distance back to work to get his Kawasaki Ninja and go home. He was still chewing over Quinn's tempting offers when he rode down into the carpark under his apartment building in Leichhardt, but the moment he saw the car parked in his second allotted space, all thoughts of Quinn fled.

Not a car enthusiast, Jack nevertheless had a soft spot for Victoria, a black Aston Martin Vanquish S Coupe. An absolute dream to drive, she was smooth, responsive, and gobsmackingly fast. It also helped that finding her here meant her owner was upstairs.

Jack parked beside Victoria and got off the bike, his hand automatically going out to stroke the silky surface of the car. It was ridiculous to associate Ethan so closely with the machine, but it was inevitable, really. Driving was Ethan's release, his Zen place. There had been a time when Jack had doubted Ethan's devotion to his supercars—he had six —but any misgivings had vanished the moment Jack had seen him behind the wheel. Ethan Blade, assassin, spy, warrior, was a hopeless car nut and speed junkie.

Jack didn't precisely run up three flights of stairs, but he definitely took them two and three at a time, managing to slow down to a casual walk as he neared his front door. No matter how desperate he was to see Ethan again, the crazy bastard had been silent for *four months*. He didn't deserve to hear Jack running towards him.

So, he unlocked the door and went in, like it had been any other long day at work. After putting his code into the alarm system and rearming it, he set his helmet on the end of the kitchen counter and grabbed a bottle of water from the fridge. The open-plan kitchen, living, and dining areas were empty of lurking assassins, and the shower wasn't running, so that meant Ethan was in the bedroom.

Chastising his dick from reacting too noticeably, Jack wandered into the hallway leading to the bedrooms and bathroom. The door to the master bedroom was open, and a soft glow fell through it, spreading golden and warmly inviting across the polished wood floor. Jack stepped into the light and leaned against the doorframe, idly opening his drink as he glanced around the room.

Suit jacket and pants hung neatly on the front of his wardrobe, leather dress shoes tucked precisely under the tallboy, weapons harness with twin Desert Eagles secured in their holsters draped across the back of the old recliner in the corner. And lying on his usual side of the bed, reading one of his silly action books, was Ethan Blade.

Jack absorbed the sight, letting it both calm and excite him. Calm him because any doubts he might have had about Ethan's commitment to him had vanished the instant he realised the man was in his bed. If Ethan had come to end things for good, he wouldn't have undressed. Excite him because all the man wore was a pair of black boxer briefs and his socks. Always his socks, but that little foible had stopped amusing Jack ages ago. It was the least of Ethan's issues, and probably the most sexy of them.

Jack never failed to be thrilled by seeing him. Pale skin marked with familiar scars. Long, strong legs, slim hips and a powerful yet lean torso. Broad shoulders, long-fingered, calloused hands. Head of dark hair, a little bit shaggy. Slightly plump lips, narrow nose, fine, arching brows. His eyes, rimmed in long, lush lashes, with their perpetually wide pupils and unnaturally white irises.

Taking a small drink to lubricate his suddenly dry throat, Jack said, "Ethan."

Ethan looked up from his book, a little half quirk on his lips. "Jack."

Jack was grateful his hands were occupied with the bottle, otherwise he would have been ripping his clothes off already. Especially since Ethan's undies were doing absolutely nothing to hide his reaction to Jack's appearance.

"It's been a while." Even as it came out, unconsciously echoing Quinn, Jack winced.

Ethan closed the book and set on the bedside table. "For which I'm sorry. I certainly hadn't meant to take so long to get here. Thank you, though, for respecting my request."

Jack focused on the bottle in his hands. "Yeah, about that. I was going to call you tonight."

Arms crossing his bare chest, Ethan didn't quite fall into the motionless predator mien Jack had become so well-acquainted with, but it was a close thing. "You were?"

Fuck. This was so awkward. It shouldn't be awkward. Jack should already be on the bed—be *on* Ethan—but four months plus temptation from another man quelled his usual response to seeing him. Well, his emotional response, anyway. His dick had already leapt ahead to the reunion sex, or make-up sex, depending on the direction this conversation took.

"I needed . . . to know you were okay." Hell, he might as well have just stopped after "needed." His "need" where Ethan was concerned hadn't required a qualifier in a long time.

"Well," Ethan said softly, smiling around the words, "it's lucky I needed . . . to know you were all right, as well."

Only towering rage had ever stopped Jack from returning one of Ethan's smiles, something that hadn't changed in the last four months, it seemed. One crooked finger away from throwing himself at him, Jack said, "Can I ask why it took you so long to . . . enquire about my wellbeing?"

"You may. The clean-up took longer than I anticipated. Afterwards, there were a few personal matters I had to take care of."

Once, the word "personal" would have stopped Jack's questions about Ethan's past or whereabouts, but no longer. They weren't just fuck buddies anymore.

"Such as?"

Ethan looked away, taking a few deep breaths as his arms tightened over his chest. Then, letting out a long sigh, he dropped his arms so his hands landed, loose and empty, in his lap. The hopeless gesture was so out of Jack's experience with Ethan, he came on instant alert.

Taking a step into the room, Jack looked around again, confused enough he automatically scanned the room for hostiles. "Ethan?"

"I quit, Jack."

NINE
AFTER

Being back in the Office HQ was like pulling on old, favourite clothes—familiar and comfortable. For the first time since the police had snapped the handcuffs on him, Jack felt in control, like an effective part of the team. He was able to start moving, with one of the most powerful investigative tools at his disposal. Given free range on the Judge, it wouldn't be long before the Office tracked him down and destroyed his psychotic little world view.

He could also set about finding Ethan. Find out if the man was holed up somewhere, licking his wounds, or out on a mission to hunt Jack down. Jack didn't care which activity he found Ethan at, so long as he found him.

The lift doors opened on the familiar, much-missed sight of the eighth floor where ITA was based. Packed with individual desks in the middle of the wide space, surrounded by the operations rooms, and filled with the bustle and noise of people dedicated to protecting the Meta-State from dangers within their own boarders. Jack had mixed feelings about each person who worked here, and he'd had some misgivings upon occasion about how they got the job done, but generally, he felt positive about ITA and their overall aims. Ethan would purse his lips at Jack's sentiment, telling him it was just that— sentimentality. The assassin had his own hard-earned opinions about such organisations, but only twice had he tried to lure Jack away from the Office. After that, he'd made his peace with Jack's loyalty to the red tape and bureaucracy, satisfying himself with teasing and jokes, usually at Jack's expense.

And on that thought, Jack made up his mind.

"Ma'am, can I make a suggestion?"

McIntosh eyed him curiously. "Of course."

"Let me call in Ethan Blade."

That sharp, direct expression she'd turned on him in the garage came back. "Why?"

Jack's stomach churned with his usual precombat uneasiness. He'd always trusted it, knowing it would go away the moment he got the green light, leaving him calm, clear-headed, and determined to move, to fight, to win. He trusted it now, too.

"Part of it is personal. I want to know where he is, what he's doing. But that's not the only reason. He can help us."

Christ, this wasn't unlike telling his mother he was gay. The same trepidation, the wariness about her response, but the same resolution to be honest. This was the first time he'd verbally acknowledged his relationship with Ethan to anyone within the Office. He was fairly certain they already knew, though. At least, about the physical side. Now he'd find out how she really felt about the whole thing.

McIntosh's eyes went chilly. Not the full Artic blast he was expecting, thankfully. "What can he provide in this situation?"

Jack took a deep breath and instead of saying "some peace of mind," went with, "The mindset of a killer. He's not a psychopath like the Judge, but he understands the practicality of it better than anyone, especially now Adam is . . . gone. I got a crash course in serial murderers, but it's not going to help us much. The Judge isn't just a serial murderer, he's . . ." He didn't know exactly what he was, but Jack knew there was something more to the bastard. Something Ethan knew. "He's got other motives."

"Other motives you think Blade can illuminate for us?"

Jack shook his head, not trusting himself to voice the lie. "Blade can help us track him. He could be the difference between catching him before he kills again, or not."

Another long, considering stare. Jack met her gaze fearlessly, done with trying to hide everything from everyone. Office assets had done worse in the name of the Meta-State, Jack included. Of course, those assets probably hadn't felt about their "worse" things the way Jack felt about Ethan. Right now, he was incredibly pissed off with Ethan, and he couldn't help but wonder if he'd killed Adam, but until he knew for certain, Jack still wanted him back. Wanted this new, nebulous thing they'd started to keep going.

And if McIntosh decided she didn't like him wanting that, then perhaps it was time for Jack to leave the Office. Once the Judge was a bloody lump at his feet, of course.

McIntosh's expression was unreadable beyond what she wanted Jack to see, a serious deliberation over his proposal. God, what he wouldn't give for some of Adam's insight right then. The sweat was gathering between his shoulder blades when she spoke.

"Do it. If he can provide something useful, it will be worth it."

Agreement didn't mean he'd got away with anything. McIntosh was a master at this game. Proving it, she took a phone from a pocket and handed it over. She didn't want him using his implant, where he could *think* his words into the connection, words she couldn't hear or control.

Taking the phone, he dialled the number from memory and put the phone on speaker. It rang several times, then clicked over to another line, then another. Finally, it was answered. A dull electronic voice asked them to leave a message and informed that any response would be delivered within twenty-four hours.

"Blade, it's Jack Reardon," he said, highly aware of McIntosh's attention on him. "We have a situation we'd like your input on. Please make contact as soon as you can."

That was it. Nothing personal, no demands for explanations, no pleas for understanding. No hint he'd spent six months falling deeper and deeper in *something* with this strange, unsteady man. Or four months in growing frustration, waiting for his return. Or four weeks making up for lost time, only to ruin it all by a single, bad choice.

"It's up to him now." Jack handed back the phone.

McIntosh gave him a single nod. "Let me know the moment he gets in contact."

"Of course, ma'am." A promise he actually meant. Ethan wouldn't want to come here, so Jack would have to go to him, wherever he was, and that would mean begging, demanding, or simply telling his director he was leaving the building.

With an indelicate snort, McIntosh nodded again. "In the meantime, you have work to do. I wasn't just trying to piss Dumay off.

We're going to find the Judge. Go. Lewis is waiting for you. I'm going to have a talk with Donald."

Jack watched her go to politely but firmly tell off the senior Ex Mon supervisor, once more glad he'd accepted a position with ITA over ETA. Director Alex Tan of External Threat Assessment had a well-deserved reputation for bending the rules until they fractured. ETA jobs were always given the widest possible operational parameters, and the assets were, for the most part, unconditionally covered by Tan when they overstepped those boundaries. Jack had banked on Tan's habit of retroactively approving unsanctioned activities to cover him during the whole Harraway deal. And it had been Tan's idea to "keep Blade happy" so he might consider working with them in the future. Tan had even offered Jack a place in ETA, weighting it with promises to make it worth Jack's while.

Not exactly giving Tan a definite no, Jack hadn't yet regretted his decision to stay with ITA and McIntosh. For the first five years of his career with the Office, Jack had believed his director to be a straight-down-the-middle player. She abided by the rules and enforced them when required. Tough but fair, direct but compassionate. Leading up to Jack's fifteen months undercover operation with Valadian, and in the year that followed his return, he'd seen another side of Donna McIntosh. She respected the rules and followed them diligently—until they didn't work for her. When that happened, McIntosh quietly and calmly did what was required to get the job done. She didn't flaunt it, like Tan, or do it for her own benefit, as Harraway had. McIntosh's goal was that of the Office. To protect. Righteous was how Harraway had described her, and in the midst of all the filth and evil Jack had to suffer during his job, he needed to know McIntosh's honour was there to guide him out of the shadows.

Buoyed by the fact McIntosh had come personally to get him out, Jack headed towards Lewis's operations room. As he crossed the floor, he got a series of pats on the back and welcome-homes from his fellow ITA assets. This, too, buffered his mood, knowing these people were happy he was back.

All of which was reinforced when the door to the operations room banged open and Lewis stepped out, eyes shining and one hand clenched over his heart.

"My boy," he proclaimed in weepy relief for all to hear. "Finally released from the clink. I don't care what you did wrong, just so long as you're home now!" Arms spread, he gestured Jack in for a hug.

Jack rolled his eyes but had to work hard at not grinning at his friend. One thing he could always rely on from Lewis was a joke to lighten just about any mood—and a serious, glad-you're-back chin lift when Jack avoided the embrace and just squeezed his shoulder in thanks. Which nearly reverted to a full-on hug when Jack noted Lewis was wearing the same clothes as he had been yesterday. His mate had pulled an all-nighter, and it was now nearly 5:00 p.m. Jack mollified the sudden warm rush with a gruff "Missed you, too, dickhead."

Lewis gave the spectators a final "My boy will always be innocent to me," and then ordered Jack into the operations room.

The team had rapidly expanded since Jack had been arrested that morning. The room, which had comfortably held them all the previous week, was now bursting at the seams. People crowded around the big table in the middle of the room, working diligently with a minimum of fuss and noise. Jack did a quick count as they made their way to where Lydia stood, and noted that there were more coffee cups than humans in the room, a testament to how long and hard they'd all been working.

"Jack," Lydia said, genuinely pleased. "Good to have you back. How are you?"

Knowing he looked like twice-pummelled crap, but grateful for her concern, he said, "Better now I'm here. Pity I don't come bearing good news. The police know Lewis and I were in Bangkok. They questioned me about it."

Lewis's eyes widened, and Lydia's narrowed.

"Any idea how they discovered it?" she asked.

"They have pictures of us there. Someone got shots from the city CCTV feeds. McIntosh is already down at Ex Mon, snap-freezing Robson's nuts off."

Lewis cringed. "Poor bastard."

"Don't feel too sorry for him yet. Detective Connors recognised you from your ASIO days."

"It was a possibility," Lewis said, instantly serious. "Ted Connors. We looked into him at the start of the operation and knew he'd attended some of the antiterror exercises we did with the New South Wales police a while back. After the joint exercises, he kept applying to ASIO, and they kept finding one reason or another to knock him back. He's an able investigator, but he takes it all personally. Swears undying vengeance at least twice a week."

"You must have made an impression if he remembered you."

Lewis snorted. "I doubt it. He's the sort of person who 'keeps tabs' on those he finds 'suspicious,' and to him, anyone who's smarter, better-looking, or richer than him is 'suspicious.' In this case, it's my looks."

"Of course," Lydia murmured dryly.

"Well." Jack stretched the word out suggestively. "I wouldn't be too dismissive about it. I mean, in an effort to cover our presence in Bangkok, I had to tell him you're gay now."

While Lydia laughed, Lewis said darkly, "You didn't."

Jack patted his pockets. "I have his personal phone number for you."

The closest assets snickered, and Lydia had to walk away to get herself under control.

Lewis glared at the assets, then at Lydia, then at Jack. "Absolutely last time I let you organise *anything*, Reardon."

"Either way, we're both on his radar now. If he decides to look into Bangkok, how much damage could he do?"

"He'd be well out of his jurisdiction, but that doesn't mean he can't pass whatever he finds on to someone in a position to chase it."

Jack took a steadying breath. "Do we need to take him out of the game?"

The Messiah case was too sensitive to risk. If Connors went blundering in and actually found something, the potential disaster resulting from the exposure of the Messiah's current whereabouts wouldn't bear thinking about.

"We'd risk sending up flares that there's something important to find."

"Let's feed him false information," Lydia suggested. "Let him run, but we make the course for him to follow. Steer him away from the Messiah."

Jack nodded. "It's about our best option."

"I'll go talk to Wade," Lydia said as she headed for the door. "He's running the ETA team on Theta Subject now."

Still glad they didn't have to deal with the Messiah directly, Jack returned to their immediate concern. "We might have some help with the Judge, at least. McIntosh gave the go-ahead to call in Ethan Blade."

Despite the general hum of people working industriously around the room, Jack's quiet words were heard. Everything went silent, and a dozen pairs of eyes focused on Jack. Even people who hadn't been there at the time of Ethan's sojourn with the Office knew all about it. The next big drama for everyone to fixate on couldn't come soon enough for Jack.

"Are things that bad?" Lewis's expression was wary and a bit disappointed.

Jack could understand. Lewis was very good at his job, but hearing your bosses were thinking of bringing in your sworn enemy because you weren't getting results fast enough was disheartening.

"Bad enough, and we're coming late to this party," Jack said grimly. Lewis would get over it. "Blade might be our best chance of catching this psycho before he kills again."

After a long moment, Lewis nodded, then smirked. "Not to mention helping you with that nasty case of Garrote you picked up."

And he was over the hurt.

He was also wrong. Even if Ethan didn't hate Jack now, the fact he'd "retired" meant he could very well be out of the country and unwilling to return to help them with a problem he was partially to blame for.

TEN
BEFORE

he quiet words arrested Jack's pointless search. Gaze snapping back to Ethan, he frowned. "You what?"

"I haven't taken an official job in over eight months, Jack. There's been no . . ." His lips twisted into a self-conscious grimace. "I haven't *needed* to work since we started seeing each other. The—for want of a more accurate word—compulsion just hasn't been there. You once asked me if I liked what I do. *Did*. The better question would have been, *why* I did it."

Jack recognised the force behind the sudden rush of words. Ethan was nervous and uncertain, and for someone with a driving need to have things ordered and precise, such wild emotions were strange and overwhelming. Once, Ethan's go-to response in similar circumstances was a deadly detachment, the same unfeeling, remote mindset he used in order to kill. Somehow, Jack had elicited a different reaction. There had been times when Jack's unrelenting contrariness had pushed Ethan into his stone-cold killer persona, but at other times, he had been on the receiving end of this—a guileless word ramble that revealed far more than Ethan was probably comfortable with.

"I have certain things I have to do," Ethan continued. "Things that have kept me alive all this time. Things that I *trust*. Like scrambling after a job. Getting away, getting secure works, so it's what I always do. Then there are things I must do because without them, I would lose myself. For the longest time, Jack, I believed working, picking up tickets and hunting targets, was one of the latter things. I stopped once before. Years ago. It was when I decided I couldn't work for anyone else. That I didn't want to be *run*. I wanted to make my own choices. So I broke away and stopped doing what they wanted me to do. What they'd trained me to do."

Jack knew Ethan had been in some sort of military organisation in the past. Had suspected they were the ones who'd taken an already troubled young man and turned him into a remorseless killer, but this was the closest Ethan had ever come to admitting it. Hearing it spoken aloud kicked Jack's protective streak into high gear. If he ever found out who was responsible for doing this to Ethan—to Paul St. Clair— he wouldn't stop hurting them until they were as damaged as Ethan. More so.

"But something in me wasn't right. I couldn't *not* do anything, Jack, and the only thing I knew how to do was stalk and kill. Only when I was on a job did I feel balanced. Like I was real. So I went back to it and two years ago, I found something else that made me feel balanced. Someone who made me feel real."

Unable to hold it in anymore, Jack whispered, "Ethan."

Ethan held up a hand. "Please, Jack. Let me finish. I'm self-aware enough to know swapping one crutch for another isn't healthy, and it does scare me how much I want to be with you. But not enough to turn me away, clearly. Coming to accept that helped me realise that what propelled me to work wasn't one of the things I have to do to stop myself from getting lost. It was simply something I'd done for so long, it was habit. Like scrambling after a job. So, I've stopped."

Jack eyed him warily. "Just like that? You stopped?"

Lips twitching with a couple of false starts, Ethan settled on, "It's been eight months in the doing, but yes, effectively. I just had to sever ties with my associates and ensure certain people wouldn't take exception to my decision. But it's done, Jack. I'm here and I don't want to leave—oh!"

All pretence at restraint gone, Jack hurled himself onto the bed. After a mad struggle to untangle arms and legs, to align bodies, and then tangle arms and legs in a more pleasing configuration, Jack sighed and sank into Ethan's body. Face buried in the warm, safe haven between his neck and shoulder, Jack reassured himself Ethan was really here, that it wasn't just some wish-fulfilment dream.

Long, long minutes later, stroking Jack's back, Ethan murmured, "Jack, are you all right?"

He lifted his head enough to move his lips. "You're not going to leave after a week?"

"Not unless you kick me out."

"Good."

Jack turned the word into a kiss on his neck. Then another kiss and another. Ethan shivered, his strong fingers digging into Jack's back. Jack worked his way up the firm line of his neck, to the corner of his jaw and his earlobe, nibbling and sucking until Ethan was breathless. Then he abandoned the ear for the soft, sensitive spot behind it. Jack ran his hand through Ethan's hair, shifting his head for easier access as well as looking for, and getting, the man's instinctual response to push into his hand and shudder.

"Jack" Ethan squirmed under him. "You need to get undressed. Now."

It had to be the fastest horizontal strip in history. Definitely a personal best, especially considering that while at the foot of the bed, shoving his pants and underwear off, Jack also helped Ethan wiggle his way out of his briefs. All the records went flying out the window, however, because Jack stalled where he was, captivated by the vision stretched out on his bed, stunned by how much he wanted this man.

It wasn't just the pale skin with its scars—each a tale of survival, a mosaic of his life—over sleek, lean muscles and not one iota of spare flesh. Or the dark hair flopped over his forehead and a faint touch of pink colouring his cheeks. Or the way long lashes swept down as he squirmed under Jack's scrutiny, biting his lower, plump lip.

It was the way he trusted Jack, how he made himself vulnerable for him. How he would laugh when Jack teased him, or unleash his rare, wicked sense of humour. It all made him *beautiful*.

Christ. A burst of heat and light went off under Jack's ribs. It had happened so many times in the past, he'd come to think of it as his personal grenade, exploding at times like this, or when Ethan was being particularly endearing or innocent, even sometimes when they argued. Fingertips against his neck, or a hand on his thigh, often pulled the pin, too. Or a laugh, or a smile. Or watching Ethan drool in his sleep.

Each time it exploded now, Jack knew what it meant, had accepted it, had meant to act on it, but then Canberra happened, followed by four agonising months alone, and when Ethan did appear it was to bare his soul, leaving them both too raw for anything other than what they knew worked. Namely, mind-blowing sex.

Starting at Ethan's socked feet, Jack worked his way upwards with hands and lips. He kissed and stroked and licked and tickled until Ethan's pale skin was blushing and Jack could all but hypnotise himself with the contrast of it against his brown fingers. He spread them out over the inner curve of Ethan's thigh, feeling the muscle quiver at his touch. It fascinated him, this clear delineation between their bodies, so obvious right now, but later, when Jack was lost to the motions and sensations, it would all blur and mix until he didn't know where he stopped and Ethan began.

Abandoning that pleasure before it could overwhelm him, Jack nuzzled into the crease between thigh and groin, drowning himself in that strong scent of blood-warmed skin, a hint of sweat, pure musk, and, as always with Ethan, just a touch of gun oil.

"God," Jack moaned. "I've missed this."

Ethan laughed, startled and a little ragged. "That doesn't make the rest of me feel superfluous at all."

Suppressing his own chuckle, Jack licked a long, curving route to Ethan's belly button. "Don't worry, there are other bits I missed as well."

The body under him tensed, and Ethan's breathing shortened. His navel was highly sensitive, and he was always wary of Jack paying it too much attention. Jack teased the rim of it with his lips and tongue, loving the way Ethan squirmed and bit back groans. Strong fingers curled through Jack's hair, just holding on for now. When Jack dipped his tongue in a little too deep, however, Ethan's hand fisted and tugged Jack's head up and away.

"No?" Jack asked to be sure.

"No." Ethan gave a gentle pull, and Jack went with it, sliding up until they were face-to-face.

"Then what do you want?" Though he could guess, by the way Ethan's legs lifted, knees clamped to Jack's ribs, hips rising, rubbing their dicks together. Jack pushed back, a slow, meaningful glide. Yes, it said, we'll get there, but first . . . "Anything you want and I'll do it. Anything."

Jack had offered this a couple of times in the past, hoping Ethan would take advantage of the open invitation. Maybe he'd want to top, or possibly try blowing Jack, to see if his dislike for sucking dick had changed at all. Or perhaps, he'd accept what Jack was really offering and ask for a kiss.

Kissing on the mouth was the line Jack had drawn. Fucking could be just physical, or it could be intimate, but for Jack, kissing was *always* intimate. The lips, the mouth, the tongue, these were the things that shaped a person, that most readily told you who they were. How they spoke, what they said, if they laughed or scorned. So much of who someone was came through the mouth that Jack sometimes wondered why everyone didn't feel as he did. Sex was great. Sex with someone he really liked was even better. It was mind-blowing with someone he cared for deeply. But a kiss meant so much more.

Ethan had always respected Jack's wish. Other men had teased and cajoled and outright tried to force it, but never Ethan. He'd simply accepted it and happily taken everything else Jack had willingly given. Just as Jack would never push Ethan about the blowjob thing. But his issue, the kiss thing, was starting to feel pointless and silly. Jack wanted it, wanted Ethan to want it, but it had been so long. Twelve years since Jack had last kissed someone like that. It had been Jack's fault Hamish left him, clearly and unarguably, and that mistake had left a scar. Wounded Jack deep enough he'd believed he wouldn't ever recover. Now, however, when he knew he wanted to kiss like that again, he couldn't make himself cross the line. The memory of the pain, of the guilt for failing Hamish, was a razor-sharp barrier holding him back. He needed someone else to push the blade into him.

So, he offered. He told Ethan he would do *anything*, and he hoped and waited and prayed.

Ethan looked up at him, white eyes inexpressive but lips curled into a soft smile and cheeks flushed just a little bit more. He unwound his fingers from Jack's hair and drifted them down over his temple, traced under his eye, along the side of his nose and let them linger on Jack's mouth.

"I want you," Ethan whispered. "Just you. Don't drive me wild. Don't make me so crazy with lust I don't know what I'm doing. I want to be *with* you, Jack."

Not a kiss, but holy shit. It was perhaps the next best thing.

Throat clotted with so many unspeakable words, Jack could only nod. Ethan's answering smile was slow and sweet and pulled the pin on Jack's grenade all over again.

Feeling like he should be glowing from the internal explosion, Jack kissed him, technically on his cheek but so close to the corner of his mouth the smallest move from Ethan would have knocked down that last hurdle. But he didn't and Jack lingered there, letting the moment wash through him. This right now was perfect for them. Nothing had to be forced because it would happen when they needed it to.

For the next however long, they simply moved together, touching and kissing and whispering. Eventually, Jack found himself back where he'd begun. He skirted his mouth around the contested zone of the navel and, forgoing any teasing, slipped his lips over Ethan's dick. He kept it light and tender, not aiming to get Ethan off, just doing something they both enjoyed. A lot. Ethan arched and whimpered, stroking Jack's hair and shoulders, murmuring his name over and over, then exclaiming it loudly when Jack sank right down on him and swallowed.

Pulling off Ethan with a slow, deep suck, Jack sat back on his heels and tugged on Ethan's hips. "Roll over."

Dazed and languid, Ethan complied. He stretched, arms reaching over the headboard, spine curling, legs spread on either side of Jack, calves tightening, toes pointing.

"Jesus." Jack squeezed himself to keep things from tipping over then and there. With his other hand, he slapped Ethan's arse lightly. "Don't do that again. It's distracting."

"Hmm, I certainly wouldn't want you to be distracted." Ethan relaxed and melted into the mattress. "Do continue. Please."

Chuckling, Jack propped Ethan up on his knees. "Just for that..." he promised ominously, then leaned over and bit one taut, wonderfully displayed cheek.

Ethan's startled gasp encouraged him to keep going. Jack ranged across his perfect rear, down his thighs, and up his spine, all the while working one, two, three saliva-wet fingers into him. It was also gratifying to watch Ethan, usually so sure and deliberate, fumble in the bedside table drawer, taking an inordinate amount of time to find what he was looking for. When he came up with a foil wrapper, he held it for a speculative second, then flicked it so it went spinning across the room and disappeared under the tallboy. Jack muffled his part amused, part so-aroused-no-blood-was-feeding-his-higher-functions laugh in Ethan's skin. The second attempt found the lube. Ethan shoved up and back, making Jack sit on his heels. Ethan followed him until he was sitting on Jack's lap, knees spread to either side, back pressed against Jack's chest.

Fuck. This was nice. Jack wound his arms around the man, holding him in place.

"Like this." Ethan wiggled against him. "No condom. Just us. Like this."

They'd gone bare a couple of times before, so Jack agreed wholeheartedly. It necessitated some distance to slick up his dick and to find a comfortable angle, but the moment Ethan sank down on Jack, it was perfect. Being inside him, flesh to flesh, just enough lube to ease the passage, was as explosive as Jack remembered. More so because memory was fallible and few things came close to this immediate, visceral contact. But even that paled in comparison to watching and feeling Ethan slowly, beautifully, move on him.

He rocked back and forth, gentle motions that worked Jack in deeper and deeper. His spine curved, shoulders cradled on Jack's, head tossed back. Jack touched him, couldn't stop touching him—running his palms down his chest, over his tight abdomen, along his straining thighs; up his sides, under his arms, urging them up so they reached for the ceiling, fingers twining together as Ethan lifted himself up and slid back down. Again and again and again, driving them both closer to the edge, then up once more, and he paused, waiting.

"Yeah," Jack moaned, and one arm around his man's chest, he braced himself with his other hand on the mattress and thrust up into Ethan.

"Jack," Ethan gasped, shuddering. "Yes."

Jack kept his pace steady, wanting it to last forever, at least for longer than a couple of minutes, but it was hopeless. It had been four months and this was just so fucking hot and Ethan was . . . he was . . . Hell, he was right there, moaning Jack's name and moving with him, rising as Jack fell, falling as Jack rose. The sight, the sounds, the sensations overwhelmed him, and wrapping his hand around Ethan's dick, Jack abandoned himself to the fucking.

Neither of them lasted long then. Ethan went first, hands gripping Jack's thighs for balance. He arched sharply, dick pulsing as he came, which rocketed Jack over the edge as well, sending him tumbling through a white-out orgasm.

ELEVEN
AFTER

"Where are we on finding the Judge?" Jack asked as the team resumed work.

"Not very far advanced," Lewis said. "We're chasing leads on how he may have got into the police station. Since your little demonstration to them about how easy it is to bypass their security measures, they've been frantically upgrading. That's where you come in. You're the closest thing we have to an expert on the Judge at the moment, as well as being very familiar with the Local Area Command..."

Jack groaned. "You want me to work out how he got in and out."

"Exactly. I've got everything you need over here." Lewis beckoned Jack over to the corner, where a desk had been set up.

With the laptop and rolls of schematics and blueprints, it looked very similar to his usual spot in the room with the strike force. So much of his time with Infinity had been spent doing this—going through building plans and security systems to work out how the killer got in—that he had the urge to look around for Adam. Of course, the man wasn't there. Jack wouldn't be able to glance up from his work to find Adam across the table, thumbing through his phone or sleepily sipping his coffee. Steph wouldn't be there to tease him with being thrown out a window, or to send him off to fetch lunch just to give her and Jack a few moments of peace. Jack wouldn't be able to bypass Adam in favour of going to Steph with a question so he could get a succinct, innuendo-free answer.

Which made him angry again. He hadn't gone through all that shit at the LAC that morning just to come back here and keep doing what he'd been doing there for the past month. Work that, while worthwhile, hadn't found them the Judge in time to stop him from killing one of the strike force members.

But right then, there was little else he could do. The fact that the Judge had gotten into the LAC was the newest lead they had, and Jack had watched Adam work long enough to know the answer was in the details. In a lot of cases, the killer was already known to the police investigating the murders. It was just a matter of stacking up the evidence to prove it.

Clamping down on his anger, Jack sat and began the process all over again.

It worked for an hour or so. The puzzle consumed his mind, gave him something to focus on. It was like a virtual obstacle course. Jack had always enjoyed them. Not just physical courses, but those that presented problems to be solved. It was why he didn't mind his cover job, why he enjoyed it when he was required to do something for the ISO. But the more he worked, the more frustrated he got.

The NSW police had substantially increased their security measures over the past month. They'd taken his demonstrations to heart and perhaps gone a bit too far in the other direction. Then again, considering the calibre of their opponent and the fact he had gotten in and killed someone, perhaps not. As a result, this was a course he couldn't work his way through. No matter how long he looked at the plans, or which way he approached the problem, he couldn't work it out.

"Fuck this." Jack pushed away from the desk sharply. The motion knocked a couple of rolls of paper off the far side.

Annoyed and unsettled, Jack stalked out of the operations room, giving Lewis's concerned "Jack, you okay?" an acknowledging wave on the way.

Running up two flights to the tenth, Jack bummed a couple of cigarettes off Miller, and when he came back into the stairwell, found Lewis waiting for him.

"You okay?" Lewis's expression dared Jack to brush him off again.

"Yeah. No." Jack brandished his smokes and lighter and stepped around Lewis to head up to the roof. "I need a break."

"Fair enough, but, mate, maybe try the garage. I did some reading on Eve Garrote and she's a noted marksperson."

"God fuck it." Jack turned around.

"When you come back, find me," Lewis called after him.

Ten flights later, Jack came out into the garage, which was the very last place he wanted to be. He needed open space, fresh air, a line of sight longer than a couple dozen meters. A distant horizon he could aim for, or a broad expanse of stars he could navigate by. Something other than walls on all sides, restrictions and restraints. Lies and half-truths.

God. He hadn't felt like this in over a year. It was making a lie of McIntosh's earlier comments. Well, not entirely. Ethan *had* grounded him. Given him something other than work to focus on. A reason to go home, to talk, to smile.

It wasn't too hard, then, to work out why he was feeling unsettled. He needed Ethan back. Or at least to know how he was and if Jack needed to fight for him.

He'd been out of that interview room at the station for nearly four hours, and what had he managed to accomplish? He'd put a call in to Ethan's number, exposing his relationship with the man to his director at the same time. She hadn't fired him or locked him away, so that was a plus. He'd poured over the LAC security plans and found nothing. They were no closer to the Judge and hadn't made any progress on resolving the ticket.

The cigarette flared down to the filter, and Jack stubbed it out on the cement wall. It hadn't done much to help settle his guts, hadn't tricked his body into thinking he was ready for whatever might come his way. He lit the second one, forcing his thoughts back to the case. He certainly wasn't going to get anything done if he spent all his time lamenting about how much he hadn't done.

It had been an hour since Jack had called Ethan and nothing. The message had said twenty-four hours, but this was different. This was *Jack* looking for a response, not some anonymous buyer wanting Ethan for a job.

The second smoke wasn't helping either. He discarded it rather than continue with the pointlessness and headed back upstairs.

Assets pointed Jack towards the tearoom when he asked after Lewis.

"Great," Lewis said when Jack joined him. "Now you smell like sweat *and* smoke."

"You like it."

"Yeah, baby, give it to me." Lewis opened the fridge and perused the shelves stacked high and deep with people's forgotten lunches, missed dinners, and yogurts way beyond their best-befores.

Jack beelined for the coffee and made himself a strong cup and a weaker one for his friend. By the time he'd turned back to the table, Lewis was hauling a largish container of pasta out of the fridge.

Jack eyed it sceptically, ignoring the way his stomach cramped and reminded him it had been a good while since he'd last eaten. "This is why we're in here? To steal someone's else's food?"

In a highly stressful job, such as theirs, tearoom etiquette was vitally important. Cups and cutlery should be washed and dried, rather than left dirty in the sink. Chairs belonged tucked into the table; they shouldn't be trip hazards. Newspapers folded and put on the counter, not left strewn across the table. And when the only bright spot a person might have in their day was homemade pasta for lunch, finding it missing was reason enough to draw blood.

"I bet you haven't eaten in the last day. Sit." Lewis shoved a fork at Jack. "Eat. Now."

Still, Jack hesitated. Christ, it looked good, but there were few things powerful enough to make him eat Lewis's cooking.

"For fuck's sake," Lewis muttered. "Lydia made it, okay. Not me. It's perfectly edible."

Lydia was smart, organised, and level-headed enough to offset Lewis when he got carried away. She was also the fiercest foodie Jack knew and the one most likely to throw the first punch in any tearoom disagreement. Knowing she'd made the pasta made it both easier and harder to resist.

"What the hell." Jack grabbed the fork. "I've got one ticket already, what's another one."

The pasta, even cold, was really good. Jack ate the lion's share, realising as he scraped the last of the congealed sauce from the bottom of the container that it had been nearly twenty hours since he'd last eaten.

Dinner with Ethan. The food had been good. The rest of it hadn't.

"Feel better?" Lewis asked.

Finally understanding, Jack nodded. There would be no reprisal from Lydia. She was probably the one who'd sent Lewis to make sure he ate. It made him think of Adam's commitment to helping Steph when no one else could.

"Thank her for me."

Lewis grinned. "Will do. I get bonus points if I do what she says."

Chuckling, Jack said, "You're so whipped."

"Am not."

Jack just raised his eyebrows.

"Oh, and you're not?" Lewis asked dryly.

"No." Jack scoffed, then, "Maybe."

"Knew it."

"Yeah, well, at least I top."

It took Lewis a moment, but when he got it, he scowled, then snorted laughter. "Lyds would agree."

"She is very smart."

Lewis swirled the last of his coffee. "I guess this means your guy showed up again."

Maybe it was the soporific effects of the complex carbohydrates settling into his belly or he was primed by his semiconfession to McIntosh, but Jack didn't immediately run from the question. And maybe that was why he answered as he did. That, or he really was getting tired of all the lies and subterfuge.

"Yeah, he did. He's been back the entire time we've been on this job."

"Cool. I had sort of wondered, actually. You've been less cranky."

Jack tried to scowl, but the blatant truth of the matter just wouldn't let him. He and Ethan had been happy. Mostly. Just the usual trials and clashes of two people learning how to live with one another, made all the more precarious by Jack's job and Ethan's past. Oh, and the monumental secret Ethan had been keeping. But then, Jack hadn't been entirely honest with Ethan, either.

"And he doesn't know about the job?" Lewis skirted around the actual question he probably wanted to ask.

Maintaining a relationship while working as they did was hard. Lewis and Lydia had solved the issues of constantly lying to a partner or spouse by falling for each other. It helped, too, that they weren't field assets. Neither of them were out there, risking their lives or their relationship with some of the things field assets occasionally found themselves doing in order to get the job done. Which brought Jack right back to the question Lewis hadn't asked.

Because he was in an odd mood, Jack answered the unasked question. "He didn't know."

He did now, though.

"I'm sorry, man." Lewis contemplated the bottom of his coffee cup, giving Jack a quiet, unobserved moment to deal, then asked, "Do you think he's in any danger from the Judge? Should we pick your bloke up and get him to a safe house?"

Jack almost laughed, but the impulse was strangled by the sudden tightness in his throat. The unlikely event of Ethan allowing the Office to protect him was quickly overrun by the thought of what Lewis would say if he knew the man he was offering to protect was Ethan Blade.

"No," Jack managed to scrape out. "He'll be okay. We don't know that the Judge is after me."

"Are you sure? He killed one member of the strike force. The other member is missing, either on the run because they know the Judge is after them, or we just haven't found the body yet." It was blunt but true.

"I'm sure," Jack said firmly.

Lewis eyed him sceptically, and Jack suppressed a wince at the expression. The reason Lewis was so good at his job was because he could make intuitive leaps between scattered bits of seemingly unrelated information. Giving him a couple of half-truths was no guarantee he wouldn't find the right conclusion. Christ. Perhaps Jack should lay it all out there. Lewis was his best friend. Maybe he would understand.

Even as he opened his mouth to say it, to tell someone that he'd fallen for an assassin, someone technically on the Office's long list of interesting subjects, the words dried up in his throat. The mess in Canberra was still too raw for him to risk it happening again.

When Lewis did speak, it was to say, "Okay, you've been fed. Time for bed, mister."

It was so unexpected, Jack could only gape at him.

"You've been up for I don't know how long, and if you're going to be of any use to us, then you need some sleep. Frankly, I won't have you cranking all over my team when you take us through everything you know about the Judge." He stood and pointed imperiously in the general direction of the breakrooms. "Go to bed. Now."

TWELVE BEFORE

hank heaven for full-face helmets. Jack couldn't stop grinning as he wove his black Ninja through the morning traffic in Surry Hills. Waking up with Ethan beside him had negated so many of Jack's grumbles about the new job, he was having trouble remembering he was supposed to be cranky about it. He'd laughed his way through a shared shower, smiled over a quick breakfast, and even now, away from Ethan and on his way to work, the simple joy wouldn't go away, which was nice.

A *ping* from his implant threatened his happy mood. It was a clear reminder of where his focus should be.

Jack accepted the call, then had to swerve around an abruptly braking SUV, sidling the bike between the big car and a small MG convertible on the other side.

"Jack? You there, mate?" Lewis's voice came into his head.

"I'm in the middle of traffic, dumbarse." Squeezing between a couple more pairs of cars, Jack edged up to the line at the intersection, hoping the light went green before he had to come to a complete stop.

Lewis chuckled, but when he spoke he was all business. *"Just a quick comms check before you get to the LAC. You get a chance to go over the file again last night?"*

"Yes, mum," Jack muttered aloud, his voice muffled by his helmet. "I did all my homework." Over breakfast that morning.

The light miraculously turned green, and Jack roared away, getting in front of a delivery truck and cutting across the lane to turn into Goulburn Street.

"Ha-ha. Don't kill yourself on the way in, okay. If you do, they'd probably want to send me in your place."

"God save the country if that ever happened."

"Right? Okay, Home is going silent. Don't get cranky, record everything, and good luck."

Smiling wryly at his friend's agreement, Jack confirmed the orders and signed off. Moments later, he turned into the visitor's carpark of the Local Area Command for Surry Hills. He parked and, helmet under his arm, went into the building.

The interior was government-building typical. Fluorescent tubes overhead, bland walls interspersed with posters promoting the police force and community involvement, the utilitarian carpet worn down in places from millions of feet, a line of people already snaking away from the reception counter. He had to wait for ten minutes before he reached the head of the queue.

Jack pulled out his ISO ID and handed it over. "Jack Reardon. I was requested to come in by Senior Sergeant Phelps."

The man behind the desk looked his ID over critically. "We don't see you guys much around here. I thought you were all in Canberra." He then checked Jack's face, making sure he matched the photo beside the badge.

"That's what we want you to think."

After a little pause, the receptionist got the joke and sniggered. "Yeah, right. Let me just get you a native guide to take you upstairs. Can't have you wandering around freely, *spying* on things."

"That's fine." Jack accepted his ID back and tucked it away in an inner jacket pocket. "We know it all, anyway."

Another pause, this one mildly sceptical, mildly worried it was true. "Yeah, right," he repeated. "You can take a seat, Mr. Reardon. Someone will come get you shortly."

It wasn't long before he heard his name being called. A uniform stood just this side of a door labelled "Authorised Personnel Only."

Jack sauntered over, his ID making another appearance. "That's me."

The constable, a sun-bleached blond at least a couple of inches taller than Jack, though he slouched self-consciously, motioned for him to follow. "This way. The strike force is on the third floor. Everything beyond this door is restricted access. You will need an escort to move around."

That was the entire commentary he got all along the corridor, in the lift up two floors, and along another corridor. At a closed door, the constable knocked and waited.

Senior Sergeant Stephanie Phelps wasn't what Jack had been expecting. Not that he'd had much of an idea either way, but the rounded, medium-height woman with a steel-grey bob and sharp, piercing brown eyes wouldn't have been his choice. She wore plain clothes, pink and grey sneakers, jeans, and T-shirt with the slogan "Ew, people."

"Yes?" she asked distractedly, focusing more on the screen in her hand than either of them.

"Ma'am, this is your guest, Mr. Reardon." The constable's shoulders hunched in further.

Phelps looked up, her initial welcoming smile fading into confusion before she managed to smooth it over. "Jack Reardon?" she asked as her gaze went over his shoulder. Perhaps the real Caucasian Jack Reardon was hiding behind the Indian man.

"Yes, ma'am," Jack said dryly. This was why he generally went by Nishant in casual situations. It was just easier. If this had been a normal UC operation, he would have gone with a name like Raj or Jaidev, something no one would ever think to question. He began to reach for his ID again. "I can show you my ISO identification, if you wish."

The poor woman blushed. "Ah, that's not necessary. I'm sorry, it's just that . . ."

In the spirit of a good working relationship, Jack smiled. "It's okay. I get that a lot. Think nothing of it."

Smiling once more, Phelps said, "Thank you and welcome. We're very happy you're here." To the constable, she added, "Toomey, if you see Adam, give him a kick in the bum. He's late, again."

Toomey grunted acknowledgement and shambled away.

"Come in, Mr. Reardon." Phelps ushered him through the door. "Thank you so much for agreeing to see us."

"I wasn't exactly given a choice, ma'am," he said as he went in.

The room was longer than it was wide, mostly filled by a table that was two separate ones pushed together. Its surface was covered in files and papers, two laptops, and three different phones. There was a mobile whiteboard at one end, covered in writing in several different colours and hands. At the other was a big wall-mounted screen, displaying several of the crime scene photos. On the wall opposite the door were a couple of windows, looking out over the park behind the building. There were only three chairs at the table.

Phelps, in the process of clearing off a corner of the table, stopped and looked at him, eyebrows raised. "I'm sorry. I thought I made it clear it was a request, not a demand." She sounded apologetic, not indignant.

"No, it's okay," Jack hastily said. "It was a bad attempt at humour."

Her wide eyes didn't waver for a long moment, and then she blinked. "If you say so. I think you're going to fit in here, at least."

"Really?"

"It's the attempted humour. Adam tries but rarely gets there."

"Sounds familiar." Jack counted up the chairs again, just to be sure. "Where's the rest of the strike force?"

"Running late, as usual." Then Phelps seemed to pick up on his meaning. "Oh, they cut us back, again. Right now, it's just me and Adam and he's only on loan from AFRG. Oh, and now you, as well. Another loaner, but trust me, if you prove you can read and reason at a high school level, I'll do my best to keep you around, too."

Jack would have laughed if she didn't look so serious. "And Adam is?"

"Our profiler." Phelps motioned him to sit where she'd cleared some space. "Don't call him that to his face, though. He says it makes him feel like he's a dog doing tricks at a party." Once he was seated, she pulled a chair up opposite him.

"Right. A psychologist." Shit. He'd had enough of psychologists for a lifetime.

Phelps gave him a sharp look. "Not all profilers are psychologists, you know. In fact, few of them are."

Suitably chastised, Jack asked, "So if I call this Adam a shrink, that'll be wrong, too?"

"Well, no. He is actually a forensic psychiatrist, but that's his dirty little secret." She shuffled some bulging files around. "Okay, this is most of what we're working with at the moment. I'd rather Adam was here to give you the serial murder talk first, but beggars, blah blah blah."

The serial murder talk? Christ.

"As for why you're here, Mr. Reardon," she began.

"Jack, please."

"Right, Jack. Call me Steph, or Stephanie. Just don't call me Fanny." She accompanied that with a stern look. Reassured he got the hint, she continued. "You, my new friend, are my secret weapon. Technically, you're here to provide expert advice on how our offender got into the scenes without alerting anyone. Something which our own investigative teams are more than capable of doing, by the way."

Jack nodded along. It seemed McIntosh's theory about why Jack was here was turning out to be right.

"Your real purpose is to give us an insight into the military side of things. *Officially*, we are not investigating Captain Morrissey's murder, but if Adam has any chance in hell of producing a working profile, he needs an expert to advise him on that side of things." Steph gave him a frank look. "Do you have any objections to that?"

Before he could answer, the door opened and a man rushed in. "I'm here." There was a laptop bag under one arm and a cardboard coffee tray in the other hand. "I bought coffee for everyone. Hope the mysterious Mr. Rear..."

Oh. Fuck.

Jack's stomach dropped all three floors. Quinn, too, looked like he'd been abandoned by his internal organs, and if Jack hadn't been so fucking shocked, he would have taken a moment to appreciate how thrown the man was. In about three seconds flat, Quinn's expression went from rueful, through confusion and uncertainty, to end, like a car crash, on pained resignation.

"...don likes a long black," Quinn finished.

Probably attributing Quinn's vocal stumble as shock at Jack's ethnic appearance, Stephanie hustled over to help him with his cargo. "About time, Quinn." She took the coffees and came back to Jack, offering him one. "Jack, this is Adam Quinn, our *profiler*." Obviously said to annoy him. "Adam, be nice to Mr. Reardon—we want him to stick around."

Taking the drink, Jack wondered what he'd done to piss off God, karma, and Murphy so badly. Why, of all the people in the world, did his occasional hook-up from months ago have to be the profiler on this case? Why was Jack, *not* the only ex-solider with ISO, the one picked by Steph to help them out? Why hadn't that truck taken him out on the way here? So many whys and no ready answers.

Adam set his bag on the table and approached Jack. "Mr. Reardon, it's a pleasure." His tone showed no sign of recognition.

Calling on every measure of undercover training to keep a straight face, Jack stood and shook his hand. "Likewise. Call me Jack. Adam, was it?"

"Dr. Adam Quinn, to be precise. But Adam's fine. Jack, huh?" He tilted his head, and that penetrative gaze hit Jack. "Paternal family name, right? And a Hindi middle name."

If Adam didn't want to feel like a dog doing tricks, he shouldn't act like one. "Correct. My father's of English descent, mother was Indian."

Eyebrows arching slightly at the "was," Adam thankfully let it pass.

That moment, however, didn't go by Stephanie unnoticed. "I said don't piss him off, Adam."

Not breaking eye contact with Jack, Adam grinned, wide and unabashed. "I don't think this one scares that easy."

"No, but piss him off and he could throw you out the window." Stephanie gave Jack a sympathetic look. "The last consultant we had threatened to do that to him."

Jack shrugged like it was still a possibility. Adam smirked and then dragged the last chair over and sat next to Jack. Again, Adam's cologne sparked some pleasant memories, but that was all. Their time together had been nice, but it was well and truly in the past.

"Right, now that we're all acquainted, let's start." Stephanie handed Jack a couple of folders. "Are you aware of a serial killer we've dubbed the Judge?"

They went through all the information Jack already knew. Steph filled in most of the details the Office didn't have the night before, and even before she'd finished, Jack knew why they needed his military expertise. Captain Shane Morrissey had been killed in his residence on base.

"The offender is escalating" was Adam's first offering to the discussion. "Not in terms of needing more gratification from his victims, yet, but rather in the difficulty of getting to the victims. If he'd kept to housewives and suburban slobs, we would have no need of you. The original profile would still fit, but this changes things. A lot."

"You're sure these latest two are the same guy?" Jack asked.

"As sure as we can be," Steph said. "Which in this business is never one hundred percent."

"Okay." Jack was used to working with less than total certainty.

"That's the basics of our case," Steph said. "Do you think you can help us?"

"I should be able to offer something—fingers crossed it helps."

"Good." To Adam, she said, "Unless you had any stunning revelations last night . . .?" When he shook his head, she sighed. "All right. I'm going to go see Dumay. See if I can't shake a constable or two free of her clutches to help us."

Adam chuckled. "Good luck. Remember what happened the last time you did that."

"You nearly got thrown out a window. I'm hoping for a similar outcome." She swept out of the room.

"Dumay?" Jack's belly tightened at being alone with Adam.

"Superintendent Julia Dumay," Adam intoned, like he was introducing Darth Vader. "Our evil overlord. Actually, that's not fair. She's just a victim of an evil chain of command. Every time ADFIS presses their boot down, Dumay's the one who has to take whatever staff or equipment away from us they disapprove of. Still, if you get the chance to sit in on a meeting between her and Steph, you should. Dumay is a rock, and Steph is the falling rain."

Grateful Adam didn't seem inclined to bring up personal issues now they were alone, Jack asked, "So, now what?"

"Now, my friend, you get a crash course in psychos, from yours truly. Buckle up, buttercup. This is gonna get rough."

THIRTEEN

AFTER

Jack didn't think he'd be able to sleep so he didn't try. He did the next best thing.

In the break room, he stripped to his undies and, still too twitchy to get into the headspace he needed, started a tai chi sequence. At first, it was hard to get Ethan out of his head. Too many memories from the last month of moving beside him in slow, delicate motions, of watching the tension ease from Ethan's body, of how the peace it gave them both led to some of the best nights in Jack's life. But as he concentrated on his breathing, on flowing from one stance to the next, those distractions slipped away. By the time he eased to a stop, a half hour had passed and he felt calm, ready and able to carry on.

Lying down on the lower bunk, Jack worked his way through his body, as he had in the police interrogation room, and relaxed muscle groups one by one. Done, he slipped *sideways*. The overlay for his implant appeared before his inner eyes. Sitting patiently in one corner was the file Jack had complied in the interrogation room. Not really wanting to acknowledge some of the contents, Jack nevertheless opened the file so its contents could be accessed by a different program.

The cognitive modelling application of the implant wasn't as powerful as computer-based programs, but it was good enough to help soldiers in the field, and it had helped Jack in his work for the Office, as well.

He set up the goal and parameters of the search, both wanting and dreading the answer it might give him. He was banking on Adam's assurance that a lot of the time, the answer to a serial murder case was right in front of them, just buried amongst so much other information it took time, and sometimes chance, to uncover it. Jack had been immersed in the case for so long that surely, if they'd already had the answer to who the Judge was but just hadn't been able to see it, this would work. Perhaps subconsciously, he knew who the killer was and was just incapable of seeing it. Or perhaps, acknowledging it.

Letting the model run, Jack dropped into a deeper trance state. With a model working on a subject so close to Jack's personal life, it was possible it could incite flashbacks, and Jack didn't want to be aware if that was the case. If the filing cabinet in the back of his head, filled with all the dark and terrible things he'd witnessed and done over the years was going to bust open, the less mobile he was, the better. No one needed him to wake up punching and kicking, or find him rolled up in a foetal position, sobbing his heart out.

No matter the depth of the trance, nothing would entirely keep the bad memories out Once more, Jack burst into the foyer of the ISO building in Canberra. The assassin named Porsche was making a break for it towards the courtyard and Harry . . . Harry swung around the end of the desk ahead of Jack. It was a memory. Jack knew it even as it all unfolded before his eyes again, and yet he couldn't stop it. Knowing what was coming, carrying that sick, fatalistic knowledge in his guts, he still wasn't fast enough to save Harry.

Ping.

The alert from the implant replaced the sound of gunfire and jerked Jack out of the ill-fated scenario. Swimming up through visions of flashing silver and endless pools of blood, Jack shook off the clinging tendrils of the flashback. As he surfaced, he noted that the cognitive model hadn't finished, just paused while he took care of whatever external problem there was. Going *sideways* again, Jack opened his eyes and focused on the springs of the bed above him.

Another knock at the door, the sound that had made the implant wake him up. Jack rolled off the bed, automatically reaching for his gun. For a moment, he was back in the ISO HQ, exchanging fire with several bad guys, then Lewis's "Jack? You awake?" solidified him in the present.

"Yeah." Jack let the gun drop back to the mattress. "Come in."

"You don't look rested at all," his friend announced when he came in.

Jack hauled on his crumpled jeans. "Just the image I was going for. Anything new? What's the time?"

"Nothing substantial and just after 10:00 p.m. You got about four hours." Lewis wandered over and perched his arse on the edge of the small table. "Word filtered up from the depths of the fourth floor. Apparently McIntosh went through Ex Mon like a dose of salts. She left them shitting themselves about failing to catch those CCTV images. You could almost hear Robson crying from up here. The entire department is scrambling to cover their collective arse. Imagine how it looks. They didn't do their job and now one of our assets has caught a ticket, picked up by no one less than number five on the JSL. I don't have to tell you, but the name Harraway is being whispered around the place."

Of course people would be thinking about Glen Harraway. It had only been a year since the traitor had been exposed and arrested. The Office as a whole was still under intense review, Intelligence more so than the rest of them. Investigations into the extent of Harraway's corruption were still turning up nasty secrets and betrayals, and probably would for years to come. Jack could sympathise with the poor assets down in Ex Mon. He knew very well what it was like to be under suspicion when he'd done nothing wrong. Well, wrong within a certain definition of the word, at least. He was sympathetic, but at the same time, as the asset with the ticket on his head, waiting for Eve Garrote to show up, he just hoped the problem in Ex Mon was rooted out before someone else died.

"It's got me thinking about the photos," Lewis continued.

"Yeah?" Jack sniffed his shirt. Christ, it still stank but it was all he had, so he slid it on and buttoned up. "What about them? Didn't they get your best angle?"

"Apart from that, they don't fit."

Lewis's tone was serious. No hint of his usual joking attitude. His mind had been working just as furiously as Jack's had while he'd pretended to sleep.

"How so?" Jack asked, just as serious.

"Ex Mon hasn't dropped a ball this big, ever. Not even when Harraway was doctoring information. Unless someone there deliberately let the photos through, which I very much doubt, I think they were planted deliberately. It's too much of a coincidence, otherwise. We've been out of Bangkok for nearly a month now. The Messiah's been recruiting the best hackers across the world for years. If those photos had been somewhere easily enough accessible the *police* could find them, then hundreds of that slimeball's Disciples would have found them long before now. They show us outside of that brothel, where the Messiah disappeared. Even Detective Connors could put that together and get a clue."

"It makes sense," Jack reasoned. "The Disciples *did* find the photos, they worked out we're the ones who got their precious digital terrorist, and now I have Eve Garrote after me. What's your point?"

"My point is this." Lewis waved his hands up and down his own body. "Where's my ticket? I'm in those photos with you and yet, nothing. Not one person on the JSL wants me dead. I'm a little miffed."

Despite the deadliness of the subject, Jack snorted. "You're the only person I know who'd be upset at *not* getting a death threat."

"It's insulting but telling. The photos implicate both of us in the disappearance of the Messiah, therefore it's not the Disciples who bought the ticket."

"McIntosh said it was a best guess only, not definite."

"But it's what people are fixating on. The biggest mess you've been in over the past year is Canberra, and we managed to keep that one sealed tight."

Shoving aside his gut reaction to the mention of Canberra, Jack grumbled, "So what's your theory, then?"

"Stick with me," Lewis said in a placating tone. "The ticket came out two hours before you were arrested. When did Connors say he found the photos?"

Jack eyed him warily for a moment, then closed his eyes. Without needing to go into a trance, he accessed the constantly running, passive surveillance app of the implant, searching through the conversation with Connors in the interrogation room.

"He didn't specify. Only said he'd found them when looking into my history. That would have been after the Judge killed one of the Infinity crew."

"So, somewhere between 9:00 p.m. and 6:00 a.m., let's say," Lewis mused.

Jack shook his head. "Probably from about 10:00 p.m. at the earliest. I left Adam just before then and, if he's the victim, he would have needed some time to get back to the LAC."

Lewis studied him for a moment. "You really think it's him, don't you."

"From what Connors said, yeah."

"I'm sorry. You two seemed to be getting on well." The carefully chosen words echoed the unasked question from the tearoom.

Stomach twisting into a painful knot, Jack nodded. "He was a good man." Shit. He was talking about Adam in the past tense. "Hurry up and spill the rest of your mad theory."

"Yeah, okay. So, the photos don't make sense. The other thing that doesn't add up is Garrote. No offense, mate, but you're well below her pay grade."

Jack would have been insulted if he didn't think it as well or know how true it was.

"On top of Garrote stooping to your level, she picked that ticket up so fast no one else got a chance at it. We found out you'd been arrested because as soon as Intel got the news of her picking up the ticket, they did an active search for you. She was on it before they'd even closed the cuffs."

Jesus. This was what Jack got for consorting with an assassin. Maybe Ethan did know Eve Garrote and had told her how shitty Jack had treated him, and this was her coming to her fellow paid killer's rescue. Jack had to find Ethan before Garrote found *him*.

"What if—and promise me you'll think about it before shouting it down—but what if the ticket isn't about the Messiah *at all*," Lewis said, tone lowering portentously. "What if it's someone who doesn't want you to actually catch the Judge?"

There was no point in arguing with Lewis. Once he set his feet on a certain path, he wouldn't get off it until he was either vindicated or proved himself wrong. Besides, Jack was of two minds. His friend was right in that it was too coincidental for the ticket to surface now if it was the Disciples who'd bought it, but why the hell would anyone go to all that trouble to protect a serial killer? Lewis hadn't developed his theory that far, but Jack let Lewis hurry him up to McIntosh's office. After a brief wait, they were let in and Lewis explained it to their director.

McIntosh barely let him finish before she authorised Lewis to follow the tangent, giving temporary operational command to Lydia. The speed with which she'd responded said McIntosh either trusted Lewis's deductions implicitly, or she knew something they didn't. Neither was more likely than the other, and both were probably true. Despite that, Jack was still hesitant about the whole idea as they headed back down to the eighth. If it was true, then that meant the whole mystery around the Judge was bigger and deeper than just one man fulfilling his own twisted desires. Which blended all too well with Jack's suspicions after his last argument with Ethan.

"Where are you going?" Jack asked Lewis as they hit the landing for their floor and the other man kept going.

"Down to Ex Mon to find whoever's in charge of investigating those photos and hope something there backs up my theory."

"Okay, Don Quixote. Have fun with the windmills."

A couple of steps down, Lewis stopped and frowned at him. "What's that supposed to mean?"

Jack sighed. "I'm not making fun of your theory. More that I just hope it couldn't be possible. If it's true, then . . ."

Knowing the conclusion of that sentence as well as Jack did, Lewis nodded solemnly. "It would explain a few things, though."

"Yeah, but not enough things. If you're going to bother the good folks on the fourth, what am I doing?"

Lewis smirked. "It's seminar time. We have a lot of new people on the team, and they need to be brought up speed. Lydia should have them assembled by now. Go, my son, and spread the good serial killer word to the faithful."

"Can't they all just read my reports? And why do you get out of it?"

"They could, but reports don't answer questions as well as you do. As for me, I'm the boss, and my job is to delegate, not do."

FOURTEEN
BEFORE

Jack was a killer. Both with the Office and the armed forces. As an SAS lieutenant, he'd given the go-ahead to set charges around a Taliban barracks. He'd depressed the trigger himself, killing dozens of soldiers in one move. He'd shot the enemy, cut their throats, strangled them. As a field operative for the Office, he'd poisoned people, sniped them from a distance, broken necks from behind.

But none of it, absolutely *none* of it compared to what Adam described for him now.

Adam threw out words like manipulation, domination, and control as driving forces behind the actions of serial murderers. He explained the development of the "fantasy"; went through the careful planning, the living and breathing of the desire; the eventual progression to enacting the dreamed-up scenario; to the act itself. He went through the difference between *modus operandi* and *signatures*, between *staging* and *posing*. Described organised versus disorganised killers, impulsive versus targeted killers.

All of it in excruciating, *juicy* detail. The depth Adam went into was painful, pulling dozens of examples straight from memory to illustrate various points.

And that was just the introduction.

By the time they stopped for lunch, Jack's head was busting with so much information and imagery he couldn't meet Adam's gaze for longer than a moment or two. Thankfully, the profiler volunteered to fetch sandwiches from a café down the road, took their orders, and left him alone for a precious few minutes.

"I'm sorry about Adam." Steph surfaced from her work to smile at him comfortingly. "He likes to show off, and, well, it's a bit of a ritual, hazing the newbies. You kept up really well, though."

"So, it's not him . . ." *Making me pay for turning him down last night.* "Not just me, then?"

"Oh, no. He does it to everyone. The guy before you had to leave about halfway through the opening speech to 'take an important call.' The trick with dealing with Adam is to give as much as you get. Once he knows he can't walk all over you, he backs off a bit."

Jack nodded his thanks and took a walk around the perimeter of the room to stretch his legs. Stephanie seemed to understand his need for a bit of silence and left him to it.

He ended up by the window, looking out at Sydney, stretching away into the distance. Spent a while concentrating on something other than the work, to give himself a breather from it all. None of the big landmarks were visible from his position, but they were the superficial parts of Sydney. They weren't the things Jack looked to when he needed to be grounded. He homed in on the sand of the beaches, the tangle of the streets, the skyline, the people going about their lives. This time, though, he had the added weight of knowing Ethan was out there, in the same city. Here, with him.

It worked to fix him in the here and now, fetching back the last part of him that was still in Bangkok, hunting down the Messiah.

After lunch, he felt ready to continue, and Adam took him through the details of the Judge's victims. It was easier going this time, as Jack found that using the terms Adam had given him in the morning helped distance him from the raw brutality and sickness of the scenes. The technique was one he was familiar with. Occasionally, in order to get a job done, thinking of the enemy as something other than a person with hopes and dreams was necessary.

"What about the newest victims?" Jack asked when Adam stopped after the first two victims in Melbourne.

"I haven't completely worked the new victims out," Adam admitted sourly. "Part of that, I think, is because the scenes feel like they're not entirely about the victim. Like I said this morning, he's escalating, but not in the usual direction. He's a 'mission-orientated' killer, meaning he's there for the actual killing and getting a certain outcome. He leaves the Bible verses to make sure that we know what outcome that is. Punishing his victims because they're bad. He is policeman, *judge*, and God."

At Steph clearing her throat meaningfully, Adam added, "But he's not delusional. It's not like he thinks he's God, or a judge or a policeman, because frankly, they're below him. He's operating on an entirely different level to everyone else."

"Conceited," Jack offered.

"Without a doubt." Adam gave him a proud smile. "You just got your passing grade. Welcome to the wonderful world of profiling."

"Thought you didn't like that word."

"I don't. Too many incorrect assumptions hang off it. But for you, it's fine. You're an armchair profiler." He grinned cheekily.

"My, my." Steph didn't take her gaze off her laptop. "I think it's love."

Adam threw a pen at her, laughing. She dodged without looking up.

Jack looked from one to the other, enjoying the clear comradery and teasing affection between them. "How long have you pair been working together?"

"Since the dawn of time," Adam said at the same time Steph said, "Far too long."

Chuckling, Jack said, "Seriously, though."

"This time, we've been on this case for nearly two weeks now, but it's like living in each other's pockets," Steph said. "Since it's been just us most of the time, we've been working long hours."

"Long hours," Adam agreed. "Have worked together before, though. Then there was that steamy vacay we took to America together."

Jack quirked a curious brow.

"FBI training course," Steph cleared up. "That's where I first met him. Are you done trying to traumatise the poor man?" she asked Adam.

"For today."

"Good. Jack, I think you can call it a day. Tomorrow, we'll put you to real use. Could you be here by eight?"

"No problem. I can stay longer if you need."

She waved him out. "I'd rather we not burn you out too quick. Go, try to sleep. Just let me call for an escort."

"Don't worry." Adam stood and indicated Jack get moving. "I'll see him out."

"If I'm a loaner and not allowed to roam on my own, why are you?" Jack asked as they headed towards the lift.

Adam winked. "I'm special." He flashed a laminated card that hung around his neck under his tie. "I'm AFRG, so I'm like 'affiliated' staff. Australian Forensic Reference Group," he explained when Jack looked puzzled. "We're a bunch of professionals the BAU put together to help them out with serial cases. Based in Melbourne and we don't normally go *to* jobs. I'm not usually this hands-on, but since Steph was getting so much flak from ADFIS and Dumay, I offered to come up and help."

That made Jack pause. "You're here on your own? The BAU didn't send you?"

"Nope."

Shaking his head as they stepped out of the lift on the ground floor and headed towards the foyer, Jack said, "Are you doing more here than you would back home, though?"

Adam stopped walking, and Jack saw a new expression on his face. There were no winks, no smiles, no forthcoming jokes. He was deadly serious. "Yeah, I am. I'm supporting a friend in a difficult situation. That's more than worth the expense."

Jack felt like shit-heel. In his defence, he'd only seen the smart-alec, irreverent, smirking man, even during all the dark and sick subjects they'd touched on today. Seeing this side of him was a bit of a surprise.

"How do you stay so . . . *happy* doing this for a job?" Jack was genuinely curious.

Adam studied him with those searching eyes for an uncomfortable minute, then he grinned, once more the joker. "It's either this or madness, right?"

Letting out a long breath, Jack turned and kept walking. Adam caught up and stayed with him all the way outside and over to his bike.

"Nice." Adam ran an appreciative hand over the seat of the bike.

"Know anything about bikes?" Jack asked.

"Not a thing."

Jack laughed, preparing to put his helmet on.

"I think we should go somewhere for a drink," Adam said.

Jack put the helmet on the seat. "We talked about this, remember."

"I'm not angling for anything other than a few drinks. Remember what *I* said? About being friends." He did lean closer, though, voice lowering. "And the other offer is still there, too."

It was interesting how what had been tempting the night before was now amusing. All because Ethan was here.

"I don't think so," Jack said blandly.

Adam smirked. "About which offer? The drinks or the blowjob?"

"The BJ," Jack found himself answering without thinking about it. "You might still get the drinks, if you work at it. Goodbye, Quinn. I'll see you tomorrow."

Adam laughed and gave Jack a mock salute as he got on the bike and rode away.

Jack spent the ride to the Office trying not to feel guilty about not shooting Adam down completely.

After what felt to be an inordinately long first day debrief— mostly because he was compelled to admit his prior connection to Dr. Adam Quinn, sparking a discussion on how beneficial, or detrimental, it would be to the case—Jack got home after nine. Disappointingly, Victoria wasn't in the garage and the apartment was empty. The sting of Ethan's absence was mildly mitigated by finding a note in his precise handwriting, saying he would be back "later."

Feeling dirty from the day's information overload, Jack showered, ate a quick dinner of toast and cereal, then watched a late news broadcast to see if anything interesting had happened elsewhere in the world. Nothing had, and eventually, he had to concede defeat and go to bed. Though he didn't think he'd be able to have a good night's sleep with Adam's lecture swirling around his brain, Jack was dozing when he heard the alarm system beep. Before he'd cleared the sheets, it beeped the all clear, and a moment later, Ethan's lean shadow appeared in the doorway to the bedroom.

"This is 'later'?" Jack sank back onto the bed.

"Arguably." Ethan slid out of his jacket. "I did mean to be here sooner, but I lost track of time."

While Ethan padded silently around the darkened room, Jack got comfortable again, watching as clothes were removed and neatly folded onto the recliner.

"You can use the wardrobe." He liked the idea of Ethan's clothes hanging next to his. "And we can reorganise the tallboy to fit your undies in."

All movement stopped, and Jack's stomach tightened. What had sparked Ethan's fight-or-flight mode? Before he worked it out, Ethan moved again, drawing in a deep breath and letting it out, then finished unbuttoning his shirt.

"You wouldn't mind if I did?"

"Of course not. I thought this was what we were doing. What we talked about. You being here for more than a flying visit. Staying here."

After a long, strained moment, Ethan nodded. "I suppose I wasn't sure if that was still what you wanted."

Tension uncoiling in his gut, Jack groaned. "Jesus, Ethan. Just toss your clothes in the laundry basket and get your stupid arse in bed."

Ethan chuckled as he balled up his shirt and threw it blindly over his shoulder. "As you wish, Jack." A second later, he landed on the bed, momentum rolling him right to Jack's side.

Grunting at the impact, Jack shoved him away, then made his own attack. They play wrestled and laughed and tickled until at some shared signal, it turned to caresses and moans and kisses. Jack got Ethan pinned on his belly, wrists cuffed by one of Jack's hands at the base of his spine. He kissed and nipped his way from one straining shoulder to the other, nuzzled into the dark hair, teased his entrance with a couple of fingers. Then he spent a while tracing the scars on the pale skin, letting the anger and protectiveness they inspired wash through him. It dulled the edge of his arousal enough he let Ethan's hands go and lay down, covering him like a blanket, as if by being here now he could somehow deflect the whip that fell twenty years in the past. Under him, Ethan relaxed into the mattress.

"I do hope that eventually you will do something a little more productive while you're there," Ethan murmured.

"Eventually." Jack pressed his lips to the back of his neck.

"Just don't go to sleep first."

"It was a long, disturbing day. Sleep might not actually work for me tonight." Jack heaved himself up onto his elbows, taking some of his weight off Ethan. "What did you do today?"

"Hmm, nothing terribly scintillating, I'm afraid. I spent the morning giving Victoria a thorough going-over. It's been some time since she was driven. This afternoon I had some other matters to attend to. What was so disturbing about your day?"

Jack could spot a subject change when it all but clobbered him over the head. He decided to give Ethan this one, knowing the man wouldn't be able to stop dissembling cold turkey, no matter his good intentions.

"This new job I started." He rolled off Ethan and onto his back. "It's not a normal job. Not something I'm used to."

Turning to his side, head propped up on one hand, Ethan stroked Jack's chest. "You said this morning you were going undercover."

Normally, Jack's job wasn't pillow-talk material, but this was Ethan, the one man Jack had been with since joining the Office who knew not only exactly who Jack was, but what he did for a living. Also, this was Ethan Blade, a man who could probably do Jack's job better than he did. For once in his career with the Office, he'd found someone who could listen and understand.

"Yeah. It's not a regular undercover job, though. No assumed identity, no fake history. I'm just SSA Jack Reardon, ex-soldier, advising on a case the Office usually wouldn't touch. It doesn't feel . . . right."

"I can understand that." Ethan traced patterns over Jack's body, soft and smooth and tingling. "Will it be a long case, do you think?"

Gaze following the mesmerising vision of pale fingers framed against tan skin, Jack muttered, "Too soon to tell. I hope not, though. After Bangkok, I feel like I need a break. A week, even a couple of days, but this job came up and . . . Christ." Succumbing to his rising arousal, Jack grabbed Ethan's hand and hauled until the man was pretty much right on top of him. "Quit teasing and just get on with whatever you want to do."

Laughing, Ethan squirmed into a better position. "As you wish, Jack."

FIFTEEN AFTER

When Jack found Lydia, she had gathered all available team members in their operations room and left him a place at the head of the table. Considering he'd once thought he would become a teacher, like both of his parents, Jack didn't have issues with talking in front of people. What he did worry about was the subject matter. He'd been working the case for close on a month, spending so much time with Adam it had been hard not to absorb more information about serial murders than he ever would have wished to know. Still, this wasn't his area of expertise, and he dreaded any of the questions the team might throw at him.

After making sure Lydia had lined up the crime scene photos in order, Jack took his place at the head of the table. The screen in front of him linked to the large wall-mounted one at the far end of the room. Flicking the first photo to the big screen, Jack began.

"Three years ago, two murders in Melbourne pinged on the national database as a possible serial."

A dozen keen expressions turned to stare at the picture of the first victim. Jack had stared at it so often over the past weeks he was numb to the instinctual reactions of horror and sadness, but he gave the team half a minute to deal with their own feelings, then continued.

"The murder happened in the woman's bathroom—in the shower, so most of the physical evidence was washed away. Eleven stab wounds, all with the same six-inch blade. The attack was methodical, not erratic, and fast, giving the victim no time to defend herself. She was then moved to the bedroom and posed as you see here. The killer left a note with the body. A passage from the Bible." Jack flicked to the picture of the note, and read, "'Parents are not to be put to death for their children, nor children put to death for their parents; each will die for their own sin.' He's saying that this woman committed a sin and he's punishing her for it."

"What did she do?" a tech from halfway down the table asked. They all had comprehensive files on the victims, but it would be quicker for Jack to answer.

"Nothing wrong," Jack said grimly. "In our opinion. To her killer, though, she represented something he hated."

"A woman?" a young female tech asked.

"All but one of his other victims are male," someone else reminded her. "Gender isn't a link between them."

"Correct," Jack said. "But this woman's crime against her killer was something she was just as powerless to change. She had a son who suffered from schizophrenia with violent tendencies. He was convicted of manslaughter after pushing a woman in front of a car during one of his bouts. Our victim's only sin, in her killer's eyes, was to 'create' a damaged child. The killer knows he's not normal, for want of a better word. There's something wrong with him, and he blames someone else for it. Popular opinion about serial killers is that their mental illness is a result of childhood trauma. It excuses their actions, rather than forcing them to take responsibility for them. This is our offender saying it's always the mother's fault. Or the abusive father's. Someone else is to blame, not me."

As he carried on to the next victim, "A middle-aged man, killed in the same manner. A drug dealer and pimp who'd get young girls addicted and then force them to hook for their drug money." He realised he was all but repeating Adam's words from Jack's first day on the strike force. It gave him some solace to think that even if Adam was dead, at least his work was still being done.

"This one's pretty straightforward," Adam said in his memory, and Jack echoed it aloud. "The Bible passage reads, 'But the eyes of the wicked will fail, and escape will elude them; their hope will become a dying gasp.' Basically, the only hope the wicked have is death. At the same time, our offender is showing us he *isn't* wicked, because he's doing our job for us."

"Cocky bastard," a man at the far end of the table muttered.

Jack smiled sadly, recalling Adam proclaiming him an "armchair profiler" after saying pretty much the same thing.

"All right," he said gruffly, moving past the moment. "On their own, the first two victims make sense. The Judge is punishing them for their crimes, real or imagined. He's, in a sense, trying to prove that his desire to kill is justified. Then we get the next victim, Brandt Williams. Not only is he in Sydney, but he's also much younger than the other two. He's got gainful employment in a legitimate field. He doesn't have a criminal record and, apart from some slightly unusual porn on his home computer, is so vanilla he fades into the background. He was killed and posed at work. The Bible verse left with him should be recognisable to most of you. 'And lead us not into temptation, but deliver us from evil.'"

Every head around the table nodded, but it was Lydia who spoke up.

"The verse itself is pretty self-explanatory, but how does it fit with the victim?"

"We don't know. Adam couldn't find a connection that felt right to him. We simply do not know why the Judge chose Williams."

The team tossed ideas around for a while, most of them centred around the porn—which featured furries—while Jack listened patiently. Adam had gone down all these paths, and many others, over the weeks, and still not come to a conclusion he was happy with. It had frustrated him no end, wondering just what temptation or evil death was saving Williams from, or stopping him from committing.

When the speculation had tapered off, Jack moved on to the fourth victim.

"Captain Shane Morrissey, Australian Defence Force Intelligence Corps. He's the victim who facilitated our inclusion in the case. ADFIS refused to share information with the strike force and actively worked to stop them from investigating Morrissey's death. So the strike force leader had to go outside of the box to get the expertise they needed."

"Namely, you," Lydia said. "However, we have more access to military records than the police do. More than some of the higher ranks in the military wished we had sometimes. Everyone here is well-informed on Morrissey's personal history and career."

"Which, again," Jack continued, "we couldn't quite reconcile with the Judge's apparent agenda. His verse was 'You are the salt of the earth. But if the salt loses its saltiness, how can it be made salty again? It is no longer good for anything, except to be thrown out and trampled underfoot.'"

"Corruption," was one tech's immediate response. "Salt stops corruption in food. The Judge is saying that Morrissey was corrupted somehow, and that killing him was the only way to stop him from doing whatever he was doing."

"Or," another piped up, "killing him was the only way the Judge could see to make him pure again."

Both ideas Adam had toyed with, but again, hadn't been able to find a suitable conclusion.

"We looked into Morrissey weeks ago," Lydia interjected. "There's no hint of corruption in his career. He was perfectly committed to his job."

Silence for a moment, and then Jack said, "Adam also thought it may have meant someone else had corrupted Morrissey. Not necessarily in his work, but in his private life. He was gay and had no known partner, but that doesn't mean there wasn't someone. Perhaps Morrissey cheated on him." His stomach tightened reflexively. Was that what Ethan thought? That Adam had corrupted Jack? Or maybe that Jack had corrupted Ethan?

"But if we don't know or can't find out about a possible partner, how would the Judge?" someone asked.

Putting Ethan in his own drawer in the filing cabinet, Jack shrugged. "Who knows. It's possible the Judge was stalking Morrissey for weeks before killing him. He could have seen things that no one else did. Morrissey was an officer in the Intelligence Corps. If he wanted to keep something a secret, he would know how to. And we've already shown that the Judge is an above-average operator. Basically, anything is possible."

The fifth victim, Brenna Luntz, had been murdered the day before Jack was arrested and was so similar to Williams Jack could have just "dittoed" everything he said for the young man. Single, young, employed, no criminal record, nothing remarkable about her on the surface, other than being targeted by the Judge.

"Her verse was 'Then the Lord God said to the woman, "What is this you have done?" The woman said, "The serpent deceived me, and I ate."' As with Williams, this appears to be about temptation. The investigative team was still compiling information on her when . . . well, they were still working on it yesterday."

After the team threw out a few ideas, one of them asked Jack and Lydia, "Do we know what verse was left with the last victim at the LAC?"

Lydia fielded it. "No. So far, we have no information other than the victim was either Dr. Adam Quinn or Senior Sargent Stephanie Phelps. Kate, you keep working on trying to get us more information from the police. Ryan, your group is now on Morrissey, and Mel, yours is on Williams and Luntz."

While Lydia continued to assign tasks, Jack put Adam's last version of the profile up on the main screen. Hopefully it would help spark something in the team as they kept digging into the lives of the various victims. Jack's only real hope right then was that with his firsthand knowledge combined with the collective IQ of the room, progress would be made, sooner rather than later.

Maybe if the Office had done this from the start instead of just monitoring Jack and the case peripherally, they wouldn't be here now. Adam would still be alive and maybe Ethan would be at home, and happy.

Jack returned to his schematics and blueprints in the corner. His mildly freshened mind might see something he'd missed earlier. As he worked, various team members came over with questions about bits of information they found, or asked his opinion on their burgeoning theories. Around midnight, Lydia forced Jack out of the room with half of the team so they could get some sleep. Grumbling but thinking he could use the time to let the cognitive model finish, Jack went. He was asleep the moment his head hit the pillow, however, and only woke up when the alarm set by the tech in the top bunk went off.

Sleepy-eyed, Jack trundled into the tearoom for coffee. He was blinking confusedly at the clock on the wall which said it was now nearly 10:00 a.m. when Lewis burst into the room.

"Jack! Come on, we've caught a break. Hurry up!"

Instantly awake, Jack left his coffee behind and followed his quickly moving friend. Lewis, like Jack, clearly hadn't been home for a shower or change of clothes, but he looked surprisingly energised. Which was probably due to the crinkles pressed into the side of his face from where he'd slept on his shirtsleeve.

"What's going on?" Jack demanded as they came to a stop at Lewis's desk.

A skinny guy sat in Lewis's chair, fingers flashing over the keyboard as he muttered to himself, mostly about how slow the system was and how could anyone ever work with just the one screen?

"Jack, this is Fabian Haggedo... Hagglethorne... Haggis?" Lewis frowned at him. "Sorry, how do you pronounce it again?"

Leaving off his typing with a resigned sigh, Fabian said patiently, "Heggenhougen."

"Him," Lewis finished, gesturing grandly to the guy. "He's from Ex Mon."

"I guessed." Jack held his hand out to Fabian. "Jack Reardon. Pleased to meet you."

Fabian gave his hand a slightly perplexed look, then turned back to the computer screen. "I was told that finding out where the contested images came from was top priority and to not give up until I knew everything about them. It took me fourteen hours, but I did it."

Behind the man's back, Lewis made drinking motions and mouthed, "Red Bull."

"Great." Jack leaned over the back of the chair. "Can you show us what you found?"

Another weary sigh from Fabian. "I can't *show* you anything new. Unless you know how to interpret digital signatures of different image capturing systems." The way he just barrelled right on meant he clearly didn't think they could. "I can *tell* you what I found. External Monitoring *didn't* royally screw anything up. The images the police have didn't come from Bangkok CCTV systems. I checked feeds from all the cameras around the entrance to the hotel, and the angles don't match. It's close but not exact."

Jack's guts went cold. "Someone was physically tailing us."

"They obviously weren't there for anything other than pictures," Lewis reasoned.

"And only for pictures of him." Fabian pointed at Jack.

"What? But we're both in them," Jack said.

Fabian gave him a partly patient, partly exasperated look. "It's obvious. The centre of each image is you. Thomas is incidental. Besides, there are the other pictures, too."

Lewis nudged Jack. "See. I told you. This has nothing to do with me. It's all about you."

Scowling, Jack asked, "What other pictures?"

"These ones." Fabian brought up the new images.

Jack at a poker table in a bright, glittering casino. He was grinning and flipping a chip to a waitress. Jack leaning against a marble wall, having his cigarette lit by the same waitress, who was biting her lip sexily. Jack outside a slightly less ornate building, head close to a small Thai woman's, listening as she spoke with her hands. Jack, at another table, this one bare of green felt but with higher stacks of chips. A final one of Jack across the street from the brothel he would later drag Lewis to.

There in crisp, clear images was his search for the Messiah.

No wonder he'd picked up a ticket. He hadn't thought he was being careless, but clearly he had been if he hadn't noticed someone following him around Bangkok every day for two weeks. Every second person there had a camera. And those who didn't have the big obvious ones hanging around their necks used their phones. It would have been hard to spot a tail in that environment, but from the angle of the pictures and the variety of places, this person must have been on Jack's arse like a boil.

"One thing's for sure," Lewis said seriously. "Whoever it was isn't working for the Messiah or his Disciples."

"Yeah. If he was that close to me, no way he would have missed what I was doing. We got the Messiah, so no one warned him off."

Lewis got his deducting face again. "Fabian, did you get the first lot of photos from the police servers? Or did you find where they originated from?"

"I had to get them from the New South Wales Police server first so I knew what I was looking for. Then I found them on a server in Jakarta, which is where the police got them from, as well. But they didn't originate there. I haven't traced them back to their original upload site yet."

"When were they uploaded to the Jakarta server?"

"4:22 p.m. on the sixteenth."

"Two days. And how hard was it to find them?"

"Any mid-level analyst could find it."

"They were planted," Lewis said to Jack. "Clearly and deliberately planted for the police or some other interested party to find. Like say, someone who wanted to buy a ticket on you. Do you believe me now? This is about the Judge."

Jack ran his hands over his face. "Fuck. You're right. Whoever it is, though, they've been planning this since Bangkok. Since our second week in Bangkok, when I started hunting the Messiah. Two weeks *before* I was seconded to the strike force. We need to find out who pointed Phelps towards me when she went looking for a consultant."

"The first two murders in Sydney both happened before we went to Bangkok," Lewis mused. "Infinity was formed three days after they found Morrissey and systematically blocked and derailed over the next three weeks until they put in a request to the ISO for SSA Jack Reardon, as soon as he was back in country."

Jack's hands curled into fists. "It was all a delaying tactic. They didn't want Infinity making any headway until I was there and fucking incriminated myself with every bloody thing I did and said."

Christ. Not again. Jack hated being manipulated. The anger was growing with each second. After everything he'd gone through in the desert, then in this fucking building, thanks to Ethan, McIntosh, and Harraway, he'd sworn he wasn't going to be used like that again. Yet, here he was.

How many of the other coincidences over the past several weeks had been deliberate? Fuck. How could he trust anything now?

"Um, excuse me?"

Jack opened eyes he hadn't realised he'd closed and found Fabian looking at him.

"I didn't even get to the interesting bit," Fabian said.

Lewis looked like he was going to say one thing but then changed his mind and simply asked, "And what's the interesting bit?"

"The digital signature of the images." Said like it was plainly obvious from the start. "The images weren't captured on a camera. Or least, not a mechanical one."

Jack's guts shifted uneasily. "What do you mean?" Though he had an inkling.

"They came from a processor attached to an optic nerve."

The person following Jack hadn't been taking actual photos. They'd simply been looking at him and taking shots with a neural implant. Just like Jack did.

SIXTEEN

BEFORE

Jack was both disappointed and happy to find Ethan dead asleep the next morning. The lack of morning sex was balanced out by knowing Ethan now felt content and secure enough to *sleep* in Jack's apartment. Whatever had caused his hesitation the night before had been smoothed over. Fingers crossed they could get on with this wild experiment in living together now.

With no personal delays, Jack was back at the LAC right on eight o'clock. Adam was late again, leaving him alone with Steph, which he didn't mind. She put him to work within moments of the impossibly tall Constable Toomey once more dropping him off at the room.

Steph sat him at one end of the table and gave him a stack of blueprints, schematics, digital 3D renditions of the Williams scene, staff schedules, security checklists, witness statements pertinent to the ingress and egress of their offender, and a pile of secondary information she put to one side in case she had missed something he might need.

"Since you're here in the capacity of a security expert, we should actually have something to show for it," she explained apologetically. "If you could at least jot something down, I'd really appreciate having something to show Dumay. *Then* I'll let Adam pick your brain about the Morrissey scene. Is that okay?"

"Happy to do what I can to catch this creep."

She smiled brightly. "Such a refreshing attitude in someone from the military. I was starting to think everyone even vaguely associated with them were all uptight, arrogant, condescending little . . . little *twerps!*"

Jack laughed. Twerps? So like Ethan, whose deadliest curse was "blast."

Not really looking it, Steph said, "Sorry."

"Don't be. I'm feeling a bit ambivalent towards them myself, these days."

"I read in your file you were discharged on medical grounds."

Sufficiently open-ended, he could expand on it or ignore the subtle invitation to share. Jack didn't like talking about his final days with the service. There was precisely one person outside of those involved Jack had told about it, and there were days he regretted spilling it all to Ethan in the desert. Yet, there was the urge to tell Steph *something* more, something to explain his own bitter feelings about it all. He managed to shove that thought aside and pass on her comment with a shrug and gratitude that Adam hadn't been there to witness it.

The problem, he realised as Stephanie considered him with a sympathetic expression, was that there was no distance. There was no insulating persona to buffer him from the demands of the job. This, where he was a single, thin pretence away from being himself, was too close for comfort.

"Do you have everything you need?" Steph asked instead of pushing.

Jack swallowed the discomfort. "Enough to get started, at the very least."

"Don't hesitate to ask if there's anything you need." She retreated to her end of the table, letting him get busy.

By the time Adam rocked up, looking tired and nursing an extra-large coffee, Jack had appropriated half of the table and had it covered in blueprints and schematics. His "employment" as an SSA might be a cover, but the technicalities of the job weren't. He was expected to be able to prove his qualifications at the drop of a hat and did actually use it as part of his real work, as well. He wasn't just pretending to help Steph, and he did think he would be able to give her what she expected. Still wasn't certain how it would help overall, but he wasn't going to do a half-arsed job for her.

Absorbed in his process, Jack barely spared Adam a "good morning." He was, however, peripherally aware of the profiler watching him for a while. Adam sat, coffee in front of him as he flicked idly through his phone, keeping a surreptitious eye on Jack's work.

Aware of the fault in his walls, Jack worked to shore them up, putting a professional distance between him and these people he had to work with for now. Once, it wouldn't have got to him so easily. Once, though, was before the desert, where so many things had been broken. His ability to compartmentalise all the distasteful, horrible things he saw—and did—in the process of getting the job done had been tested and shattered out there. Building it up again was a slow process, but he was getting there.

Unlike the Melbourne victims, Williams had been killed at his place of work, in the IT department of an internet-based company that provided design and printing services. He'd been discovered on the floor of his section in the main building by the early-morning staff. Killed in the shower in the men's toilet, then posed. The building had been fairly secure, especially after hours, but it hadn't been foolproof. Jack highlighted several possible ingress points for the killer, which had already been picked up by the police.

In an effort to actually be helpful, Jack extended his study beyond the obvious and into the realms of "highly trained operator" and looked for ways he would have used if an Office job had required him getting into the building undetected. *Then* he looked for ways Ethan would have used. Those two searches overlapped and showed Jack a small window in the building's security. The timing would have to be exact, but once found, Jack knew it was how the Judge got in and out without leaving a mark on the security.

Pleased with his efforts, Jack looked up and discovered himself alone with Adam. Steph's workspace was tidy and her laptop missing.

"Her day to pick up the grandsprog from day care." Adam answered the unasked question as he gathered up his few things. "Let's call it a day, too."

Slightly disappointed he couldn't do a big reveal, Jack settled for making a detailed note on the Williams file and emailed it to Steph. Adam waited, slightly impatiently, and as he was escorting Jack out of the building, declared, "Drinks tonight. No excuses."

"Sorry, but I don't mix business and satisfactory pleasure." Jack enjoyed watching Adam's comically aghast response a bit too much.

"Come on," Adam pleaded. "Just a drink. Two work colleagues getting to know each other a bit better over a beer or two. Don't say no, Nishant."

No one on the team had been able to come up with a reason for Jack pursuing his personal connection to Adam, but neither had anyone decided it might be damaging to the job. Either way, going for drinks with the man wouldn't be personal. Even knowing each other's proper names, what was happening between them now was less real than the hook-ups had been. Back then, the attraction had been honest at least. Jack was still attracted to Adam, but nothing was going to come of it, not now he and Ethan had solidified their arrangement. But encouraging a friendship would be a lie. All part of the job Adam wasn't aware of.

Telling himself it was to protect Adam, Jack said, "I actually have dinner plans tonight. Sorry." Well, he was hoping he did.

Adam schooled his expression into a bland smile, but not before he let slip a touch of his disappointment. "I understand."

Determined to not apologise again, Jack simply said, "See you tomorrow," and got on his bike to go into the Office.

After a substantially shorter debrief than the day before, Jack was leaving the operations room when someone called, "Reardon!"

Jack spied Jesse Feitt approaching through the mostly empty cubicles in the centre of the room. Since Ethan had directly involved himself in the Office's operations, it had been decided they had to find out everything they could about him. Under the guidance of the new Intelligence director, Special Investigator Jesse Feitt had been given the unenviable job of finding every skerrick of information out there on Ethan Blade. Seen as the resident Blade expert, Jack had been sought out for his opinion and knowledge several times. He always felt a little creepy talking about Ethan with Feitt, especially if the subject of the investigation was currently in his apartment.

"Sorry to bother you on your way out," the special investigator said. "I would have waited, but Director McIntosh said you're on a UC case at the moment. It won't take long."

With no excuse, Jack followed Feitt down to the sixth floor, Intelligence's main hub. Feitt's small operations room was empty at this time of day, just a couple of screens on the table glowing in the dim lighting.

"We found some evidence I need you to confirm," Feitt explained. "We're not one hundred percent, but I think we might have a real piece of Blade's history here. I was hoping you could say yay or nay."

Jack sat before the indicated screen. "I'll give it a go."

Feitt sat at the other screen and tapped at the keypad. "I'll warn you, it's not pretty. The guy who discovered it has ten years of investigating mass killings and he threw up."

"Fuck. That bad?"

"That bad. If you want, we can skip the worst part of the video. The actual details aren't that important."

Second-, third-, and fourth-guessing his offer to help, Jack let Feitt bring up the video on the screen in front of him. It opened on what was either an apartment or very expensive hotel room. The view was from across a street and through a wall of floor-to-ceiling windows. The room it looked into was plush with several soft couches, glass coffee tables, and a dining suite big enough to have an annual general meeting around. Lit with soft yellow light, everything appeared burnished and smooth.

A man sat on a couch, laptop beside him. Dressed in a designer suit, he sprawled back, legs spread, tie loosened, the top buttons of his shirt undone, showing a thick patch of chest hair. He was dark-complexioned, with a Mediterranean cast to his features. A snifter in one hand, idly swirling an amber liquid around the bowl, he flicked through images on the laptop. Jack couldn't make out the pictures, but it had to be porn of some sort, judging by the prominent tent in his pants.

"Athens." Feitt wasn't watching the video but sitting back in his chair, as if distancing himself from the images. "During the constitutional amendment eighteen years ago, there was a proposal for the total separation of state and church. A lot of public protests and arguments. Even more private disagreements and threats. The man in the video is Stefanos Moraitis, a self-made man of rather substantial numbers. Mostly through legitimate investments, but there was some insider trading going on, some under-the-table deals. He was one of the most vocal voices calling for the separation. Didn't mind throwing an awful lot of money at the cause, either. Made himself a few enemies along the way."

Getting a sense of where this was going, Jack asked, "Married?"

"Divorced. Publically, it was amicable, but only because privately he paid his wife a whole heap to keep quiet about his extramarital activities. Had an addiction to paid companionship. Male, female, didn't matter."

On the screen, Moraitis put the snifter down and blatantly rubbed his dick while checking his watch. A moment later, he looked over at the door, and the smile he gave it was enough to make Jack grimace. It was all predator, and not a predator looking for food, but for something to play with. The subject got up and went to the door, opening it. A man in a plain black suit spoke to the subject for a moment, who nodded impatiently, handed over a wad of cash, and beckoned someone into the room.

Jack swallowed hard. The boy was fourteen or fifteen at most but dressed to look younger. His hair was cut short in back but long at the sides, so it swished over his face as he came into the room, hesitant and wary, shoulders hunched, head bowed. Once he was inside, the subject shut the door and locked it. When he looked at the boy, his expression was pure hunger.

Wanting to skim already, Jack forced himself to watch as the boy was encouraged to go sit on the couch. The subject followed the kid closely, touching him constantly, on his shoulders, his back, his head, a seemingly accidental bump of his groin against the boy's lower back. Over the next twenty minutes, the subject plied his prey with Sugar, a synthetic amphetamine pressed into little cubes and dropped into a drink strong enough to cover the flavour, usually highly alcoholic. It was frustrating because the kid kept his face down, hair a shield, even as he gulped down booze and Sugar. When he was sufficiently doped, the subject got him naked and pulled him onto his lap.

That was when Jack saw it. The boy's back was striped with red marks, from his shoulders down to his hips. Long lash marks, scars barely healed.

"Shit," Jack whispered.

"That's what flagged it for us," Feitt said just as softly. "If Blade was telling us the truth about his age, he was fourteen there. Fifteen at most. It gets worse."

Jack's stomach churned. Watching any more of this would make him puke, and they hadn't even got to the really bad part yet.

On the screen, the boy was a pliant toy for the subject. He was lifted and turned, touched and posed, head a loose weight on his neck. As it went on and on, Jack thought there was very little left that could make him any more horrified and furious than he already was.

He was wrong.

The subject put the boy on his knees and opened his mouth.

Jack shut the screen down. Sat for several minutes in complete silence. He was numb, inside and out. It was good, because if he felt anything right then, he would probably be arrested with no hope of parole.

"Do you think it's him?" Feitt asked.

It was difficult, but Jack managed to get most of the footage into the deepest, darkest drawer in the filing cabinet in the back of his head. He sealed it shut knowing it wouldn't stay that way.

"Yeah." His voice was rough. "Pretty certain. The scar patterns match. Age is right. Triggering trauma." Jack shoved away the memory of Ethan saying he would never fellate him.

"I can tell you what happens, if you'd rather." Feitt's tone was sympathetic.

"No. I'll watch it. Make certain it's him." Jack turned the screen back on. The footage was still playing. He focused on the time bar at the bottom. "Where do I skip to?"

"About ten minutes further."

Jack slid the bar across to the right time and the image jumped to one nearly as rage inducing. The subject stood at the window of the room, looking almost directly at the camera. He had another glass in his hand and a satisfied smirk on his lips. Behind him, on the floor, the boy was lying facedown, head turned away from the camera. From the utter slackness in his limbs, he was either asleep, or more likely passed out. The subject slowly savoured his drink, and Jack hoped that whoever had set up the camera had a sniper rifle as well. It would be the only fitting end.

Just as Jack was considering moving the video along again, the boy pushed up to his hands and knees. There was no hesitation, no softness about him. He moved with sure, efficient motions as he got into a crouch. Hair still covering his face, he reached for the empty cognac bottle on the coffee table. Standing, he flipped the bottle and caught it by the neck, then slinked around the table and came up behind the subject.

The subject had no idea. Didn't hear a thing, didn't suspect anything. The boy came up directly behind him so as to show no reflection in the window. Once he was in place, it went so fast Jack barely caught it. Smashing the bottle on the window frame. Catching the subject around his face. Pulling his head back. Stabbing the broken bottle into his neck.

"Still think it's him?" Feitt asked.

"Definitely."

Feitt opened a file and typed. "Right, Ethan Blade's first confirmed kill was when he was . . . let's say fifteen."

SEVENTEEN AFTER

After dropping his knowledge bomb, Fabian hightailed it back to the fourth floor and Ex Mon. Jack and Lewis retreated to a spare operations room to talk in private.

"We speculated the Judge was ex-army, but it's worse. He's fucking special forces," Jack ground out. "SAS. We're the only ones given the implant."

"In the ADF, yes." Lewis sat on the table, feet up on a chair, elbows on his knees and hands dangling between them. "Don't narrow your focus too soon. The tech in your head was developed here in Australia, but if we did it, don't think other countries out there haven't, as well."

Jack shook his head. "It has to be someone I knew in the SAS. It's too coincidental. Someone's been targeting me since Bangkok. Someone with an implant like mine. He comes back here and watches while I pretty much point to myself as the Judge, and when it looks like we might catch *him* before I'm accused, he buys a ticket on my head. It fits. Who else but the psycho himself would want the protection of an assassin taking me out. He's been after me the entire time."

"That's a fair assessment." Lewis frowned at him worriedly. "But do you really want him to be someone you knew? Someone you fought side by side with?"

"Anyone else doesn't make as much sense. He's ex-military, with my skills, my training—someone who is targeting me. And who else would do that but someone I know?"

Jack had lost touch with most of the people he'd known in the service. He didn't really know them anymore. The only guys he might still call friends were Nigel Kruger and Trent Dupont, the other survivors of the Chota Nagpur plateau. He would bet his life it wasn't either of them.

"All right," Lewis conceded. "We'll get a list of every SAS member given an implant for, say, two years on either side of your induction in the unit. Run them down and see what we find. Was there anyone who you think might want to see you dead or locked up for some reason?"

"Nothing immediately comes to mind. There were a couple of guys I didn't particularly get on with. The gay thing and—" Jack waved at his complexion. "—the terrorist comments, mostly, but it wasn't anything I considered like serious hate. Those of us in the Unit were . . . elite. We didn't socialise much with general infantry. There was some resentment on their side, but none of them would have been given an implant."

"Try to remember some names, all the same. Let's not narrow the parameters just yet. What about your CO? The one who sent you into India."

The last time Jack had seen him, he'd been lying on the floor of his office, face bloodied and staring up at Jack with a mix of horror and rage.

"Yeah, him, too. Though he was too old back then for an implant."

Lewis nodded. "How about a pissed-off lover?"

"No one in the Unit. Couple of infantry guys before I joined the SAS. Couple of pilots when I was doing my chopper training." Jack hesitated. Hamish definitely qualified as someone with a big enough grudge against him. God, if Ham was still that pissed at him after all this time, then Jack had hurt him more than he'd realised, and what he'd felt back then had been like open-heart surgery without anaesthesia. If it was Ham coming after him, no wonder Jack hadn't been any good for Ethan—he was horrendous at relationships.

Grimly, he told Lewis about Ham, as well.

"It's a start," Lewis said.

Jack ran his hands through his hair as he paced. "I have to get out of here. I need to start hunting this fucker down."

"Jack, you can't leave. Garrote is probably in country by now. In *Sydney*. Let us take care of this."

"Fuck. I need Ethan."

Seventeen hours since he'd put in the call to him, and still nothing. Maybe he had scrambled. Maybe he was in Kuala Lumpur, holed up in his lair there, watching from a safe distance.

Lewis, who'd been inputting information into his screen, snapped a look at Jack. "Ethan? As in Blade?"

Wondering where the hell his command of his emotions had gone, Jack grunted sourly. "Yeah. I told you before I think he can help us on this. Well, this turn of events only makes it more pertinent."

"Sure." Though Lewis didn't sound convinced.

Jack blamed it on too much bad news all at once.

With the new information, Lydia whipped the team into a fresh fervour as they hit the thirty-hour mark of the current investigation. Tired people swapped out for fresher ones, but Lydia and Lewis kept going. Jack spent hours with Lewis listing people he remembered from the Unit, and around midday, information started feeding back to them. They began eliminating names immediately—the deceased; the infirm; those still in the military and their location confirmed as overseas. The list whittled down further throughout the afternoon until they had a much smaller suspect group.

One of whom was Nigel Kruger.

"It's not him," Jack said firmly.

Lewis, who'd caught another couple of hours of sleep, eyed him tiredly. "We can't rule him out just because you said so."

"I know it isn't him. Or Trent Dupont. We went through hell, the three of us. That . . . bonds you. I couldn't hurt either of them; they couldn't hurt me."

"Sorry, Jack, we can't discount them. Not yet."

Jack stalked away. He kept thinking they would find the vital bit of information in the next minute, ten minutes, half hour, and the longer it went, the worse his mood got.

Then McIntosh appeared with a list of new names to add to the suspect pool.

"Who are they?" Lewis skimmed it quickly. "They're not military."

"No," their director said. "But they have neural implants. Private citizens who paid very handsomely for them, either personally or their employer did."

Lewis very carefully didn't say "told you so" to Jack, just handed the list over to Lydia to assign to a couple of techs.

"So much for restricted technology," Jack muttered.

"Even restricted has price tag, Jack," McIntosh said kindly. "All of us here are well aware of that." Then she left.

As everyone got back to work, Jack felt useless. All this fuss and activity because someone wanted him either dead or locked up. And he had no idea *why*.

Jack really couldn't imagine someone from the Unit doing this. It wasn't that he didn't believe one of them could snap and go totally bonkers—he'd had enough close calls himself to understand just how easy it would be—but that this wasn't what he would expect from one of his fellow soldiers. Jack knew that if he did cross that final line, he wouldn't fuck around staging murders or leaving clues. He would just grab his gun and hunt his prey directly. Fast. Efficient. Effective. Of course, McIntosh had just opened them to a whole new world of potential suspects.

He got a copy of the new list and returned to his desk in the corner to read through the names, personal stats, and work histories, trying to find something that leaped out at him. Nothing did and the more nothing he found, the more distracted he got.

It was coming up on twenty hours since he'd put the call in to Ethan. His silence, though warranted, hurt. Ethan hadn't let one of Jack's calls go through to his answering system in nearly a year. Had one bad decision really broken that sort of trust? No. It hadn't been a conscious choice. Jack hadn't been thinking. He'd been reacting. Reeling from Ethan's words, hurt, angry, and confused. And Adam had been nothing but honest with Jack the entire time.

Fuck. Jack needed to know where Ethan was. What he was doing. Why he'd lied. Was he killing again?

Before Jack could torture himself with that path of thought, the door to the operations room slammed open and Lewis stuck his head in.

"Jack," he called across the general chatter, clacking keyboards, and crunching of snacks. "Come on. Something else has come up."

Oh God. What now?

Jack slowly stood, not sure he wanted to know what could make Lewis look so bloody serious. Surely things were already as bad as they could be.

Feeling like a man walking to his execution, Jack followed Lewis into the empty room they'd talked in earlier. Lewis had obviously appropriated it for his own tangent investigation into the chance the ticket was about the Judge, not the Messiah. He had a couple of laptops set up side by side, three coffee cups in various states of fullness and warmth, and a bowl of jelly beans, a few bright coloured escapees scattered across the tabletop.

"What's going on?" Jack's stomach had knotted itself up, and it got worse when Lewis silently pulled a chair out and indicated for Jack to sit. "What the hell, Lewis?" he demanded at the gesture.

"Just fucking sit, Jack."

Jack sat. He was about two seconds away from shouting at Lewis to just tell him what was going on.

Taking his own seat, Lewis leaned on his elbows and let out a long, slow breath. "We've found out why Ethan Blade hasn't contacted you."

Suddenly, Jack's guts weren't tied up anymore. Everything inside him had gone liquid, sloshing around in a sickening wave. Had the Judge gone after Ethan? He killed Adam and then decided to really rip Jack's chest apart and get Ethan, too. Knowing now why Lewis had insisted he sit didn't stop Jack from surging to his feet and grabbing his friend's shirtfront and hauling him close.

"Tell me," Jack whispered hoarsely.

Lewis, so close he had to lean his head right back to focus on him, looked between his eyes. He obviously saw the mania close to the surface, because he gripped Jack's arms, gentle but firm. "Calm down. We'll sort this out, like the other one."

"What other one?"

"The other ticket."

Jack let Lewis go and stared at him. "What do you mean, other ticket?"

"A second ticket came up on you fifteen minutes ago. We have no idea what for, but, Jack, it's been picked up already."

Shaking his head, Jack denied what he knew was coming.

"By Ethan Blade."

EIGHTEEN
BEFORE

"**D**o we know who bought the ticket on Moraitis?" Jack asked. Feitt looked up. "There was no ticket."

"That was clearly a planned hit. Everything was staged." It explained why they never saw the kid's face. He knew the camera was there, and he'd kept the subject front and centre for the whole ordeal, making sure there was no doubt about who the man was and what he was doing.

"It was. The footage was used to destroy Moraitis's reputation and gutted his entire campaign to separate church and state. But there was no ticket, and the Greek authorities didn't investigate past what the video showed. Moraitis was murdered by one of his tricks. They barely searched for the killer." Feitt flashed a half-hearted smile. "Anyway, that's all I needed. Sorry for the nightmare material."

Jack took his time going down to the garage, but by the time he reached his bike, he wasn't ready to go home. There were too many thoughts, too many images chasing around his mind. When he came out of the garage, he turned north and headed across the Harbour Bridge. Within twenty minutes he'd reached Middle Head. The park was closed for the day, but after leaving the bike in the carpark, Jack walked out to the old fortifications.

The Australian military had had a presence at Middle Head for over a hundred years, from the first gun battery in the 1870s to the current Royal Australian Navy base. Well before Jack had made his grief-stricken decision to join the army, Middle Head had been one of his favourite places. His father used to bring him and Meera out here on weekends and school holidays, to get them and their constant bickering out of their mother's hair. Jack had loved roaming through the ruins, imagining those long-gone soldiers manning their guns, watching the wide expanse of the harbour for sign of the enemy or racing through the underground tunnels. Meera, uninspired by the ruins, would sit on the very edge of the peninsula with her sketch book and ignore her stupid little brother. Chris Reardon had enjoyed it for the history, for the palpable sense of the depth of time, for the lessons he tried to impart to his warring children about how fighting never solved anything.

Jack hadn't been back in years. Not since he'd brought Dad out in a desperate bid to awaken his memories, to revive the man Jack had grown up worshipping. His father had grumbled the entire time, wanting to know why some stranger was making him walk around a bunch of pointless old ruins. Sad and defeated, Jack had turned them around and started back to the car. Just as they were passing the tiger cages, where soldiers had been trained to resist torture, Dad had stopped and stared at it for several minutes.

"That's where I imagined you were," he'd whispered, talking not to Jack, but to some memory of the son he believed to be dead. "They said it was some training exercise that went wrong. Faulty equipment or something. But I knew. I saw it in their eyes. You were captured by some enemy somewhere. Being held prisoner. Being tortured, or already dead. I thought . . . I thought, I hope he's with Usha. I hope she told him not to feel guilty anymore."

The sun was still up when Jack reached the outer ruins. He bypassed the tiger cages his father had fixated on and went to the old gun emplacement. It was quiet. No tourists, no guided tours going on around him, no families out to enjoy the summer day. A breeze came off the water, cool with a hint of salt. The only disturbance on the bay was a slowly expanding wake of a passing boat. Seated on a smooth cement wall, Jack let himself think.

The name Ethan Blade had been around for seventeen years, and Jack believed the man he knew had been a killer that long. To have it so viscerally proven left him breathless, though. Horrified and angry and disgusted. Not at Ethan, but at the world that allowed such things to happen. At the monsters who put a boy into that position. Moraitis, the man who'd delivered the boy, whoever had trained a kid to take that much drink and drugs, to let himself be so terribly abused, and to then get up and so easily kill.

The whole thing put Ethan's words of the other night into stark relief. Jack had assumed a troubled, abusive childhood had led a young Paul St. Clair to those who would then shape him into the assassin Ethan Blade. But what Jack had just seen wasn't a kid forced to defend himself in the worst way possible. It had been calm, methodical. Cold. That boy had walked into the room knowing the required outcome and exactly how to get it. Fifteen and already a trained and proficient killer. Nearly two years before the name Ethan Blade had been entered onto the John Smith List.

Then there were the scars. Healed in the video, but only just. Ethan had claimed the whipping had been "discipline." For what indiscretion, he'd never confessed. Could this be it? Was that how they—whoever *they* were—made a kid walk into that room?

Did the fact Ethan was a Sugar Baby have anything to do with it? Eighteen years ago wasn't so long after the common myth about Sugar Babies being born sociopaths had been disproven. Someone out there might have wanted to . . .

No. Jack couldn't go there. Not right now. He couldn't think of the wider range of implications, not when he was so concerned with the immediate. Namely the man he'd invited so intimately into his life.

There were elements about Ethan Jack chose to ignore, as most people did with those they cared about. Being an assassin wasn't quite akin to snoring or eating noisily or starting every sentence with "I was just going to say," but Jack was no innocent in that department, either. There was also no doubt in Jack's mind about Ethan not being a sociopath. He had, understandably, some compulsions and obsessions, and Jack had learned, and still was learning, how to deal with them. Which Jack was more than willing to do because those things didn't entirely define Ethan. They didn't account for his love of all animals, or his passion for fast cars, or explain why he read the books he did. Ethan's past didn't matter when it was just them, talking or touching or simply being together.

What Jack had seen this evening didn't change how he felt about Ethan. It just explained a few things.

Feeling more settled than he had when he arrived, Jack stood and stretched. The sun was disappearing over the horizon behind him, blazing across the city in a final wave of orange and red and dark cobalt blue. The buildings were starting to light up as he made his way back to his bike, and by the time he cruised through the CBD on the way to Leichhardt, Sydney was alight with all the colours of the spectrum, a constellation of rainbow stars that were as much a guiding force as the Southern Cross.

When he got home, he was pleased to find Victoria in the garage and Ethan in the apartment. The lights were off and the blinds drawn on the sliding door to the balcony. The brown leather couch had been moved back and the coffee table set to the side. In the middle of the room, dressed in a pair of gi pants and socks, Ethan moved through a stately, elegant tai chi sequence. The shadows were by turns both concealing and revealing, sliding around his lean torso and strong arms like a lover's caress. A flash of a tight six-pack, shifting into darkness to expose the taut planes of his back. The almost dainty flex of a wrist, extending a firm arm, the motion followed by his shaded face.

"Hello, Jack," Ethan said, not missing a beat, his voice low and breathy.

"Hey," Jack managed around a suddenly dry mouth.

This, too, Jack realised as he watched Ethan's precise moves, was why seeing that video didn't change the big picture. Ethan had learned to deal with his past and come through it as well as anyone could expect to. He had his mechanisms, his rituals, his needs. Somehow, in the midst of all that, he'd made a special space for Jack. And fuck if he didn't look sexy doing it, too.

"Join me?"

It was no great dilemma, and Jack was out of his suit almost faster than if he'd been offered sex. In a pair of track pants, he stepped up beside Ethan, leaving enough room for them both to move. Ethan had turned a lamp on to give Jack some light, but not enough he had to put on his glasses. Smiling at him, Ethan returned to the starting position, and Jack mimicked him.

Tai chi was something Jack had learned in the army, using it as both a low-impact exercise and a destressing technique. He hadn't practiced in years, but the moves came back quickly, his motions only seconds behind Ethan's. Focusing on his breathing, in with the rise, out with the sink, took his mind away from not only the video, but the more disturbing aspects of the Judge case. By the time Ethan shifted gracefully into a final position, Jack was blissfully relaxed.

"You had a long day," Ethan commented as they put the furniture back into place.

"Ah, yeah." Jack spent an extended moment ensuring the couch was the perfect feet-resting distance from the coffee table.

Should he tell Ethan he saw the video or not? When informing Jack he wouldn't ever be sucking his dick, Ethan hadn't given a reason and Jack hadn't asked for one, not wanting to risk Ethan running away. He was reasonably sure that if he mentioned knowing why now, Ethan wouldn't scramble out of the country, never to be seen again, but was it worth bringing up the memories? Jack had tried to inspire some good memories in his father by taking him to Middle Head and had instead made them both sadder. He couldn't imagine making Ethan confront what had happened in Athens would end any better.

"Long debrief." Satisfied with the furniture, Jack suggested dinner, and after a rummage through the fridge and pantry, they resorted to the stack of menus from places that delivered.

"Not Indian." Ethan firmly put aside those menus. "If I'm going to eat butter chicken, you will have made it."

Jack hid a smirk. Butter chicken was one recipe of his mother's he'd perfected. Cooking was a turn-on for some, and *everyone* liked butter chicken. During the six months of Ethan's intermittent visits, Jack had learned to keep the dish for those times Ethan was around, as he was rewarded very enthusiastically afterwards for his culinary efforts—or the following day if Ethan overate.

Settling on burgers and salad from a local café, Jack lounged on the couch with a beer while Ethan padded about on silent feet, tidying. Jack couldn't really see what needed neatening up, but letting Ethan fiddle with minor things had become second nature to him. Having no firm thoughts on why something should be here or there, Jack had no desire to derail the behaviour.

At one point, Ethan stopped in the middle of transferring a framed photo of Jack's parents from one shelf to the other. It was Jack's favourite memory of his parents together. Usha was smiling sedately at the camera, primly posed in a white and gold sari which set her dark skin to glowing, masses of black hair curling around her slender shoulders. Chris lounged back beside her, his dinner suit rumpled, looking not at the camera, but at his wife, his face split by a wide grin and his love and absolute devotion to her shining in his crinkled eyes. Ethan gazed at the image for a long moment, expression closed down. Before Jack could decide if he needed to say something, dinner arrived and Ethan disappeared into the hallway while Jack answered the door. Ethan emerged once the door was closed and locked and Jack had set cardboard boxes of salad and heavenly smelling burgers on the coffee table.

Seeing the casual arrangement, Ethan's fingers twitched, but he fetched a couple of beers and sat beside Jack.

"You don't mind, do you?" Jack wasn't waiting for an answer. Earlier he'd felt as if he might never be hungry again, but at the sight of the burger he was suddenly ravenous. The first bite caught a bit of every overstuffed filling, and only Ethan's quick reflexes got the box under it to catch the eruption of sauce, tomato, and lettuce from the other side.

"Perhaps we should decamp to the table." Ethan began gathering up boxes of food.

Jack hastily chewed and swallowed. "Nah, just forgot to get my pinkies into place. See." He curled his little fingers around the end of the burger and pushed the errant fillings back between the toasted buns. His second bite was more successful.

Shaking his head doubtfully, Ethan removed a few of the innards from his burger before taking a bite.

"Cheat," Jack admonished. "You took the beetroot out."

"Beetroot on a burger is something we will never agree on, Jack." He displayed his debris-free lap. "And at least I'm not wearing half of my dinner."

"That's the whole point of having a real burger. How do you know you've enjoyed it if you can't look at the stains on your shirt and recall how good it was? And no one in Australia will take you seriously until you've proudly displayed the purple heart." At Ethan's askance expression, Jack added, "A beetroot stain on your shirt."

"I'm not wearing a shirt, Jack."

Jack leered. "I noticed."

"Shut up and eat your messy burger."

By the time dinner was finished, Ethan's pensive mood had been chased away. He was chuckling at an old episode of *Black Books* when he picked up one of the empty beer bottles and began flipping it absently. Jack had seen him do it with knives in the past, an unconscious habit of keeping his hand busy while his mind was focused on something else. But seeing the bottle turning end over end threw Jack right back into the vision on the video. The boy picking up the cognac bottle, flipping it to get a grip on the neck. What he did with it then. What Moraitis had done with it before he'd turned his back on his drunk, drugged, used trick.

"Jack?" The bottle was put down, and Ethan touched Jack's arm. "Are you all right?"

Contact broke the reverie, and Jack blinked at Ethan. Older, safer Ethan. "Yeah, sure. Of course. Why?"

"You went very quiet and pale."

Jack tried for a snort and got maybe halfway. "I don't go pale."

"You do, Jack." Ethan's hand migrated from Jack's arm to his forehead. "Are you getting sick?"

Brushing him off, Jack stood and gathered up the empty bottles. "I'm fine, okay?" If he discounted the fact he couldn't seem to stop replaying parts of the Athens video. He needed a distraction.

Ethan came into the kitchen, watching him warily. His expression turned to one of surprise when Jack grabbed him by the waist and lifted him onto the counter.

"Jack!" Despite the alarm in his voice, Ethan's knees parted to let Jack push in close. "What the devil are you doing?"

Licking a line from Ethan's shoulder up the side of his neck to his ear, Jack mumbled, "Think that's pretty obvious." He nibbled on Ethan's earlobe, then abandoned it for sucking on the sensitive spot just behind it.

Ethan squirmed against him, moaning low in his throat. "Indeed. However, I should probably have asked, why?" Though his hands were clearly on board with current events, stroking up and down Jack's back. His legs, too, didn't care *why* and locked around Jack's waist.

"I thought I was the one who was supposed to fish for compliments." Jack switched sides. "How does 'you're so fucking hot I can't resist' sound?" Which was, generally, true, but right then Jack's dick wasn't quite feeling it. And it hadn't stopped those bloody pictures from bursting out of the filing cabinet and across his inner eye.

With an effort, Ethan pulled back and, hands on either side of his face, stopped him from following. His white eyes studied Jack's for a long moment, a frown creasing his brow. "Jack, something's wrong." Gaze flickering beyond him, Ethan asked, almost guiltily, "Was it me? Do you not like me moving your things?"

God. That stabbed Jack right in the heart. "No. Fuck no. I don't care about that. You do whatever you need to feel comfortable." Right then, he would go out and burn down the world if Ethan needed him to.

After a moment, Ethan nodded, looking neither happy nor sad about the offer. Instead, he traced his thumbs along Jack's jaw and asked, "Then what upset you?"

He wasn't going to give up on this until he got an answer, and Jack knew he couldn't admit to knowing about Moraitis and Athens. Grasping for something to give him, something that felt real enough to pass Ethan's uncanny lie detector, Jack found only one thing.

"It's this case for work. I'm so far out of my depth I can't really process it. I've been seconded to a police strike force hunting a serial murderer. Have you ever done that?"

Ethan shook his head but kept quiet, giving Jack the room to fill up.

"Jesus, he's a sick fuck, this Judge. I kill and you kill, but not like this. It's like he believes he's doing a good thing by getting rid of these people he doesn't like." Too late Jack remembered the conversation he and Ethan had had at the homestead in the desert, about why Ethan did what he did.

Yes, Ethan had said then, *what I do is wrong. But for me, I'm doing it for the right reasons.*

Judging by the slight stiffening in the body against Jack's, Ethan too was recalling that moment.

"He's different from us," Jack said firmly. "Adam says he's playing God, like it's his *burden* or something. Proof of wrongdoing isn't required. And he's so bloody righteous about it, quoting fucking Bible verses." He barely felt Ethan's hand slip down over the tattoo of a Saint Thomas Cross on his left shoulder blade. "I don't know how I'm supposed to help them catch him. I feel . . . useless. All I've done so far is tell them shit they already know."

Somehow, Jack's desperate bid to distract Ethan became a real thing. He found himself unloading all of his issues with the current job onto Ethan, right up to his grumbling about McIntosh turning him around too quickly after Bangkok. Jack eventually ended with a mumbled apology for dumping so much confidential stuff on him.

Ethan pulled him close and kissed his temple. "It's all right, Jack," he whispered into his hair. "You can trust me. I'll help you any way I can."

NINETEEN AFTER

Unwilling to wait any longer, Jack went to see McIntosh. Miller sent him through immediately, so his director had probably been expecting him.

"Jack, sit." She gave him a sympathetic look as he did so. "I promise we'll get to the bottom of this as quickly as we can."

He nodded.

"Yesterday, you seemed inclined to believe Blade would be amenable to helping us. Has something changed since then?"

"No, ma'am," Jack admitted. "I had *hoped* yesterday that Blade would help us in spite of what he thinks I did to betray him."

McIntosh's eyes weren't cold yet, but he suspected it wasn't far away. "And did you betray him?"

"That doesn't matter if he thinks otherwise."

"Indeed." She glanced at her screen for a moment, then said, "We're still looking into who bought the second ticket. Hopefully, once we find that out, we'll be able to neutralise it."

"That won't make a difference. The ticket's an excuse. If Blade wants to kill me, he will, money or no."

McIntosh eyed him thoughtfully. "What about Garrote? If we manage to void the ticket she picked up, will she stop? Or is that personal as well?"

Jesus. This was almost like the times his mum had gently but painstakingly interrogated him about whatever misdemeanour he'd committed as a kid. It all sounded calm and rational, but by the end, he would be gutted and ashamed of choices that had felt so right at the time.

"Nothing personal there, ma'am."

"Good. What do you propose to do about Blade?"

Jack gave her a tight smile. "I'm only here to give you the chance to approve it. Either way, I'm going out there. I have to find Ethan and sort this out. Convince him to help us get the Judge, at the very least. I know him; I can get him to give me a chance to talk to him."

At least he bloody well hoped so. He was risking an awful lot on the fact he'd once believed that when Ethan looked at him, he didn't see a target.

McIntosh nodded. Not an approval, just an acknowledgement. "And Garrote? She's still a rather large issue."

"I'll deal with it." Jack was careful to keep his emotions hidden. If she thought he wasn't steady, there was no way she'd let him out of the building. "I'm not doing any good inside this building. I need to get out there and do what I'm best at. Adam's probably dead, Stephanie's missing, and it looks like it might be all my fault. This psycho is after me, for whatever reason. Maybe we should let him get me."

"You don't know who you'd be going up against."

"If he's SAS from my time, then I'm going up against myself. A cracked, unstable version of myself. I can get him. I can beat him."

"He might not be SAS," she reminded him.

"Then he won't be a challenge." How easily it was to slip back into that elite mind frame they instilled in the special forces soldiers. Jack didn't care. He would need the added grunt it gave him.

McIntosh studied him, quiet and contemplative. Their working relationship had been improving in leaps and bounds since Harraway's arrest. That was the only reason he'd come to her now. A year ago, he would have simply got out of the building any way he could—and had—and worry about asking for forgiveness later. This new tactic seemed to be working. She had listened objectively when he knew he wasn't offering an objective option. The most telling sign was that her eyes hadn't shifted from warm and soft to hard and cold.

"Thank you for your candour, Jack. As you aren't officially under detainment, I cannot stop you from leaving the building." She gave him a pointed look over the top of her glasses. "I can, however, advise extremely strongly against it."

"Duly noted, ma'am. And thank you."

Standing, she came around the desk to open the door for him. He was surprised when her hand landed on his arm, warm and supportive.

"You're not going out there alone. The Office is behind you. Remember that."

The words caught in his chest, and all he could do was nod his gratitude.

McIntosh gave him a tight, understanding smile. "Stop at the armoury on your way out. I'll call ahead and authorise anything you might want." Then, with a hint of her usual hard line, she added, "Within reason, Jack. This is a hunt, not urban warfare."

"Of course, ma'am. I'll leave the RPGs behind."

The door was opened and he was waved out with a familiar, curt gesture. It only made her prior support all the stronger.

"Good luck," she said as he walked away. The "you'll need it" was implied.

As promised, Jack was given—mostly—free rein in the armoury. He was trailed around by a young asset who carried Jack's selections with a sort of quiet awe. It wasn't *that* spectacular an arsenal. A P90 that was easier to hide than his preferred F88S-A2 Austeyr assault rifle. A second USP plus a Springfield XDM Compact as a hidden backup and extra rounds for all of them. He added two tactical knives and a handful of flash-bang and smoke grenades, mindful of McIntosh's warning about urban warfare. Then he headed into the restricted section. He only took one thing from there, a lightweight, illegal Assassin X sniper rifle. They weren't great weapons by anyone's standards but used because they could be broken down into small, easily concealable and all-but-undetectable pieces. All of it went into a pair of panniers for a bike.

The final piece of equipment he wanted was wearable, and he was stripped to the waist when Lewis found him.

"McIntosh told me what you're planning," he said. "I'm here to give the obligatory 'are you completely deranged' talk and see if you need a hand with anything."

"You could pass me the undershirt." Jack pointed to the lightly padded shirt lying on the table next to the door.

Snorting, Lewis did so. "I meant on the outside."

Lewis had been an analyst and, later, an operations manager, with ASIO, much as he did with the Office. He'd had all the field training, though, and when time and work permitted, kept up his hand-to-hand skills. But he wasn't at the level Jack needed for this.

"Thanks, but I'd rather have you on this side of the wall, watching the big picture."

Expecting the knockback, Lewis nodded. "Are you taking a strike team, at least?"

"Too conspicuous. I won't get anywhere with six heavyweight champs hanging around me."

Office strike teams were some of the best frontal assault units available, baring a full SAS squad, but they weren't exactly understated. When they spent the vast majority of their work time in the gym or knocking in doors with battering rams, subtlety wasn't too high on their skill list.

"All right. How about one guy, then? Someone to have your back?"

There really was only one person Jack wanted at his back these days. And he was part of the reason why Jack needed someone at his back.

"Too risky." If he ended up clashing with the Judge, or Garrote, and if he couldn't have Ethan there, then he didn't want to be responsible for anyone else. He'd need all of his focus on keeping himself alive.

Jack pulled on the undershirt, then motioned for the body armour. It was thinner than the usual hard-plate vests, but denser and therefore heavier, and wasn't as obvious under regular clothes.

"At least turn on your active tracking." Lewis helped Jack buckle up the armour.

"Yeah. Give me an hour first, okay? There's something I need to do."

Pausing in picking up Jack's button-down, Lewis raised an eyebrow. "Something personal?"

Jack grabbed his shirt and slung in on. "Just something I have to check, and I'd rather not have any prying eyes on me. You can rant all you want, I'm going to do it."

"Ranting is Lydia's contractual obligation, not mine."

"Why do you think I'm avoiding going back to the eighth?"

Lewis smiled proudly. "And they said you were all brawn." Getting serious, he added, "One hour, not a second more. If you don't turn on your tracking, I'll get McIntosh to authorise an override."

Remote access was an element of the implant Jack wasn't particularly fond of. There was a clause in his work contract specifying the Office could only actively access the implant during field operations, and then only in extreme emergencies. Like so many clauses, the definition of "extreme emergency" was left to the discretion of the overseeing director.

"One hour is all I need. I swear." Jack put his jacket back on and rolled his shoulders, settling all the layers into place.

Panniers in hand, Jack left the armoury, ready to get moving at long bloody last. Lewis kept pace with him.

"You're taking your bike? Wouldn't you prefer something they won't recognise?"

"I can move easier on the bike." Before Lewis could raise more objections, Jack said, "Don't worry, mum. I'm taking one from the transport pool."

Lewis snorted. "Let me guess, a green Ninja, as opposed to your black one."

"I wish. They didn't have any Ninjas last time I was down there. I'll have to settle for a Honda."

Whatever Lewis's response was going to be, it was cut off by his phone. He answered and spent most of the conversation grunting affirmatives. When he ended the call, he gave Jack an apologetic shoulder pat. "Sorry, but you're going to have to risk a rant from your other mother. Lydia's got something and she wants your opinion. And before you grumble at me, she *insisted* you come up to the eighth."

Sufficiently trained, Jack knew not to ignore a summons from Lydia, so he went with minimum grumbling. Besides, she might have found something to give him a clue about, well, anything would be appreciated at that point.

Contrary to the usual clamour created by unearthing a new, vital piece of information, the operations room was subdued, everyone quietly going about their work. Lydia sat at the head of the table, focused on her laptop to the point of needing Lewis's hand on her shoulder to realise they had arrived.

"We finally had a bit of luck." She stood to face them. "The police commissioner grew a conscience and has ordered the local investigators to start sharing information. Of course, it doesn't mean they're giving us everything up-front. So far, we've had a few of their case files from the earlier murders, stuff we mostly had already. They claim they can't understand why the ISO would want it, since a serial murderer isn't even remotely related to their purview." After a deep breath to cool the irritation, she added, "But, we *are* getting somewhere now."

Knowing why she wanted him there now, Jack asked, "Do we know who died at the LAC?"

Lydia shook her head. "That one they're really keeping a tight hold on. However, we did find out what Bible verse the Judge left with the victim. I was wondering, since you spent so much time with both of the potential victims, if you'd look at it and see if you can get a hint or a clue from it."

Swallowing hard, Jack managed, "Sure. I'd only be guessing, though."

"Better than nothing." Lydia showed him an image of the note.

Like the others, it was on plain white paper, printed from a standard inkjet. Nothing unique or unusual about it. There were a couple of brown stains on one corner, though. Blood from the victim. Jack doubted the Judge would be so careless as to leave his own blood behind. He read the verse.

"She gave this name to the Lord who spoke to her: 'You are the God who sees me,' for she said, 'I have now seen the One who sees me.'"

Jack's first thought was that this had been meant for Adam and his far too perceptive eyes. Adam who'd scoffed at Jack saying he "got inside the killer's head," claiming instead that he simply had a better capacity to "see the world through someone else's eyes." Adam, who would also berate Jack for jumping to conclusions. Similarly, just because the verse talked about "she" didn't mean it was Stephanie, either.

"I think it's about seeing something," Jack murmured. "Not literally, maybe. I'm not sure. Maybe realising something?"

"Finally knowing who the killer is?" Lydia suggested.

"Maybe. Adam always interpreted the verses in relation to what he knew about the victim, and what the offender saw in the victim to make him pick them." He handed back the image. "I can't really say anything more until we know who this was found with."

"Thanks for trying, anyway. Hopefully we'll get that information sooner rather than later." She looked at the panniers he'd put on the floor at his feet. "I should just save my breath, shouldn't I?"

"Yeah. You might be able to talk me into going out in public in just my underwear, but you can't talk me out of this."

Lydia nodded. "Turn on your tracking, and if you need backup, yell. Don't go all macho and try to get out of any mess on your own."

"See," Lewis murmured. "Your other mother."

Jack's chest tightened suddenly. He had good friends here. People who cared for him, not just as a fellow asset, but as someone whose personal welfare they were concerned with. People, he knew, who would run into a fight for him.

Though, as he headed down to the garage, he had to wonder what they would say if they ever found out about him and Ethan.

TWENTY BEFORE

Once again, Jack didn't beat Steph to work, but he did arrive well before Adam. Considering Adam was there off his own bat, he supposed he couldn't really fault the man for not keeping to a strict eight-hour day.

"He's really not a morning person," Steph explained. "If it weren't for me imposing a diurnal work day on him, he'd sleep all day and work all night."

During their brief liaison, Jack hadn't actually *slept* with Adam. They'd fool around for a couple of hours, Jack would dress, and Adam would try various means of convincing him to stay. On their final night together, Jack had found himself contemplating it. Back then, he'd had no idea how regular Ethan's visits would be, or how integral to Jack's life they'd become. Hadn't realised having something real and solid, something almost *normal*, with Ethan was possible, or that he'd want it as much as he did now. Back then, Adam had been the logical choice of partner. If his mates at the Office had found out about Adam, Jack would have copped shit for being with a psychiatrist, but even that would be pleasant compared to what would happen if they learned about Ethan.

Settling into his usual seat, Jack asked, "What's my mission for today?"

"I want you and Adam to go over what tiny bits of information we have on the Morrissey scene. Hopefully, with your knowledge, you'll be able to expand on what we have and help Adam work it into his profile. Without the information ADFIS has about it, we're really just spinning our wheels here. Adam could work up a perfectly good profile from the three other murders, but it wouldn't be useful in the long run because he didn't have all the available information."

"And the Morrissey case is the odd one out, so I guess it would help highlight different aspects of the pathology, right?"

"Exactly. I'm so glad you're here. If it weren't for Adam, and now you, I'd be doing this all on my own. Even the investigative team has been cut down. Sadly, without another murder, we've run out of evidence to process and witnesses to question." She rallied with a grin. "But, thanks to your notes on the Williams scene yesterday, we're actually following another lead. The blind spot in the security camera coverage is being looked into. I knew you'd do more than brighten the place up."

Jack waved aside the praise. He just felt better knowing he wasn't a complete waste of space for Steph.

Adam arrived not long later, slouching in with another tray of coffees. Phone ringing, Steph grabbed a drink, told Adam to take Jack through the Morrissey information, and then left the room, answering the phone with a breathless "What did you find?"

All but falling into his chair, Adam took a long slurp of coffee, pressed the heel of his palm to his forehead, groaned, took off his sunglasses and peered at Jack.

"Either you really *aren't* a morning person," Jack muttered, "or you're hungover."

A finger pointed vaguely in Jack's direction. "First one. And maybe a bit of the second one."

The Office had a full background on Dr. Adam Quinn, which Jack had read after his first day on the strike force. Adam contracted for a psychology service as a forensic psychologist, working with offenders in prison and after their release. It most certainly didn't involve sitting in a leather chair while a patient lay on the couch and unloaded about their childhood. Most of Adam's work was with violent offenders, and apparently his papers on the subject of criminal psychology were always very well received. He'd been interviewed on *60 Minutes* after being taken hostage by a patient for five hours.

Jack didn't judge Adam for his condition. He could sympathise with the toll it took to commit oneself to such a hard path. To then take time off to chase a serial murderer as a favour to a friend could only add to the load.

"Don't give me that look," Adam said, a half smirk on his lips.

"What look?"

"The 'poor you' look. The 'you've looked too long into the abyss' look. My job has nothing to do with today's malady. If a certain *someone* had merely consented to drinks last night, I wouldn't have spent so long at the bar trying to find anyone else who had even a smidge of a chance of living up to my expectations." He gave Jack a mock glare. "This is your fault."

Both eyebrows raised to banish the sympathetic expression Adam didn't want to see, Jack drawled, "It's *my* fault you couldn't pick up?"

"You've ruined me for all other men."

Jack gave that the derisive snort it deserved. "Aren't we supposed to be going over the Morrissey scene?"

Adam scowled, then winced, and after a fortifying gulp of coffee, muttered, "Spoilsport. All right, if you insist on working. Captain Shane Morrissey of the Australian Defence Force Intelligence Corps. Thirty-eight years old, a fine vintage indeed. Seventeen-year career with the armed forces, loads of medals and commendations, upstanding officer and all-round good bloke. Oh, and gay."

Jack settled back in his chair. "Is his sexuality significant?"

"It might be. Don't know. At this stage, with the very small amount we know about the Morrissey murder, we can't afford to not consider everything as significant. The Judge's other victims all appear to be heterosexuals, but also considering that they don't have a lot else in common, the odd gay man out might mean absolutely nothing, or something, or everything." Warming to the subject, Adam continued in an almost fervent manner. "Before Morrissey, we weren't exactly ready to link Williams to the Melbourne murders because of the change in city, location of the kill, and the victim's background. The move from Melbourne to Sydney is a big factor. Most serial murderers are creatures of habit. If something works once, they keep with it until it doesn't work. Melbourne worked for the Judge. I can tell you now, even though they haven't been linked to the other two victims, our guy killed more than those two in Melbourne. The very first one would have been opportunistic. Almost an accident. An angry confrontation that went a bit too far, but the killer liked it. He got a rush from it. Seeing that person die, being the instrument by which they died, fulfilled something in him. He would have had to go looking for the next rush, manufacture a situation that mimicked the first one so he—"

"You went over this on day one." Jack didn't need to hear it again, especially not in Adam's impassioned tones. "The developing of the fantasy, the evolving MO. All of that psychology stuff."

Adam grinned. "You remembered. Gold star."

Jack flicked a pen at him. "Get on with it."

Laughing, Adam tucked the pen behind his ear and did as instructed. "Okay, so Williams seems the odd one out, then we learned about Morrissey. An army intelligence captain *murdered*, on *base*, in the officers' residence. Suddenly, Williams isn't the strange case anymore. And with *two* murders in Sydney, the coincidence became too big for the PTB to ignore and they were willing to admit Melbourne and Sydney are the same murderer. If we have any chance of getting this guy before he kills again, I *need* to know about Morrissey. I need to know why him. Why would our killer take such a big risk of getting into a secure army base and confronting a trained soldier? What was it about Morrissey that made the Judge decide he must die? This is your job, Nishant. If you can give me the *how*, it will help me with the *why*. And ultimately, the *who*."

Unable to argue with that, Jack gathered the few bits of information about the Morrissey scene Steph had managed to keep hold of. They worked solidly for several hours, Adam asking questions about base life, routines, and the intelligence division. Jack hadn't had much to do with Military Intelligence, but he could answer most questions with some measure of confidence. Of course, the discussion had to include the subject of being gay in the armed forces.

"Officially, the Australian military is non-discriminatory. Gay, straight, queer, it doesn't matter. Even different gender identities. When I left there was at least one transwoman in an officer position."

Adam quirked an eyebrow. "Officially?"

Conceding with a nod, Jack said, "Yeah, of course not everyone is as accepting as the official policy. There were those who didn't care and those who did."

"Did you have any problems?"

"Nothing too bad. Less once I was in the SAS. Even the biggest meathead thinks twice before insulting a special forces soldier."

Adam's gaze dropped lazily over Jack's body. "Mm, yeah. There are better things to be done with that body than insulting it."

Squashing down the warmth rising in his belly, Jack threw another pen at the leering man. "Eyes up here, thank you."

"Don't make me beg."

Jack's laugh was genuine. "As I recall, you're not really good at begging. It's sort of more like whiny commands."

Eyebrows shooting up, Adam scoffed. "Whiney commands? Bite me."

"Case in point."

Adam tried for indignant, but his usual grin broke through. "Did it work? Do you want to bite me now?"

"Don't know about *bite*, but *something*, sure." Jack smirked.

Before Adam could demand specifics, the door opened and Steph came in, followed by Officer Toomey.

"I hope there's some work happening between the hilarity," Steph admonished them, carrying on before they could do anything more than look contrite. "Jack, you know Constable Toomey." The tall blond nodded in Jack's direction, trying his hardest as usual to hide between his shoulders. "Apparently he and some other officers have been at the Williams scene all morning, trying to recreate your suggested means of entry. They say it's not possible."

Toomey shrugged apologetically, looking at the table between Jack and Adam.

"It is," Jack insisted, but trying to talk Toomey through his scenario proved difficult. The man kept shaking his head at everything Jack proposed and saying flatly it wouldn't work in practice.

Eventually, they all ended up down at the scene where Jack demonstrated how it was possible to slip in between the overlapping camera fields, scale the wall, and get into the building through the roof. Not that it necessarily proved his point, as Adam reminded everyone Jack came from a special forces background. Once shown the way, though, Constable Toomey was capable of making it, even if he was caught on the edge of one camera sweep or the other.

Whether it was the memory of Adam's condition that morning, or the excursion out of the room in the LAC, or a combination of both, Jack gave in to Adam's pestering and agreed to a few drinks when they were done for the day. After digging up a spare helmet, Adam got on the back of the Ninja. Having the man pressed to his back, arms around his waist, invited a few nice, if unwanted, memories, and not just for Jack, apparently.

"Whoo!" Adam exclaimed when they'd come to a stop outside a pub not far from his hotel and he'd wrestled the helmet off. "Who would have guessed being in that position fully clothed would be such fun?"

Jack elbowed him in the ribs. "Don't go getting any ideas, Quinn. This is *just* drinks."

"I wouldn't dream of *anything* else." But as he got off the bike, he made sure to press his erection into Jack's hip.

Ignoring it, Jack followed him inside the small bar. They scored drinks and found a quiet table in the back. In silent agreement, they chatted about everything but the case, and it didn't take Jack long to remember why he'd agreed to more than one night with Adam back then. He liked the man, a lot. However, that like didn't turn into lust this time. When he did catch himself thinking about sex, it was Ethan who automatically populated the vague images in his head. As one drink turned into two more for Adam and his flirting ratchetted up several notches, Jack's thoughts kept going back to Ethan, and in the end, he had to admit defeat and call it a night. Not before making sure Adam got to the hotel, though.

As Adam fumbled his way off the back of the bike outside the Oaks, less coordinated than he had been the first time, he looped an arm around Jack's neck and planted a kiss on the lower part of his helmet, over his lips.

"One day," he murmured against the smooth surface, "you'll let that happen without anything in the way."

A shiver ran down Jack's spine. During their first hook-up, when Jack had explained that he didn't kiss on the mouth, Adam had given him one of his piercing looks and, after an uncomfortably long evaluation, said, "Sure. I get that. Just let me know when you're ready for it."

Now, Adam stepped back, his hand trailing down Jack's arm. "See you tomorrow, Nishant."

"Later, Quinn."

Jack's debrief at the Office had to be some sort of speed record, and yet, when he got home, Ethan was already in bed. He wasn't sleeping, but when Jack crawled in with him and made some exploratory moves, Ethan murmured, "In the morning, Jack," and rolled over, snuggling his back into Jack's chest. Disappointment mitigated by the promise of morning sex, Jack wound an arm around Ethan and tucked his face into the warm skin of his shoulder.

Even this was better than anything else.

TWENTY-ONE
AFTER

Jack's first destination was his apartment. He left the Honda Interceptor he'd taken from the Office transport pool in the visitor carpark, entered the building through the front doors, and took the lift up to his floor. Anyone who knew him even vaguely should be aware he usually took the stairs. Avoiding traps was all about breaking habits. Still, Jack felt confined and restricted in the lift. He took the time to pull his USP and hide it inside his helmet. The hallway on his floor was empty when the lift doors opened. Stepping out, Jack moved slowly, searching for something out of place or new. Nothing leapt out at him, but he kept up his cautious pace until he reached his neighbour's door.

Mr. Cesare answered his quiet knock within moments. "Nishant." Relief relaxed his face. "I'm so happy to see you, what after the commotion yesterday morning. I knew it was a mistake, those police—"

"Thanks, Mr. Cesare." Jack felt bad for cutting him off. He'd always taken the time to listen to his elderly neighbour, knowing the man didn't have many visitors and only his dachshund, Short Round, for company. "But it's not all cleared up yet, I'm afraid."

"Oh." His weary, lined face creased further into a worried frown. "I'm very sorry to hear that. Is Ethan with you?" He peered down the hallway.

"No. He's somewhere safe, don't worry." It warmed him to know Ethan had made friends with the sweet old guy. "I didn't want to disturb you, but I need to know if you've noticed anyone around my place since yesterday morning."

If the Judge was as good as he appeared to be, and if Ethan or Garrote had been around looking for him, Jack doubted his near-sighted and partly deaf neighbour would have noticed them, but it wasn't in Jack's nature to make assumptions.

"No, son. Of course, I'm not as sharp as I used to be. Were you expecting someone?"

"Not exactly. What about Shorty? He notice anything?" The dachshund was a good guard dog and absolutely devoted to his human.

Mr. Cesare's expression crumpled. "Shorty's not here. He had to go to the vet yesterday afternoon."

"Shit." Jack gripped the old man's arm compassionately. "What happened?"

"They think he was poisoned. I found him chewing a toy I'd never seen before yesterday, and an hour later, he was vomiting and couldn't stand up." Tears glimmered in his faded eyes.

Fuck. Whichever of the heartless fucks who'd resorted to hurting an animal would have Shorty's and Mr. Cesare's pain taken out of their hide. One thing Jack knew for certain, it hadn't been Ethan. He would put himself in harm's way before letting an animal get hurt. Besides, he and Shorty were old friends, and Ethan wouldn't have had to poison the dog to get past him silently.

"The vets think they got it in time." Mr. Cesare tried to sound positive. "We just have to wait and see if there will be any lasting damage."

Jack's hand curled tightly around the butt of his gun inside the helmet. "I'm sure he'll be fine. Do me a favour, okay? Don't answer the door to anyone you don't know, and if you see anyone or anything suspicious, call this number any time, day or night." He handed over a card with Lewis's direct line on it. "He's a friend of mine. He'll be able to help you with anything that comes up."

Mr. Cesare took the card but frowned at it. "This all seems very dramatic."

"I know, sir, but please humour me."

Patting Jack's arm, the old guy nodded. "Of course, son. Of course. I hope you get this trouble sorted out soon."

"Me too."

After Mr. Cesare had closed and locked his door, Jack continued his cautious way to his apartment, wondering if he shouldn't just have his neighbour taken to a safe house. Even as he thought it, Jack dismissed it. Rocco Cesare had assured Jack he would only leave his home feet first and not before.

By his door, Jack set down his helmet and, USP in hand, unlocked it. Anyone waiting for him inside would have been able to bypass the security system and as such could turn on the screen hooked up to the camera on the door. They'd know he was outside. Shoving the door open, he dove into his apartment, going into a low roll and coming up with his back to the kitchen counter, crouched below the overhanging top. He tracked across the living room and dining area with the gun. There was no movement, no bodies visible. No sounds of someone behind him in the kitchen, but when dealing with the level of operator he was, that meant next to nothing.

His nerves were steely calm as he slowly eased around the counter, scanning the kitchen and finding it empty. Efficiently and thoroughly, Jack checked the rest of his place, uncovering no hidden assassins or psychopaths and no signs of disturbance. There was, however, blood in the bathroom.

It was dried in small splatters across the vanity, like they'd dropped there while whoever it was leaned over the sink. Jack opened the mirrored cabinet above it, finding nothing out of place. Thanks to Ethan's obsessive tendencies, everything was ordered by size so it would be easy to notice if anything had been disturbed. Closing the cabinet, he caught sight of his own face.

Surprisingly, he didn't look too bad. Not too tired and not too stressed, considering the tickets and serial murderer with some sort of grudge against him. There was a touch of worry about his eyes, but mostly he just looked grim and determined. Sure, he had very few facts right then, but he knew the outcome he was aiming for, and that gave him confidence and purpose. Whatever, *whoever*, was out there, waiting for him, wasn't anything he couldn't handle.

Even if his biggest obstacle turned out to be Ethan.

From the back of his linen cupboard, Jack retrieved a small forensic kit. All assets had one or two of them in their personal residences for times such as this so they could collect evidence for the Office before the police showed up. With no intention of involving the cops at all, Jack went back to the bathroom and swabbed each of the blood drops, clearly labelling each sample. That done, he sprayed a light layer of fluorescent solution around the rim of the mirror, then shone the small black light torch on it. As expected, there was a cluster of smudged fingerprints around the lower left corner, where it was gripped to open the cabinet. However, further up the side were a set of two clear and one partial print, as if someone had rested their hand against the glass, perhaps leaning there after a fight that injured them. It was far from conclusive, but Jack used the small, disposable camera in the kit to take photos of them all the same.

As he was packing up his gathered evidence, another thought struck Jack. Clearing his gear out of the sink, he turned on the hot water, full bore, and waited. After a minute, the steam billowing up from the sink coated the mirror and condensed on the cool surface— except for where someone had written a message.

Eight numbers on three lines. The first two lines were most likely latitude and longitude. The third wasn't as clear but probably specified a time. 10:30 p.m. that night? Or last night? Was it a message to him from Ethan? Or whoever had poisoned Shorty? Was it a trap?

Jack snapped a photo with the camera and with his implant as well. Trap or not, meant for him or not, it was a point on a map he could target.

Jack left and, after checking the bike for tampering, headed to his next stop. Bathurst Street was about a fifteen-minute ride from Jack's place, but if a man didn't want to be followed it was about twice as long, which gave Jack a ten-minute window on his hour before turning on his tracking. Coming here, though, was precisely why he hadn't wanted to be tracked.

The penthouse apartment was exactly as he'd last seen it. Immaculate, stylishly furnished, his hastily removed tie and jacket still hanging over the back of a chair and his unfinished beer on the table.

For a minute he let the memories flood his body. The relief of finally being together after so much frustration. Of finally being able to relax without anyone knowing where they were, or that they were together. Christ. It had felt so fucking good to not have to think about anyone else. Just them and how bloody good it was to hold each other. All the restraint and barriers gone.

Inevitably, Jack was drawn to the big, plush leather couch, facing the perfect view of Hyde Park. It had been night, of course, when he was pushed down into the corner of the couch, his body slowly awakened and electrified by skilled hands and lips. Then, Jack hadn't seen the outside view he gazed at now, paths dissecting the vibrant green of Hyde Park, the majesty of St. Mary's cathedral in the distance. He'd been consumed with the most amazing blowjob of his life.

Jack dragged himself away from the view and locked all those memories in the filing cabinet. Memories that had once been glorious, but now so potentially painful. Done wallowing, he searched the penthouse.

There were no clues, no signs of habitation, no hints as to where anyone involved in this mess might be.

Leaving, Jack couldn't decide if the lack of evidence was a good or bad thing. Good because it meant the location was still a secret. Bad because he really needed every hint he could get right then.

As promised, Jack turned on his active tracking and sent a ping to HQ, letting them know where he was. Which wouldn't mean much to them because he was on the move, cutting through the traffic and bending road rules to a point just shy of breaking them. The more erratic he was, the harder he would be to follow, to predict—to ambush. He took the evidence from his apartment to a drop point for the Office, sent a message in to have it picked up, then continued on to the Oaks Goldsbrough Apartments.

The door to Adam's suite was crisscrossed with blue and white police tape. As with most security, it worked only to keep out honest people, and Jack had the lock picked and was squeezing through the largest gap in the tape within a minute.

There were, of course, more memories here. Good ones—the fun, playful fucking; the glimpses into Adam's life and personality. And bad ones—the argument; unconsciously seeking comfort in Adam's presence; Ethan's expression of hurt and betrayal. These, too, got locked away as Jack searched.

The police had clearly been through the suite from top to bottom, the signs of their thorough passing hiding any evidence of someone else tossing the place, either before or after Adam was killed, or went missing. Hopefully, the investigative team would hand over their report on Adam's place to Lydia sooner rather than later. Knowing if the suite had been searched before the cops got here would help Jack define a timeline.

Again, he came up skint for any clues, but he'd had to come here. Not just in case there had been evidence to find, but to satisfy the expectations of anyone following him.

He'd left the bike in the lane behind the building and was just straightening up from checking it when the bullet hit him.

TWENTY-TWO
BEFORE

"**W**hat's this?" Jack asked as he wiped the soap from Ethan's back.

Twisting lazily under the shower spray, Ethan craned his neck to see the spot Jack's fingers were drifting over. "Hmm. Just a bruise."

Jack slapped his bicep gently. "I can see that. How did you get it?"

"Victoria's bonnet. I was working on her yesterday and straightened when I shouldn't have."

Absorbing that as Ethan rinsed, Jack settled for watching the water sluice down the lean body before him. Still mellow from wake-up sex, Jack squirted shampoo into his hand and, hauling Ethan close, worked the product into his wet hair. As planned, the scalp massage made the man melt against him. It was one of Ethan's quirks Jack took shameless advantage of whenever he could. Running his fingers through Ethan's hair, nuzzling into it, or just stroking the back of his head. The resultant almost-purr was enough to make Jack's dick warm and thicken. Before the shampoo was washed out of his dark hair entirely, Jack had Ethan pressed up against wet tiles, lips feasting on his throat, their hard dicks in one, slowly moving hand. Having come once in bed, the build-up was leisurely and tender, the hiss of the water joined by Jack's gasps and Ethan's husky "Jack," repeated at least a dozen times. Jack went first, his orgasm feeling like it came from somewhere deeper inside him than just his balls. Somewhere that had been closed off for a very long time, somewhere next to the grenade in his chest, which exploded along with his climax, so it was his turn to melt into Ethan's body.

It was Ethan's lips on his neck and shoulder that brought Jack out of his glowing haze, and the prod of his erection against Jack's belly that made him sink into a crouch. It wasn't until the head of Ethan's dick was at the back of his mouth that Jack remembered the Athens video. He hadn't blown Ethan since then and nearly choked now, his body automatically rejecting the act in its entirety. Pulling away, Jack coughed on the unusual reaction.

"Jack?" Ethan ran a hand through his curls. "Are you all right?"

Jack looked up into his half-lidded eyes. Once, the white irises had unsettled him, but now they comforted, especially when accompanied by brows quirked in concern. The Athens vision was tucked away into the filing cabinet with no trouble.

"Yeah, just got a little too enthusiastic. I'm fine now." And proceeded to prove it until Ethan was shaking and moaning and coming.

After drying off, Ethan pulled on a pair of gi pants and left Jack to dress alone, during which Jack discovered that Ethan had taken him up on his offer to share space in the closet and tallboy. In fact, he had reorganised everything from top to bottom. The amount of clothes hadn't quite doubled in volume, but somehow Ethan had managed to arrange it all so nothing was squashed in or jumbled together. Marvelling at the thoroughness with which Ethan had attacked the task of moving in, Jack found undies, socks, button-down, suit, and tie without too much hassle, then dressed and joined Ethan in the kitchen.

"You reorganised the closet and tallboy." Jack accepted a mug of coffee from Ethan.

Freezing with his own cup of tea halfway to his mouth, Ethan said, "I can change it back if it's not all right."

The sudden uncertainty in Ethan's voice and expression caught in Jack's chest. This wasn't what he'd wanted when asking Ethan to live with him, but perhaps he should have expected it. The whole situation was completely new to him, and added to the fact he'd stopped working, it wasn't surprising Ethan might feel unsettled.

Jack wrapped his free hand around the back of Ethan's tense neck and dug his fingers into his damp hair, needing to reassure him. It took a moment, but Ethan pushed into the touch, as he always did, and relaxed a fraction.

"It's perfect," Jack said firmly. "Exactly what I wanted."

Resisting his instinctive reaction to the touch, Ethan morphed his hesitation into scepticism. "Exactly?"

Fingers fisting in Ethan's hair, pulling his head back and exposing his throat, Jack smirked. "Exactly." He dove in and kissed from clavicle to jaw.

Ethan's moan quickly changed into a mocking sigh. "Don't you have a job to get to?"

"Eventually." Jack nipped the tender skin under Ethan's jaw a couple of times, then released him. "I had to give them a little demonstration yesterday, to prove my point about the perp possibly slipping through the security cameras. It went over so well I'm planning another one for today."

Free, Ethan opened the fridge and retrieved bacon, eggs, and tomatoes. "Which entails being late?"

"Actually, yeah. Did you go shopping yesterday?"

"I did. Eating takeaway every night isn't ideal."

Meaning Ethan didn't like the apartment being regularly visited by random strangers. Jack didn't mind but a second reason came to him as well.

His suspicions were confirmed after a look at the stocked fridge. "And the makings of butter chicken just happened to leap into your trolley."

"Perhaps." He fought it, but a grin broke over Ethan's face. "Maybe you could make it tonight?"

Resisting the urge to do something extra stupid, Jack shrugged. "Maybe. If I get home at a decent time."

Between them, they got breakfast underway and as they sat at the table—Ethan firmly steered Jack and his plate away from the couch— Jack was content enough to ask something he'd been curious about for a while now.

"What is it with the hair?" He watched Ethan carefully for a response. "You love it when I touch your head."

Ethan went still, only for a moment, though, but when he relaxed, he kept his gaze on his food. Breaking the wobbly yolk on his fried egg, he dipped the corner of his toast into it, then put it down and pushed his plate aside. Just when Jack thought he should apologise for upsetting him, Ethan spoke.

"I don't recall much from my early childhood. I believe I told you once I was blind until I was six, or thereabouts."

Jack just nodded. Ethan talking about his past was so rare he didn't want to disrupt the flow.

Sugar Babies were born with tissue across their eyes. These days, the surgery to remove it was much more successful and readily available. Back when Ethan was born, it had resulted in a high percentage of permanent blindness. As such, they'd held off on operating until the babies were older, but six was still much older than most kids were when undergoing the procedure.

"As such, I have no memories of my mother's face. I have a vague memory of her singing. At least, I think it's her. It's a lullaby, so I choose to believe it was she who sang it to me. By far the strongest memory I have is her running her hand through my hair. Sometimes it was to comfort me. Sometimes to comfort her."

Ethan went silent and motionless again. Once more, though, Jack only had to wait about half a minute before he found the words—or perhaps the courage—to keep talking.

"Sometimes it was neither of those things. Those times, she would stroke my head as I was falling asleep, and say, Paul, *ma petite erreur.*" Slowly, Ethan raised his face to meet Jack's gaze, a faint challenge in his expression.

Keeping his face neutral, Jack processed the information encompassed in Ethan's words.

He was French, not British. Jack had more than half doubted the English accent was real right from the first time they met. A fake accent was an easy way to throw people off the mark while in disguise. Ethan's French accent was perfect to Jack's unaccustomed ear, but then so was the English one. That was the obvious revelation and one Jack could accept easily enough. It was the second one that made his stomach tighten in sympathy and shared pain.

Ethan had been separated from his mother before the surgery. Before he was six years old. His memories of her weren't as numerous or clear as Jack's were of his own mother, but the loss had left a scar as deep, as painful—as disabling. And perhaps Ethan hadn't had a loving father to help with the grief. Jack could only hope that at such a tender age, Ethan hadn't also had the crippling guilt, as well.

Jack had to say something. The longer he didn't, the more Ethan's expression smoothed away, heading towards his cold-hearted killer persona. If it got all the way to dead-eyes and steely mouth, Jack feared that would be it. Their little experiment in cohabitation would be over, and Ethan would leave for good. If Jack said the wrong thing, then the outcome would be the same.

"What was the lullaby?" Jack asked casually.

For a moment, he thought he'd blundered; then Ethan's lips curled up slightly at the corners.

"I don't remember all of it, but it was about a chicken. A grey one, or a brown one." Ethan frowned in thought. "Or perhaps there were many chickens. Either way, it or they laid eggs in very unusual places and a little boy would eat the eggs while they were still warm."

"Warm from the chicken's bum or from being cooked?"

Ethan blinked at him. "Do you know, I have no idea." Then he laughed.

Relief more than anything else made Jack laugh as well.

Breakfast done, Jack tidied the kitchen. When he was done, Ethan emerged from the bedroom dressed in a dark charcoal suit.

"Those look like going-out clothes." Jack tugged on the back of Ethan's collar as he passed him on the way to the bathroom.

Ethan followed, fastidiously straightening his jacket. "I have a meeting today."

"With your banker?" Jack smirked.

"Not exactly."

Any more answers were stalled by teeth brushing.

"Then who?" Jack persisted on the way back to the living room.

Pocketing Victoria's key and slipping on his sunglasses, Ethan returned Jack's smirk. "Perhaps it's a surprise."

Jack frowned at his back as Ethan led the way out of the apartment. "For whom? I hope not for the not-exactly-a-banker person. Didn't you say you retired?"

Ethan's chuckle was pure evil, and once more, answers were forestalled by Jack's neighbour opening his door. As soon as it was wide enough, Mr. Cesare's dachshund, Short Round, bolted out and aimed himself at Ethan's feet.

"Shorty!" Rocco Cesare scolded, stepping into the hallway.

Ethan was already crouching, hands full of excited, yapping dog, so Jack reassured his elderly neighbour it was all good.

"You're off late this morning, Nishant," Mr. Cesare commented while Ethan and Shorty reunited.

Back at the start of his semiregular visits, Ethan had installed a security system in Jack's apartment that met his requirements for feeling safe. In the process, he'd come into contact with Mr. Cesare and Shorty. Ethan and any animal were destined to be firm friends, and Jack suspected Ethan had allowed himself to be seen by the old man just so he could get his hands on Shorty. He couldn't help but wonder how Ethan would react to Mr. Cesare knowing about his presence now, though.

"Worked late last night." Jack kept one eye on the pair on the floor. Shorty was on his back, stubby legs waving ecstatically as Ethan scratched his belly. "You guys going for a walk?"

"Before it gets too warm. Hello," Mr. Cesare added as Ethan stood, a happily wiggling sausage dog in his arms. "I remember you. You installed Nishant's alarms."

Ethan smiled. "Yes, sir. Ethan Saint." He held out a hand.

Mr. Cesare shook his hand. "Rocco Cesare. Call me Rocco, and perhaps you can convince Nishant to do the same. Is that your Aston Martin parked next to Nishant's noise machine downstairs?"

Christ. A dog and appreciation of his car. Mr. Cesare was certainly hitting hard on Ethan's weaknesses. Jack suffered through the gushing for a minute, then pointedly put his hand on the base of Ethan's spine and pressed gently. "Don't you have your mysterious appointment to get to? And I can't be much later than I already am."

Ethan stiffened and stepped away from Jack's touch. "Of course, Nishant." His tone was pleasant, but he didn't look at Jack as he handed Shorty back to Mr. Cesare. "Goodbye, Rocco, Short Round. Enjoy your walk."

Jack added his goodbyes to Ethan's, then followed him along the hallway, down the stairs, and into the garage. By the time they reached Jack's bike and Victoria, the tension had eased from Ethan's shoulders, and he threw Jack a soft smile as he unlocked the car. As such, he caught Jack's expression. "Jack?" He could imbue a wealth

TWENTY-THREE
AFTER

Jack was thrown off his feet, and he crashed against the stairs he'd just come down. The sharp edge of the risers snapped into his armour, jolting his whole body. Despite the radiating agony across his chest and the roaring of blood through his ears, Jack heard the next shot, a muffled crack at the same time the cement by his head blew into shards. Instinct rolled him over and off the stairs, falling into the narrow space between them and the wall of the building. Another shot followed him, sparking off the wall as he dropped.

Adrenaline flooded his body, and he scrambled into deeper cover. His USP was in his hand without a thought. Sitting up, Jack peered over the stairs. The shooter had to be somewhere in the alley with him. Not on a roof because the angle of the shots had been too shallow. There wasn't a lot of cover in the narrow, dead-end street. A couple of industrial bins and a car were parked at the far end. A fourth shot ricocheted off the brick a few millimetres to the side of Jack's head and he dove back down, grunting as the motion set off another series of painful waves through his chest.

Breathing through the discomfort, Jack called up the few seconds of footage his implant got of the alley and replayed it. In the split moment before he ducked down, he saw a small movement on the edge of the image. Focusing in on it revealed a blackened shape suggestive of the business end of a silenced rifle. The entrance to the alley was covered by an overhead carpark, its underside a cat's cradle of girders and supports. The shooter was up there, nestled into the deep shadows with a rifle.

Shifting around to get a line of sight on where he'd glimpsed the rifle, he wondered if it was Ethan up there, and what Jack would do if he scored a hit. Actually hitting the target would be a bloody miracle, and either way, Jack was pretty sure it wasn't Ethan. The man he knew wouldn't have wasted his first, surprise bullet on a body shot. Or missed on the follow-ups.

Jack, unconcerned about the noise he made, fired off three rapid shots into the girders. They boomed in the confined space, echoing off the walls. One bullet sparked off a metal strut, and within the shadows, a darker shape jerked and rolled over a precarious perch across several horizontal bars. Jack didn't think he'd scored a direct hit because a second later, the subject returned fire, three more shots, and then three more, the timbre deeper. He or she had emptied the rifle and moved on to a larger-calibre handgun.

Waiting out the volley, Jack dug a smoke grenade from his jacket pocket and, when he got a chance, raised up and fired with one hand while pulling the pin with his teeth and tossing the grenade with the other. It hit the bitumen under the overpass, and smoke bloomed. Jack kept up a steady rate of fire while the white cloud grew to encompass the space under the overpass, billowing up into the girders.

"Drop your weapons," Jack called as he made an explorative move out of cover. If the assassin had thought to bring a gas mask and thermal goggles, then Jack was out of luck. "Come down slowly and surrender. Backup is already on its way."

Nothing. Not that Jack had expected anything, let alone compliance. But since "nothing" included no more gunfire, Jack made his slow, cautious way along the wall of the building, covering the smoke-shrouded girders. His chest and back ached, but the armour had done its job, thankfully, even if the weight on his abused torso was now more annoying than ever.

"Identify yourself," he tried, still not disappointed when he got no answer.

By the time he reached the covered passage, the smoke had dissipated enough he could see up into the girders. They were empty. Following through to the entrance of the alley, Jack saw a dangling rope hung over the side of the carpark. It twitched once as the escaping subject disappeared over the edge.

In the distance, sirens were wailing and getting closer, undoubtedly called by someone, or many someones, in the surrounding buildings.

Not wanting to get caught up in official business, Jack hurried back to the bike and made his own hasty getaway. As he sped down the road, he contacted Lewis.

"Several cars are heading your way," his friend said by way of a greeting. *"There were eight reports of gunfire. Someone found you, I presume."*

"Yeah," Jack thought back to him. *"Contact was made in the lane behind the Oaks Goldsbrough. First shot from the other party."* Coolly, Jack made his report so Lewis could pass it on to the appropriate authorities and answer their most immediate questions. Anything more than that would be subjected to a "need to know, and you don't" line.

"Did you get a look at them?" Lewis asked when he was done.

"Just the wrong end of their gun and the underside of their shoe as they disappeared over a wall above me. It wasn't Blade, though."

"How can you be sure?"

"I'm still alive. He wouldn't have missed under those circumstances."

"Good to know. We got your package, and it's with the lab right now. Should have a prelim on the blood in another hour or so. I have a location on the coordinates you found as well. You're going to love it," Lewis predicted in a wry tone.

Jack's sore stomach sank. *"Where?"*

"The Cenotaph at Martin Place."

One of the oldest WWI memorials in Sydney. Whoever had left the coordinates on Jack's mirror wanted him there, no fucking doubt.

"We checked all CCTV footage around ten thirty last night and the night before. Nothing suspicious, so whatever's happening there hasn't happened yet. I'm about to mobilise a strike team to set up a watch—"

"No." Jack had to concentrate on getting through a slow patch of traffic and couldn't immediately continue.

In his head, Lewis waited a moment, then asked, *"Why not? If you're going to spring the trap, at least do it with a team there to give assistance."*

Jack grumbled as he wove the bike between a couple of cars and found a clear stretch. *"You even think too hard about setting up in Martin Place and they'll know it, Lew. They won't touch the place with a* remotely controlled drone. Trust me. They're operating at a level we can't touch, as sad as it is."

There was a grinding silence on the other end of the line. Then Lewis muttered, "I don't like it."

"Neither do I. I've got seven hours until then. I'll think of something."

"Okay. I'm going to have three strike teams on standby here, ready to roll if it goes sideways. They can get there in seven minutes."

Knowing he couldn't veto it, Jack agreed with a grunt and turned off the road into a parking structure. Easing the bike around the boom gate, he took the ramp going down. Before he lost the signal, he told Lewis where he was heading and what he needed; then the call cut out and he was alone with his thoughts and aching chest.

First contact with the enemy was over and done with. About all he'd learned for certain was it hadn't been Ethan. According to her JSL listing, Eve Garrote was as good a marksman as Ethan, but his fleeting glimpses of the shooter hadn't been enough to tell if they were female or male. All things considered, Jack settled on it having been the Judge. Not every soldier in the SAS was a perfect shot. Very few of them were. They were better than average, but not extraordinary. And if the psycho was really starting to lose his grip on reality, then that might affect his skills as well. At least Jack could hope. Anything to give him an advantage over the bastard.

On the lowest level of the carpark, Jack rolled the bike towards the corner furthest from the exit. The area was permanently unlit, covering any comings and goings through the access to the underground tunnel network. Swinging his leg over the bike, Jack winced at the sharp increase in the ache in his chest. He unbuckled the panniers, unwilling to leave them behind this time, and found the secluded door to the tunnels and pressed his palm to the hidden scanner. The door opened silently.

Jack didn't have long to wait. About ten minutes later, he heard the soft pad of someone approaching. They were singing the song Lewis had told him to expect, which was, of course, "One Night in Bangkok." Still, Jack kept his USP out and ready until they'd confirmed IDs and the medic had produced her kit.

The medic, Karen, was good at her job, restraining herself to a single "You really should come in and get this looked at properly," before shutting up and assessing the damage done to his chest from the bullet and his back from impact with the stairs.

"Nothing cracked as far as I can tell," Karen informed him after a couple minutes of somewhat painful poking. "You'll bruise up nicely and hurt like hell for a while. Arms up."

"About that." Jack lifted his arms obediently so she could wrap a wide bandage around his ribs. "Can you give me something for the pain?"

Karen gave him the look every medical person Jack had ever encountered had perfected—the "my trained opinion is clearly wasted on lunatics like you" look—but after finishing with the bandage and helping him back into the armour, she gave him a shot that worked within a minute. Very reluctantly, since Jack's medical file noted he only had the one kidney, she also handed over a green whistle.

"For emergencies only. And if you need it, then you *absolutely*, no excuses, *need* an ambulance, anyway."

Jack tucked the three-milligram tube of anaesthetic into an inner pocket on his jacket. "Fingers crossed I won't need it. Thanks for this." He gingerly patted his ribs. It didn't hurt and he tried standing, which worked rather well, so he headed back out to the bike. It was precisely where he'd left it and showed no signs of tampering. As he emerged from the underground carpark, he called Lewis again.

"Any sign of Blade's Aston Martin?"

Jack didn't really think Ethan would be using Victoria now. She was too conspicuous and the Office knew she was his, but knowing where she was might just give Jack a direction to head in.

"Not even a hint. We've got a KLO4 on any black Vanquish, though. There aren't too many registered in Sydney." Lewis rattled off a list of names in case Jack recognised one of them as an alias Ethan might use. None of them sounded familiar or stood out as something Jack associated with Ethan.

"Extend the KLO4 to cover any sort of supercar," Jack suggested. *"Porsche, Ferrari, McLaren. Anything that goes from zero to holy fucking shit in under five seconds."*

Lewis swore under his breath. *"Yeah, okay. Any ideas on where to look for him?"*

Jack turned the Interceptor to the west. *"That's my next objective. I'll let you know if I find him."*

"Let's just hope you find him before he finds you," Lewis said, deadly serious.

Revving the engine, Jack roared away.

Lewis could hope all he wanted that Jack found Ethan first. True to form, Jack had fucked up. He'd ruined every other serious relationship he'd ever had, why should this one be any different? All he could hope for right then was that Ethan still thought Jack was worth the pain.

TWENTY-FOUR
BEFORE

Ethan finally looked at Jack, and the fist on top of his car loosened, fingers spreading out over the black duco. "Jack, I'm sorry. I didn't mean to worry you. You're right. I don't have experience with any of those things, and I can't promise that I won't make mistakes upon occasion. I can, however, assure you that regardless of what anyone else thinks or says, I want to be here. With you."

Jack wanted to believe him. Desperately. Yet, he could still clearly feel the way Ethan had reacted to his touch, the same way he did when threatened. If he wasn't worried about being openly gay, then what had caused him to pull away?

"I want you here, too." Jack took a couple of steps towards him, testing his limits. "It's why I asked you to come and stay. I know it's not going to be easy. I don't have a great track record with relationships. *I'm* undoubtedly going to mess something up at some stage."

The corner of Ethan's mouth quirked up. "We're not incapable men, Jack. I'm sure we can weather the rough patches. And if you were to leave me, I should remind you, I'm retired, not disabled."

Jack snorted, that involuntary draw he constantly felt for Ethan, especially at times like this, bringing him another step closer.

"Too soon?" Ethan leaned back against Victoria's side.

There was barely ten inches between their chests. "Too cheesy." Jack let his voice drop into a husky rumble.

The panes of Ethan's glasses angled downward, judging the distance. "Jack, am I required to remind you we're not exactly in private?" His little smile turned brittle, and his tone flattened.

And there it was. What had made Ethan pull away from Jack in front of Mr. Cesare. Ethan didn't want to be touched in public not because he feared being seen as gay, but because it was a risk to his control. Jack was fascinated and aroused by how tranquil and easy Ethan could be when they were together, but only when he felt secure. Outside of his lairs or Jack's apartment, he was constantly on alert, wary, ready to face any threat. Having someone touching him hindered his ability to react, and perhaps having *Jack* touch him was distracting on other levels, as well.

"No," Jack whispered and backed off. "Just wanted to tell you that I'll miss you today."

Before he got out of range, Ethan put his palm on Jack's chest as he said, "And I you," then let it drop, unspoken thanks for understanding.

Exchanging smiles, they got onto and into their respective vehicles. Jack watched while Ethan backed the Vanquish out and turned her towards the exit. He wasn't a publicly demonstrative person, but he took a moment to mourn the loss of simply holding hands as they walked together, then started the bike and headed in to work.

His welcome at the police station wasn't quite as warm as Ethan's parting smile. Steph and Adam were both on their phones, having tense conversations. Adam was pacing the length of the room while Steph sat at her laptop, phone held between cheek and shoulder while she tapped keys angrily.

"It's okay," Adam ground into his phone when he saw Jack. "He just showed up."

Steph, too, ended her call with a "He's here," and stood, hands on hips.

"Where the hell have you been?" Adam demanded.

"I'm not that late." He was. Ethan was very distracting. Still, he hadn't expected showing up late would cause such a strong reaction.

"So?" Steph asked, sounding calm. "Do you have an explanation?"

"As it happens, I do." Jack casually strolled to his usual seat and sat. This was the perfect opener for his demonstration. "Steph, would you care to call the front desk and make sure I've arrived, please?"

Eyeing him sceptically, Steph called down and after about fifteen seconds, turned a furious glare on Jack. "He hasn't checked in? No, that's okay," she said into the phone, tone low and tight. "We'll sort it out up here." Then she slammed the phone down and glared at Jack.

"And that," Jack said mildly, "is how easy it can be to bypass security, even in a secure place like this, or a military base."

Adam gaped from him to Steph and back again.

"Explain," Steph said.

"The best way to get around most security measures is familiarity, confidence and—" Jack produced a laminated card and put it on the table in front of Adam. "—forgeries."

Picking up the card, Adam glanced at it, then at Jack, then did a double take with the card. He swore and tossed it back at Jack. "This is why you came out for drinks last night? To get my AFRG card and copy it?"

"And you didn't suspect a thing. I got a photo of it and had a forgery made." By Office techs. "I've been in and out of this building for several days now. A lot of the staff in this section have seen my face. They're familiar with me being an 'approved' visitor. Today, I simply walked up to the back door at the same time as someone else, flashed my new card, and they happily let me in with them."

Silence greeted his speech, neither of them looking appeased.

"This is why you wanted me here, to explain how your offender got in and out of the military base. And it is easier than you think." Jack looked between them. "Do you want to hear it or not?"

"By all means." Steph had regained some equilibrium. "Tell us your theory."

Jack took them through his analysis of the Morrissey scene. He had personal experience with the base in question and described how it was possible to circumvent the outer security, which was similar to what he'd done that morning. Familiarity, confidence, and forgery.

"Once inside, it's easier to move around. There is nothing simpler than blending in with military personnel. Everyone in uniform, drilled into acting just as uniformly as they look, coached in exactly what to say to anyone who crosses their path. Enough people cycle through those places not everyone is familiar. As sad as it is, this was the easiest and least risky entry faced by your killer.

"Adam, on day one, you said serial murderers often have a fascination with the police. That could extend to the armed forces, right? Your offender knows enough about the military to blend in. He probably tried to enlist but was knocked back for failing the psych evaluation. Or maybe he did get in and was discharged due to psychological issues. I'd say he's physically fit, if he subdued Morrissey, though."

"Shit," Adam whispered. "This is why ADFIS didn't want us looking at Morrissey. They know the offender could be one of theirs."

Armed with a new perspective, Adam's perpetually lazy mien vanished, and Jack got to see the profiler in action. He buzzed through the gathered information with a new vigour, looking at it all from a new angle. Several times he threatened to kiss Jack for "breaking the case wide open." Steph regarded these declarations with a tolerant smile and a quiet thanks to Jack for giving Adam exactly what he needed.

If Jack had been worried his part was over, he was soon disabused of that notion. Steph made good on her promise from the first day and set him to work going over witness statements, looking for anything that might stand out in light of the new information.

Likewise, once convinced of Jack's theory about how the Judge got into Williams's workplace, Connors set the Scene of Crime team to the task of scouring the route for evidence. Between Jack and Toomey making the run, there was a substantial amount of disturbance of the area, as well as five weeks of accumulated weather and wildlife to deal with. Still, a couple of days later, Steph reported that the SOC team had found a partial print under the skylight the Judge probably used to gain entry. Thanks to Jack, the investigative team had a new lead, as well.

The excitement of Jack's revelations seemed fleeting, followed as they were by days of tedium. There was a staggering amount of information from the three civilian victims to go through, and it was only compounded when every day or so, Adam would give Jack and Steph a new piece of his evolving profile to chase down in the case files. The whiteboard quickly filled up with Adam's scrawl, listing traits he believed the Judge possessed. A lot of them were rather generic—abusive childhood, cruelty to animals, fascination with fire—but some seemed oddly specific—he would drive a statement car, either expensive or overly modified; he would be charming and make himself attractive to others; he would be physically fit, perhaps obsessively so.

Jack continued to give in to Adam's invitations for drinks every couple of days, and by the end of the second week, drinks had extended to dinner just so Jack knew Adam was eating something substantial.

Things at home, too, settled into a comfortable pattern. Ethan was there most nights when Jack got in, and they usually spent some time doing tai chi together. It helped Jack ease out of the mindset work put him in and also mellowed Ethan out. The nights Ethan wasn't there, he invariably showed up after Jack was in bed. Occasionally, when Jack walked into the apartment after having dinner with Adam, he would find something changed. Usually something small, like the order of his books on the shelves, or the cutlery in the drawer, or the towels in the linen cupboard.

Sometimes, Jack would purposefully put something back out of place and see how long it took Ethan to correct it. That stopped after the day Jack came home early, hoping to surprise Ethan with butter chicken for dinner. Expecting to find the apartment empty, he was startled to come across Ethan in the bedroom. Every drawer on the tallboy was pulled open and all the clothes were on the bed, half of them folded neatly, the other half strewn across the bedspread chaotically.

"What happened here?" Jack asked.

Ethan didn't look at him, totally focused on folding T-shirts. "You put the underwear away wrong, Jack. Again."

Cranky from Adam's passive-aggressive demands for something more and annoyed that his surprise was ruined, Jack's mood soured further with the knowledge he'd caused Ethan to get deeply lost in his compulsions. Rather than possibly make it worse, Jack backed off. He tried to start dinner but ended up just stewing over everything. All the while, he could make out the soft opening and closing of drawers as Ethan continued working through his own problems. Eventually, Jack made a cup of tea and took it in to him. Most of the clothes were back in their drawers and Ethan was pairing socks, and ignoring him. Jack left the tea on the corner of the tallboy and retreated again. Ethan didn't speak to him for the rest of the night, and while he didn't sleep, he did lie beside Jack in bed, without touching. In the morning, Jack woke up groggy and cranky, only to find Ethan had made him breakfast and was ready to communicate again. That night, he let Jack touch him. Lesson learned, Jack was extra careful with the clothes afterwards.

Then there was the day Jack came home and found Ethan in Mr. Cesare's doorway. He wore an old T-shirt of Jack's and a pair of jeans that clung to his thighs and arse as he crouched to measure the bottom of the doorframe. Around his trim hips was a battered tool belt, pulled low with the weight of hammers and screwdrivers. Short Round was there, little butt planted beside Ethan, devotedly watching everything the human did like the world's creepiest supervisor.

Unable to help himself, Jack wolf-whistled as he sauntered up.

Ethan looked up, sunglasses on, lips curled into a little smile. "Hello, Jack." He stood and wrote a number on a small notepad. At his feet, Shorty picked up his arse and looked between them expectantly, tail waggling so hard his long body wobbled.

"What are you doing?" Jack asked.

"Rocco asked if I'd look at installing an alarm system for him."

"And you actually are?"

"I don't see why I shouldn't. He's a lovely gentleman, and I don't mind helping him. Don't worry, I'm only charging him for the cost of the system."

Before Jack could say anything else, Mr. Cesare shuffled out of the kitchen and joined them.

"Your drink, son." He handed Ethan a glass of iced tea. "Hello, Nishant. I hope you don't mind, but I stole your young man today for my own purposes."

"It's all good, Mr. Cesare. Just check his pockets before he leaves. I fear I'm going find Shorty held hostage in our place soon."

At the sound of his name, the dog jumped up on his back feet, pawing at the air. For once ignoring the dachshund's antics, Ethan stared at Jack, mouth open in surprise.

Chuckling, Mr. Cesare admitted it was good advice, then wandered back inside to turn on the news. Jack put a finger under Ethan's jaw and gently shut his mouth.

"What?" he asked, partly worried, partly amused.

"You said 'our place.'"

Shit. He had. Jack's belly rolled uneasily. "Yeah. Is that okay?"

Ethan just nodded.

"Good." Jack sounded like he meant it, which he did, but it was still a bit startling to realise it. "You going to be much longer here?"

"I have a few more measurements to get, but that won't take long."

Jack stepped back and turned towards their apartment. "I'll be waiting for you, then. Oh, and when you come in, leave the tool belt on."

That turned into a very good night, but then there was the day Jack came home, a bit late, and found Ethan closed off and silent. He spent a lot of time at the door to the balcony, carefully standing so he didn't silhouette himself in the glass, and stared out at the city. His stiff posture discouraged touching, and his vague, single-syllable answers to Jack's questions stopped any chance of meaningful conversation. It made it hard for Jack to relax and he spent the night restless, waking several times to find Ethan gone. Jack usually found him at the front door, watching the screen hooked up to the external camera, but one time, he was fastidiously checking every window lock.

"Is there a problem?" Jack muzzily asked.

"No." Ethan didn't pause in testing the pressure mat under the window in the spare bedroom. "Go back to bed, Jack."

Wrecked from a long day of going through evidence reports and then a few too many drinks with Adam, Jack did so.

Then there were the bruises. In Jack's regular explorations of Ethan's body, he found a new one every couple of days. Ethan's excuses got thin pretty fast, and when Jack stopped accepting them, Ethan turned his talent to distraction. When that wouldn't work anymore, he settled on, "It's nothing to be worried about, Jack. I'm just . . . it's a surprise. For you."

Jack feathered his lips over the newest bruise, a purpling patch under Ethan's ribs. "What sort of surprise entails this?"

"A good one, I hope."

Abandoning Ethan's lower torso, Jack slid back up until he could look him in the eyes. "Nothing is worth you getting hurt."

Ethan cupped his hands around Jack's face, holding him still and staring into him so deeply Jack thought he saw something flicker for a second in Ethan's fixed pupils.

"Some things are worth it," Ethan whispered.

Feeling raw and exposed, Jack asked, "Like what?"

"Like you, Jack."

TWENTY-FIVE
AFTER

Jack had no real expectation of finding Ethan at the Sydney Motorsport Park, but he couldn't not check it out. He used his ISO ID to get into the restricted areas, flashing a picture of Ethan from the Office's file at every staff member he could capture. A few recognised him as Roy Carter, Ethan's amateur racing nut persona, but no one recalled seeing him in over a year.

Realising that, once again, it had been too long since he'd eaten, Jack got a coffee and a sandwich from a café and watched V8 cars pelt madly around the track while he ate.

It was hard to think of the sport as relaxing, and certainly the few times Jack had been in a racing car with Ethan, the experience hadn't exactly left him tranquil. But it was the opposite for Ethan. It was like the single-minded focus he needed to control the car and judge corners let him put everything else about his life out of his mind. Everything narrowed down to right there, right then, and all the paranoia and stress of his dangerous world didn't fit into that space.

God. Jack was an absolute shitheel. He'd been too distracted by Adam, and yes, guilty about it all, especially about thinking he was "helping" Ethan, to really hear what Ethan needed from him. The signs had all been there—the distance, the obsession, the compulsions. The bruises. Ethan had talked a good game, but he'd been stumbling when Jack wasn't looking.

Fuck. He discreetly rubbed away a few tears.

About the best he could expect was that Ethan had left the message on the mirror and they would meet up that night. Until then, Jack had other mysteries to solve.

Feeling a bit aimless as he left the SMSP, he had a sudden urge to go back to Middle Head. His recent visits had reminded him how much he used to enjoy the park. If he hadn't had his head up his own arse these past weeks, he should have taken Ethan. Perhaps he would have found some of the peace there that Jack did.

Jack headed for Mosman. He wouldn't get there before the park closed, but that was probably a good thing. If the Judge was still following him, then an empty space filled with old fortifications wouldn't be an entirely bad place for a fight, at least.

He was cruising along the M7 when his implant *ping*ed.

"Jack." Lydia sounded excited when he answered. *"Are you sitting down?"*

"Of a sort. You have news?" He didn't want to tempt fate by saying "good news."

"Of a sort," she repeated in the same wry tone. *"The blood sample from your place came back. It's Blade's."*

It was a both a worry and a relief to know Ethan had been back home after the arrest. Had he gone there looking for comfort? How had he been hurt? *Who* had hurt him? And was that person the same one who'd been inflicting the bruises?

"Also, the fingerprints on the mirror match that found at the Williams scene. We're treating them as the Judge's. So far, no hits on any databases, but we're still looking."

Jack felt sick that the psycho had been in his home. Now he understood why Ethan needed so much security around him.

"Any other news?" As he asked, he noticed a red motorbike westbound on the highway. It was weaving through the traffic, clearly doing far more than the posted speed limit.

"Actually, yes. The police finally coughed up a report on Quinn's suite. Apparently, it was disturbed before they got there. A physical altercation."

Jack listened with half an ear. He flashed quick looks at the speeding bike as it whipped past him, going in the opposite direction. Once it was behind him, he checked on it in his rear-vision mirror.

"They found blood splatter that turned out to be Quinn's. Jack, it looks like—"

In the distance, the other bike's brake light flared, and the rider threw it into a tight turn. Barely missing being taken out by a car, the bike left the road and, dirt spraying up behind it, cut across the grassed divide between the highway lanes.

"Fuck!"

"Jack?"

"Got a situation here," Jack said aloud. It would be muffled on Lydia's end, but right then he didn't care. "Suspicious red bike, was heading west, is now on the eastbound lane of the M7, coming up behind me. Fast."

Cutting the connection so he wouldn't be distracted, Jack revved the Interceptor's engine and shot away. Behind him, the other rider kicked their bike into high gear and chased him.

It was entirely the wrong time of day to be having a high-speed chase on one of the main arterial roads into and out of the inner city. There was slightly less traffic heading east than there was going west, but that didn't make it any easier to evade both crazy commuters and crazier pursuer. Jack forgot everything else and concentrated on dodging cars, risking quick looks for the other rider every thirty seconds or so. Despite Jack's efforts, they were rapidly gaining on him, taking risks he wouldn't, pushing speeds he would only dare on an empty road. Whoever it was, they wanted him bad.

Who was it? The Judge? Garrote? Although Ethan had never said outright, Jack was certain he could ride, and probably at a skill that matched his pursuer. Anyone with as big a fixation on fast, dangerous things as Ethan had would know how to ride. Besides, being proficient with all sorts of vehicles would only benefit an assassin. Similarly with soldiers. Which didn't narrow down his options any.

He checked over his shoulder. The red bike was relentlessly closing the distance between them.

Without a second thought, Jack pushed the Interceptor faster and, planning his moves three cars ahead, shot into the thicker traffic. It was wild and very risky, putting his trust in so many unknown quantities, but he knew his own instincts, his own reflexes. It was like running a new obstacle course. Just faster. Much, much faster. Leaving the other rider behind, both literally and figuratively, Jack flew through the cars, their shapes blurring in his periphery, his awareness expanding out as it did in combat situations.

A car braked and he went left, swinging out in front of a small truck, throttling back to keep from smacking face first into the SUV in front, then revving forwards into a widening space in front of the car he'd just passed. He cut through a narrow gap between two more cars and, spying a wide gap between another two, rocketed up between them. In front of him, the highway opened up, a rare distance between this pack of vehicles and the one ahead.

Jack roared into the relatively empty space and risked a look over his shoulder.

"Fuck!"

Red was still on his exhaust. Not close enough to be a danger, but closer than they had been when Jack took off. Coming into the clear, Red powered up and the gap started to get smaller.

Jack reached the next pack of traffic, and he dove into another obstacle course. He took bigger risks and cut through smaller spaces and kept his speed right up there. A few grey hairs later, he shot back out into the relative clear.

Red sidled up beside him.

Shit.

There was nothing he could do. The traffic ahead was thicker and slower, and Red was right there, keeping pace easily. Experimentally, he dodged left and they followed, matching his move perfectly. He slowed, so did they. He moved right, into their space and they waited until the last moment before moving over as well. Fantastic. Synchronised motorbike manoeuvres. He hoped the people in the cars around them were enjoying the show.

The rider wore a full-face helmet, as Jack did, a set of black riding leathers and a pair of big boots, black of course. They were shorter and leaner than Jack, smaller than Ethan.

Red unzipped the front of their leather jacket. As they reached under their arm, probably going for a gun, the sides of the jacket flapped back and the wind of their speed outlined breasts. Small but definitely there.

Eve Garrote.

Jack was almost glad to have her show up at last. And fucking hell, he was impressed. She could *ride*.

Sure enough, she pulled a gun. A compact piece she could handle easily while steering with one hand. Something that wouldn't be immediately visible to the commuters around them. Jack had to get this off the highway, away from all these potential victims.

Garrote had the same idea, apparently. She held the gun on him steadily and eased over, forcing him to the left. Garrote made little hurry-up gestures with the gun, urging him to speed up. There was an exit coming up, and she clearly wanted them to take it.

Following the little instructions, Jack increased his speed, Garrote keeping pace perfectly. She had them in the left lane, approaching the exit, and Jack dutifully veered towards it, speeding up again. The assassin matched him, perhaps a second behind. The car in front of them sped up, taking the relatively clear exit. Jack moved into the space it created, throttling up even more. Garrote was right beside him, the gun giving him a don't-mess-around motion. Another gap opened up on the ramp, and Jack raced into it. This time when Garrote pulled in beside him, the gun was fully visible, pointed at him directly. No more games.

So Jack stopped playing.

He sped up, once more, threatening to ram the back of the car before them, and Garrote matched him, the gun jerking out, ready to shoot. Then Jack touched the brake, lightly, but enough so Garrote rocketed ahead. To a chorus of alarmed car horns, Jack swerved over to the left and out of the direct line of traffic. Ahead, Garrote had also braked, but she was locked in between two cars and couldn't do more than come to a complete stop.

Given a couple of seconds, Jack throttled the Interceptor back up and, when a big enough space opened up, he darted back into the traffic. He turned right sharply, planting his foot onto the road and skidding the back tyre of the bike around in a tight turn. Straightening up, he jetted back down the ramp, heading towards the highway, in the wrong direction. Another assisted turn and Jack was back on the M7, heading east with the rest of the evening traffic.

Of course, all Garrote had to do was continue up the ramp, cross the intersection, and take the on ramp back to the highway. Under the cover of the overpass, Jack cut back to the westbound lanes and tore off in that direction. He took the first exit he came to and rode right into a convoy of cop cars, lights flashing and sirens blaring.

He was disarmed, cuffed, and sitting in the back of a patrol car when the implant *ping*ed.

"*Jack?*" Lydia sounded frantic yet relieved. "*Where the hell are you?*"

"*In the back of a cop car. Possibly in North Rocks.*"

She sighed wearily. "*Not a great move, I have to say.*"

"*I didn't have a lot of options, and I figure a phalanx of armed and angry law enforcement might keep Garrote away. She's shown up.*"

There was a bunch of swearing and muffled chatter, and then Lydia came back clearly. "*That's just the cherry on the crap cake, then. You might not find the police very happy with you right now.*"

Jack groaned, letting his head thump back against the uncomfortable seat. "*What now?*"

"*Well, as I was saying before you rudely cut me off, we got the report on Quinn's suite. They found, naturally, Quinn's DNA, but also that of two others. One was yours, Jack.*"

"*That's no great revelation,*" Jack countered. "*We were working together at his place. Who was the other one?*" Was the last one Ethan's? Left behind when he . . . Jack cut off that thought savagely.

"*The other one was, oddly enough, Constable Richard Toomey.*"

Jack let out an explosive breath. Not Ethan, thank God.

"*Makes sense,*" he thought to Lydia, relief letting him sag back, his cuffed hands pressing into his lower back. "*I know he and Adam had gotten . . . friendly.*"

"*Yeah, friendly. I guessed from where they found the DNA.*" As she continued, her tone got serious. "*But the thing is, Jack, they can't find Toomey now. He's gone missing too.*"

Now he understood why being in the back of a police car wasn't a great place to be right then. One of their own dead, two missing, and their best suspect currently causing havoc all across the city. They weren't going to let him go so easily this time.

Then his brain caught up to Lydia's exact words. "Wait. What do you mean, too?" He spoke aloud in surprise.

"*It was in the conclusion of the report on Quinn's place. It looks like he was taken from his suite, alive. It's Stephanie Phelps who died in the Surry Hills LAC.*"

TWENTY-SIX
BEFORE

Jack set down the next round and sank gratefully into the booth opposite Adam. "Fuck me. I'm exhausted."

"Both things me and my hotel room can help you with," Adam said cheerfully.

Absurdly, sitting most of the day reading and talking on the phone was draining Jack's energy, while it appeared to invigorate Adam. He no longer slumped into the LAC later than everyone else, but showed up first thing, bright-eyed and eager to keep going with the hunt.

Jack scowled. "Jesus, anyone would think you'd gotten laid."

Which was part of his current problem. The ready supply of sex at home had all but dried up. Ethan's mood swings had continued, and when Jack tried to talk to him about it, he got the cold-hearted killer treatment. If Jack didn't pry and waited patiently, then Ethan came around within a couple of days and things got back to normal—for a while. Then it would all begin again, usually when Jack tried to start things in the bedroom. Or living room, or bathroom. At times, Ethan reciprocated his advances, and events would progress in a naked, fun direction. Sometimes it got to the messy, happy end. Other times, Ethan would pull away and get distant, and Jack would be back to waiting. Not knowing which conclusion he would get made Jack reluctant to try over the past week.

Adam winked over the rim of his tumbler. "What if I said I had? Would you be jealous?"

"No." He held out his glass, and Adam clinked his to it. "Cheers. Must have been a good one."

"Meh." The dismissiveness was ruined by Adam's grin. "Just okay. He didn't have much fight in him, but you know, he was there and his arse was . . ." He grunted and made squeezy motions with his hands.

Trying not to laugh, Jack asked, hesitantly, "Do I dare ask who the poor bastard was?"

Adam's grin passed wicked and hit positively debauched. "You get three guesses, but I'll give you a hint. You know him."

Jack's eyes rolled. He had developed a certain dislike for hints after Ethan's cryptic little efforts. Still, the clue narrowed the potential victims drastically. There were very few men in the small overlap between his and Adam's acquaintances. Jack went with the most absurd in the hope it would make Adam just spit out the name.

"Connors."

Whisky sprayed across the table as Adam spat the wrong thing out.

Finding something to smile about, Jack called, "Bib here!" to the bartender, who looked over with a tolerant smile. They'd become something like regulars in this little bar, and the guy currently tending bar was on most nights.

"Or him?" Jack nodded towards the young man behind the bar as Adam mopped up his face and the table with their serviettes.

Adam glanced over. "I wish. Straight as a bloody arrow, that one. One more guess."

Willing to throw away his last chance, Jack went with the next most ludicrous option. "Constable Toomey."

Smile going a little bit strained, Adam merely held his glass up for another toast.

"Holy shit. Really?"

Adam nodded, suddenly very closed-mouthed.

"Wow. My gaydar's on the fritz." Jack couldn't imagine the tall bloke expressing much of anything, let alone responding to Adam's brand of club-to-the-back-of-the-head flirting.

"Right?" Adam took a fortifying drink. "Since you decided to piss off early last night, leaving me alone to carry the burden of hunting down this remorseless—"

"Get on with it."

"Fine. I was on my own and Toomey comes in, asking if I need anything. I'm tired and annoyed, so I say, 'Someone to suck my dick' . . ." Adam's eyebrows very eloquently finished the sentence.

"Jesus," Jack hissed. "And that worked?"

"I was surprised, too. Less so when he got up and bent over the table, though."

Jack's bourbon nearly went down the wrong pipe. "I worked at that table today."

"Don't worry, he didn't come on it."

Christ. Jack shook his head in disgust, and then the snicker he was fighting got through. Moments later, he and Adam were roaring with laughter.

"So," Jack asked when he could, "when's the wedding?"

Glaring at him, Adam muttered, "If he turns out to be a stalker, I'm blaming you." Leaning across the table and in a softer tone, he added, "You really aren't jealous, are you."

Jack sobered instantly. "No. Amused but not jealous." It was on the tip of his tongue to tell Adam about Ethan. About how he had a solid and good thing happening. And it was a good thing. Despite Ethan's current issues, Jack was happy to have him in his life more completely than fleeting visits. Whatever was going on with him was something they could deal with because what they had was worth it.

"Hmm," Adam mused, "I'll have to find another excuse to turn him down if he comes at me again."

"You could have just not fucked him in the first place." Though Jack was a fine one to talk.

"I suppose, but I'd still be horny as hell if I hadn't. Again, your fault."

"That's getting old."

Adam shrugged and changed the topic. An hour or so later, Jack finally found the guts to ask something that had been lurking in the back of his mind for a while.

"Do you know much about Sugar Babies?" He felt like he was betraying Ethan just for asking, but the strange moods, occasional paranoia, and bruises were bothering Jack.

"Sugar Babies?" Adam sucked in a deep breath. "Not really. No one much cares about studying them anymore. Poor bastards were picked on enough thirty, forty years ago. With the in-utero treatments these days, I think the instances of true Sugar Babies are pretty negligible. Why? You don't think the Judge is one, do you?"

"No, I was just curious." And wrong. Studies had proven Sugar Babies were no more likely to be sociopaths than anyone else. Jack didn't know if it predisposed them to any other mental issues, but the angle he should have tried was childhood trauma. No matter the physical defects Ethan may have been born with, the abuse he'd suffered as a child had to be the source of some of his problems.

Adam's gaze turned keen, studying Jack with the razor-sharp insight that saw far too much, even as he lifted his beer and drank the last of it down. When he finished, he stood and picked up Jack's mostly empty bottle. "This is going to require more alcohol."

Jack cursed himself while Adam was gone. He should have known better. An ill thought out question was like blood in the water to Adam. Jack could go before he got back. But he was Adam's ride, and abandoning the man wasn't in Jack's nature.

"Right," Adam said when he returned with beers and bourbon. "No one thinks about Sugar Babies anymore. Why do you?"

Jack scowled. "God, you're such a psychiatrist. Can't you turn it off?"

Hand over his heart, expression solemn, Adam said, "I can't just stop caring about people, Nishant. Especially people I really, really, *really* like." He finished with an exaggerated wink and leer. Then, serious once again, leaned forwards and lowered his voice. "Come on. You asked for a reason. Now tell me the truth."

Fuck it. Jack was here, Adam was persistent, and getting some advice could only help Ethan, surely.

"Fine." Jack threw back the bourbon, chased the burn with some beer, and leaned in. "It's someone I know. He's a Sugar Baby, but I know that doesn't mean much compared to his other problems. Or maybe it does, I don't know. All I do know is he's having some trouble at the moment. Bouts of paranoia, obsessive-compulsive tendencies. He closes himself off and doesn't talk, for days sometimes."

"Is he seeing anyone professionally?"

"No." Did Jack know that for certain, though? Ethan kept disappearing and wouldn't tell Jack where he was going or what he was doing. He'd claimed he was aware of his issues, so perhaps he was getting help and just didn't want Jack to know. Jack couldn't convince himself of it, though. Ethan had been isolated for too long to suddenly want help from a stranger.

"Then perhaps you should suggest it to him. I can talk to you about him, but that won't help him. I know some good people in Sydney I can recommend."

Jack was shaking his head before Adam had finished the sentence. "If he's not going now, he won't just because I ask him to." He'd probably only get even more closed off and erratic.

"You really should try, nonetheless. For his sake."

"Can't you just tell me what to do to help him?"

Adam slumped back in the seat. "It doesn't work like that. I can't counsel by proxy."

"All right. Fine. Then just help me understand what he might be going through." Now he'd stepped onto this path, Jack couldn't seem to steer himself off it. "He was abused as a kid. Horrifically. Physically and emotionally. I know he lost his mother when he was very young, and he's never mentioned a father. It was after he lost his mum that he was hurt. I don't know by who, but I think they forced drugs on him as well." The memory of watching that kid take the booze and Sugar Moraitis offered swamped Jack for a moment, making his hands curl into fists and his teeth grind, until he got it back into the filing cabinet.

Rather than look disgusted at the idea, Adam merely nodded. "One benefit of being a Sugar Baby is an incredibly high tolerance for most illicit drugs and alcohol. But that doesn't excuse his abusers," he added hastily when Jack glared at him. "Look, from what you've said, it sounds logical. Anyone suffering that sort of abuse isn't going to survive unscathed. You said he had obsessive-compulsive tendencies. He doesn't like being touched in public, does he?"

Jack gaped at him. "No, but I thought that was—" Unable to say exactly what he'd thought that was due to, Jack finished lamely with, "because of me being gay."

Adam shrugged. "Maybe, maybe not. Does he get upset when he can't completely control a situation?"

"God, yes." It was like a weight off his shoulders. "He gets stiff and silent, like he's having this internal debate." A lot of the time, Jack suspected he was debating which weapon to go for.

"He probably is. I'd guess he's not exactly impulsive, either."

"No. Given a choice, he usually has everything planned down to the nth degree."

"And when he doesn't have a choice?"

So it went for the next several drinks. Adam kept them lubricated in between asking questions that had Jack spilling his guts about Ethan's quirks and idiosyncrasies. Even as his words became slurred and Adam's attentive face grew fuzzy, Jack made sure to keep his comments as platonic as possible. He might be discussing Ethan's personal issues, but he wasn't about to reveal the intimacy of their relationship.

Much, much later, as they stood on the footpath waiting for taxis—neither was fit to ride—Adam said, "Your friend. He's gotta see someone, profreshnly. The man is sick, Nishant." He frowned. "Nishant? Nishy? Nisha?"

Jack blinked at him. "What?"

"What what?" Adam threw an arm around Jack's neck and pulled him close, nearly toppling them both over. "Are you ready to kiss me yet, Nisha?"

He was so close Jack couldn't focus on him. Or he was too drunk to focus on anything. Either way, Jack's gaze caught on the sloppily leering mouth, and for a moment, he was ready. He'd been getting ready for a while now. To take that last step. To leap over the final bridge and burn the hurdle behind him. All the barriers were down now. He wanted to kiss . . .

Jack got a hand over Adam's face and shoved him away. "Not you. Call Toomey if you want to kiss."

Adam made a scoffing motion. "He's okay, I guess. 'Snot you, though. Come on, don'tcha wanna fuck my mouth again?"

Not so drunk he missed the startled looks from a few other people on the footpath with them, Jack shushed him. "You need to go home before someone hits you."

"Home's stupid Melbourne." Adam exaggerated a pout. "If I lived in Sydney, I'd be home already." His face lit up. "I could buy a home here. I'm *going* to buy a home here. No! I'm going home with you."

"Not tonight, tiger." A taxi pulled up, and Jack steered Adam into the car. As Jack gave the driver the name of the hotel, Adam hauled out his phone and pulled up Toomey's contact.

Unsettled, like something was wrong with the whole situation, Jack watched the taxi pull away. Knowing Adam was actually calling Toomey for a fuck bugged him, but not because he was jealous. He wasn't. Not in the least.

Another taxi arrived and Jack piled in, giving his own address and tuning out for the ride home. By the time he was trudging up the two flights to his apartment, the uneasy sensation in his belly had turned to full-on dread.

What the fuck had he done? He shouldn't have told Adam anything about Ethan. Christ. He was such a dickhead. Ethan would kill him for it. Maybe literally.

Hoping like hell Ethan wasn't home, or already asleep, Jack crept in. Unfortunately, the lamp by the balcony door was on and Ethan was standing opposite it, staring moodily out at the city lights. When Jack closed the door, Ethan turned and his white eyes were unmistakable in the dim light.

"Jack, you're late."

Very carefully walking to the fridge and making sure he pronounced his words properly, Jack said, "I never said what time I'd be home."

Ethan was quiet while Jack got a bottle of water. He was still wrestling with the cap when Ethan spoke.

"I hope you didn't ride home in this state."

Oh *God*. Another man in his life who saw far too much. And knew just how to open him up like he was filleting a fish. Jack had to get out of this conversation pronto.

"Got a taxi." Giving up on the water as too complicated, Jack beckoned Ethan over with a sexy tilt of his head. "Missed you, baby. Let's fuck."

It didn't have the expected response. Instead, Ethan took a step backwards. "Jack? Are you all right?"

"I'm great. And horny. Come on, let's go to bed."

After another uncomfortable silence, Ethan eventually nodded. "Yes, Jack. Let's go to bed. You're clearly coming down with something. You only call me 'baby' when you're sick."

"I don't," Jack scoffed.

With a patently sceptical expression, Ethan approached, deftly avoided Jack's grabby hands, and manhandled him into the bedroom. Getting undressed was also kept strictly functional. Ethan encouraged him to drink the water, then refused to get under the sheet with him, sitting on the side of the bed and trying to feel Jack's forehead instead.

"I'm fine," Jack grumbled. His distraction wasn't working. "I'm just drunk."

Keeping his hands to himself at last, Ethan considered him patiently. "You went drinking with Adam, I suppose."

Jack rolled over so he wouldn't have to look at him and cave under that expressionless expression. "He's part of my job. Gotta pretend to be his friend." Except it was past pretending now. Jack liked Adam. Not the same way he liked Ethan, though maybe once it could have been that way.

"That's all right, Jack. I understand. I was, however, hoping you could spend tomorrow with me."

"Can't. Working. You know that."

"Could you take a day off? Don't you Aussies pride yourself on taking 'sickies'?"

Jack groaned. "I'm on an important case. I can't just pretend to be sick for you." Christ, would this interrogation never end? The sooner Ethan left him alone, the sooner he could put that night's massive betrayal into the filing cabinet and stop feeling so fucking guilty.

"I've booked track time at Wakefield tomorrow. It takes a couple of hours to get there, so going is a whole-day endeavour. I'd very much appreciate it if you would come with me." His voice was tightly controlled, and the hand he put on Jack's shoulder was hesitant and light. "I need to drive, Jack, and I think I need you there with me."

Fuck. Jack squeezed his eyes shut. The very thought of being inside the tight confines of the car with Ethan for hours just to get to there was terrifying right then. To then sit in a mixed state of panic and exhilaration as Ethan lit up as he raced, becoming so bloody glorious and peaceful it would break down Jack's walls like nothing else. He was barely keeping them up as it was. There was nothing between him and Adam and Steph. They were getting to know *him*, and now Jack had pushed down one of the few remaining barriers just to get Adam to talk to him about Ethan.

God fuck it. If Ethan ever found out what Jack had done, he'd leave at best, fight to kill at worst. His past was something he was so careful about revealing, doling out tiny portions, judging Jack's reaction warily, forever poised to run if Jack made the wrong move. Jack couldn't risk Ethan finding out.

"I'd like to go with you," he said, voice rough with both the truth and the coming lie. "I can't, though. Things are at a vital stage of the case." They were actually stagnating to the point Jack thought McIntosh would call it off sooner rather than later. Jack fumbled till he found Ethan's hand and tugged it in for a kiss on his knuckles. "You go. Do a lap for me, too, okay."

Ethan didn't answer for a long time, then his hand went slack and slid out of his hold. Standing, he murmured, "As you wish, Jack," and walked out of the bedroom.

Relieved he hadn't said anything incriminating, Jack fell asleep within moments.

TWENTY-SEVEN
AFTER

Jack cut off the call from Lydia and pressed his forehead to the back of the seat in front of him. He breathed in deep, trying to kickstart his brain with fresh oxygen. How the fuck could he so viscerally feel like he was being torn in two when there was no blood?

Steph was dead. Oh God. She had a family, a grandchild she looked after at least one day a week. Smart, tough, dedicated Stephanie. And the fucking Judge had killed her. What was her sin in his eyes? Being too good at her job? Too close to catching him? Jack dredged his memory for the note left with her body.

She gave this name to the Lord who spoke to her: "You are the God who sees me," for she said, "I have now seen the One who sees me."

Could it be as simple as that? Steph had seen the Judge as he killed her, obviously, but that didn't feel deep enough. What else had Steph seen? Who had she seen? Or perhaps, who had she *spoken* to? Or had spoken to her? There were still too many unknowns for Jack to guess at what it meant. Christ, they needed Adam and his insights.

At least Adam was alive. Or had been thirty-six hours ago. But the fact he'd been taken from his suite, not killed there, meant whoever had him wanted him alive. For what, though? The Judge was a killer, not a kidnapper. Unless it wasn't the Judge who'd taken him.

Jack straightened sharply. Lydia said Toomey had also gone missing. Adam's comment about Toomey being a stalker had just been a joke. Hadn't it? If anyone was going to see through a public façade to the true person underneath, it would be Adam. What if . . . ?

Christ. Jack was grasping at straws. If there was something off about Toomey, Adam would have seen it sooner rather than later, considering the amount of time they'd spent together. After a couple of hours with Adam, Jack had been scrambling to batten down his personal hatches in an effort to keep the man's intuition out. He doubted Toomey would have found it any different.

The more likely scenario was the Judge had come for Adam after killing Steph and found Toomey there as well. Both men were probably the psycho's prisoners. At least they were together. Jack knew what it was like to be in desperate circumstances on his own, and with allies. The latter always made it easier to deal with the situation.

Pulling in several more deep breaths, Jack sat back. Reacting wasn't going to help him here. He had two potential abductees to find and rescue now, as well as an errant assassin to track down and convince to come back to him. A thought that sat easier in his heart now he knew Adam wasn't the Judge's latest victim—or Ethan's first after coming out of retirement. It was time to act. And being hauled into a police interrogation room and not let out until he'd confessed to everything wasn't going to be part of the plan.

He was squirming his plastic-cuffed hands down over his arse when his implant *ping*ed.

"Kinda busy," he grunted once he'd answered the call.

"*Yeah, I bet,*" Lewis said dryly. "*What's your current sitrep?*"

"Still in the back of a cop car, but. . ." Jack strained and got his hands over his booted feet and back on the most useful side of his body. "But about a minute away from getting these fucking cuffs off." He began searching the hem of his pants for the pin he always carried for just these sorts of situations.

"*Maybe you could hold off on that for a bit. McIntosh is already on her way to Surry Hills to give Dumay another serve. She's got the minister on hold.*"

"Too late." Jack twisted his wrists around, working the fine point of the pin into the ratchet-lock of the cuffs, pushing the plastic teeth apart. "I'm pretty much out of the cuffs. My bike's not far from the car. Once I'm out of here, I'll—"

The sudden rev of a powerful engine cut Jack off mid-escape plan. He flinched at the deep, gravelly roar, like an off-pitch rock slide.

"*Jack?*" Lewis asked cautiously.

"Something . . ." Jack looked around and sure enough, found the source of the sound.

He'd been pulled over at the base of the off ramp, and the cops had shut the exit while they sorted out Jack's mini arsenal. About a hundred meters further along was an intersection with a cross road. Beyond the intersection was the on ramp to the highway. At the intersection, a canary-yellow Monaro with black racing stripes had come to a stop. A bonnet with twin scoops faced the conclave of four cop cars. The car rumbled at them menacingly.

All eight cops currently inspecting the contents of the panniers stopped and turned as one towards the car, like a gang of meerkats sensing danger.

The car growled again, the engine revving so hard the front end bounced on the bitumen.

"Secure these," the senior officer snapped, shoving the panniers at one of the others. The sergeant gave out more orders, sending four of them to their cars, the remaining three taking up positions behind the other two cars, including the one Jack was in.

As the Monaro challenged them again, the sergeant faced the vehicle and, one hand on his holstered weapon, held the other one up, palm out. Walking slowly forwards, he yelled, "Please turn the vehicle off and step out of the car."

"Jack?" Lewis tried again. *"What's happening?"*

Jack held his breath. Did he dare think Ethan had come for him? Who else would face down so many cops in a souped-up car? And if it was Ethan, was he here to help Jack escape, or kill him?

"Please turn the vehicle off and get out of the car," the sergeant commanded again, getting closer to the Monaro, which settled into a steady growl, the whole chassis vibrating visibly. "If you fail to comply, I will be forced to—"

With a sudden roar, the back tyres of the car spun, smoke curling up from the bitumen, rear end shaking from the power of the revs.

"Move, man," Jack hissed a second before the driver unleashed the car and it leaped forwards.

Shouting wildly, the sergeant dove for the side of the road. A bright yellow blur raced through the air he'd just vacated and sped between the parked cop cars so fast it was gone before Jack had fully comprehended it was even there.

The Monaro went the wrong way up the empty off ramp, and about halfway, it came to a shuddering, black skid-mark-birthing halt and appeared to . . . wait.

The cops emerged from cover, warily watching the Monaro as they gathered to strategize.

Up on the ramp, the yellow car's tyres began smoking again. The police started to scramble, but before they got too far, the Monaro lurched into motion. From a standing start, the car drifted in a tight circle until it was pointed back at them. Rear fishtailing, it slammed into motion and charged forwards.

It had to be Ethan. The coincidence of finding another crazy car nut right here, right now, was too bloody great.

Contrary to its first pass, the Monaro didn't fly by at top speed this time. Just before it reached the parked cars, it braked sharply, then spun and drifted sideways between the police cars. Officers scattered again, unable to know if the driver was in control or not. Jack didn't flinch as the bonnet of the yellow car came within mere inches of the vehicle he was in. He trusted Ethan's control implicitly. Once beyond them, the Monaro straightened up again and rocketed away. It pelted through the intersection, dodging cross traffic, and disappeared up the on ramp.

"Go!" the sergeant yelled at the men in the cars. "Go, go, go!"

The police got their cars underway in an impressively short amount of time, but they were still miles behind the Monaro as they gave chase. The sergeant sent a third car after them, leaving just the one with Jack in it behind. One car and only two cops. Much better odds than he'd had previously.

"Thank you, Ethan," he whispered, only remembering the open line to Lewis when his friend demanded an explanation.

"Blade," Jack said tersely, getting back to work on his cuffs. "He just drew off most of the cops for me. I'll be out of here in minutes."

There was a speculative pause. *"Are you saying he helped you, rather than tried to collect his money with your head?"*

"Yeah, or he's waiting to get me on my own."

"Or that. So get moving. Do you need anything?"

Jack finished uncuffing himself, out of sight of his two remaining guards, both of whom were on their radios, furiously calling for backup. "I should be able to get the bike, but the weapons are a bust. I'll need to restock. I'll let—"

Another throaty rev cut him off.

Surely Ethan wasn't so good he lost his pursuers this quick?

Jack scanned for the new disturbance. Likewise, the sergeant and his remaining constable went on alert. Even as they found the red motorbike charging for them, black-clad rider holding a gun up and pointed right at them, the constable was hit. He staggered back, looking more stunned than hurt, then slowly toppled over.

Gun out, the sergeant shouted at the rider as he moved to stand over his fallen mate. The bike whipped past him, and he tracked it. As the car had done, the bike travelled a little distance up the ramp, then skidded around and came back towards them. Sergeant and rider exchanged fire, and the officer got lucky. A bullet hit the front of the bike, and it wobbled wildly.

The bike twisted into a skid, then overbalanced and crashed to the bitumen. Momentum carried it towards the sergeant, trailing sparks. The rider had rolled before it hit the ground, tumbling over and over across the hard surface. She sprang to her feet, guns in both hands, and got off a couple of rounds before having to duck for cover behind the now still bike. The sergeant had got behind the bonnet of the remaining car and was taking shots when he could, all the while yelling at her to desist and surrender.

"Jack!" Lewis demanded once more.

"Can't talk," Jack said, working on the lock of the car door.

Ethan not wanting to kill him was a risk Jack was more than willing to take. Garrote being here out of a sense of chivalry? God, even he wasn't that dumb.

"Okay, I will, then. There are two more cars heading to your location and four more joining the chase on the M7. Jeez, Jack, when you do something, you don't mess around. I've mobilised two strike teams. If you don't get clear of the police in the next ten minutes, they'll be there to extract you. Thanks to your little circus out there, Dumay isn't budging this time, no matter how many ministers McIntosh throws at her."

"Great." Jack got the lock open on the door. "I'll be clear in under five and will let you know where I am when I'm safe." He cut the connection and, before opening the car door, did a quick sitrep.

Garrote was crouched behind her fallen bike, and the sergeant was keeping her pinned down effectively. With Garrote taking all of his attention, the sergeant shouldn't be a problem.

Jack eased the door open and slithered out into a crouch, using the door as cover from the cop, and the car as cover from Garrote. Hopefully she wouldn't see what he was doing until it was too late to stop him, giving him a good head start out of this mess.

The gunfire boomed back and forth, the sergeant alternately yelling at Garrote to cease fire, at his radio for an ETA on backup, and at his fallen officer. "Parks! Give me a sign, mate!"

Dropping to the sloping ground on the side of the road, Jack peered under the car, and sure enough, the downed cop was moving. Sluggish twitches of his head and hands, but he was definitely alive. Jack looked closer and found a black-tufted dart hanging from the material of the man's sleeve. Garrote hadn't shot to kill, just to knock out.

What the hell?

Jack was eeling towards the bike when his conscience got the better of him. Garrote might have started out with tranq darts, but she was using real ammunition now, and the drugged man was lying in the middle of the firefight.

Creeping around the back of the car, Jack watched the exchange for half a minute, judging numbers of shots and lines of fire. When he saw an opening coming up, he rolled out onto the road and sprint-crawled to the downed officer.

"Shit!" the sergeant shouted, clearly catching sight of Jack. He stopped firing. "What the bloody—"

"Just cover me," Jack yelled back as he shoved his hands under the cop's shoulders. "Please!"

The sergeant swore some more but covered Jack's retreat. Garrote stayed hunched down behind the bulk of her bike. Her helmet visor followed Jack's progress, but she didn't risk taking a shot at him. Praying she continued to be bashful, Jack worked his way back into cover, dragging the groggy man with him. Once they were both tumbled down into the ditch on the side of the road, the sergeant stopped firing and ejected his empty mag. While pulling a fresh one from his belt, he turned, mouth open to ask after his mate.

He didn't get a word out. Instead, he came face to barrel with Parks's Glock, which Jack had grabbed from the man's holster as they rolled.

"Your man's going to be okay," Jack said tersely. "But I can't stick around. Don't worry, when I go, she'll follow."

With nothing but an empty gun in hand, the sergeant gritted his teeth and after a moment, nodded. Returning the gesture but not taking the gun off the officer, Jack moved towards his bike. When Jack was about to break cover from behind the car, the sergeant slammed the new mag into his gun and sent a couple of warning shots towards Garrote.

Silently thanking the man for the moment's respite, Jack dashed for the Interceptor. He'd learned long ago to always carry a second, hidden key for whatever transport he had. While the sergeant covered him, he slung a leg over the seat and jammed the key home. As the bike came to life, Jack grinned. He was going to get away with—

The warm barrel of a recently fired gun touched the back of his neck.

TWENTY-EIGHT BEFORE

"**S**hoot me now," Jack moaned as he stared at the ceiling of his bedroom.

He was too old for this. There was no rebounding from this hangover with a greasy breakfast. His stomach churned at the mere hint of food, and the pounding in his head tripled at just the thought of moving. Of course, it wasn't just the dregs of an ill-spent night pinning him to the mattress. Guilt and shame and heartbreaking fear were all there as well.

Ethan was gone. He hadn't come to bed after Jack passed out, and he wasn't in the apartment now. Jack knew because he could check the logs on the security system with his implant. The effort had cost him the last portion of brain matter that wasn't already hurting, but at least he now knew how much wallowing was required.

With a monumental effort and serious risk of ruining his sheets, Jack rolled over and buried his face in his pillow. God fuck it. He'd really screwed this up.

Honestly, he should never have thought it would work. His history with serious relationships—or casual ones—was not a solid foundation. How could he have believed it would be different this time?

He'd naively opened the gate for his first boyfriend, Ian, and then couldn't believe it when he bolted. Only a colossal dickhead would have ever let Hamish go. For fuck's sake, if he couldn't make it work with Ham, the world's most considerate and caring guy—he'd joined the army to do his bit for the nation, but to also get the experience he needed to then teach in third-world nations—then surely he was doomed. Jack *had* believed he was doomed after Ham walked away. Hadn't even tried.

Then Ethan Blade had shot, lied, and seduced his way into Jack's life, and right on schedule, Jack was failing again.

Pursuing anything with Adam, even just friendship, was clearly the wrong path. It wasn't required for the job. Jack didn't need a new friend in his personal life who had no idea about who he really was, or what he really did. He most certainly didn't need the temptation of talking about Ethan behind his back anymore.

His only recourse was to put distance between himself and Adam, and by extension, Stephanie. No more chatting as they worked, no more cooing over Steph's granddaughter, no more drinks and dinner with Adam.

Wincing at the throbbing in his temples, he got up and staggered into the bathroom. Under a cold spray, he worked himself the rest of the way into wakefulness and when he got out, felt marginally better for it. On his way back to the bedroom to get dressed, he called Ethan.

"Jack." His answer was clipped and frosty.

"I'm sorry." When all he got was silence, Jack rushed on. "I was a total dickhead last night. No excuses. Except for, well, I told you I would fuck something up sooner or later."

"Mm." It didn't sound any warmer, but not any colder, either.

"I'd really like to make it up to you. Can you come home?"

"I'm afraid not, Jack. I'm not in Sydney."

Jack sank to the bed in defeat. "Fuck. I'm really sorry. I don't want you to leave."

After a moment, Ethan sighed. *"I'm still in the country, Jack, at Wakefield. My track time starts in fifteen minutes. I will be back this evening."*

"Jesus." Jack fell back on the mattress. "Don't scare me like that."

"Oh, I think you have a few more scares coming."

The slight softening of tone made Jack smile. "Yeah, I reckon I do. I'm glad you are getting to race."

"Yes, well. The booking fee is non-refundable."

Just hearing Ethan's voice was a balm to Jack's head. He felt better already. Impulsively, Jack said, "I'm going to take the day off, like you wanted me to. I could meet you down there." He'd beg McIntosh's forgiveness later.

After a small silence, Ethan murmured, *"I don't think so, Jack. Right now, I'd rather be alone."*

"Okay." Jack tried not to be disappointed. "Anything else I can do to show you how sorry I am? Do you want butter chicken for dinner?"

"I'm not sure. I will let you know."

All right. Jack was pushing too hard. "I'll see you tonight, then?"

Another small sigh, then in a whisper, *"Yes, you will."*

"Drive safely."

"Where's the fun in that?" And he was gone, but at least Jack hadn't totally ruined everything.

Determined to put his other plan into action as well, Jack popped a couple of paracetamol, dressed, and was headed out the door when he got a *ping.*

"Mate," Lewis said when he answered, *"where are you? We've had a couple of calls from the strike force, wondering if you're coming in today. Phelps sounded a bit worried, actually. I think she thinks you're planning another demonstration."*

Jack groaned. "No demonstration. Just running late. Had a few too many last night." Which was when he remembered he didn't have his bike. "Shit. I have to pick up my Ninja before I get there, as well."

"Wow, you actually left your precious somewhere insecure?"

Jack told Lewis what he could do with this own precious, then cut the connection and called a taxi. The car was just pulling up when Lewis called again.

"Change of plans. Come in to the Office on your way. McIntosh wants to see us."

Stomach churning more than it already was, Jack confirmed and rather than keep his director waiting, went straight into work. Also conceding to his tender head, he took the lift up to the tenth instead of running the stairs as usual. He got a little happy when he surprised Lewis by coming up behind him as he was waiting at the door to the stairwell.

"Shit." Lewis glared from Jack to the scattered photos he'd dropped in shock and back to Jack. "Thanks a fuck bunch, dickhead."

Chuckling, Jack crouched and helped him pick up the photos. "Are these the Bible verses from the Judge's crime scenes?"

"Yeah. I've been studying them."

"Why?"

Standing, Lewis shrugged as he sorted them back into order. "I just have a feeling like we're missing something in them."

"Quinn's been over them with a fine-toothed comb. If there was something, he would have seen it." Part of his plan to put space between himself and the job was to use surnames. No more Steph and Adam when he wasn't with them. They were Phelps and Quinn, as it would have been on any other job.

"Sure, I guess. He is the expert, after all . . ."

Jack knew how Lewis could pull together disparate-seeming bits of information into a cohesive whole that more often than not turned out to be right. So, instead of dismissing the trail off, Jack prompted him. "You're clearly seeing something he didn't. What is it?"

"I don't know," Lewis moaned. "Something's pinging on my radar, but I can't quite get to it." His frustration was almost palpable.

Patting his shoulder, Jack said, "You'll get there. You always do. Come on, let's see what the boss wants."

Mumbling to himself, Lewis followed, and they were only made to wait a couple of minutes before Miller ushered them into McIntosh's office.

"Gentlemen, thank you for your time," she said as they sat. "Lewis, do you have something to show me in those photos?"

Lewis quickly put the photos facedown on her desk. "No, ma'am. Sorry. Just thinking about a few things with the case."

McIntosh eyed the photos for a moment, then focused on them each in turn. "Whatever thoughts you've had or are having, forget them. I've just come from a meeting with the other directors and Minister Simmons. It's been agreed that your operation is no longer worth the Office's time or money."

Jack couldn't say he was entirely surprised. Relieved, yes, but definitely not surprised now that the investigation had all but staggered to a halt.

"But, ma'am." Lewis shuffled the photos as if looking for something. "I really think I'm onto something with the Bible verses. I *know* they all mean something apart from the obvious."

"Unless it's proof of who the Judge is, then I'm afraid it isn't enough, Lewis." McIntosh's tone was sympathetic. "I took a chance on our participation helping them find and detain the Judge, and while Jack fulfilled the purpose they requested him for, nothing else has come of this to convince the minister that it's worthwhile. I will, of course, keep the investigation on our radar, and if anything significant happens, we'll follow up then. Until such a time, however, you will both be moving on to more pressing operations."

Relief washing away, Jack groaned. Another instant turnaround. He was going to go mad if McIntosh kept this up. And he'd have no chance of really making things up to Ethan if she hustled him into something new now.

"Don't worry, Jack. I'm giving you a week off before your next operation." Her tone was dry but on the cusp of sharp.

Jack ducked his head contritely. "Thank you, ma'am. I appreciate it."

"You too, Lewis, and your core team."

She dismissed them, and once in the corridor heading for the lifts, Lewis gave Jack's shoulder a not-so-soft punch.

"What the hell?" Jack rubbed the sore spot.

"You could have backed me up in there, you know." Lewis stabbed angrily at the Down button.

"I could have, if I wanted to keep going on a pointless operation. McIntosh is right. This thing hasn't been making forward movement in over two weeks. *And* catching serial murderers isn't our job."

Scowling, Lewis muttered, "Precisely. It's different and interesting."

"Then you go sit in that room day after day, read the same reports over and over looking for something slightly different each time."

The lift doors swished open and they stepped in.

"I wish I could," Lewis muttered. "I'm tired of being cooped up in this building all day and night."

Jack snorted. "Being out there isn't much fun, either, sometimes."

"Probably, but it didn't seem too tough this time. You weren't being shot at, or doing the shooting, and you did pretty good going out and drinking on the *Office's dime*."

"Not even that's all it's cracked up to be." Jack heard the bitterness in his own tone, so there was no way Lewis could miss it, either.

"What do you mean? Did something happen last night?" When Jack didn't answer, Lewis added, softly, "With Quinn, maybe? Like... *you know*." He made a suggestive gesture.

"Jesus, Lew. No." It even sounded false to Jack. "Get your head out of the gutter."

"It's just that you've got history with him," Lewis defended his assumption. "Then what is it? You've never backed out of an op before. Not even that time in Melbourne when you dressed up like the—"

"Dressed *up* is a bit of a stretch," Jack interjected sourly. "Look, you're partly right. It's because of that history I need to get out. You don't know what it's like going undercover. And it's worse going out there as myself when one of the subjects knows me."

Lewis chewed it over for a moment, then nodded reluctantly. "Yeah. I guess you're right." Then he smiled. "At least we get a week off, right?"

"Right," Jack agreed, then frowned. "A whole week seems a bit generous, doesn't it?"

"Probably. Which means she's got something nasty waiting for us when we get back."

Jack just hoped it was a bit more exciting than sitting in front of a computer reading witness statements all day. He thought he might enjoy a few pitched gunfights after this.

The team broke up happily enough, already making plans for what they were going to do on their time off. Lewis called John Axworthy at the ISO HQ, Jack's official boss, and updated him on the situation, leaving it up to him to break the news to the strike force that SSA Jack Reardon's services had been rescinded. Judging by Lewis's side of the conversation, Axworthy wasn't that impressed with the task, but then there was little to do with the Office that impressed Axworthy. On paper, he could field a small army of ISO security personnel, but in reality, he had barely enough permanent staff to fill a bus. A small bus. That, like Adam and Steph and the Judge, was not Jack's problem, so he said his goodbyes and went home.

Wanting to present Ethan with the best possible welcome, Jack cleaned the apartment. That done, he spent a while chatting to Mr. Cesare and playing with Short Round, and distracted himself in the gym in the garage. Partly because he'd missed more workouts than he'd accomplished lately, but mostly because there was a glass wall with a usually uninspiring view of the garage. He was running on a treadmill when he spied Victoria coming in.

Mouth dry despite taking a long drink from his water bottle, Jack headed over to meet Ethan. Things had felt more positive than not on the phone, but a lot of time had passed since then for Ethan to think and ponder and possibly change his mind.

Ethan's hands were empty when he got out of the Aston Martin, but that didn't mean he wasn't deadly. Jack stopped by the back of the car, waiting to see how he was greeted before making a move.

Sunglasses on, Ethan turned to face him. "Jack."

"Ethan." Jack waited a bit longer, then said, "I'm sorry."

"I know you are."

Fuck. Awkward. If only Ethan had pulled a gun on him. Jack knew what to do with that.

TWENTY-NINE

AFTER

Jack froze.

"Hello, tall, dark, and handsome." Garrote had a faintly South African accent, and the hand that reached around him to relieve him of the Glock flashed a band of dark skin between glove and sleeve. The back of the Interceptor shifted as she got on behind him. "Nice and easy now. We're getting out of here before Officer Plod realises he's shooting at an empty helmet."

Sliding his eyes to the side, Jack tried to get a look at her face, but she was planted firmly behind him. "Eve Garrote, I presume."

"Well, well. The information I had on you didn't say you were so smart. Good guess, handsome. Let's get out of here first, then exchange pleasantries."

Unable to help himself, Jack snorted. "Excuse me if I'm not too keen on your sort of pleasantries." He turned the bike on, drowning out Garrote's bark of laughter.

The sound of the engine drew the sergeant's attention, and he did a startled double take at the sight of them on the bike.

"Don't worry," Garrote said over the growl of the bike, slipping an arm around his waist as he turned the Interceptor onto the road. "I've been told you're off bounds."

Her hand, however, settled low on his abdomen, under the lower edge of his armour and a few fingers width from things he'd rather she not get any closer to. The gun pressed into his lower back, also below his armour.

Garrote directed him with little taps of the hand on his abdomen, indicating which corners to take as they raced away from the lone sergeant. They avoided the highway where, presumably, Ethan was still giving the police merry hell. Which brought Jack to the next revelation. Ethan had to be working with Garrote. There was no way they'd both show up at the one spot so close together, with the same goal.

To help Jack escape the police.

If Garrote wanted him dead, she would have shot him instead of getting on the bike with him. There was the possibility she was fucking with him, as Ethan had done in the desert. But something about this felt different.

Pretty certain she wasn't going to shoot him like this, Jack silently dictated a quick message to the Office. When he tried to send it, however, a jolt of pain lanced through his head.

"Fuck!"

The bike wobbled as Jack reflexively tried to curl up and protect his head.

"Careful," Garrote yelled, pressing closer to his back so she could grab the handlebar and keep the bike going. "I'm not dying for this job."

The pain faded almost as quickly as it came. Jack blinked his eyes back into focus, feeling the late-afternoon rays bite into his retinas. They were coasting along just fast enough to stay upright, Garrote steering them into a partially empty carpark of a small row of shops. As they came to a stop, Jack got a foot down to keep them from toppling over.

"What the hell?" he ground out, rubbing at his temples. An echo of the searing pain lurked behind his eyes.

"I would have told you sooner, but I didn't think you'd be bold enough to use the implant while riding with a gun at your back." Garrote's tone was exaggeratedly patient. "So I'll tell you now. Don't try to use your implant. I have a jammer with me."

"Assassins and their gadgets," Jack muttered under his breath. Louder, "Messaging while riding with a gun at my back is nothing. I can even walk and talk at the same time."

"You're going to be fun. I like it when my toys bite back." The gun shifted against him but didn't pull away. "Now, how about you hit that kill switch you boys come equipped with and we'll be on our way again. We really shouldn't linger out in the open. The cops know you have this bike now."

There was no doubt. Ethan had to have told her about the kill switch in Jack's implant. He had accepted that the supposedly secret neural implants given to the SAS weren't all that secret anymore. The kill switch the Office had programmed in, however, *was*. Jack had never specifically told Ethan about it, but he had to have worked it out for himself, considering the jamming device he'd used in the desert hadn't affected him after Jack killed the implant.

Knowing Ethan and Garrote were working together still didn't answer the most vital question though.

Were they going to kill him or not?

If he had Ethan on his own, he'd do anything to get the truth across and convince the man to drop the ticket. Garrote, however, was a whole other risk category, one Jack wasn't quite ready to take.

"Fine," Jack grumbled. "Just give me a minute to get into a trance state."

"Pull the other one, handsome. I know you don't—"

Jack slammed his head back and his skull connected solidly with her jaw, pain cracking through the back of his head this time. Garrote wasn't expecting it, though. She rocked backwards, unbalancing the bike, the pressure of the gun disappearing from Jack's back. Foot already planted, Jack swung his other leg up and over, knocking the woman the rest of the way off the Interceptor. He lunged after her as she hit the bitumen of the carpark. They landed hard, Jack on top, Garrote's head bouncing off the ground, dazing her. Jack grabbed the hand with the gun and twisted her wrist. The weapon popped free, and he scrambled away with it.

By the time he had some distance, gun held ready and pointed at Garrote, she had pulled another weapon and had it trained on him from her lying position.

Panting, they stared at each other.

Eve Garrote was probably around Jack's age, lean and ropey with small but taut muscles. Her skin was darker than his and possibly of Cape Coloured ethnicity, a sleek pixie cut of black hair capping her head. She had a wide, full-lipped mouth, magnificently high and sculpted cheekbones, and eyes hidden behind a pair of aviator sunglasses. A faint scar ran down the left side of her face, over her jaw, and ending in what was probably a very close call next to her jugular.

Her dossier said she was a markswoman, most of her confirmed kills either sniper shots or point-blank hits in close quarters. Jack wouldn't discredit her in a fight, though. She looked tough and capable, and just because no one had witnessed her taking a target down hand to hand didn't mean she couldn't do it easily. One of the things Jack had come to know during his relationship with Ethan was that the information any organisation had on Ethan Blade was far from comprehensive. Underestimating him would prove deadly, and Jack got the same feeling from Garrote now.

Somewhere to Jack's right, a woman gave a startled cry, then, "They've got guns," and the clatter of shoes on concrete.

Shit. If Jack closed with Garrote here and now, not only would he probably not survive, but there was a big chance of civilians getting hurt, or worse, in the process. His best option was to just pull the trigger.

Yet, for some reason, she still hadn't pulled hers.

His thoughts must have shown in his expression because Garrote said, "You know she's on the phone to the cops right now. We have to get out of here."

"We?"

Surprisingly, Garrote lifted the business end of her gun skyward. "Yes, we. I didn't go to all the trouble of getting you away from the cops just for you to run right back to them."

Jack didn't take his sight off her. "I was doing swell on my own. With or without you I would have gotten away. Now, though, it's going to be without you, one way or another."

Garrote shook her head. "You're being an idiot."

"Not the first time I've been accused of that. Your choice, Garrote. You let me get on the bike and leave, or I shoot you and leave, anyway."

"You can't face him on your own."

What the . . .? Did that mean she and Ethan *weren't* working together?

"You'd be surprised at what I can do." Jack got to his feet and backed up to the Interceptor. "See. Walking and talking at the same time."

Another bark of laughter and Garrote sat up, casually crossing her arms over her knees, gun dangling from a finger by the trigger guard.

"You *are* fun." The amusement vanished with her next words, though. "He'll kill you."

Now Jack really didn't know what to think. Was she worried Ethan would get him first and rob her of the money? Then why not kill him now? Garrote had never been squeamish about public kills in the past.

In the distance sirens sounded. Now wasn't the time for guessing games. If they were still here when the cops showed up, things would probably go tits up faster than they already were.

Backing up the last step, Jack threw a leg over the bike seat, still keeping the gun on Garrote, though she'd made no move to aim at him again. She just shook her head in an it-was-nice-knowing-you way. Her entire attitude was baffling. He was halfway convinced she wasn't going to kill him. He'd felt the same way about Ethan when they first met, and sure, Ethan *hadn't* killed him, but Jack doubted he could win this woman over with some mind-altering sex.

The sirens were growing louder, but Jack hesitated to turn on the bike. He was probably going to regret this, but . . .

"The ticket you picked up on me. Who bought it?"

The mirrored panes of Garrote's sunglasses didn't waver. "You don't want to know."

"Probably, but they want me dead. I think I have a right to know."

Garrote gave a mildly conceding shrug. "Perhaps. Ask me again, the next time we meet."

A loud blurt of a siren was probably a cop car demanding right of way through an intersection, and close enough to be just around the corner.

Time had run out. Jack turned the key, and the Interceptor roared to life. As he kicked off, Garrote gave him a jaunty salute with her gun. Back prickling as he deliberately put a predator behind him, Jack headed away from the sound of sirens. Just before he turned a corner, he looked back at the carpark. Garrote had vanished. He doubted he'd seen the last of her.

Quickly gaining his bearings, Jack headed, in a roundabout way, for the nearest drop point for the Office. Clear of Garrote's jamming device, he sent a message to Lewis, got a confirmation in return, and when he reached the drop point, had to wait for barely a half hour before his contact appeared.

He was surprised when he instantly recognised the voice singing "One Night in Bangkok."

"Lewis?"

His friend appeared out of the dark tunnel, wheeling a new bike. "Holy crap, are these things heavy, and that's not the correct response. How do I know you're my contact if you don't give me the right response?"

Jack scowled and grumpily trotted out the required line. "Happy now? Jesus."

"Very happy," Lewis said patiently. "All right. Tell me all about it. How did you escape Miss Trigger Happy 1999?"

Between taking drinks from a water bottle Lewis supplied, Jack told him everything. Lewis absorbed it all, nodding in places, grimacing in others. No doubt he was analysing it all in conjunction with what they knew about Eve Garrote and the ticket.

"Yeah, it's hard to tell," Lewis said when Jack finished. "We've got absolutely no hints of Blade and Garrote teaming up in the past. Garrote did work with that Ugandan warlord and a couple of 'liberation' groups in Africa, but Blade's always been a solo operator. You said she said, 'You can't face him alone.' Does that mean she's willing to go against Blade for you?"

"I have no idea. If she's anything like Blade at all, then she'll enjoy making cryptic little comments and hints."

Lewis frowned. "Why would you think she might be like Blade?"

"Our information is far from complete. I know for a fact there are jobs Ethan pulled that no one has ever attributed to him."

His friend's frown went from confused to quizzical, and Jack cursed himself silently. "Ethan" was too familiar for a subject of one of their operations. It personalised him, made him human, and that was often a detriment to getting the job done—whatever that might entail.

Jack was making too many slips. All of his walls were crumbling around him, just as they had in the desert when he'd let a dead-eyed assassin into his head and heart. The moment he'd done that, he should have quit the Office. It had only destabilised the foundations of every other wall he'd built to protect himself, professionally and personally. The walls were falling, and the filing cabinet was busted.

Lewis studied him for a moment longer, then asked quietly, "Did you tell Feitt about these unknown jobs of Blade's?"

Of all the walls Jack had built, the one that was crumbling between him and Lewis now was the one Jack should have knocked down himself. Or perhaps never built in the first place. Its foundations had been there for a long time, but after Canberra, Jack had slapped those bricks into place so fast and high he hadn't recognised the darkness for what it was.

Guts twisting up in instinctual fear, Jack shook his head. "I didn't tell Feitt, and I won't."

"Why not?"

Even in the dim light of the tunnel, Jack could see his friend's expression struggle to stay neutral. Jack had just admitted to withholding evidence in an ongoing investigation. It was more than enough for Lewis to report him. Charge him, even. More than enough to have him dragged back to the Neville Crawley Building and kept under forceful detainment.

Lewis was his friend, though. Had been the entire time they'd been with the Office. They'd worked jobs together, done them well and successfully. They'd drunk together, eaten together, teased and laughed at each other. Jack was the first person Lewis had told about his growing feelings for Lydia, had shared his worries about working and living together. If Jack told Lewis everything, this wouldn't be another Canberra.

It could be worse.

THIRTY BEFORE

N ot wanting to make things any worse, Jack struggled for something to say that would smooth over the edges between him and Ethan.

"How did Victoria go?" As long as he was complimentary or interested, the Aston Martin was always a safe topic of discussion.

"Very well. I believe I sorted out the timing issue when she gets into sixth."

"That's great."

"Mm. It is."

More uncomfortable silence. Jack suddenly wished he'd paid more attention when Ethan talked about the car. Fuck. He'd mentioned something about a new clutch cable, hadn't he? Or was that for the Roadster? Or Ferrari?

Christ. He didn't need to talk about the fucking car. All he had to do was be honest.

Before he could act on that thought, Ethan said, "Perhaps we should go upstairs and talk somewhere a little more private."

The garage would give them plenty of room if it came to a fight, but Ethan was right. It wasn't very private with people coming and going in their cars, as well as the few residents in the gym. And if Ethan wanted privacy, maybe he really wanted to talk. Whenever Ethan had spilled about his past or secrets previously, it had been when he felt safe.

Jack agreed and they headed upstairs. It was a quiet walk, but not as uncomfortable as it had been facing off in the garage. They'd made this walk enough times lately to be familiar with each other's pace and habits. Jack would open the door, Ethan would go through and wait for him, falling into step again. Sometimes, their hands would brush together, and occasionally, Ethan didn't pull away. Sometimes, Jack intentionally "accidentally" touched him and Ethan let it happen. He didn't try this time, but Ethan's perhaps purposeful proximity was welcomed, and by the time they got into the apartment, Jack wasn't angry anymore. He was resigned.

Jack had fucked up, and guilt had coloured his reactions. Ethan was a keen observer. He read people every day—read his targets—and he knew Jack better than anybody else did. Of course he knew something had happened behind his back.

While Ethan slid out of his jacket and draped it over the back of a chair, Jack steeled himself for the truth, only realising he'd put the kitchen counter between himself and Ethan when he leaned on it, bracing for impact.

"Okay." He figured if he offered up his mistake, it would look better than Ethan exposing it.

"Please, may I go first?"

Startled, Jack looked up. He'd expected Ethan's killer voice. The flat, neutral tone that meant all emotions had been switched off, or buried so deep they may as well not exist. Instead, he got a soft, hesitant query, something expecting to be shot down or laughed at.

Jack nodded.

Ethan leaned back against the dining table, arms crossed, and seemingly stared at a spot on the floor between him and the kitchen counter. He still had his sunglasses on, even though the only light was the dull glow of the setting sun through the closed blinds on the balcony door. He wore jeans and a royal blue T-shirt, hair still messy from the helmet he wore while racing, dark strands around his neck a little damp from sweat. Jack would never forget just how lethal Ethan was, but right now, he looked nothing like an accomplished assassin. He just looked . . . lost.

Jack's chest grenade went off, but it wasn't the burst of heat and light he had grown used to. Had come to want so badly. This time, it wasn't an explosion, but an implosion, sucking all the warmth out of his body, leaving him hollow and stunned. Not even when Ethan had talked about leaving the only life he knew to come here had he appeared so vulnerable.

And Jack had done this to him.

"I want to be here," Ethan said into the silence. "I came with the expectation that this was it for me. We'd be together and nothing else would matter." The corner of his lips curled up, but it wasn't the sign of fondness it usually was. This time, it was bitter and sad. "I should have known better. There are things that can't be escaped, and the past is one of them."

Jack's mouth was open, to apologise for hurting him, or to reassure him, or both, but without lifting his gaze, Ethan stopped his words with a raised hand.

"I'm trying. I really am, but I don't know what I'm doing. You know your place in the world. You have your work, which you believe in, and a family you want to protect, no matter how distant they are. You have friends that care about you. Right now, all I have is you."

What had Ethan said that first night? That he knew he couldn't replace one crutch with another. What was Ethan about to tell him? That he *had* gone back to killing for money? Please, God, if he had, let there be money involved. Jack had spent too much time learning about people who killed for their own twisted pleasure to not make connections between serial murderers and assassins. Specifically, between Ethan's history of abuse and that of most serial murderers.

"I thought I could do this. Be what you wanted. Needed. But clearly, I'm failing."

Nothing had hurt quite like this. Not being shot or stabbed or believing his army CO had deliberately sent his squad into a no-win situation. Not even watching Hamish walk away had felt so much like his heart being ripped in two.

"Ethan," Jack choked out, but whatever else he was going to say was blown to atoms with Ethan's next words.

"Are you sleeping with Adam Quinn?"

His heart froze mid-cleave. "What?"

Ethan took off his sunglasses and pinned him with his cold, white eyes. When he spoke again, his tone was the steely hard paid-killer one Jack had expected earlier.

"You talk about him all the time. He's part of your current job, yes, but you spend a lot of time with him outside of the demands of the strike force."

"Yeah, but it's still part of the job. Being friendly—"

"You don't have dinner with Senior Sergeant Stephanie Phelps, but she's part of the job."

"No, but—"

"And unless you're hiding something big, I don't believe you ever slept with her before."

Jack blinked at him. "What the fuck are you talking about?"

Ethan uncrossed his arms, hands loose, body shifting into a ready stance. To run or fight, Jack didn't know. Didn't know which he would prefer. He was having trouble keeping up with the change in topic. It had been a while since Ethan had so completely flummoxed him like this. Stupidly, Jack had thought they were past all the manipulation and mind-fucking.

"I know you've slept with him before," Ethan continued smoothly.

Jack hadn't seen him so calm and collected in a long time. Hadn't, in truth, seen Ethan Blade, assassin, in all that time. Well, he was back. He was also wrong. Sort of.

"Okay," Jack said slowly. "Yeah, I fucked him a couple of times, way back before you and I got serious. You knew I saw other men sometimes back then. How did you know about Adam, though? Were you spying on me?"

"You don't want me to answer that."

Jack spluttered, finally feeling something. It was anger, but at least it was something other than shock and numbness. "Actually, I think I do."

Ethan pursed his lips for a fraction of a second. It was a crack in his armour, but Jack saw it. "You haven't answered my question. Are you sleeping with him now?"

The crack let a tiny point solidify in Jack's swirling thoughts. Ethan hadn't said his name once since they'd reached the apartment.

Ethan's overuse of Jack's name was a quirk Jack was rather fond of. All the different nuances Ethan managed to squeeze into the simple word was something special, something that belong just to them. No other man in Jack's life had ever put so much meaning into his name. Of course, it hadn't started out so sweet or welcoming. When they'd first met, Jack had been Ethan's target, and targets weren't human. They were objectives. They didn't have names. To convince Jack he *wasn't* a target, Ethan had used his name. Incessantly. And it had stuck.

As disturbing as not hearing his own name now was, Jack found the fact that Ethan hadn't used Adam's name more than once telling, as well.

Jack threw that thought into the filing cabinet and slammed it shut.

His anger evaporated. Ethan had done this before. Tried to distance himself, to make what he had to do less painful. This wasn't Ethan Blade preparing himself to kill. It was Ethan desperate to protect himself. There was only one thing Jack could do in the face of that.

Plainly, honestly, he said, "No."

Tension coiled between them for a moment longer, then Ethan sagged against the table, barely holding himself up with a death grip on its edge. Jack was around the counter and in front of him without thought. Wanting to touch, to hold, he nevertheless kept his hands to himself. Ethan had come back from the edge, but Jack knew better than to think it was all good just yet.

"I'm not sleeping with him, or anyone else. I don't want to." Jack willed him to meet his gaze, and when Ethan did, he continued. "I want this, too. Us. So much it scares me sometimes."

Ethan pulled in a shuddering breath. "Me too. I never used to get scared, Jack. Not for a very long time, at least. Then I met you, and suddenly there was so much I didn't know, *couldn't* know, and that . . . frightened me. I didn't know if whenever I went to you I would be welcomed or not, or perhaps find you already with someone else."

They both shivered, and Jack wondered if that was how Ethan had found out about Adam. Had he come for one of his visits, and not finding Jack at home, tracked him down to Adam's hotel suite and saw him getting fucked and sucked? Not sure he wanted it confirmed, Jack kept his mouth shut and let Ethan carry on.

"I didn't know, still don't, if you would get tired of my . . . oddities and want nothing more to do with me. Each time you let me into your home, into your life, I didn't know why you would do that for me. And *he* is so much better for you. He's not a liability to you. He's not here on a fake passport. He's not messed up."

"Shit," Jack hissed, hearing his own thoughts spoken at him.

"That's what I did today, Jack. I drove and it helped me decide that if you were with him, I'd walk away. You'd be safer. And happy. And I could stop being so scared."

Jack blinked rapidly, wondering why he was worried about bawling like a baby in front of this man who was eviscerating himself.

"But when I got out of the car and saw you waiting for me, I changed my mind. In spite of the pain and the risk, in spite of everything and every*one* else, I want this. I don't know what I'm doing, Jack, but I want to keep trying. With you."

Eyes blurring, Jack reached for Ethan. He was going to kiss him, on the mouth, show him that he too wanted this, with him and no one else. It all went awry when Ethan lunged for him at the same time. Noses clashed, arms collided, and legs tangled. They ended up on the floor, Jack on his back, Ethan sprawled across him.

After a startled moment, Jack muttered, "Well, I don't know about anyone else, but I think we're certainly a danger to ourselves."

Ethan snorted, then buried his face in Jack's chest, as if levity was inappropriate. Jack squirmed until he could get his arms around him. They lay in easy silence for a while.

"Hey." Jack ran his fingers through Ethan's hair. "Are we good?"

It took Ethan a few moments to answer, though that could have been because he was busy pushing his head into Jack's hand, seeking comfort in the familiar touching. "Yes, we're good."

"Great. Can we get up, then? I'm lying on something that's digging into my arse."

With a few frantic apologies, Ethan got off him and helped Jack to sit up. They discovered the offending object was a small shifter. Sheepishly, Ethan surmised it had fallen out of his pocket when they fell. Jack studied the little tool for a moment, then solemnly tucked it back in Ethan's jeans pocket for him.

"The last time something fell out of one of your pockets, it was a tactical knife," Jack mused.

For some reason, Ethan blushed. Then he threw a leg over Jack's hips and settled onto his lap. The blush made sense when he draped his arms around Jack's neck and rolled his hips. "I have other things in my pants you might prefer."

Jack cracked up, nearly toppling them over again. When Ethan tried to be sexy, it was either endearing or hilarious. After a moment, Ethan joined in, winding his arms around Jack tighter as they laughed. It was amusing, yes, but most of it was relief. Something that could have gone so badly had ended in the best way possible, and yet Jack knew he couldn't risk it happening again.

In that vein, he pulled back so he could meet Ethan's gaze. "I've got some good news."

Sitting back on his heels, Ethan tried to school his expression into something serious, but his lips kept curling up at the corners. "I'm all ears."

Cheekily, Jack tweaked one of said ears. "You aren't, thankfully. I do really like your other body parts, as well. Especially those ones in your pants."

"Get on with it." Ethan swatted his hand away playfully.

"Fine. McIntosh called me in today. They've decided working with the strike force isn't worth our time anymore. The Office is no longer interested in the Judge or Infinity."

Ethan's expression lost all signs of amusement. He didn't quite get to totally expressionless, leaving a small crease between his brows, but it wasn't the jubilant response Jack had expected.

"Ethan? Isn't that good news?"

"Of course it is." His frown morphed into a pretty good imitation of a smile.

A little concerned, Jack tried, "How about if I sweeten it with the bonus of me having a week off work?"

Fake smile changing into a genuine grin, Ethan slid off Jack's lap and got to his feet. "*That* is incredibly good news." He pulled off his T-shirt and headed for the bedroom. "Let's celebrate."

Flummoxed again, but in a very nice way this time, Jack scrambled after him.

THIRTY-ONE
AFTER

Jack sucked in a deep breath as he contemplated Lewis's question. There were a couple of different ways he could answer it, but only one was the truth, and it was the one that would probably end his friendship with Lewis for good. Whatever the outcome, though, he had to be honest for once in this whole mess. He'd lied through his teeth to Feitt all year. To McIntosh and Tan whenever Ethan was brought up in reports. To Lewis when he'd asked about the mysterious boyfriend. But worst of all, he'd lied to Ethan.

"Because," he started, and stalled. Swallowing the hard clot of dread and doubt in his throat, he tried again. "Because I've been seeing Ethan Blade for about a year now. On and off. A couple of days here and there. Tan requested it. After everything with Harraway, Tan wanted to keep Ethan happy with the Office. He wants to use him."

Lewis frowned. "Use him how?"

"To do the jobs his other operatives are too squeamish to do." Jack shrugged. "At least, that's what I think. He never outright said, but what else could he want from an assassin?"

"But I thought about half of ETA field assets were classified sociopaths, anyway."

There was some professional rivalry between ITA and ETA, naturally, and gossip about the External Threat Assessment assets had always focused on their flexible morals. It was all just rumours, though. Jack had worked with ETA assets in the past and found them no worse or better than those in his own department. Most of the operational differences between them stemmed from the directors. Jack didn't often agree with Director Alex Tan, but he had found him useful in the past.

"The joke's on Tan, though," Jack said. "Ethan has some strict standards. He doesn't just consider the money when taking a job."

Lewis was looking more thoughtful than horrified, but that was probably because in his straight-centric mind, he wasn't equating Jack "seeing" Ethan with "dating," or "fucking." Lewis had no hang-ups about Jack's sexuality, so the delay in understanding here was probably more about him not thinking an assassin of any sex could be deemed relationship-worthy.

Of course, if Jack was really going to be upfront, he would have to clear it up for him.

"Has Tan asked him to do anything yet?" The cogs were turning in Lewis's complex brain.

"Not yet."

"Strange."

Jack hadn't really considered it before. So long as Tan was willing to cover Ethan's presence in Australia while he and Jack were together, Jack had no real interest in Tan's motives. Or rather, Tan had been silent for so long Jack had forgotten to worry about them.

Before Jack could find the words to tell Lewis everything, his friend shook his head as if clearing it, and spoke.

"The reason I came to meet you is that we got the full report on the disturbance at Quinn's suite." He gave Jack a sympathetic look. "It's not good."

Guts clenching, Jack asked, "What is it?"

"It looks like Quinn didn't run. He was taken by the Judge. They found a Bible verse."

Ice drenched Jack. Fuck. So long as there hadn't been a note, the Judge's involvement in Adam's disappearance hadn't been confirmed. Likely but not definite.

"What does it say?"

Lewis pulled out his phone and read from the screen. "This is why I speak to them in parables: 'Though seeing, they do not see; though hearing, they do not hear or understand.'" He paused, then asked, "Any insight?"

Nothing immediately jumped out at Jack. Except, maybe . . . Christ. How many times had Jack joked with Adam about him "seeing through the killer's eyes"? It was too much of a coincidence, surely.

No. This note was simply playing off the one the psycho had left for Steph. He was taunting them. The people most able and likely to catch him *hadn't*. He was showing off, the arrogant bastard. Jack grimly repeated his thoughts for Lewis.

"Which fits with Quinn's profile," he said.

"And doesn't really shed any more light on the whole thing."

"I'm not so sure about that," Lewis muttered.

"You've discovered something about the verses?" Jack asked.

Lewis made an indecisive sound. "Not really. It's just . . . I don't know. They feel too specific?"

"They are specific," Jack reminded him. "The Judge picks them to illustrate his fucked-up reason for killing that particular person."

"Yeah, but it's flawed logic. The only verses Quinn was able to definitively link to the victims were the Melbourne ones. He wasn't able to do that with the Sydney victims. At least, not that he told anyone before he was taken."

"Are you saying you think it's not the same killer?" The thought made Jack sick. Two nutjobs of this quality on the loose? Christ.

"No," Lewis said firmly. "It's the same killer. Or well, I'm pretty sure it is. Everything else is too similar. Wound patterns. The posing of the body. The placement of the verses."

It was like Adam was right there, feeding Lewis his expertise. Perhaps they should have sent Lewis in right at the start. Between him and Adam, they probably could have found the Judge well before now.

"Then what are you thinking?" Jack coaxed Lewis towards his point.

"That the Sydney notes have a different purpose to the Melbourne ones."

It made sense. Adam's inability to link the new Bible verses to their victims had been puzzling and frustrating for Adam. For the first time in his career he'd started to doubt his own skills and knowledge. Again, Jack regretted how the Office had cut off their involvement in the strike force so early. If they hadn't, Lewis may have had these breakthroughs earlier and none of them would be here right now. Brenna Luntz and Steph would still be alive, Adam wouldn't be—hopefully—being held captive by a psychopath, and Ethan . . .

"Which is?" Jack asked.

Lewis drew a deep breath, as if gearing up for a big reveal, then shrugged. "No idea."

Jack groaned. "If your half-arsed theory is right, then it probably means the victims are being chosen for different reasons, too."

"Yup," Lewis agreed, then scowled. "We're going to have to start from scratch, aren't we?"

"Not exactly," Jack assured him. "This is what I spent all those weeks doing, remember. Everything we've done up to this point isn't wasted. It's just excluded one angle of interpretation. We have a new one, now. All we have to do is apply the new perspective to the information we already have. Hopefully, it will highlight something we didn't know was important before."

Lewis groaned, and Jack smiled heartlessly.

"Now you know how I felt all that time."

Lewis scowled at him. "All right. Any more ideas on what we're looking for this time?"

Jack shook his head, then stopped mid-shake. In light of Lewis's speculation about the notes and victims, a memory sparked newly bright. With it came a resonance of the seething anger he'd felt then, but he breathed through it until it faded. That rage had made him do the stupidest thing he possibly could have, adding to the shit pile he was currently wading through.

It was Lewis's turn to prompt him. "Jack? What did you think of?"

Focusing on his friend, Jack reminded himself of his conviction to tell Lewis everything. Well, maybe not everything right now. Just the pertinent things.

"It's something someone said to me the other day. I was told to look at the victims as two groups, not as individuals."

Lewis repeated it several times, emphasising different words each time. After nearly a minute, he nodded. "I think there's something in it." Glaring at Jack, he added, "You've been sitting on this for two days?"

"They haven't exactly been a pleasant couple of days. Truth to tell, it kind of got lost in the mix of everything else that happened. And it wasn't until *you* decided the Sydney victims were different to the Melbourne ones that it made any sort of sense to me."

"All right. I'll give you that one. So, this is our new perspective. We discount any connection to the Melbourne murders and look at the Sydney victims as a group, rather than disparate individuals. Does that sound right?"

Jack nodded, wondering if he'd dodged a bullet. Lewis seemed to have dismissed Jack's earlier mentions of Ethan. He was relieved but also annoyed with himself. Sooner rather than later, he had to tell Lewis about Ethan and hope like hell it didn't turn into another Canberra.

"Okay, that's what we do now," Lewis muttered resignedly. "What are your immediate plans?"

"Actually, I think I'll come in."

Lewis's eyebrows nearly reached his hairline, and he reached over to put his palm on Jack's forehead. "Are you sick?"

Jack dodged his hand. "I've been out and made contact with Garrote and, most likely, the Judge. Looking for me will keep them occupied for a while. Blade hasn't actually come in, but he is out there, too, doing something. There's not much more I can do until the Cenotaph tonight."

"That actually sounds logical."

Jack gave him a withering grimace. "Come on, let's get going."

Lewis groaned as he faced the bike he'd wheeled all the way from the Neville Crawley Building. "Can we just leave it here?"

"And walk all the way back?" Jack got on the new bike and waved Lewis over. "Hurry up or I'll leave you behind."

Eyeing Jack, the bike, and the narrow tunnel stretching away in front of them, Lewis grumbled but got on the back. "Just so you know, if we make it back alive, we're going to discuss the matter of Ethan Blade. At length."

Fuck. Seemed Jack hadn't quite ducked fast enough. He started the bike, and the rumble of the engine echoed through the confined space, magnifying it and making conversation impossible. With the headlight illuminating the way ahead, Jack got them going, half hoping this stupid idea would kill them both. That way, he wouldn't have to deal with Lewis knowing about him and Ethan.

THIRTY-TWO
BEFORE

than's hand drifted lazily down Jack's ribs, over his hip bone, and down his thigh. Halfway to his knee, it paused, fingertips idly playing in his leg hair; then the hand slipped down the outer curve of muscle and began the slow return journey. The hand had done this several times over the past ten or so minutes. It was the only movement in the bed. In the room. Probably in the entire apartment.

Three days of his week off gone already and Jack couldn't bring himself to care that they hadn't left the apartment in all that time. Didn't mind that the most clothes he'd worn in that time was pyjama bottoms or shorts. Not that it had been a sexfest the entire three days. There had been a lot of lying in front of the telly, catching up on the world or shows or laughing at how the player statistics for the cricket looked like dating profiles. Ethan had read and Jack had pestered him to read aloud, often falling asleep after a chapter or two. Not because the story was boring but because he felt so content with Ethan's voice in his head.

The change in Ethan was welcoming, as well. He slept like he used to, deep and intense, only surfacing when he was ready or if Jack was too horny to wait and blew him awake. The last couple of bruises were fading nicely, barely yellow tinges under his pale skin. He smiled easily and laughed with Jack, and at him. He teased and tempted, and his attempts at deliberate seduction were getting better. Which didn't matter because Ethan was at his most desirable and irresistible when he wasn't trying.

The hand made another slow circuit. Each time it did, it got just a little closer to Jack's dick. They'd already fucked twice today, and the way this was going, a third was soon to happen. Maybe this would be the time Jack kissed him.

God. He'd been ready, determined to do it after the not-an-argument, but the make-up sex had been so frantic, so desperate, it hadn't felt right. And each time after, Jack thought sex wasn't the right time. The perfect time to do it was when Ethan couldn't misconstrue it as something that just happened in the heat of the moment. But then Jack would wonder if planning it wasn't as bad. It should be spontaneous, natural, because then it would mean more. If it happened to occur while Ethan's legs were wrapped around his waist, his back arched in ecstasy, eyes wide and mouth gasping Jack's name . . . well, that would be natural, too, right?

As the hand headed south again, the heel of its palm brushing along the length of Jack's dick, he thought about other things he'd been waiting to happen naturally, but hadn't. Things, or one in particular, that Jack now decided needed some prompting. Waiting until the hand was making another downward sweep, bringing more contact to his warming dick, Jack spread his legs a little, just enough to make Ethan's hand dip down between them.

The hand paused there, as if contemplating the new territory open to exploration. Slowly, it cupped the inside of Jack's thigh, sending a pleasant wave through his muscle and up into his groin. Fingers flexing, Ethan dallied for a while, then resumed his route. The next time, he moulded his hand around Jack's shaft, stroking down it softly. Jack widened his thighs, and the hand dropped between them, grazing his balls. So it went for several more minutes, until with each pass, Ethan was giving him a few firm pumps before fondling his balls and then tease his taint.

Jack was finding it hard not to squirm. He didn't want to upset the current sequence of events, wanted this to reach its eventual conclusion. But *Christ*. His whole body was aching with the need for more. More hands—well, at least one more—more pressure, more heat, more mouth—*any* mouth—more . . . more Ethan. And Jack wasn't alone in his vibrating frustration. Ethan made small motions that pressed his dick against Jack. It was hot and hard, and the feel of the thick shaft rubbing on Jack's skin quickly became too much to resist.

"Jesus." Jack reached for Ethan's dick and gave it an appreciative squeeze. "When the hell are you going to fuck me?"

Ethan froze, except for the part of him in Jack's hand, which pulsed with unmistakable eagerness.

"Yes." Jack let him go, but only so he could tumble Ethan to his back and straddle him. Catching both of their dicks in one hand, Jack leaned over and nuzzled into Ethan's neck. "Do you know how long I've wanted this? Wanted you to want this?"

Under him, Ethan bucked, shoving himself harder against Jack. His hands pressed into Jack's back, his sides. They slid up either side of his neck, pulling Jack's face closer so he could kiss his chin, his nose, his temples. He murmured agreement and whimpered when Jack brushed the tip of his dick with his thumb, smearing pre-cum around and around and down. Then, with a strangled moan, he put his hands on Jack's chest and pushed him up and away.

"Wait," he gasped.

Befuddled with lust, Jack sat back on his heels and nodded. "Yeah. Lube. We'll need lube."

Ethan barked a single, breathless laugh and sagged into the mattress. "Yes, I suppose. Eventually."

Scrambling for the bedside table drawer, Jack muttered, "Not eventually. Now. We've had a whole year of foreplay."

A warm hand landed on Jack's back. "Jack, please wait."

Words and tone got through the fog in Jack's head. He faced Ethan, sitting cross-legged on the bed. His dick was still hard, but some of the urgency had disappeared. "Why? You want this. I know you do."

Ethan pulled in a deep breath, eyes closing as he let it out. "I do. Desperately. You are unique, Jack. You make me want so many things that I didn't know I could have." A smile softened his mouth. "You made me enjoy sex. A *lot*. You made me want, for the first time in my entire life, to . . ." He sighed and, skin blazing with a fierce blush that spread down to his chest, finished with, "To fuck a man. Specifically, you."

Initially, Jack was amused. Ethan didn't say "fuck." Not as a curse or a verb. Jack had coaxed it out of him a couple of times, loving how it made Ethan squirm and redden. And then the context caught up to him.

Jack frowned. "You mean you've never topped before?"

"I've never felt a desire to."

He looked so worried Jack wanted to smother him in kisses. Instead, he said, "That's okay, you know. You're a natural bottom, that's all."

Ethan chewed that one over for a moment, then shook his head. "No. That's not it. Or at least, not completely." He sat up and mirrored Jack's position. His dick had softened noticeably, and the flush of blood under his skin had faded. "Perhaps I am a natural bottom, but that doesn't change the fact that I'm not attracted to men."

Jack blinked. Then again. "Um . . . what?"

"Hmm. I worded that wrong." He shifted onto his knees and, when Jack didn't stop him, straddled his lap. "I'm incredibly, scarily, desperately, attracted to you. The fact that you are male is secondary to the fact that I very much like how you make me feel." He rolled his hips over Jack's groin. "Physically." He cupped Jack's face in his hands and stared directly into his eyes. "But most importantly, intellectually and emotionally. I have never felt so alive with anyone else. So . . . human."

Throat closed up, in compassion and fear and the need to kiss him, Jack could only nod. His arms wrapped around him and tugged him closer.

Ethan settled into the embrace. "I've been with very few people. Two women and three men, before you. I found sex easier with the women. More . . . tolerable than with the men. With them, things only worked if I let them do to me whatever they wanted. Not being erect during penetration isn't so unusual they suspected I wasn't enjoying it. I could fake everything else well enough."

Helplessly, Jack wondered if Moraitis was counted as one of the three men Ethan had been with. The thought sickened him even as it made him hold Ethan tighter. Unaware of the grim direction of Jack's thoughts, Ethan relaxed against him, pliant and warm and smiling as he continued.

"Then I met you. You were cranky and sad and really wanted to punch me."

"With reason," Jack grumbled into his shoulder.

"With very good reason. Yet you didn't. You walked with me, you talked with me. You made me laugh. You laughed with me. *At* me.

You never hesitated to get angry at me, despite believing I was Ethan Blade, feared assassin. And I wanted you because of all that."

Tilting his head to look at Ethan, Jack asked, "Really?"

"Really."

"When did you first want me?"

Cheeks pinking faintly, Ethan looked away for a moment, then back again. "The first night. When you let me clean your wound."

Jack snorted. "No. Really, when did you first want me?"

"Then. I swear it's true. I'll grant I didn't exactly understand what I was feeling. All I knew was you had made yourself vulnerable to me even knowing what I was. Exposed your wounded back. That meant something to me. No one had ever done that for me before. Even Valadian, when he . . . dominated me, made me strip naked every time, so he knew I wasn't hiding a weapon. He didn't want me to touch him or look at him during it. And yet you, a soldier and spy, lay down and let me tend you." He bit his lip, and his blush deepened. "It helped, too, that the firelight made your skin glow like old gold. Made me want to touch it. Touch you, to know if you were as warm as you appeared. You were."

"That was the fire and infection," Jack muttered gruffly.

How would Ethan feel if he knew Jack had done all that because he'd been so confused and on the edge of a deep, dark hole, that he hadn't cared if Blade had meant to plunge a knife into his back?

Ethan started to move on him again. They were both flaccid, but that wouldn't last long. "Long story short. I want to top you. I just don't know how."

Did how it all started matter when they were here now? Probably about as much as knowing about Moraitis mattered when it came to how Jack felt about Ethan. Not greatly. Both topics could wait a while longer. Because right then, Jack wanted Ethan inside him more than he ever had in the past.

"Well, that's a load of rot." Jack nipped his chest. "I've fucked you enough you should have picked something up by now."

Ethan chuckled. "True. That, however, doesn't mean I won't require some instruction." His voice went husky and low. "A *lot* of instruction."

Just like that, Jack was hard again. After a swift check, he discovered Ethan was, as well.

"Right," Jack growled. "This is getting done. Now."

"Indeed." Ethan matched his rumbling tone and lunged for the bedside table.

Unable to resist, Jack scraped his teeth over the perfectly displayed rear. Ethan shuddered and laughed and fumbled the drawer open.

"You shall pay for that," he promised.

"God, I fucking hope so."

Knock knock.

Ethan froze and Jack groaned.

Knock knock knock. "Boys? Are you home?"

"Mr. Cesare," Jack muttered.

"Hello? Nishant? Ethan?"

At the sound of his called name, Ethan went completely still. He was getting better, but old, life-preserving habits died very hard. Jack sighed and hauled himself off the bed.

"I'll see what he wants. You stay here."

Ethan didn't exactly relax as Jack found a pair of clean pants and a T-shirt, but he didn't go for his guns, either. Hoping this was an innocent interruption and that things could get back on track as soon as possible, Jack headed for the front door. Perhaps some of Ethan's paranoia had rubbed off on him because he checked the screen to make sure the elderly man was alone before opening the door.

"Jack!" Mr. Cesare smiled in relief. Short Round squirmed for attention in his arms. "I was worried you weren't home."

Jack scratched Shorty's head. "We're home. Just . . . busy."

"Sorry, sorry. If it's too much trouble, I can always ask Melanie on the first floor to look after Shorty for me."

Shorty licked his human's chin. Then he started wriggling so hard he was in danger of squirting free and tumbling to the ground.

Chuckling, Jack said, "It's fine. We'll watch him for you. Put him down before he breaks his silly neck."

The moment his little paws hit the floor, Shorty pelted towards the bedroom, instinctively seeming to know where Ethan was. He yapped excitedly, and Ethan's startled but happy exclamation made Jack smile.

"It's just overnight," Mr. Cesare explained. "My grandson's in hospital in Newcastle—nothing serious—and my daughter is coming by to pick me up so we can go see him." He handed over a bag with Shorty's stuff, assured Jack he would be back late the following day, and headed downstairs to wait for his daughter.

A shirtless Ethan, convinced there was no threat, appeared with Shorty in his arms. The dachshund was on his back, legs waving as Ethan rubbed his belly. But for the interruption, that could have been Jack.

He explained the situation, and before he'd finished, Ethan had tucked Shorty under his arm, opened the bag, and started pulling bowls and cans and toys out. More than a little disappointed, Jack settled for pressing against Ethan's bare back and resting his chin on his shoulder, watching as their guest's gear was sorted out.

"Great," Jack muttered, "now I'll never get fu—"

"Jack! Not in front of the pup." Ethan covered Shorty's flappy ears. "Besides, the quicker we get Shorty situated, the sooner we can lock him out of the bedroom."

"Put some water in a bowl and let's go." He rubbed his stiffening dick against Ethan's arse.

Ethan's groan was throaty as he set Shorty on the counter, then reached back with his now free hand to grip Jack's hip. "Do you plan on locking the front door at any stage?"

"At some stage." Jack nuzzled into Ethan's neck.

"Jack." The word was part wanton, part exasperated. He pushed back against Jack, but the rub of his arse over Jack's groin seemed more stay-right-there than go-away. Between that and the fact that the hand on his hip held tighter, Jack couldn't move. He felt magnetised to the man.

Butt planted on the counter, Shorty watched them grind, head tilting one way, then the other. He gave a curious little yap and nudged Ethan's arm for attention.

"Mm, Jack, you need . . . oh, yes . . . to close the . . . ngh!" With a firm push, he shoved Jack's hips back, but only far enough so he could turn around, hoist himself up onto the counter, and reel Jack back in with his legs around his waist.

Hands in Ethan's hair, chest to chest, Jack forgot everything else and leaned in to kiss him.

Shorty's rumbling growl cut through the fog surrounding Jack. Ethan froze. A second later, Jack was propelled back so hard he collided with the dining table. Ethan rolled over the counter and dropped behind it as Shorty skittered along the smooth surface towards the doorway, barking madly.

Jack followed the dog's trajectory and discovered Adam standing the entrance, bottle of bourbon in one hand. He looked ragged. Tired and harassed with his tie askew, hair messy and sleep-deprived eyes wide in shock.

Then Ethan stood up behind the counter. His face was closed down. Lips in a hard line, eyes narrowed. This was Ethan Blade, ready and capable to kill. He had a gun in each hand, and both of them were trained unerringly on Adam.

THIRTY-THREE
AFTER

Jack and Lewis made it back to the Neville Crawley Building safely. Once above ground, messages came in for both of them, sending Lewis to the eighth to catch up with Lydia and the team, and Jack to the tenth, to McIntosh's office.

"You managed to cause quite a stir in the space of a couple hours." She motioned for him to sit.

"That was the plan, ma'am."

Her smile was tight and didn't quite reach her eyes. "It was a rousing success, then. Dumay has a rather diverse vocabulary when inspired. I'm having Miller look up the meaning of some of the words she used to describe you."

"She's a smart woman."

McIntosh agreed with a nod. "And in a difficult situation. Which I made that much worse for her. Not only does she have the commissioner and ADFIS breathing down her neck, but I left her on the phone to Minister Simmons, as well."

"Hopefully we'll catch the Judge tonight and they'll all leave her alone."

"Nothing is ever that easy, Jack, especially when it comes to politics. Give me a rundown of what happened while you were out."

Well-trained in giving concise reports, Jack had his director caught up within fifteen minutes, explaining the new insights he and Lewis had discussed in the tunnels.

When he'd finished, she asked, "And Garrote's intentions?"

"No bloody clue, ma'am. She could have killed me several times and yet . . ."

McIntosh leaned back in her chair, fingers laced together over her belly. "Hopefully her motives won't matter for much longer. We've found out who bought the ticket she picked up."

"Who?" Jack tried not to get too excited. Finding the ticket owner was one thing. Getting them to void it was another. Depending on why they bought it, they might not be willing to give in to any of the Office's usual tactics—money, coercion, or threats.

"Sun Zheng, an importer/exporter based in Hong Kong. He *appears* to be a Disciple of the Messiah, but we've yet to confirm it. His company is just a front for a smuggling organisation, which in turn might be part of an as yet unidentified Triad. We haven't ruled out the possibility of a black society group from the mainland, either. What it boils down to is that someone is going to a lot of trouble to make us think the ticket is retaliation for your capture of the Messiah."

"You're clearly not convinced."

"Not yet. I'm tending to agree with Lewis's theory that it's all too convenient. As for the second ticket, we've narrowed it down to originating within the Meta-State, most likely from Australia. Intelligence is close to finding the buyer. I understand you've refused backup when you go out tonight."

"Yes, ma'am." He gave her the same reasons he'd given Lewis.

"I'm overriding your decision. Two strike teams are going to be in the tunnels at the closest entrances to the mall." Which put them only fractionally closer than the Neville Crawley Building. "A third will be here to provide backup if required."

Knowing he couldn't argue with her, Jack simply said, "Yes, ma'am."

She merely looked at him over the tops of her glasses, letting him know she'd caught his tone. All she said was, "Go give Lewis a full debrief."

Jack escaped before she had him scuffing his foot on the carpet and promising to be good from now on. When he reached the eighth, Lewis directed him to his private operations room for the debrief. Lewis had been to see Fabian in Ex Mon again. The tech was homing in on the originating host server for the photos that had incriminated Jack in the Messiah's disappearance.

"He says he'll know within the next hour. There are so many Red Bull cans in his workstation, it's a wonder he hasn't been crushed in an avalanche. How did it go with McIntosh?"

"Knuckles mostly un-rapped." Jack told him about closing in on the ticket buyers.

The actual debrief didn't take long, leaving the floor open to Lewis's promise to pick up the "matter of Ethan Blade."

"It's more than just work, isn't it," Lewis said, tone neutral. At least it wasn't one of disgust or horror. "He's the 'not a boyfriend,' right?"

Jack let out a long breath. "Yeah. He's different to how you'd think he would be. Almost innocent in some ways. He didn't choose this path. Some fucked-up military group moulded him, taught him this was all he could be."

Lewis shook his head. "No. I don't get it. There's always a choice."

With a bitter smile, Jack said, "He said the exact same thing to me, actually. But sometimes, you don't know that there is one. Lew, he was fifteen . . . no. He was fourteen the first time he killed someone. Not in self-defence, not manslaughter, but deliberately. A proper hit. And he'd been trained to do it. I don't know how old he was when they—whoever *they* were—got him, but it had to be *years* before that first time. Their idea of disciplining a child involved a whip and scars that survived into adulthood. They told him, *convinced* him, that because he was a Sugar Baby, he was a monster. So yeah. There was a choice, but he couldn't make it back then because he didn't know he could."

In the silence that followed, Jack thought perhaps this wouldn't be any different to Canberra. Well, he was fairly sure there weren't terrorists hiding in the woodworks, but the longer Lewis avoided meeting his gaze, the more he thought he'd lost another friend. Still, he had to try.

"The moment he *could* make that decision, he did. He walked away from it."

"Because of you?" His friend struggled to stay impartial, but there was a touch of sarcasm in his question.

Crossing his arms so they wouldn't do anything stupid, Jack said, "No. This was before we met. He did it for himself." Before Lewis could point out the obvious, Jack continued. "Yeah, he went back to it, but on his own terms. He only took the jobs he wanted to do, ones where he could confirm that the target needed to be taken out. You can't deny that we're better off without Valadian running loose."

"An assassin with a heart of gold?" Lewis cocked a sceptical brow.

Jack chuckled. "Fuck no. Just one with a bit of a conscience. Hard-won but there. I'm sure if you just got to know him . . ."

Lewis put his elbows on the table and rested his face in his hands, his groan coming out muffled.

"Can't you just trust me on this? We've been friends for seven—"

"Eight." Lewis dropped his hands and looked Jack in the eyes. "All right. He's a top bloke according to you. For your sake, I really hope he is. If you go out there tonight and he shoots you, I'm so rubbing your dead face in this conversation."

Jack muttered, "Well, about that . . ."

Lewis stared at him. "What the hell did you do?"

"I fucked up. Big-time."

"Shit. So, Blade really could be gunning for you?"

"It's my fault." Confessing made Jack feel sick, but relieved too. Lewis was still sitting there, actually listening to him, sounding reasonable. "I should have seen it coming. He'd made too many changes too fast. For me. And I didn't realise how close he was to an edge. God. He pulled guns on Adam when he showed up at my place."

"What?" Lewis demanded. "Adam Quinn showed up at your place? When?"

Fuck. This was taking a sudden nosedive. "A couple of days after McIntosh pulled us off the Infinity case."

"Holy crap. That's why my holiday was cut short, wasn't it? And you lied through your bloody teeth to me about it."

"Not just you. Everyone."

"Doesn't make me feel any better." Lewis shoved his chair back and stood. "For fuck's sake, Jack. I'm your friend. Your best mate! You could have told me sooner than this. Before the shit hit the fan. I could have helped you sort it all out before it went nuclear."

Jack got to his feet as well, feeling the need to be ready to either fight or run before he messed up further. "If I'd known you would help rather than freak out, I would have come to you, but I didn't know."

Jabbing himself in the chest with a finger, Lewis muttered, "Best friend, Jack. It was bad enough when you kept all the Valadian and Harraway shit to yourself. This? It's worse."

"How is this worse?"

Lewis backed away. "Because this isn't about work, Jack. You were the first person I told about how I felt about Lydia. Before I even told her. And you felt you couldn't tell me about this. I guess you really have forgotten what it means to have friends or family."

He was at the door when Jack worked through the fiery rage Lewis's final jab inspired to find some words to say.

"Do you want to know why I didn't tell you?"

Shoulders stiff, Lewis turned to face him. "Sure. Just don't lie this time."

"Okay. No lies. It was because of Canberra."

"Oh," Lewis said, then when full understanding hit, "Oh, shit. Harry."

"Yeah. He found out, didn't take it well and . . ." Jack shrugged, unable to say the rest aloud. Which he didn't need to. Lewis knew what had happened then.

Lewis came back to his chair and sat. After a moment, he sighed. "You're still a dickhead. I've known you for how long now? I trust you. If Blade's not all that bad, then I get it. Dude was hot."

"Still is."

"Even if he's gunning for you?"

Jack huffed. "Let's not go there."

"You've got it bad."

"Yeah." Jack was done lying or hedging.

"Does McIntosh know? Tan?"

"Sort of. I haven't told them directly, but I'm sure they've got an idea."

"Probably. I won't blab to anyone else. Except Lyds, because it's my nuts on the line if she finds out I knew and didn't tell her."

It felt strange, but Jack laughed. "Fine. Go save your nuts. I've got something else to do for a while."

"What?"

Jack told him about the cognitive model, and Lewis agreed he should let it finish. He was going back down to Ex Mon to check on

Fabian and left Jack to it. In an empty breakroom, Jack rushed the relaxation procedure, went *sideways*, and set the model going once again.

This time, thanks to his talk with Lewis, his subconscious threw images of Ethan at him. Calmly working his way through Valadian's army, face expressionless as he shot man after man. Lying on the deckchair, touching himself in the golden-pink light of dawn. Behind Victoria's steering wheel, relaxed as the world blurred by the window. Jack's brown hand splayed across his back, fingers lined up with old scars.

When the model finished and Jack came out of his deep trance, he was uncomfortably aroused. That state disappeared rather fast when he checked the results, though.

After throwing open the door to the breakroom, Jack nearly ran over a panting Lewis.

"Jack! Fabian did it. He's found out who originally uploaded the images to the internet. You won't fucking believe it!"

"I bet I will," Jack said grimly. "Who was it?"

"Martin Conway of Melbourne, Australia. He's a nobody, literally. It's a fake identity. But get this. Martin Conway is also the name of the buyer of your second ticket."

Jack absorbed that and found it fitted with what he'd just learned. "Do you have a picture of this Martin Conway?"

"Not yet. Fabian is trawling every state and territory for a driver's licence, but I don't reckon he'll find one."

"No, probably not." Jack stalked down the hallway. "Let's go see McIntosh."

"She already knows about the Conway connection." Lewis hurried after him. "My theory is that when Garrote picked up the first ticket so quickly, whoever's trying to protect the Judge bought the second one under the Conway identity but made sure Blade knew about it before he did so Blade could get this one." He patted Jack's shoulder as they entered the stairwell. "Sorry, mate. But I really think your boyfriend's serious about taking you out."

"I'm still not convinced. And I'm not convinced there's a third party trying to protect the Judge." Jack took the stairs up two and three at a time.

"Why not?" Already winded, Lewis puffed his way up behind him.

"Because who is the one person in the world absolutely guaranteed to want to protect the Judge?"

"His mother?"

"No. Himself."

Lewis staggered to a stop on the landing between the ninth and tenth floors. "What? Are you saying Martin Conway is the Judge?"

"Yes." Jack stopped as well. His thoughts had been racing from the moment he read the model results. Things were snapping into place at long last, and he took a moment to line up the final piece. "The Judge hasn't only been three steps ahead of us all this time, but he's playing a game we didn't even know about. It all comes down to the victims. They're all connected."

"But Lyds and the team have been looking into that. They aren't connected. The only common thing any of them have is Williams and Luntz both have a storage unit in separate facilities. That's it. Morrissey doesn't, so the theory is bust."

Jack frowned. "No. There has to be something else." The last few clues added up, and he spun around, racing upwards once more. "That doesn't matter, anyway. Just come on!"

"Why doesn't it matter?"

"Because I know who the Judge is."

THIRTY-FOUR

BEFORE

Jack threw himself between Ethan and Adam. Two guns now aimed directly at his spine, Jack glared at Adam.

"Get out of here," he said grimly.

Adam blinked slowly, his expression shifting from shock to understanding. As if there weren't two firearms pointed in his general direction, he just shook his head.

"I should have known," he muttered instead of leaving.

The weight of Ethan's deadly presence pushed at Jack's back. He knew Ethan wouldn't shoot him, but Adam's wellbeing wasn't nearly as secure, even with Jack between them. Shorty stopped barking, falling into a series of little confused whimpers.

God. Was Adam really so arrogant he thought he wasn't in danger?

"Just go," Jack snapped.

Adam shook his head again, mouth open to respond.

The barrel of a gun moved into Jack's peripheral vision.

"Fuck." Jack spun and locked his arm around Ethan's, jerking the gun downwards. "Run, Adam. Now!"

He couldn't check if the stupid man had finally listened and left, because Ethan twisted out of his hold and darted away. Desperate to not let him get through the doorway, Jack threw himself at Ethan. He caught the assassin around the thighs, and they crashed to the floor by the fridge. Ethan tossed one of his guns, freeing a hand to wrap around Jack's throat. Ignoring the grip, Jack wrestled to keep the other hand pinned.

"Jesus, Ethan," he ground out against the fingers closing around his windpipe. "Quit it. He's gone. You're safe."

Empty, cold eyes pierced Jack, silently rejecting the lie. But a second later, the hand around Jack's neck let go. Ethan stopped struggling, letting his remaining gun drop to the floor. Jack grabbed it and tossed it after the other one. For a long moment, he lay on top of Ethan, half expecting a sneak attack. When it didn't come, he slowly got to his knees, straddling Ethan's thighs.

"You okay?" he asked gently.

Ethan just blinked, gaze locked on the ceiling.

"All right." Standing, Jack found the guns and tucked both into the back of his pants. Then he closed and locked the door. At least Adam had left.

Shorty trotted back and forth on the counter, whining. He licked Jack's hand furiously when Jack picked up him and put him on the floor.

"Good boy," he told the dog. "Go lick Ethan. He needs it more than I do."

Before Shorty reached his second favourite human, Ethan was up and leaving. He disappeared into the hallway, and a moment later, the door to the bathroom slammed shut. Shorty's bark told Jack the dog hadn't been fast enough to join him in there.

As the adrenaline swirled, potent and unused, Jack got angry. At Adam. At Ethan. At his goddamned fucking self. At McIntosh. If she hadn't put him on this bloody job as *himself*, none of this would have happened. He wouldn't have made Ethan think he was cheating. Ethan wouldn't have nearly shot an innocent man. Adam wouldn't have shown up at his fucking home.

All of his wild rage coalesced into a single, hard point.

Stalking into the bedroom, Jack stripped so hard he tore the seams of his shirt. Dressing in jeans and clean T-shirt, he shoved his feet into his boots while Shorty worried at the bathroom door. The dog's almost pained cries nearly made Jack change his mind. Nearly.

He made sure he locked the front door behind him. The last thing he wanted to do was leave Ethan vulnerable again.

Jack ran at least two red lights getting to the Oaks. He didn't care. Barely remembered to put the stand down on the bike when he got to the hotel. Ignored the concierge's enquiries and took the stairs up to the top floor. The exercise only focused his anger even more, so that when he reached Adam's door, he didn't hesitate to bang on it with his fist. After two sets of three, the thought that Adam might not have come here caught traction. Jack backed off, sucking in deep breaths so he could think straight. Where else would he have gone? To the police to report the madman with the guns? No. If Adam hadn't sensibly run at the first appearance of the weapons, he wouldn't think to go to the cops for protection. The bar? It was more likely. Jack knew how much the man drank, so it was likely he would have sought comfort in alcohol. Then Jack remembered the bottle in his hand.

"Goddamn it." Jack moved to the door again and banged on it. "Open up, Adam, or I'll kick the door in."

A moment later, the door jerked open. Adam glared at him. "You didn't bring the boyfriend to shoot it down?"

Slamming the door wide, Jack pushed his way into the suite. Adam's lip curled into a sneer, but he gave ground, letting Jack close the door behind him.

Adam stalked over to the chair by the balcony, threw himself into it, and picked up the open bottle of bourbon, taking a long drink. A third of it was gone already. He'd tossed his suit jacket to the floor, shirt untucked and half-unbuttoned, as if he'd got that far before giving up and not caring if he spilled his drink on it. He looked defeated.

Now that he was here, Jack lost some momentum. The vague idea that he'd come here to punch Adam had propelled him this far, but seeing him like this stole most of his impetus. He was still angry, couldn't imagine not being angry right then. But he'd never seen Adam like this before. Bored. Restless. Anxious. Excited. Positive. All of them, but not this. Not crushed and hopeless.

Stalled in the middle of the room, Jack rubbed a hand over his face, hoping that when he spoke, he didn't just start yelling.

"What the hell, Adam?" It came out hard but modulated to a reasonable level. "How the fuck did you find out where I lived?"

Usually piercing blue eyes looked at him, unfocused, bloodshot, weary. "How did you know what room I was in?"

"You told me you were in the same suite as when we hooked up," Jack snapped. "On any number of occasions when you tried to get me to come here with you. After I told you no so many times. Don't you ever fucking give up?"

"Sure. It's all my fault I didn't know you were lying to me." He took another drink.

That cut deep. The truth always did.

"I didn't lie to you about him. I just didn't tell you." Why was he trying to justify himself to Adam?

"Oh, that's fine, then. Just call him a 'friend' when you want some free advice on how to deal with your crazy boyfriend. Jeez, a fucking Sugar Baby."

"Watch it," Jack hissed.

"The man pulled *two* guns on me. I think I have a right to comment." Adam lifted the bottle to his lips.

"Christ." Stalking over, Jack grabbed the drink, spraying sharply scented drops of bourbon across them both. "You've had fucking enough of that." He took a long drink himself, then took the bottle to the kitchenette and poured it down the sink.

"You owe me for that," Adam muttered.

"Take it out of what you owe me for coming to my home and royally fucking everything up. Tell me, how the hell did you find me?"

Home addresses of Office assets weren't national secrets, but they were far from advertised. They all had PO boxes, private numbers, and secure lines. Not once in eight years had Jack's home privacy ever been disturbed. Except by Ethan, but that one he could easily, happily, forgive. This one? God, Adam was lucky his nose was still perfectly shaped.

"How do you think?" Adam asked carelessly as he got up and went to the balcony. He swayed a little as he stood looking out at the city. "I work with the police."

"Jesus." Jack locked his fingers together on the back of his head. "That's a gross violation of their authority." Then a thought hit him. "It was Toomey, wasn't it? He got you my address."

Adam shrugged.

"Does the poor bastard know you're just using him?"

"Maybe he's using me."

"If he was, he'd be the first one to ever get anything from you without having to pay for it."

That made Adam turn around. "What the fuck?"

"Don't pretend to be innocent. You sit there with that goddamn smirk on your face because you know what everyone is thinking before they do. And you use it to get what you want."

Adam's top lip curled up. "I don't need to be analysed by an amateur." He opened a cabinet under the TV and pulled out a bottle of vodka. Unscrewing the cap, he muttered, "Besides, if that was true I would have fucking found the Judge by now and all this shit would be over." He chugged back several mouthfuls before Jack got the bottle off him.

"How much booze do you have here?" Jack headed for the kitchen again.

"Doesn't matter. The concierge will get me more."

"You don't need anymore."

"No, but I want it."

Pouring the vodka into the sink, Jack snorted. "For someone who supposedly knows better, you don't have much self-control."

"Fuck you." Adam was too tired or too drunk, or too much of both, to put real effort into the words.

"No, and that's what I'm talking about. You used Toomey to scratch an itch, and now you used him to get to me, all because you *want* something you can't have."

"Wow. And you said *I* was arrogant. Who said I went to your place looking for sex?"

"What the hell else was I supposed to think? You show up, unannounced, with a bottle of bourbon. Isn't that foreplay in your book?"

When he didn't get an immediate retort, Jack shook the last of the alcohol out of the bottle, set it beside the other one, and then turned around. Half expecting to find Adam passed out, he was shocked out of his anger to see the man back in the chair, elbows on knees and face buried in his hands.

"Adam, what's wrong?"

"They shut us down."

"What? Why?"

"Because of you." Lifting his face, Adam found the strength to glare at him. "That's why I went to your place tonight. To let you know that if the Judge kills again, it's on your head. Excuse me for bringing some Dutch courage."

Jack sat in the other chair. "Why did they shut Infinity down?"

"You know why. They've been trying to stop us from the first day."

"ADFIS did this? Why now and not earlier?"

Adam gave him a withering grimace. "Before, they couldn't point to the fact that the ISO pulled their 'advisor' because of a 'lack of new evidence' and 'insufficient reason to warrant the ISO's further involvement.' That's what your boss said you reported to him when he called to say you wouldn't be working with us anymore. I can't fucking believe you, Jack. You got advice on how to deal with your psycho boyfriend and then fucked off. I didn't think you were that selfish, but what really hurts is that you gave *them* a reason to shut us down."

Jack slumped back in his chair. Goddamn John Axworthy. For someone who worked in international relations, he was about as diplomatic as a toddler with a gun.

"It wasn't me," Jack said. "I never said any of that. The decision to pull me off the strike force came from well above me." He couldn't admit that he hadn't protested, that he had, in fact, rejoiced.

Adam gave him a sceptical eyebrow quirk.

"I swear. Jesus, if anyone had suspected ADFIS would react like this, I don't think they would have pulled me out." At least, he hoped so. "What happens now?"

"Now? Steph gets reassigned, I go back to bloody Melbourne, and we wait for the Judge to kill another poor person before anything more gets done." His hand moved, as if seeking a bottle. Finding nothing, he moaned. "And I just signed a fucking lease on a far too expensive apartment right in the middle of the bloody city. Shit."

"You were really going to move here?"

Adam shrugged. "Been thinking about it for a while now. I have a friend here who's been after me to join her practice. And, you know, there are other benefits." For a moment, his gaze locked on Jack, and then his eyelids closed. "Well, I thought there were."

Sighing, Jack stood and hauled Adam to his feet. "Come on, bedtime."

"Alone," Adam said mournfully as he stumbled along, one arm slung across Jack's shoulders. Sitting on the end of the bed and struggling with his shoes, he muttered, "I've changed my diagnosis on your boyfriend. Probable obsessive-compulsive personality disorder with *definite* violent tendencies. He needs help, Nishant."

Jack took pity on him and removed the remaining shoe. "I know. I'm doing my best." Except that he wasn't. He'd felt so guilty about it, he hadn't bothered to deal with the outcome of that conversation. Not when things had seemed to be going better.

"Proper help." Adam crawled up the mattress and curled around a pillow. "I know his type. They're my specialty. He's only going to get worse before he gets better. Don't ask me, though. I have too much of a personal interest to be objective."

"Him pulling guns on you wasn't personal." Fingers crossed. "It was surprise and ingrained habit."

"Yeah, sure. That's what I'm talking about," he said sourly. "Go home, Jack. Make sure he's okay. I promise to never darken your doorstep ever again."

With the realisation that Adam was right about everything, Jack left.

The facsimile of a friendship he and Adam had was over now. Not that it would have lasted beyond the parameters of the job, anyway, but if there had been a chance it could have survived, it was crushed now. Bridge burned.

Ethan needed help. Jack himself would be a bigger mess than he was if it hadn't been for the therapists he'd seen over the years, and he'd only had to deal with a fraction of what Ethan had been subjected to. The biggest hurdle wasn't getting Ethan to agree, though. It was convincing him that the only way it could be done was through the Office. No other psychiatrist would be allowed access to the intelligence Ethan knew.

Lastly, another innocent was going to die. It was the only way the strike force would be reinstated.

As he got on the bike, Jack noticed a familiar figure coming down the footpath towards the hotel. Hands shoved in his front pockets, head down, shoulders hunched, Constable Toomey didn't notice Jack. Out of uniform, Jack finally saw what Adam had been talking about.

The man was *built*, his long, muscular legs encased in tight jeans, abs and pecs shown off by the silk shirt clinging to his torso, and when he turned to go into the building, his arse proved to be perfect.

The odd sensation the man's appearance left in Jack's stomach wasn't jealousy. It wasn't attraction, either. Mostly. Jack wasn't sure what the rest of it might be, but it wasn't an entirely comfortable feeling. He squashed it down. Adam knew what he was doing. Probably.

All the rage that had driven Jack to Adam's had changed to regret by the time he got home. Jack hadn't done enough to catch the killer or make sure Ethan was okay. So, he was saddened but not surprised to find the apartment empty when he got in. All of Ethan's clothes were gone. His books. The weapons he'd stashed around the place. The photo of Jack's parents he'd moved to a more central spot had been returned to where he found it.

"Jack," Ethan said, tone flat when he answered Jack's call.

"Are you okay?"

"I'm fine." The studious neutrality of the words said otherwise.

"I yelled at Adam for a while."

"I imagine you did."

Knowing Ethan wouldn't want to hear Adam's justification for invading their privacy, or that he hadn't known he *was*, Jack just said, "He won't be back. Will you?"

After a long silence, Ethan murmured, *"I don't know. I can't feel safe there, Jack. I'm sorry."*

Jack swallowed his guilt and worry. "Don't be. I know you can't. Are you safe now?"

"I am." His tone softened, as if grateful Jack cared enough to ask.

"Good. Can I come to you?"

Another pause in which Jack could hear Ethan breathing on the far end of the connection. *"Not yet. I need to be on my own for a while. I left Shorty with Mrs. Langridge on the first floor. Please fetch him back. You shouldn't be alone because of me."*

"Okay." Jack held back the desire to plead. He'd only just smoothed over his last fuck-up. "Just . . . let me know how you're doing."

"I will. See you soon, Jack."

His laugh was strained as Ethan cut the call. The last time he'd said that, it had taken four months.

Jack fetched Shorty, and Mrs. Langridge informed him she'd found the dachshund leashed to her doorknob, his bag of goodies beside him. Assuring her it had just been a miscommunication, he took Shorty home and watched as the dog searched every nook and cranny for Ethan. Eventually, Shorty curled up with Jack on the couch, his chin on Jack's chest, big eyes sad and confused.

"Yeah, mate," Jack whispered, scratching his head. "I miss him, too."

THIRTY-FIVE AFTER

Mc Intosh studied the results of Jack's cognitive model while he and Lewis fidgeted in their seats. Once McIntosh agreed with Jack's conclusion about the model results, he would be heading out once more. In an hour, whoever had left the message on his bathroom mirror would be at the Cenotaph, and Jack would be there as well.

"It says here there is a 71.54 percent probability the serial killer is Ethan Blade," McIntosh said.

"Yes, ma'am."

She looked at him over her glasses. "But you don't agree."

"No, ma'am."

Her gaze flickered to Lewis.

"It's not my personal feelings getting in the way," Jack said, informing her that Lewis was in the know at the same time. "I know he's come up as the top result, but it's not him."

"He fits the profile, a little too well," she reminded him gently. "How can you be so sure?"

"You said it yourself. He fits it 'a little *too* well.' Lewis's gut told him the tickets weren't about the Messiah because it was too coincidental. I'm saying the same thing here."

Lewis frowned. "You're insinuating that the Judge is not only after you, but that he knows a lot about Ethan Blade's tactics and skills, *and* that he knows about your relationship with Blade."

Hearing it spoken aloud made it all the more real. How neatly Jack had been played, once again.

"Yes. He's not an SAS soldier. He's like Ethan, and Eve Garrote. He's an assassin, not a serial murderer." When they still looked sceptical, Jack rushed on. "It fits. Before Ethan came here, he said he had to severe ties with his associates. He's never said who they are or what they do, but what if one of them took exception to him retiring? Because of me?"

McIntosh shook her head. "Are you saying he killed five people just to get to you?"

"No. Only one. The first two in Melbourne, I don't know what his motive was there. Maybe it wasn't him. Maybe he's just copying that killer's style. They were killed years ago, well before I met Ethan. They don't count. As for Williams and Luntz, I think they were *assassinated* as opposed to being victims of a serial killer. Lew said they were the only ones with something in common. The storage units. I bet whatever's in them is why they were killed. Our guy just used those tickets as an excuse to come here and play his mind-fuck games with me and Ethan. Morrissey is the odd man out. He's also the reason I was called in."

"That's far-fetched, even for me," Lewis said. "How would the Judge know *you* would be called in?"

McIntosh looked down at her screen, still filled with the results of Jack's model. "Because he was the one who suggested you to Stephanie Phelps."

Jack nodded. "He was right there in the middle of it. I can't believe we all missed it for so long. I even explained it. Familiarity, confidence, and forgery."

"The second most likely candidate from your model." McIntosh set the screen down and said grimly, "Constable Richard Toomey."

Things happened quickly then. Lydia organised a strike team to search the storage units, and Lewis began digging into Richard Toomey, revealing a stolen identity and a fake transfer from a rural police station with the first few probes. Jack went down to the armoury and restocked. He was in the garage, arranging panniers on a new bike when Lewis found him.

"Not sure if it adds much at this stage, but I worked out what was bugging me about the Bible quotes." He gave Jack an eye roll. "I'm disappointed that a good Christian boy like you missed it."

"I'm a boy and Christian, but not good. What is it?"

"I don't think the quotes were only picked because they related to the victims. All of the Sydney quotes have the number thirteen in either chapter or verse. Both for one of them. Adam's quote was Matthew, chapter thirteen, verse thirteen. It means something to him."

"Yeah." It made a sick sense in light of everything else they'd just learned. "Or to someone else involved in this."

"Blade?"

"Maybe. Either way, it's time to get this done." He got on the bike.

"The strike teams are in position. We got a clear signal off your implant. You're good to go." Lewis paused, then added, "Don't go."

"I have to. If Ethan set up the meet, I have to be there for him."

"So he can shoot you?"

"So I can tell him the truth."

"And if it's Toomey who's waiting?"

Jack smiled. "We'll get some answers at least."

Conceding, Lewis stepped back, and Jack roared out of the underground carpark. Stealth was pointless at this stage. Toomey knew so much already; trying to hide the rest was useless.

He came in along Pitt Street, turned down Angel Lane, and parked. Overhead, the birdcages were silent, the recordings of native bird calls turned off for the night. The art installation was too flimsy to support a grown person's weight, but Jack scanned the hanging cages, anyway. Now he knew the nature of his foe, he wasn't taking any chances. Convinced it was clear, he headed towards Martin Place and the Cenotaph.

Sidling between two buildings facing onto Martin Place, Jack stopped just before stepping out into the pedestrian mall. Back to the wall, he peered around the corner. The Cenotaph sat in the middle of the paved street, a stone sepulchral guarded at either end by a bronze soldier and sailor. On the face Jack could see, the words "Lest We Forget" were visible. Jack had attended several ANZAC Day services at the Cenotaph, and the thought that Toomey could defile it with his sick games made Jack furious. Several of the streetlights around the Cenotaph weren't working, leaving most of the area in vague shadows. Good for sneak attacks.

A gun barrel settled low on Jack's side.

Far from shocked, Jack merely whispered, "About time you showed up."

"Aw, as smart as he is handsome. Finally got a clue, did you?" Eve Garrote moved in front of him and pressed against his body. She followed his line of sight, her breasts rubbing across his chest. "Mm, that's not all you got. Is that a gun in your pants or are—"

"All right, enough with the bad jokes." He indicated they move into the deeper shadows. "Ethan asked you to pick up the ticket on me, didn't he?"

Garrote's teeth flashed in the darkness. "It's sweet you call him that. And yes. I owed him a favour, and this is how he calls it in. To protect *you*. I couldn't actually give a toss about you, but he is my brother and we always stay loyal to family." She twirled her gun around a finger and winked at him. "Mostly, anyway."

Jack stared at her. Without the sunglasses he got a look at her eyes. White irises, too wide pupils.

Brother? It made him think of Ethan's associate he met a year ago. A woman who'd helped them find out who the traitor within the Office was. A woman who'd treated Ethan like an annoying sibling—who'd had white eyes as well. A family of Sugar Babies, at least two of whom were assassins. Christ.

Putting that aside for now, Jack concentrated on the immediate situation. "Is Ethan here?"

"*Ethan* is around. If things go as planned, everything will be sorted out while we're tucked away safely." She heaved a theatrical sigh. "And then you two lovebirds can fly off into the sunset. If the sheer *cuteness* of it doesn't make me shoot you first."

"You're weird. You know that, right?"

"He said you do that. Just say things no sane person would when talking to one of us."

"I stick with what works," Jack said dryly. "Are we really just going to stand here all—"

"Reardon!"

Jack jerked. His name bounced back and forth across the empty street. He didn't recognise the voice, but then he hadn't spoken to Toomey a lot, and had no doubt the man hadn't been using his real voice. No doubt because the accent on the word had been British.

"Uh-oh," Garrote said. "Looks like things did not go according to plan." She shook her head despairingly and whispered, "He should've learned long ago that they never do."

Jack made sure his USP was loose in its holster, checked his backup in the back of his pants, and lastly swung the black Austeyr assault rifle around to his front. "In that case, let's wing it."

He headed into the open space of Martin Place, ignoring Garrote's hissed "You're an idiot." This meeting had taken too long to happen. Now it was here, Jack wasn't waiting any longer. Not when it meant Ethan had possibly been incapacitated—or worse.

"Here he is," Toomey said as Jack came into the clear. The tall man stood by the Cenotaph, feet shoulder width apart, hands on hips. He was a dark shape amongst the shadows, just a hint of blond hair picking up some of the distant lights. "Surprise."

Jack trained his sight on the bastard. Just because he wasn't obviously armed didn't mean he wasn't dangerous. "Not exactly surprised, *Constable Toomey*. I figured it out ages ago." What was a little white lie between enemies?

"Clever. Of course, you didn't work it out soon enough to help poor Adam Quinn. Don't feel sad about that, though. He didn't work it out, either. Until it was too late."

Advancing slowly, Jack swept the surrounding area, hoping for a glimpse of Ethan, or at least no more unknown players. "Is Adam still alive?"

Toomey tilted his head and smirked. "It's nice that you're worried about him. You must actually like him, because let's face it, he's not that good of a fuck." The conceited smile faded, and deadly serious, he said, "Not like your other boyfriend. He's good, isn't he."

Jack went cold. He came to a stop and his finger rubbed against the rifle's trigger guard. "What did you do to Ethan?"

"Nothing he didn't let me do. All to keep you safe."

Close enough to see the man lick his lips, Jack shuddered. The bruises. The secret meetings. It all made sense now. "You sick psycho."

"That's not fair. I had a traumatic childhood." Toomey grinned.

"You're about to have a traumatic adulthood," Jack snarled. "Tell me where they are."

Folding his arms across his chest, Toomey asked, "Or what? You'll shoot me? You'll never find them then."

"I worked out who you were. I can find them."

Toomey laughed. A genuinely amused sound. "You're not that smart. I practically handfed you the clues. Kill me and you'll never find them. Isn't that right, Nine?" While he was still talking, he threw himself at the Cenotaph, back pressed to the huge stone slab. A gun appeared in his right hand, and he pointed it ninety degrees off Jack.

Tracking Toomey's aim, wondering who else had joined them, Jack found Garrote crouched by one of the post office's pillars. She had a gun on Toomey, held steady in two hands.

"Don't try it, Too," she said. "You've always been a useless shot."

Too? Or perhaps Jack hadn't heard her right. Yet, they seemed to know each other. What the fuck?

Toomey chuckled. "You're right. I missed him by a mile today." He waved the gun in Jack's direction. "Of course, that was just for fun. I liked seeing him be all butch. Maybe that's what One-three sees in him. A real man's man."

"You're just jealous," Garrote said, a hint of something . . . *playful* in her words.

"Probably. I mean, he—" A nod at Jack. "—has something I always wanted but never got."

Stomach clenching, Jack settled his sight on Toomey's chest. "You *want* Ethan?"

"Wow." Toomey turned towards him. "It's all about sex with you. No wonder—"

Garrote sprang out of cover and advanced swiftly while talking in a language that may have been German.

In the same instant, Toomey shifted from smiling rogue to intent deadliness. He lunged to meet her, covering the distance in a few long strides, even though Garrote kept her gun on him. She didn't fire, and the moment they were close enough, she tossed the weapon and they clashed.

Toomey had over a foot on Garrote. His arms and legs were longer, giving his punches more reach and his kicks more power. Garrote, however, was fast. Height had some advantages, but it also slowed a fighter down. It took longer for his punches to land, whereas Garrote could dart inside his reach, deliver a short, hard blow, and get away before he could retaliate. It was mesmerising to watch as the assassins battled across the width of Martin Place. Jack tried to follow Toomey with his rifle, but the mix of bodies meant he'd be just as likely to shoot Garrote. If he managed to hit either of them at all.

Garrote kept up a running commentary in German, sounding at times teasing, pleading, or insulting. Toomey never responded, but he appeared to understand. Mostly, his face was blank—an expression Jack knew from Ethan at his most distant—but occasionally, something Garrote said got to him. He scowled a couple of times and flinched once, after which his face closed right down and his efforts to disable Garrote increased.

Jack had to do something. The combatants were too evenly matched. He couldn't risk Toomey getting the upper hand, so he swapped the rifle for his USP and moved in.

"Richard Toomey," he called. "You're under arrest. Cease and desist. If you come quietly—"

Toomey dodged a kick from Garrote and spun towards Jack. His wrist flicked, and Jack threw himself sideways. The knife struck his arm at the wrong angle, the blade slicing through material, but a sharp sting let Jack know he'd been cut.

"Toomey!" Jack firmed up his aim, but before he could take the shot, Garrote danced back in and swept her foot up behind Toomey's knee.

Leg buckling, Toomey turned the fall into a roll and came up clear of Garrote.

Jack fired, the sound drowned out by the sudden roar of a familiar engine. As Toomey jerked back from the impact, Victoria charged up Martin Place. Jack scrambled out of the sleek black car's path, dropping into a roll and coming up on one knee in time to see the Vanquish turn into a tight drift. Her back end skidded around and slammed into Toomey. The tall man tumbled away towards the Cenotaph.

Trembling amidst the smoke created by her tyres, boot towards Jack, Victoria was as beautiful as an oasis in the desert. Her passenger-side door opening was like the light of Heaven.

"Jack! Get in."

And Ethan's voice a healing balm on every one of Jack's hurts. Still . . .

"We need to secure Toomey." Jack stood and started around the car, USP at the ready.

"Jack, leave him. Nine will take care of him. Let's go."

Jack was tempted. Ethan was here, and Jack could be with him in a couple of seconds, but he had a job to do. He moved along the left side of the car, stepping out around the open door.

"Toomey," he called. "Drop your weapons and show me your hands."

The driver's-side door opened and Ethan stood up, a Desert Eagle in one hand, aimed beyond the car's bonnet. "Jack," he said grimly. "Leave it. Get in the car."

"Yes, Jack," Toomey purred from behind the Cenotaph. "Best you do as the little woman says and get in the car."

Jack bit back a snarl. He wasn't going to let this fucker know how much he was reacting to his taunts. "I'm taking you in, Toomey. You're going to tell me where Adam is."

"No." Toomey stepped into view. "You're going to leave, or I break her neck."

Garrote was quiet in Toomey's hold. He had one arm around her neck, his big hand completely covering one side of her face. The other hand gripped her shoulder. All he had to do was pull and twist and she was dead.

"Nine," Ethan said, low and steady.

Flashing a smile, Garrote said, "My fault, One-three. Get out of—"

Toomey broke her neck.

THIRTY-SIX BEFORE

Jack told McIntosh he'd run into Adam in a bar and discovered the fate of the strike force that way. He had to talk fast to convince her, but she agreed and Jack was back on the Infinity case. Lewis and Lydia had headed up to Byron Bay, but both came back when they learned what had happened. Leaving the rest of their team to their time off, they made up Jack's support at the Office.

Toomey had smuggled out a lot of the information from the LAC, and Jack and Adam spent days in his hotel suite, continuing the search for the Judge. Adam was short with Jack at first, but their old working comradery soon asserted itself, and by the third day, Adam was teasing Jack about his habit of pacing while thinking.

Each night Jack called Ethan and they chatted for hours. Wanting to be totally upfront, Jack told Ethan he and Adam were working together again. Ethan initially went quiet but made an effort to accept it at face value.

Six days into the new arrangement, Jack was leaving the Oaks when he saw Toomey on the stairs. They only exchanged grunts in passing. Adam didn't talk about his relationship with the tall constable, and Jack didn't ask. He didn't want to know, and didn't really want to explore why he didn't want to know. It was Adam's life; he could do what he wanted. Trying to convince himself of that, Jack stepped out onto the footpath and stopped in mid-thought.

Victoria idled in the drop-off zone.

Moving slow so he could relish the vision of her low-slung shape just in case she turned out to be a mirage, Jack approached the car. When he was barely a foot away, the passenger door opened.

"Hurry up, Jack."

Hesitation vanishing, Jack folded himself into the car.

God, he'd missed Ethan. Missed his shy smile and his dark sunglasses. Missed touching his face and smelling his hair and tasting his skin.

"Hey," Jack said, unable to stop grinning.

Ethan shook his head fondly. "Close the door, Jack. We have somewhere to be."

Yes, he'd even missed his snotty accent.

Jack closed the door and buckled up. Ethan put Victoria in gear and palmed the steering wheel, sliding her out into traffic. It was a shame they were in the middle of the city. Jack would have really appreciated watching Ethan unleash the car on the open road, to know that he was happy and peaceful.

"Where are we going?" Jack rested his hand on Ethan's thigh.

Ethan glanced at his hand, then covered it with his own between gear changes. "It's a surprise."

Groaning, Jack muttered, "I don't like surprises."

"I think you'll like this one."

"Did you move back in? I'd love that surprise."

For a moment, Ethan's fingers tightened on Jack's, then he lifted his hand to the gearstick. "No. I do hope it's just as good, though."

Jack brought Ethan's hand to his lips and kissed his knuckles. "It will be."

Ethan squeezed Jack's hand warmly.

Out of the filing cabinet came an old memory.

Wish you were here?

Those words, seared into Jack's mind when he was certain he wasn't going to survive the torture shack, had tormented him for over a year. For so long he'd battled them, looking for something to anchor him in one place. It still amazed him he'd found a place to stand thanks to Ethan, because it had been Ethan Blade who'd planted those words and their destructive intent in his head. But *that* Ethan was as distant as *that* Jack was now. They'd both come so far, on their own and together, that those men were like mirages in the desert.

Jack drank in Ethan's profile, loving the purse of his lips and the furrow of his brows as another driver cut in front of them. Such a small thing, and yet the pin was pulled and Jack's grenade went off.

Amidst the light and heat, Jack said, "Ethan."

Ethan glanced at him, smiling softly. "Yes, Jack?"

"I—" His throat closed up. Taking a deep breath, he tried again. "I . . . have a surprise for you, too." Shit. Not what he'd meant to say.

"You do?" He indicated and went around a corner. "Is it in your pants?"

Jack snorted. "Idiot. No." Then after a moment, he admitted, "Actually, it is."

Ethan's grin set off the secondary charge in Jack's chest. "Hmm, lucky we've arrived, then."

Startled, Jack took notice of the world outside the car. They were on Bathurst Street, at the Hyde Park end. Ethan slowed Victoria and turned into an underground carpark of a building that had only finished construction a couple of months back. A flash of a card at a reader on the wall had the boom gate rising, and they drove down into the darkness.

They parked and Ethan led him to a bank of lifts. Two were normal, but the third had a restricted sign on it and a keypad instead of a call button. Ethan showed Jack the code, and the doors opened immediately. Inside the private lift, Jack wrapped his arms around Ethan and simply held him. Buried his face in his neck and breathed in deep. Ethan sighed and leaned on him, hands fisting up the back of Jack's shirt and holding on like he would never let go.

"I missed you," Ethan whispered. "So much."

Stupidly pleased, Jack kissed his neck. "You did?"

Ethan thumped a fist against his back. "Of course I did. I'm sorry I left, but it felt like old times, and the only thing I could do was fight or scramble."

"So you scrambled. That's okay." Jack ran his hand through Ethan's hair, smiling when the man pushed into the touch, his eyes drifting closed. "You didn't go far, and you talked to me. And you weren't gone for four months this time."

Nodding, Ethan murmured, "I'm getting better."

Jack pulled him closer. "Yeah, you are."

The lift came to a stop and the doors opened onto a small elegant foyer. Ethan strode over the gleaming marble floor and, once again, showed Jack the code to unlock the next door. Made of steel, the door was heavy and solid and thoroughly practical as a security measure, but the metal had been beaten so it looked fancily distressed and sophisticated. Beyond it, the penthouse opened up into a space probably as big as Jack's entire home.

Jack wandered in a few steps, speechless. Underfoot, the floor was dark, polished wood, covered here and there with thick earth-toned rugs. The walls at either end were rough red brick. On one, a large TV hung over an electric fireplace. At the far end was a kitchen with shining appliances. The furniture in between was in shades of brown and cream, except for a large L-shaped suede couch in deep, dark red. One side faced the TV, the other looked out through a floor-to-ceiling window with an incredible view of Hyde Park, the cathedral glowing in the sunset light in the distance. Above, the ceiling beams were exposed.

"Do you like it?" Ethan moved past Jack to put his car keys in a bowl on a long sideboard.

"It's amazing. This is your place?"

"I bought it off the plans nine months ago and paid a bit more to have some extras added to the construction. Since I lost the warehouse in Ingleburn, I needed another safe place here, and this time, I thought I'd try something a bit more . . . normal."

"This much space in Sydney is *not* normal. Bedrooms?"

"Two, a bathroom, and combined laundry and home gym."

"Jesus," Jack hissed. "Just how rich are you?"

"Substantially less now that I'm spending all this money and not working."

"That settles it. My next career is kept man."

"If you wish, Jack," Ethan tossed over his shoulder with a smile. He headed to the kitchen. "Drink?"

"Just water." Jack had plans for how the rest of the night would go and he didn't want to be inhibited at all. "Did you do the decorating yourself?"

"Is it all right?"

"It's great. And the security? Done by Saint Security Incorporated?" he teased.

Ethan blushed. "Of course." He handed Jack a bottle of water.

Taking it, Jack brushed the knuckles of his other hand over Ethan's ribs, where he'd had a particularly nasty bruise a couple of weeks back. "Is this what caused the bruises?"

"It can be hard work sometimes. Do you like my surprise?"

"A lot." Jack hugged him. "Do you want your surprise now?"

"Shall I get it for myself?" Blushing hard, Ethan reached for Jack's crotch.

Jack knocked his hand aside. "How about I get it and you behave." Loving Ethan's wicked laugh, he retrieved the phone from his back pocket. "Your surprise is on here. I hope you like it." He *really* hoped it was a good surprise. When he'd first done it, it had felt right, but now, looking at Ethan's wary but interested expression, he wondered. "I did some research this week and found this." He keyed up the song and hit Play.

Soft, tinkling strains like a child's music box, then a woman's sweet voice singing in French. Jack had read the lyrics in English and could pick out chicken, white, and moon, but that was all. Ethan, however, was entranced. He stared at the phone fixedly, hands half-raised as if he might snatch it off Jack or dash it to the floor. After the first couple of verses, he whisper-sang along, his voice a little off tune but word perfect. Jack couldn't read the silence when the lullaby finished. Didn't know if he'd blundered epically or not.

"Was it the right one?" he asked cautiously.

Ethan nodded, still focused on the phone.

"Was it—oh." Jack staggered as Ethan crashed into him. Arms tight around his neck, Ethan held on like Jack was his life preserver in stormy waters. "I guess it was good, then."

"Very good."

"I'm glad. It—"

Ethan pulled away sharply, grabbed Jack's shirt, and dragged him over to the couch, where he made Jack sit in the corner.

"I had planned to do this tonight, regardless. But later. Much later, when I'd worked up the courage," Ethan said as he took off his sunglasses and dropped to his knees in front of Jack. "That was more than a lullaby. It was something I thought I'd lost so long ago. Thank you, Jack. It means . . . so much."

Daring not to hope, Jack's dick didn't get the message and hardened. "Ethan, you don't need—"

Ethan stopped him with two fingers against his lips. "I want to," he said, tone firm. "There will be some rules, though. No touching. Put your arms along the back of the couch."

Jack obeyed instantly. "Done."

"And no talking."

Silently, Jack nodded.

"Legs apart."

He spread them as far as they could, knees pushing into the seat of the couch on either side. Ethan took a couple of deep breaths, gaze focusing somewhere around Jack's belly, looking neither at his face or his crotch. He was clearly psyching himself up for this, and Jack was torn between telling him he didn't have to and wanting to stay quiet in the hopes that this was actually going to happen. He was tipping towards the former when Ethan's hands landed on Jack's thighs, just resting there; then they squeezed gently and, ever so deliciously slow, slid upwards.

God. Jack wanted to say something. *Only if you really want.* Or *Please.* Maybe *Let me go first.* But he followed Ethan's rules and didn't say or do anything. His dick was a little bit unsure as well. Hard but wary. Its doubts disappeared when Ethan's hands reached his crotch, gliding over him, one after the other, and back again, returning to his thighs. This happened several more times, moving further up Jack's abdomen with each sweep, until Ethan was reaching up to his pectorals. His palms were warm and firm, rubbing Jack's peaked nipples against the cotton of his shirt, sending jolts of pleasure through his chest, before they journeyed downwards once more. This time, they didn't move past the waistband of his jeans. They stopped instead and unbuttoned them. Fly undone, Ethan tugged and, hoping it didn't violate the rules, Jack lifted his hips enough for his pants to be pulled down to expose his undies and straining dick. Down came his boxer briefs, and Ethan's calloused hand scooped Jack's dick and balls into the open.

Jack dropped his head back and stared at the ceiling. The sight of Ethan's fingers closing around his dick was too much. His heart was already racing, his lungs heaving and his throat aching with the need to say things. All sorts of things, silly and sweet and stupidly tender. If he saw how the dark shade of his body made Ethan's pale skin glow, then it would all be over but for the tissues and apologies.

It was hard to follow the rules. Each stroke of Ethan's hand up and down his hot shaft sent waves of electricity through his groin, making his thighs shake and his stomach clench. The grenade was going off like fireworks each time Ethan rubbed his thumb over the raw head of his dick. He wanted, *needed*, to shift his hips, to thrust into the perfect grip, to ease the growing vibration in his guts. And it all just got better, or worse, when Ethan's other hand cupped his balls and fondled them.

Ethan had touched him like this before. Given him hand jobs to completion or just built the tension until Jack's only recourse was to fuck him senseless. This time, though, anticipation, and a touch of concern, flavoured the sensations with a headier spice, making each touch and caress so much more potent and meaningful. Which all went out the window when Ethan's mouth touched his dick.

Jack nearly came. A well-timed squeeze of his balls stopped it, letting him ease down and really experience the soft, feathery kisses along his shaft, the lingering press of lips to the tip. Down the other side, then back up, this time with the point of Ethan's tongue joining in. Several more trips up and down, the kisses becoming harder, open-mouthed, until he was outright licking Jack from root to tip, lapping at the leaking pre-cum and teasing his tongue across his slit and into the V under his glans. Jack had to bite his lips together to keep from telling Ethan how good it felt, how much he was loving this, how much he—

Ethan closed his mouth over the head of Jack's dick and sucked. A strangled, inarticulate sound escaped Jack. Thankfully it was so twisted by ecstasy it didn't count as talking, and Ethan didn't stop. He slid further down, moving slow but devotedly, his tongue and lips doing things to Jack he hadn't felt in a very long time.

Fingers digging into the couch cushions, Jack lifted his head and watched. He was already so close to orgasm it wouldn't matter if he went now. Amazingly, he didn't blow at his first sight of Ethan sucking him, but that was because the physicality of it faded under a new onslaught.

Ethan was gorgeous, and not just because his handsome face was so close to Jack's crotch, or his beautiful lips were wrapped around his shaft, leaving glistening trails as he moved up and down. It was because, as if sensing Jack's gaze, he titled his head and looked back at him.

Everything snapped into place. This was it. This was all Jack would ever need. Not the blowjob, but the connection. The gut-deep sense of knowing this man, of accepting all of his quirks and foibles, realising that he didn't want anyone else, on any level. And understanding right down to his marrow that Ethan felt the same way.

Closing his fist around the base of Jack's shaft, Ethan sped up his sucking. The glorious tugging on Jack's insides increased until it felt like everything was in motion. Hot, rushing waves rolled through him, driving every skerrick of Jack's being towards and into this stunning man.

With a final, hard suck, Jack came in a blinding rush.

THIRTY-SEVEN
AFTER

Ethan screamed in denial and rage and opened fire.

Toomey held Garrote's body as a shield and dived for the protection of the Cenotaph. Jack got off a couple of shots, but a deeply embedded and unshakable faith in what the Cenotaph represented stopped his finger when Toomey disappeared behind it. Ethan loosed several more rounds, none of them coming close to his target, fired off in anger and frustration. Jack had never seen Ethan shoot in anything other than calm deliberation, and it scared him.

"Ethan, let's go."

After a moment, Ethan got back into the car, and the instant Jack was in, he threw the idling engine into reverse and hit the accelerator. Victoria rocketed backwards, the Cenotaph and its hidden psychopath quickly diminishing in the windscreen. Ethan drove twisted around, looking behind them, one hand on the wheel, the other on the back of Jack's seat. His expression was blank, focused on where they were going, while Jack could only stare at where they'd been.

He'd spent most of the day fearing Eve Garrote and her intentions, and now, he still wasn't certain of her motives. Yet, Jack had felt the rawness of Ethan's reaction to her death. The sound of his scream still scraped over Jack's nerves, making him wish desperately the woman was still alive, just to save Ethan the pain.

"Hold on," Ethan said, voice rough but steady.

Knowing better than to question, Jack got a hold on the door and seat and braced.

With a squeal of tyres and brakes, Ethan spun Victoria through a tight reverse one-eighty; then they raced away in the right direction and Jack couldn't see the Cenotaph anymore.

At the end of the pedestrian mall, Ethan squeezed the Aston Martin out between the stanchions and onto George Street. Car horns greeted their surprise intrusion into the traffic, but Ethan didn't stick around, weaving through two lanes and rapidly leaving everyone else behind.

They were several blocks away when Jack asked, "Where are we going?"

Another couple of corners went by, then Ethan said, "The last safe place I know."

Jack wasn't sure if he was shocked or not when Ethan turned onto a very familiar street. They'd driven along this one together once before. Not in Victoria, but in a throwaway car Ethan had crashed through the front wall of the Neville Crawley Building. This time, however, he turned into the carpark, and Jack gave him his code to open the gate. Inside, Ethan parked where Jack indicated, turned the car off, and then sat still.

Alerted by a message Jack had fired off to Lewis when he realised where they were going, a strike team was waiting for them. McIntosh and Lewis were with them, but no one came forwards, just waited for them to make the first move.

"Ethan?" Jack wanted to touch him, but he exuded a clear not-now vibe. Besides, there were eight pairs of highly critical eyes on them.

"I'm all right."

"Are you sure you want to do this?"

With visible effort, Ethan nodded. "It's my only option."

Low and painfully, Jack murmured, "You could scramble again."

"Would you come with me?"

"Yes."

Ethan faced him. He struggled to keep his face neutral, but his lips warred between a smile and grimace. "Truly?"

"Truly," Jack said, surprised at how easily it came. "I mean, I have to find Adam first, but immediately after that."

The smile won. "Jack."

Christ. He'd missed the whole sentence-in-his-name thing. "Okay." His voice was gruff. "Let's get this over with."

Jack went first, hands empty and clearly displayed. He was patted down very thoroughly. The fact he'd smuggled an illegal weapon into the building was still fresh in everyone's memory. After Jack had warned the strike team, Ethan emerged, hands up. He stood patiently while he was searched and a remarkable amount of weapons removed from his person. There was a short argument when the team leader wanted to take Victoria away and have her searched as well. McIntosh interceded and the car was left unmolested.

Then they were escorted out of the garage. Not to the cells Ethan had been locked in previously, but to a meeting room on the tenth floor. Tan showed up and sat in on the debrief, watching Ethan with something close to desire. McIntosh led the questioning.

"It was pure coincidence," Ethan explained. "On my part at least. I had no idea the man you call Toomey was in Sydney. I arrived to . . ." He glanced at Jack, then said, "To be with Jack. I have, technically, retired and had no plans to engage in illegal activities anymore. It wasn't until Jack told me about the strike force that I realised what was going on."

Both directors gave Jack resigned expressions.

"You knew why Toomey's targets where killed?" Tan asked Ethan.

"Yes. I made contact with one of my prior associates and was told about the job Toomey had taken."

Lewis leaned forwards. "You were right, Jack. The answer was in the storage units. Both Williams and Luntz were Disciples of the Messiah. They each had stockpiles of hard drives. Caches of the Messiah's stolen information. Someone out there didn't want the Disciples exposing any of the Messiah's information. Eighty-two Disciples have been killed over the past three months, all around the world. The weird thing is there are no tickets. Not even a hint of them. We don't know who decided these people had to die, or how the assassins got the jobs."

"They're called the Cabal," Ethan said softly. "And they don't need to buy tickets, because they run the assassins who did the jobs. I left the Cabal eleven years ago. It wasn't easy or pretty, and the only way I stayed alive was to independently contract myself back to them."

"The Cabal are the ones responsible for getting rid of Samuel Valadian and exposing Glen Harraway?" McIntosh asked.

"Yes. Valadian's interference with the Russian *bratva* and the drug trade in the Golden Triangle threatened some of the Cabal's long-term goals. Harraway's treason would have eventually destabilised the power of the Meta-State."

Simply because it was something that still played on his mind, Jack asked, "And the Marines in Colombia?"

"The Cabal doesn't care about such small things. That one was just me."

"You told me you were paid for it."

"Yes. I paid myself and wrote it off on my tax."

Jack and Lewis snorted in amusement. McIntosh and Tan weren't as amused.

"So, you knew what Toomey was doing here all along and who his final victim would be." McIntosh's tone and eyes had chilled uncomfortably. "Why didn't you tell Jack?"

"I had promised Jack I was retired and felt he wouldn't like me admitting to still being in touch with that part of my life. At the time, I wasn't aware there would be another death. I believed he was done and only stayed here to stalk Jack. Toomey is the sort of Sugar Baby who reinforces the old 'born psychopaths' theory. He is severely disturbed. Of all of us, he doesn't kill because he's told to, or because he gets paid. He does it because it makes him happy. Killing someone is the ultimate form of control, and he loves controlling people."

"Then everything Jack worked out was right," Lewis said. "But why did Toomey wait so long between Morrissey and Luntz?"

Jack grimaced. "To give himself more time to torment me."

"Partly," Ethan said. "When I knew Toomey was here, I sought him out and tried to convince him to leave. The discussions did not go well."

"The bruises." All Jack could think was Toomey saying, *Nothing he didn't let me do.*

"Yes."

"Then why did he kill Luntz, his last target?" Tan asked.

"He believed Jack and I were no longer seeing each other."

"Is making him think that why you left for the week?" Jack asked warily.

Ethan nudged his knee under the table. "No. Just an unfortunate result."

"Oh," Lewis said in sudden understanding. "That's why you didn't have an alibi for Luntz's death. You were *reuniting*."

"Mr. Thomas." McIntosh cut him a frosty glare.

Lewis ducked his head. "Sorry, ma'am."

She levelled her gaze on Ethan. "And tonight's incident?"

"After Jack was arrested, Toomey wouldn't voluntarily meet with me, so I set it up. I knew he couldn't resist a possible meeting between Jack and myself. Of course, he knew it was a trap and planned accordingly. I asked the woman you know as Eve Garrote to help. She and I had a longstanding agreement that if a ticket was bought on Jack, she or I would pick it up before anyone else and void it. I asked her to go tonight to keep Jack from doing anything foolish. She didn't achieve her objective and lost her life for it."

Ethan's voice was steady, but Jack heard the grief in it. He was probably the only one who did because Tan persisted in asking questions about Garrote's identity and history. Rather than answer, Ethan simply shut up and set his focus on the far wall. As he had in his initial interview with McIntosh, Ethan used silence as a tool and, like then, he wore down Tan's patience. Not used to being outplayed, Tan backed off reluctantly and let McIntosh resume the questioning.

"Toomey bought the second ticket," Ethan confirmed when she asked. "Garrote picked the first one up before Toomey could, so he had to create his own. The Cabal is strict about obedience in its assassins, and Toomey was already in trouble for killing Captain Morrissey without approval. The Cabal wouldn't have approved of the second ticket, but he was desperate."

Tan pierced him with a direct look. "He picked it up under the name Ethan Blade."

"Yes. Three of us operate under that name, and other identities. Toomey used Ethan Blade because of how it would affect Jack."

Jack relayed the events at the Cenotaph, and when that was done, McIntosh and Tan departed to discuss options. After a few silent gestures and commands from Jack, Lewis grumpily left as well.

When it was just the two of them, Ethan stood and paced around the table. "Is this room secure?"

"Yeah, but monitored. They'll have a record of everything we do in here." He ached to hold him, to kiss him, but knew it had no hope of happening in here.

Stopping by the window, Ethan looked out at Darling Harbour for a long time, arms crossed, expression blank. Then he muttered, "I don't care," and came around the table.

Jack got up just in time to catch him in his arms. Ethan pushed into him, as if he could force them into one body. They remained locked together for so long Jack forgot where they were, what had just happened. What was still waiting to happen.

"I'm sorry," he said into Ethan's neck. "About what happened with Adam. It wasn't—"

"I don't care, Jack. I thought I did, but then I realised I was angry at myself, not you. I'm not used to this. I don't know what to do. I just feel so helpless, and I can't cope with that."

"I know. It's okay, we'll work it out. Just don't expect to be an expert overnight. I mean, look at me. I've been here before and I'm still fucking up all over the place."

Ethan nodded against his cheek.

"When this is all over and sorted out, will you talk to someone?" Jack pulled back and studied his expression. "We could go together if you wanted. It would have to be an Office shrink, though."

For a moment, he thought Ethan would bolt again, but he only pulled in a deep breath, then nodded again.

"We're not scrambling?"

Ethan shook his head. "I bought property here." Then he frowned. "And turned myself in to the authorities."

Jack laughed and gave him a squeeze. "It'll be okay. Trust me."

"I do."

They stood together for a while, silent and content. Then because he couldn't seem to shut things away like he once could, Jack had to get some answers. There was so much he wanted to know, but he picked the most immediately important one.

"Can I ask about you and Toomey? You have history, don't you."

Ethan stiffened. When he moved, he gently extracted himself from Jack's arms and stepped back to put a couple of feet of space between them. "Yes. We grew up together. Me, him, and the woman who died tonight."

"You called her Nine."

"It's her name. Toomey is Two. We were named for the order in which we came into the . . . group. All of us are Sugar Babies. Either voluntarily surrendered by the mothers, or abandoned." He couldn't meet Jack's gaze as he spoke, and "abandoned" came out so softly Jack knew Ethan was talking about himself.

"You're Thirteen, aren't you."

"The . . . carers were suspicious, so they refused to call me that. They said one-three instead, and it stuck."

Jack leaned back against the table and gripped its edge to give his hands something to do other than punch walls. "Why call you by numbers instead of your real names?"

"Most of the others didn't actually have *real* names. They'd been in the group since they were newborns. I believe I was the only one to come in at an older age. I was six and had a name and a mother I remembered and I was blind. They were all older, larger, well-established in the group hierarchy."

"You were bullied."

"To put it bluntly. After I had the surgery to allow me to see, it got both worse and better. I could see the attacks coming, but they stopped being *easy* on me."

"Didn't your carers know it was going on?"

Ethan caught his gaze, and in that moment, Ethan Blade was back. "We're Sugar Babies, Jack. They thought we were little better than animals. They knew. They didn't care."

"Fuck." Jack tried to stuff everything Ethan was saying into the filing cabinet, but Ethan kept talking.

"Two was both my worst tormentor and my protector. He could be charming and sweet, which made his attacks so much worse. I was lost and scared. All I knew was sometimes, he would pick me up and hold me, tell me he wouldn't let anyone else touch me, and I believed him. Every time. Then he would cut me, or try to burn me, or leave me at the mercy of the others."

Jesus. Jack was going kick the sick fuck's face in.

"One of the carers was different. She didn't think we were all monsters. I liked her. Perhaps loved her. I called her *mère* once. Mother. She cried. The others never cried for us. She smuggled in movies, and a little DVD player. The movies were dubbed into different languages. Only one of them was in French, and it became my favourite. *Toy Story*."

Trying for levity, Jack said, "I prefer *Finding Nemo*."

"That one was in Japanese. Perhaps we could watch it in English."

"Sounds good."

Ethan smiled, then lost it as he continued. "Two found me one day, watching the movie. He sat with me and watched it. He cuddled me, and laughed and sang, and I thought that was how it would always be with us. When the movie was over, he punched and kicked me until I couldn't get away." He sat in a chair and lifted his left foot. "While I was helpless, he wrote his name on the sole of my foot." Off came his shoe and sock, then he held up his foot for Jack to see. "With a knife."

Jack cradled Ethan's foot in his hands. There, neatly lettered, was "TWO" in thick white scar tissue.

"Two always felt as if he couldn't control me. I had experience none of them did. It made me question everything, including Two's command of the others. I believe he thought that if he wrote his name on me, I would be his."

"And they let him get away with this?"

Ethan put his sock and shoe back on. "When it got infected, they took me to the infirmary."

"And Two? Was he punished?"

"What for? I was the weak one."

"Jesus fucking shit. Ethan—" He couldn't finish the thought. It was too much to get a handle on in one go.

"I survived, Jack, and I'm here now. Not quite right, but getting better." He stood and touched Jack's arm tentatively. "And I may know where Two has Adam."

THIRTY-EIGHT
BEFORE

The rest of the night passed in quiet bliss. Jack returned the blowjob heartily, and they messed around in the shower before tumbling into bed to sleep wound around each other. When he woke, Ethan was sprawled beside him, comatose and drooling. Jack kissed his neck, got up, dressed in fresh clothes Ethan had brought to the penthouse for him, and left a note saying he would be back after work.

He was getting out of the taxi at the Oaks where he'd left his bike when his implant *ping*ed.

"Where are you?" Lewis asked when Jack answered.

"On my way to work. Why?" Right then, his phone for the job started vibrating in his back pocket. Hauling it out, he found several missed calls from the police and Adam. *"What's happened?"*

"We only found out this morning," Lewis said wearily. *"Because this isn't a high-priority case anymore, we don't have a nightshift or we would have heard sooner."*

"Just tell me." Jack stalked to his bike and slung his leg over the seat.

"There's been another death. Brenna Luntz." Lewis rattled off information that could have been copied almost word for word from the Williams file.

"As terrible as it is, this means they'll have to start up Infinity again," Jack said. *"I have missed calls from Quinn I should listen to. I'll let you know what happens."*

He cut the call and then listened to Adam's messages. The first couple were calm, just asking Jack to call back. The next two were a bit more worried, and the last one was a terse demand for Jack to go to the LAC when he finally got the messages. Jack kicked the bike into motion and when he got there, he found Adam outside waiting for him.

"About time, Nishant. Do you sleep like the dead or something?"

"Had my phone on silent. Keep your knickers on. As sad as it is, you can't save her now, but hopefully we'll catch her killer this time."

Adam glared at him. "That's not what's got me upset. Well, it has, but also something else. Come on, let's get in there before the detective blows a gasket."

Grumbling all the way, Adam led him in through the front doors. Newly implemented security measures meant "support personnel" such as Adam no longer got free range on the premises, and he never let Jack forget it. One of the detectives on the investigative team came to fetch them from the foyer and escort them, not to Infinity's old base, but an interview room on the first floor.

"What's this all about?" Jack asked as the detective directed him into one room and Adam into another.

"Just routine, Mr. Reardon. Please take a seat. I won't be long."

Jack went in quietly, and while he waited, he called Lewis and silently filled him in. The only reason Lewis could come up with for Jack's current situation was that he was now a suspect. Neither of them had come up with anything else by the time the detective came back.

"Sorry for the wait." He smiled faintly as he sat opposite Jack. "Like I said before, this is just routine procedure. You were involved with Strike Force Infinity, and now that there's been another death, we just like to touch base with everyone. Make sure you're all okay."

Jack wasn't sure he believed the man but said, "I'm fine, thanks for caring. Does this mean Infinity's been reinstated?"

"We're just waiting on confirmation from the superintendent. Infinity will be up and running by lunchtime."

"Good. I'll put a request in to my boss at the ISO to come back and help." He knew it would be approved.

"That would be great, sir. I know Dr. Quinn finds you invaluable. Now, last night. We couldn't get in touch with you, and you weren't home."

"So?"

The detective frowned at his tone. "As I said, sir, this is just routine. Dr. Quinn and Senior Sergeant Phelps have been asked the same questions. In situations like this, we need to know where everyone who's involved in the investigation is at any time. If we'd been able to reach you through the night, this would be over and we could all be looking for the killer now."

It was a load of crock. "Unless you're arresting me, I don't have to tell you anything."

"That's true, Mr. Reardon, but for your own safety, it would be best if you'd let us know how we can contact you in case of emergency in the future. Or where we can find you."

"Sure." Jack gave him his most insincere smile.

Realising his subterfuge wasn't working, the detective let him out and escorted him and an impatient Adam back to Infinity's base.

"That wasn't routine, was it?" Jack asked, when they were safely inside and alone.

"Not as far as I'm aware."

"Shit. They're checking our alibis. Why would they be checking *our* alibis?"

Adam shrugged. "I'm sure Connors has his reasons. Look, Infinity's back on track, so let's just concentrate on that."

They spent a while getting the room back to how it had been, waiting for Steph to show up and officially get them going again.

"You said something else had you upset," Jack said when they were done. "What is it?"

"Nothing. It was silly."

Jack cocked an eyebrow at him.

Adam wavered, then muttered, "Rich ended it between us."

It took Jack a moment to equate Rich with Constable Toomey. "Oh. Why?"

"Apparently I'm too controlling in bed."

Hiding his relief, Jack patted his shoulder. "I'm sorry, mate. It's probably for the best, though."

"Told you it was stupid." Adam scowled at the ceiling. "He was just a fling. A scratching post. But there was something about him. He could be charismatic. Really attentive. And a bit submissive. I thought he wanted to be controlled."

"Maybe he doesn't know what he wants."

"Didn't you say I knew what everyone wanted and used it to my advantage?"

"When I was angry."

Adam grimaced. "That's usually when the things we really believe come out. Maybe it means I'm not that good at my job after all. I couldn't find the Judge before he killed again. Couldn't give Rich whatever it was he wanted. Couldn't convince you to give me a chance." He shook his head. "I know, I know. You have Mr. Crazy Pants."

"You're a good guy. Smart, fun, sexy. Just because Toomey couldn't see that doesn't mean there's anything wrong with you."

Eyes rolling, Adam said, "Gosh, thanks for the pep talk. I know all that, and yeah, I'll find someone one day. Or maybe a couple of someones. Or a lot of someones. Yeah. A lot would be nice."

Jack laughed. Nothing much kept Adam down when he was up.

Steph arrived a couple of minutes later, and when the reunion was over, she cracked the whip and got them working on the incoming reports from the Luntz scene. Adam immediately started adding things to his profile, just little notes and questions, but he seemed energized by it, as if he'd never doubted himself. And maybe he could fool himself into thinking that, but Jack had seen a spark of honesty in his eyes when he'd spoken about his doubt. Jack just hoped it was a fleeting moment.

By the end of the day, Jack had a massive headache and couldn't say for sure if anything he had done had helped at all. He hadn't experienced the initial flood of information from a fresh crime scene before, and the rate of flow and amount of it had sent him reeling. Adam and Steph had thrived on it, exchanging rapid-fire theories and ideas that changed in an instant when a new piece of evidence was uncovered.

At the end of the day, Jack extracted a promise from Adam that he would go back to his suite at some stage, then went to Bathurst Street. Feeling a little self-conscious, Jack went up to the penthouse, still not quite believing the place existed, or that Ethan called it "their" place. Ethan was doing tai chi in the middle of the living area when Jack walked in, and, needing the soothing calm, Jack changed and joined him. He was feeling better when Ethan served up a plate of seared salmon and Spanish rice for dinner.

"I hope it's all right," Ethan said as he sat opposite Jack.

"It's brilliant."

"You must have had a hard day."

Jack washed down a mouthful with cold beer and said, "Yeah. Things got official again today. The Judge killed another person last night."

Ethan froze. "He did?"

"Woman. Twenty-three years old. He broke into her home and, *God*, he's just a sick fuck. The only good thing is it's made them start up Infinity again, and hopefully this time, they'll catch him." Jack pushed the rice around his plate, not so hungry anymore. "Hopefully in the crossfire."

"This wasn't supposed to happen."

It took a moment, but the whispered words finally got through to Jack. "What?"

White eyes met his for a moment, then Ethan stood and stalked away.

Jack got up but couldn't quite make his feet follow Ethan. "What did you say?"

Just as he had on those nights Jack found him uncommunicative and distant, Ethan stared out of the window, positioned so no one could see him from the outside.

"Do you know something?" Jack couldn't believe it. No way would Ethan keep something like that to himself. He'd listened to Jack agonise over this bloody job, so he knew just how much they needed every bit of information they could get. Jack must have misheard. "Ethan? What the hell did you say?"

"Nothing, Jack. It wasn't important. Just a random thought."

This wasn't happening. Not again.

"Don't lie to me, Ethan."

"Then I won't."

And he didn't, by the simple means of not talking at all. Jack demanded answers and got nothing at all in return, just cold silence and no eye contact. When Jack was angry enough to ignore the no-touching mien, Ethan broke his hold with a swift move and backed away. Jack couldn't get close enough to touch after that.

"For fuck's sake, Ethan," Jack snapped after nearly half an hour of pointless questions. "This psycho is *killing* innocent people."

"Like I do, Jack?"

The first thing Ethan said in all that time, and it brought all of Jack's fears about how closely Ethan's history resembled that of a serial killer.

"Not anymore, right?"

"Not anymore," Ethan murmured, so far away Jack barely heard it and hoped he only imagined the loss and regret he heard in the words.

"Jesus Christ." Jack rubbed his hands over his face. "I'm talking to an assassin about a serial killer. No wonder I don't understand what the hell you're saying."

When he looked at Ethan again, he only found empty eyes and a blank expression. He'd pushed too much, sent Ethan right back into stone-cold killer mode. And right then, Jack wasn't sure he cared.

"Just tell me what you know, Blade." He used the name to make sure Ethan knew he meant business. "Or I walk out and don't come back."

Nothing. No reaction.

Shit. Jack was going to have to make good on his promise. He gave Ethan several more minutes, then couldn't justify wasting any more time.

"Fine. I don't think I've left anything here. See you round, Blade."

Jack turned and walked towards the door. Fuck. Fuck, fuck, fuck. Ethan was letting him go.

"Look at them separately."

Thank Christ. Jack turned slowly. "Pardon?"

Ethan hadn't moved, hadn't changed expression. "The victims. Look at them as two groups, not one." Then he retreated into the main bedroom, closing the door behind him.

Relief evaporated like a drop of water in the desert. Ethan had given him something—albeit vague—but hadn't asked him to stay. Or to come back. Or to forgive him. Did he think he had nothing to feel guilty about? Anger surging, Jack spun on his heel and left. He made sure to slam the heavy steel door behind him.

THIRTY-NINE
AFTER

No one stopped Jack and Ethan from leaving the Office. Ethan had assured Jack taking a strike team would only ensure Adam's death, if he wasn't already dead, and Jack trusted him. They took the stairs down to the garage and found Victoria where they'd left her, Jack's arsenal still in the footwell of the passenger seat. Within moments, they were back on the street.

"Where are we going?" Jack asked.

"I was hoping you'd know."

Jack groaned. "You said you knew."

"I said I may know. It depends on you, though. It was something Two said during one of our . . . discussions. He said you couldn't possibly love me because you hadn't taken me to your special spot."

Stumbling over the L-word, it took Jack a moment to analyse the rest of the sentence. When he did, he frowned. "Special spot? I don't have a special spot. Did he say anything else?"

"Only that you went there to think and cry."

Jack racked his brain. Two had obviously been stalking him over the past several weeks, so where had he gone to think and *cry*? The only time he'd almost cried in public had been at—

"Oh shit. I know where he is."

Ethan settled into his seat, focusing grimly on the street ahead of them. "Good. Which way?"

Jack gave Ethan directions, and within fifteen minutes, they were at Middle Head. Ethan turned the headlights off as they cruised into the carpark. The site was completely dark. The lights had all been broken.

"We all have issues with our eyes," Ethan said softly as they gathered their weapons. "Two's are the worst, though. He wears contacts all the time because he is severely short-sighted. Even corrective lenses don't compensate fully. He's useless with guns and prefers hand to hand, and will always have many knives on him. Don't close with him, Jack. He's far better than I am."

"His night vision?"

"Not good, but he'll have NV gear."

"Of course he will. Right. Let's do this."

Jack led the way, his Austeyr at the ready, Ethan on his six with the Assassin X sniper rifle. Instead of taking the main path, Jack veered them onto a walking track that led into the trees. He knew they probably wouldn't be able to sneak around Two. The man had worked out this place was special to Jack, so he would know that Jack was very familiar with it. Two wouldn't be waiting for them to come down the main path to the fortifications. Perhaps they were walking into a trap, but Ethan assured Jack Two would take every chance he could to play with them first.

The track wound through the trees, making the dark deeper and thicker, the wind in the leaves covering any noises their quarry might make, as well as their own. Swiftly, they came up to the first of the ruins, an old gun emplacement, sunk into the ground to hide it from the enemy on the water. Jack went down into it. Exploring the fort during the day was fun and thrilling. In the middle of the night, looking for a certifiable psycho, was something else entirely. Wishing they'd had time to stop for smokes, Jack moved cautiously, approaching corners warily, scanning every square inch through the NV sight on his rifle. The green hued cement looked eerie in the little green circle, but the space was clear. Even what he could see through the bars on the gate across the entrance to the tunnels.

"We clear?" he hissed to Ethan, who'd stayed on the surface and followed Jack's progress while scanning the area around the emplacement.

"Clear."

Jack pressed up against locked gate and called softly, "Adam?" He had no real expectation of finding Adam here, but he couldn't dismiss it entirely. "Quinn? It's Nishant." Nothing.

They moved on to the next emplacement and repeated the process, with similar results. It took them nearly an hour to reach the outer fort, which was much larger than the individual emplacements, but they cleared it as well.

The longer Two failed to appear, the more Jack wondered if he was wrong. Ethan, too, questioned him with raised brows. There was nowhere else Jack had gone over the past month that was significant, though. And once he'd accepted that, he couldn't deny it anymore.

Moving closer to Ethan, he whispered in his ear, "I think I know where they are."

Ethan's white eyes gleamed in the dark as he studied Jack. "All right. Tell me."

"They're called tiger cages," Jack murmured. "They trained soldiers to resist torture in them."

"Are they otherwise significant to you?"

Fuck. Ethan had always been able to read him like a book. "Yeah. I brought Dad here once, after he got sick. I hoped it would help him remember good times. He found the tiger cages and told me that, when I was lost in India, he imagined I was in a cage, being tortured. And he hoped that I was dead instead."

Ethan gripped his arm, firm and comforting. "I'm sorry. But I think you're right. Two will have worked out that area is painful for you. Tell me where it is, and I'll go alone."

You can't face him alone, Garrote had told him, and now Jack knew she'd been talking about Two, not Ethan. She hadn't been able to best him, and that meant Ethan wouldn't have a great chance, either.

"We go together."

Nodding, Ethan didn't make to move out, though. He just stood there, gazing into Jack's eyes.

Feeling a little anxious, Jack asked, "What?"

"I want you to know, Jack, that I don't care about whatever happened between you and Adam. I lied to you. I should never have done that. If I hadn't, we wouldn't be here now and Adam wouldn't be in danger. I'm sorry, Jack."

"Me too. About Adam—"

"I don't care," Ethan insisted. "I heard you and him talking. I was there for longer than you thought I was."

"Shit." This wasn't going to be good. *Couldn't* be good.

Ethan shifted his rifle to the side and then moved Jack's as well. Stepping closer, he smiled sadly. "I understand, Jack. I do. Considering everything I've done to you, it's reasonable. But I want you to know, before we find Two and possibly not survive, that I . . ." He took a deep breath. "That I . . . Oh, blast it."

And he kissed Jack. On the mouth.

Jack was lucky his Austeyr was on a strap, otherwise it would have hit the cement and announced their presence to all and sundry. Happily, it just banged against his side as shock made him grab at Ethan's arms for stability. Ethan was kissing him. Firm presses of his lips to Jack's, making them tingle, making his entire body shake. Then Ethan parted his lips and touched his tongue to Jack's mouth.

Christ. Jack's knees nearly buckled. His arms snapped around Ethan, holding on for dear life as he opened his mouth. Ethan groaned and all but climbed on him, in him. The kiss deepened exponentially, sending a heady rush of heat through Jack's blood and bones. In amongst it all, his grenade went off, sparking a hotter fire under his ribs. God. Ethan tasted so good. Nothing Jack could particularly name right then, but fuck it was heady and sweet and narcotic all at once. He strived for more of it, stroking his tongue over Ethan's, making them both shudder, so he did it again and again. Ethan whimpered into his mouth and returned it in kind.

It had to end, and it did so as it started, with Ethan simply pressing his lips to Jack's in a series of pulses that echoed through Jack's body. When he pulled back, both of them were panting. Gazes met and locked.

"Just so you know," Ethan whispered. Then he stepped away and righted his rifle. "Shall we get on with this?"

"Sure." Jack got a hold on the Austeyr and indicated the direction they needed to go in.

As Ethan moved out, Jack hesitated. Half wondering if he'd imagined it, he touched his lips. No. They were still warm and sensitive. He licked them and they tasted of Ethan. Before he could blow their approach by yelling wildly, Jack shoved the moment in the filing cabinet, mildly surprised when it went without a fight, then followed the man who'd just kissed him.

They moved fast but carefully. The ground around the path leading to the tiger cages was open, but there was a fringe of scrub and trees on the seaward side. Ethan kept to the path, hoping to draw Two's focus, while Jack moved through the scrub and came up on the cages from the other side. Ethan kept pace with Jack's slower progress, so they reached their destination at the same time.

The cages were subterranean, and the entrance was sunk into the side of a rise. Cement steps led down to another gated entrance. Jack couldn't see into the pit from his position, but as they waited, someone coughed. The sound echoed up from the cages, ragged and hoarse.

Adam.

"Oh shoot," a British voice said from concealment. "There goes the surprise."

Jack was fond of Ethan's accent, but he hated how similar Two sounded. He supposed, having grown up together, it was only to be expected. He didn't have to like it, though.

"You overestimate yourself, brother," Ethan replied. "We knew exactly where you were."

Jack moved forwards while Ethan spoke, using it to cover him.

"Hey?" Adam's voice was rough and dry. "Help!" He barely got any volume on the word.

"Quiet, lover," Two said pleasantly.

"Shut up, Quinn," Ethan added in a disinterested tone. "I'm not here for you. I'm after *him*."

"But—"

"Shut up," both assassins snapped at the same time.

Two barked a laugh, and Jack got a bearing on his position, somewhere further along the path. Probably just on the other side of the ruins beyond the tiger cages.

"I've missed you, One-three. We used to have some fun times together."

"Yes. It was fun when you broke my ribs when I was nine." Ethan moved slowly in the same direction Jack had pinpointed.

Chuckling, Two moved positions. "It taught you to watch your six, didn't it? I made you the man you are, baby brother."

"You made me a monster, Two." Ethan tracked towards Jack's place, then stopped. Head tilting, he lowered his rifle a fraction and said pointedly, "Jack made me a man."

There was a startled exclamation from the cage, Adam likely working out who was here. It was all but drowned out by Two's heated snarl and the rustle of vegetation as he moved fast through the trees. Jack followed the sound, and Ethan did as well, with the Assassin X. He fired into the trees, closer to Jack's position than Two's probable one. Jack froze as bark exploded off a trunk a couple of feet to his right. If he shifted, he could give away his position. And hopefully Ethan's ruse worked. Two wouldn't think Ethan would aim so close to Jack.

"You used to be a better shot." Two was further away from Jack than the noise had indicated. "Maybe you should be a monster again, instead of letting that brownie corrupt you."

Jack bristled. He'd been called that before and it would sting coming from someone other than a psychopath, but he was more incensed about him calling Ethan "corrupted."

Ethan swept his rifle back and forth over the trees. "But the way he *corrupts* me." His voice was husky. "So much better than anything you ever did to me."

"Do you know he's a cheater?" Two asked. "He fucks other men while you're at home waiting for him."

Fuck! Jack should just learn to keep his mouth shut. Turn the other cheek, take the high road. But no, and now his words were snapping at his arse.

Ethan didn't sound upset. "I don't care about that, because it feels so good when he's inside me. When he comes and I feel his hot spunk flood my guts."

Jack gaped. Ethan could barely say "fuck" without blushing. It seemed to be having an effect on Two, as well. The man vented a few growls as Ethan kept talking.

"I let him take me from behind so I can't see him. So I'm vulnerable. I don't care about my six when he's pumping into me. All I know is how deep he—"

Two roared in furious anger and crashed through the trees. The sounds came from different directions. Goddamn it! The man had set up speakers, switching between them to keep them from picking his true location.

About to warn Ethan, a big body hit Jack from behind. He sprawled face-first into the dirt, losing the Austeyr as Two slammed down on top of him. Fuck! The man was heavy and powerful. Jack pulled out every move he had, but he couldn't shake the big man. A long arm locked around his throat and pulled his head back painfully. Spine forced into an arch, Jack struggled for breath against the hard forearm pressing into his throat. Two's knees were clamped on either side of Jack's thighs, holding them together so he couldn't kick or buck.

Two was silent as he swiftly divested Jack of his weapons. He wasn't even breathing hard, and he certainly wasn't losing his cool as Ethan kept up the filthy commentary, unaware of what had happened in the trees.

"Come on, brownie," Two whispered in Jack's ear when he was done. "Let's go see my dear brother."

Dark spots dancing before his eyes, Jack was hauled upright. As Two changed his hold to across Jack's chest and let him breathe, the sharp point of a knife dug into his side under the edge of his armour.

"No fancy moves, soldier boy. I bet you've seen how fast a person can bleed out through a knifed organ. It's one of my favourites because from the outside it doesn't look too bad. They think they've got a chance. Let's go. Easy does it."

They came out of the trees at the top of the stairs leading down to the cages. At the high end of the pit, Ethan trained his rifle on them. Two made sure to put Jack between him and the weapon.

"Shit," Adam moaned from below.

Peering into the dark entrance, Jack could just make out a huddled shape on the other side of the gate. He tried to make a patience gesture, but Two pressed harder with the knife, stalling his attempt to reassure Adam.

"Let him go, Two." Ethan's aim didn't waver. "I'll go with you if you do."

Two laughed, his breath hot on Jack's neck. "You've said that before. Why should I believe you this time?"

After a tense moment, Ethan let the Assassin X's barrel drop until the weapon dangled from one hand at his side. "I mean it this time. You killed Nine. I know how serious you are now."

"She bit me. She knows I don't like to be bit."

Ethan, framed against the paler sky, set the rifle down and placed his empty hands on the railing around the top of the pit. It showed he held no other weapons and would delay a grab for another one. "She deserved it."

Two nodded, the hard plastic of his NV goggles rubbing against Jack's head. "She did. Like One did."

"Just like One did. Leave Jack alone and we'll go home together."

Two hesitated. The knife point pressed in, then relaxed. "You sound honest. All right. We'll go home together. But to stop you from running off again . . ." He thrust his hand forwards.

Bright, sharp pain lanced through Jack's side. He gasped in shock, stunned by the sensation of the blade in his side. It felt both cold and hot, but turned into pure flame when Two twisted it inside him.

"Jack!"

Two laughed and pulled the knife out with a flourish, widening the surface wound. Blood soaked Jack's shirt, and his legs felt weak all of a sudden. A big hand landed on his back and shoved. Jack tumbled down the stairs to the cages. Adam was shouting at him, at Two, at Ethan, his voice a raw counterpart to Ethan's cold and deadly one, promising Two he would die. Even though the pain of the knife wound was like a flare in the dark, Jack felt every stair on the way down, coming to a stop against the bars of the gate. Overhead, the night was alive with gunfire. In an exchange like this, Two's lack of skill didn't matter, so long as he kept the enemy pinned.

"Jesus, fuck, Jesus," Adam rasped out. "Nishant? Tell me you're still with me."

Jack groaned and tried to move into a less painful position. "I'm here."

"Thank fuck." Adam reached through the bars to help him. "Where did he get you?"

"Lower right side, back."

"Not good. He probably got your kidney."

Jack laughed. Or tried to. It hurt too fucking much. "Nah, I think he missed it."

It took Adam a moment, but then he laughed too. A harsh sound, but he clearly remembered when he found the bullet wounds on Jack's back.

"Not funny." Adam sagged against the bars. "What's going on out there?"

"Pitched gunfight. They're fine for a bit. Have you got anything in there with you?"

"Not much. Shackle on my ankle and a bag of stuff *he* left in here before."

"What's in the bag?"

"He told me not to touch it. First rule of being a hostage is to do whatever the crazy guy says, so I haven't touched it."

Jack managed to sit up a bit more. He'd forgotten Adam had been in this situation before, though only for hours, not days. "Pass it out."

Adam shoved the backpack out through the bars, and Jack, trying to ignore the pain every time he moved or breathed, rummaged through it. Spare mags for guns that weren't in the bag, a phone with no battery life, a paper map of the park, a set of NV goggles, and some small canisters with pins in the top. Could be handy.

"He used one of them last night," Adam offered. "It's like a flare or something."

Oh yeah. That would be handy.

The problem was, Jack was in no shape to use them, and they were running out of time. The number of shots was dropping off as the assassins ran low on ammo. In the gaps between, Two was reminiscing about old times, encouraging Ethan to join in.

"Remember that, One-three? You were only sixteen but drove that car like a pro. We'd never had such a fast exfil."

"I remember. You killed that old woman. She wouldn't have told anyone about us, but you killed her all the same."

"It was Ten's idea."

"He's nearly as sick as you."

Two didn't like that and sent three rapid shots in Ethan's direction.

In the pit, Jack tried to get up. Pain whipped through him and he sank back down, his legs shaking.

"Don't move," Adam insisted. "You'll make the wound worse."

"Gotta help Ethan."

Adam muttered to himself about stupidity and heroics, then grumbled, "I guess there wasn't any painkillers in the bag."

Which made Jack think about the medic in the tunnel, and the green whistle.

"Come on, baby brother," Two yelled, his voice moving around the edge of the pit. "Let's agree to disagree and just go home. I promise I'll—"

Ethan fired out of the dark and Two grunted, stumbling as he moved.

"You little shit," Two snarled.

Another shot and Two ducked, coming into Jack's view. He had a gun in his right hand, his left pressed to his side. Teeth bared, he panted and scanned the surrounding darkness for Ethan. He ignored the pit, probably thinking Jack was either too weak from blood loss or dead already. With him so close, Jack had to move silently, not that he was up for fast movements, anyway. A millimetre at a time, Jack reached into the inner pocket of his jacket. The green whistle was still tucked in there, thankfully. He pulled it out and sucked on it deeply.

"Give up," Ethan said from close by. "You're wounded. I'm not. Time to end this."

Two laughed. "You think a couple of grazes is going to slow me down? You've never beaten me. Never."

Jack smiled as the strong anaesthetic rushed through his body. The pain subsided and he felt good. A little light-headed but cool. When he moved, the pain spiked, but he sucked on the whistle and it dulled again, leaving a faint prickly sensation in his side. Keeping the whistle in his mouth, Jack crawled to the stairs, one of the grenades in his hand. It seemed to take forever, but that could have been because he felt floaty and tended to bump into the wall a lot. Eventually, though, Jack was at the top of the stairs, lying on his belly to keep a low profile.

Two had moved while Jack got into place. He was now about a dozen meters away, crouched with his back to the wall of the ruins. As he scanned back and forth, the gleam of his NV goggles caught Jack's eye. Good. He was wearing them. Bad, because he was further away than Jack would have liked.

As Jack moved to throw, Ethan fired three shots, two of them sparking off the cement by Two's head. He flinched and looked sharply off to the right, then grinned. In his hand, he flipped a knife, grip to point, point to grip.

"Last shots," he called out happily. "I've been counting."

"And you even kept your shoes on."

Jack muffled a snicker in his arm. Ethan was so fucking cute.

Two didn't find it as endearing. He sneered. "Just like you, but at least I'm not ashamed of my feet."

Okay. That was it. Jack wasn't putting up with this anymore. He sucked deep on the whistle, and while the anaesthetic rolled through him, he reared up, pulled the pin, and tossed the grenade, shouting, "*Ma petite erreur!*" and hoped like fuck Ethan got the reference.

The grenade went off, an intense flare of orange light, right in front of Two. He screamed as his eyes took the brunt of the explosion, scrambling backwards, trying to claw the goggles off his head at the same time.

Ethan moved through the shifting light of the burning grenade, his steps certain as Two tripped over the uneven ruins. Two could barely see, but Ethan, who'd been blind for some of his formative years, kept his eyes closed as they clashed.

Jack couldn't watch much of the fight as the bright light bit far too hard into his watering eyes. He was blinking away the glare and tears when it happened. Two staggered as he tried to turn, and Ethan, hearing the crunch of boot on dirt, moved lightning fast and Two impaled himself on Ethan's knife. Before his "brother" could move, Ethan took the blade from Two's own hand and rammed it through his throat.

FORTY

BEFORE

Once more, rage drove Jack to Adam. He couldn't believe Ethan had done this to him again. Kept big fucking secrets and then watched Jack scrabble for the pitifully few clues he allowed. Then to just let him walk out! To hear him say he wouldn't be back and do absolutely nothing.

He left the bike in an illegal park and stalked into the Oaks. The concierge had seen him come and go enough lately that he didn't blink as Jack shoved through the door to the stairwell. Blinded by his anger, Jack barely got out of the way of the guy coming down the stairs. They passed on the landing between floors.

"He told me about you."

Startled, Jack stopped and looked down at the man. He stood on the lower steps, most of his body obscured by the next flight above him. All Jack saw was a large hand on the railing, a blue uniform, and a flash of blond hair. Constable Toomey. He wasn't looking at Jack, but as usual stood with his shoulders hunched and his head down. The only "he" they had in common was Adam, the man Toomey had just tossed aside.

As another man who had probably just been tossed aside, Jack wasn't exactly feeling diplomatic. "He told me about you, too."

Toomey grunted. "Do you want to know what he said about you?"

Pretty sure he didn't, Jack made to continue.

"He said you're the only one who's ever made him happy."

Jack stalled. Adam had told his current fuck that a past one was the *only one* who'd made him happy? Christ. Jack might have just fucked up the best thing that had ever happened to him, but at least he knew you didn't say shit like that. Perhaps Toomey had been right to end things with Adam.

"Sorry you had to hear that." Jack took another step up. This was getting beyond awkward. "See you round, Constable."

"Are you going up there to fuck Adam?"

"What the hell? Where do you get off asking that? You kicked him aside, so it's none of your business."

A little growl entered Toomey's voice. "You already have a *boyfriend*. Are you a cheater, Jack?"

The sound of his name from this guy sent an unpleasant shiver down Jack's spine. No. It didn't matter how much of a dickhead Adam had been, he was better off without this man.

"Yeah," Jack muttered and kept going. "I'm going up there to make him *happy*. Good night, Constable."

He didn't wait to see if Toomey stayed or left, didn't really care either way.

"Look, Rich, I can't do this any—" Adam said as he opened the door to Jack's knock, cutting himself off when he saw Jack. "What are you doing here?"

"Having a creepy conversation on the stairs with your ex. He's still your ex, right?"

"Still my ex." Adam stepped back and waved Jack in. "He came around to *explain* why he had to drop me. As if 'you're too controlling' wasn't enough." Returning to the small table, Adam sat and tapped his laptop to bring the screen back to life. "I was just going over the latest forensic reports on the Luntz scene."

"Anything new?"

Adam sipped from a tumbler of amber fluid. "No. This guy is a fucking robot. Did you come over to talk work? Because we did that all day, and frankly, I could use a distraction." He shut the laptop and leaned back in the chair. "Well, a distraction that *isn't* some guy telling me I'm too controlling but, apparently, have no self-control. So I don't want to hear it from you, either."

Robbed of some momentum by Toomey, Jack leaned against the counter in the kitchenette. "Did you really tell him I was the only one who ever made you happy?"

"What? No." But he wouldn't look at Jack as he said it.

Letting that one go through to the keeper, Jack said, "He's not the man I want to talk about, anyway."

"Let me guess. The significant other." Finishing off his drink, Adam said sourly, "Did he hold you up at gunpoint?"

"Jesus, no. I told you, that wasn't his fault. He doesn't always react like that."

"You can't discount the fact that he did, though."

Jack steeled himself. "I don't. And if he'll ever see me again, I'll talk to him about getting help."

Adam stood and came over. "What happened?" The irreverence was gone, leaving him serious and concerned.

"Ethan knows something." It hurt to admit it, but if any good was going to come out of this shit, Jack had to let Adam know. "About the case. About the Judge."

"What? How?"

"Because I've been talking to him about it. All the evidence and the scenes and the victims." Jack continued as Adam backed off, shaking his head in disbelief. "I don't do this shit every day, Adam. I needed to vent to someone, and he's the only person I could talk to. He's not just a normal guy. There are special circumstances. I can't tell you without betraying him, but he has insight. Like you do, but different."

Adam stared at him like he'd just confessed to being the Judge. "And this crazy, *special*, dangerous man can do my job better than me?"

"That's not what I'm saying. I mean, yes, he has this ability to read a person and pick them apart until he knows exactly what's going to fuck them up, but this time, I think he *knows* something."

"He *knows* something," Adam repeated bitterly. "What does he know?"

"I don't know exactly. He went quiet on me and wouldn't tell me anything."

"Because he couldn't control the situation, clearly. You shouldn't push him like that. Who knows what the hell he's going to do?"

"He won't hurt me." Even now, Jack believed it.

"Excuse my selfishness, but I'm more worried about me right now."

Jack grimaced and headed for the door. "I knew this was a mistake. You can't get over the fact I don't want you, so you won't help me."

The door was open and he was halfway out when Adam spoke.

"I'm sorry, Nishant. I haven't had a great evening, in case you couldn't tell. Stay. Tell me what happened, and I'll try to be sympathetic."

Pathetically grateful *this* man had stopped him from walking out, Jack went back in but didn't get far. Sagging against the wall by the door, Jack rubbed his hands over his face. "We'd just got back together. He left after you showed up at my place, said he wasn't safe there. I get it. I do, but he wouldn't let me go to him, either. But last night, he let me in, and now this."

When he opened his eyes, Adam was right in front of him and looking more than concerned. He studied Jack's face for a long while, exposing his own feelings in his eyes. The intent in them hit Jack in his guts, and not in an uncomfortable way. A warm pressure grew in Jack's stomach as Adam's crisp scent surrounded him, permeated him. Sex had been good with this man. Great, even. It could have easily become brilliant, if they'd let it. God, it was more than that, though. Jack hadn't been lying when he told Adam he was a good man. He would be an easy man to be with. Jack wouldn't have to worry about deadly mood swings or big fucking secrets—except his own.

Jack hit that stumbling block and dropped his gaze. Ethan had his issues and they couldn't seem to go long without a monumental hiccup, but he knew Jack. Knew exactly what he did, where he'd come from, and who he was. And Jack's heart was tearing in two thinking that it might all be over.

"Nishant." Adam pressed his hands to Jack's chest, leaning closer. "He needs help, and maybe that help isn't *you*."

"You're just saying that because you want me for yourself."

Lips twitching into a sardonic smile, Adam said, "Probably. But *you* came to *me*."

"To tell you about the case."

"You could have called. If you really wanted him over me, you would have stayed there."

Jack shook his head but couldn't voice the denial. He wanted Ethan and no one else, but couldn't work out how to say it to convince Adam.

"It was so good with us," Adam persisted. "It would be better now. What does he have that I don't? Apart from the obvious."

That sparked enough heat in Jack to form words. "My heart."

"Does he? Have you kissed him on the mouth, Nishant? It's not hard to work out why you don't kiss like that." He curled the hand over Jack's heart into a fist. "You have to love a person before you kiss them. You have to trust them with everything you are before you'll give them that final bit of your soul." Adam slid his hand around the back of Jack's neck, tugged him forwards until their lips were maybe an inch apart. "I know you haven't kissed him. Does he know why, though?"

Jack closed his eyes so he wouldn't have to see everything Adam was laying out right in front of him.

"Nishant. Look at me. Jack."

His first name, unusual from Adam, made him open his eyes. The raw need on Adam's face made his breath catch.

Adam pressed against him, whispered, "Let me," and kissed his jaw.

About to push Adam away, a soft sound caught Jack's attention. He looked and there was Ethan, framed in the open doorway.

Déjà fucking vu.

Ethan's expression shifted through shock, confusion, and hurt before leaving his face entirely. Stone-cold, he said, "Turnabout is fair play, after all," then turned on his heel and left.

Jerking at the sound of Ethan's voice, Adam looked at the now empty doorway. "Was that him?"

"Fuck." Jack shoved him away. He should be running after Ethan, yelling at him that it wasn't what it looked like, but the fight was gone. He felt tired and confused and wanted nothing more than to be alone. "I'm going home. I won't be in tomorrow."

"Nishant?"

Jack left. He trudged down the stairs and got on his bike. Without conscious thought, he ended up at Middle Head. He sat in the outer fortifications, thinking about all the relationships he'd fucked up in his life. His mother had died thinking he didn't care about his heritage, and his niece was growing up believing her uncle didn't care enough to see her. He hadn't tried to meet his sister halfway in so long he barely remembered why she made him so angry. Jack had technically broken up with Ian, but that was because he didn't want to fight for him. Hamish had walked away from him because Jack wanted to fight too much. And now Ethan.

God. Neither of them were capable of a normal relationship, but what they had—this crazy, amazing, strange, and wonderful thing—was right for them. It *had* been working in its own weird way. What they needed to keep it working was help. Ethan had to talk to someone, and Jack had to be honest, to Ethan, and about him. Which meant telling McIntosh and Tan everything. It also meant telling Lewis and Lydia, a thought that made him more nervous than anything else.

Somewhat settled, Jack went home. He wasn't looking forward to seeing his apartment, where he and Ethan had been happy, mostly, but it was the only place he knew he would be alone.

Except that he wasn't.

Detective Connors and four officers waited for him outside his door.

"What now?" Jack asked wearily. "Another death?"

"We just need you to come with us, Mr. Reardon," Connors said sternly.

Finding a shit to give, Jack backed up. "What's this about?"

Two of the officers got behind him, ready in case he decided to run.

"It's just a routine interview. If you wish, you can have a lawyer present, but it's not necessary. Now come along. It will look better if you don't resist."

What the fuck? Hadn't they got what they wanted from the "routine interview" the previous morning? About to resist, Jack froze when Mr. Cesare's door opened.

"Nishant?" He peered out nervously. Shorty wiggled in his arms and growled at the policemen. "Is everything okay?"

Not wanting the sweet man to worry, Jack let his fist relax and displayed his empty hands to the officers. "It's okay, Mr. Cesare. It's just a routine procedure." He turned to Connors. "All right. Let's get this over with."

"Glad you're on board," the detective muttered, then signalled for the officers behind Jack to cuff him. "Jack Reardon, you are under arrest for suspicion of murder."

FORTY-ONE
AFTER

Jack was ambulanced to Royal North Shore Hospital for emergency surgery, but once he was in recovery, he was transferred to the infirmary at the Office. His tendency to talk about anything and everything while under anaesthetic meant they couldn't risk him in an unsecure place. He spent most of the first day in and out of a drug-induced sleep. Sometimes when he woke up, Adam was in the bed next to his, receiving fluids for dehydration and antibiotics for possible infections. Other times, the bed was empty. Lewis was there a couple of times, too. Between naps, Jack learned Adam was undergoing interviews and counselling, while believing he was in an ISO branch.

Then he woke up, feeling more alert, and found Ethan with him. Unlike Lewis, Ethan wasn't sitting in the chair by the bed, but lay on it with Jack. Pressed to Jack's good side, he rested his head on Jack's chest, eyes closed and relaxed. He wasn't in a proper, deep sleep. Jack could tell because he wasn't drooling. Still, the fact Ethan felt secure enough to be even this vulnerable here, of all places, let Jack drift happily back to sleep.

Three days later, after a gentle debriefing and a visit from the Office shrink, Jack was allowed to go home. Folding himself up to get into Victoria hurt, but he dealt with it because it meant he and Ethan could be alone. While Jack recovered, Ethan had been in negotiations with Tan, McIntosh, the minister, and several other higher-ups.

"Tell me now," Jack commanded as Ethan drove them home. "What's the deal?"

Ethan focused on the traffic. "Well, it wasn't a thoroughly enjoyable experience, but we managed to come to an agreement in the end. In short, I have been *retained* by the Office of Counterterrorism and Intelligence. They will pay me to be available upon request. I do have control over what I will and won't do for them, but if they discover I have taken outside work, then it's open season on me."

Jack rested his hand on Ethan's thigh. "And us? What did they have to say about that?"

"Fraternisation *isn't* a fireable offense, thankfully, but we won't be allowed to work together. Ostensibly, I am classified as External Threat Assessment support staff, under Director Tan."

"That smug bastard always gets what he wants."

Ethan chuckled. "He didn't quite rub his hands together in maniacal glee, but it was close." After a deep breath, he added, "And I have a standing appointment with the Office psychiatrist every week."

"That's good." Jack squeezed his thigh.

"It will be," Ethan said firmly.

Home turned out to be the Bathurst Street one. Ethan assured Jack he would eventually be able to return to Leichhardt for more than a visit, but not for a while. Jack didn't care. He could get very used to lounging around the penthouse. He spent several more days recuperating by watching telly, eating everything, and gradually joining Ethan for his now daily tai chi. Ethan stayed close most of the time. Occasionally he would disappear for an hour or two, returning to Jack either smiling or pensive, and there were nights when he wouldn't talk but let Jack hold him. Jack knew the signs of grief well enough to recognise them. He hoped it was all for Nine and not Two, though he doubted it.

They didn't kiss again. Didn't mention it. Didn't even hint about it.

A week after the fight at Middle Head, Jack shooed Ethan out of the bedroom and slowly put on his dress uniform. As each dark-khaki item was settled into place, Jack could feel himself change. Spine straight, shoulders back, head high. These days, he only wore the uniform when he could attend an ANZAC Day service, which he did without fail, unless work commitments prevented it. Today was not ANZAC Day and yet he felt the same pride and confidence he always did when wearing it. How his military career had ended hadn't been great, but his years in service had been some of the best of his life and he still believed the hard work done by the soldiers, sailors, and pilots of the defence force was highly admirable.

Slouch hat the last thing to be put on, Jack took a deep breath and walked out of the bedroom. His back still hurt but he couldn't help but move with the steady, proud tread of the solider he had been.

"Oh, my," Ethan murmured, standing from where he'd been sitting and reading. Book forgotten, he took a couple of steps towards Jack.

"Does it look okay?"

After a long, silent moment, Ethan shook his head and turned away. He picked up the velvet box Jack had set out on the sideboard and opened it gently. Reverently, he lifted out Jack's medals and, with a questioning quirk to one brow, brought them over. Jack nodded and watched as Ethan's nimble fingers secured the medals to his chest.

Leaving one hand resting over the medals, Ethan smiled at him. "Now you look perfect."

Jack let his gaze rove over Ethan. He wore a fitted suit in black, with a black shirt and tie. "So do you. Are you sure you won't come with me?"

"It wouldn't feel right. I'll pick you up after, though."

Understanding Ethan's reticence, Jack went down stairs and found McIntosh already waiting for him. He settled into the passenger seat of her car and she nodded approval of his choice of clothes, then pulled back into the traffic. The drive to Rookwood wasn't a long one, but their progress was stymied by hundreds of cars outside the Rookwood Necropolis. About a third of the traffic jam was police cars. An hour later, Jack and McIntosh stood amongst a sea of police uniforms, waiting for the graveside service to start. Across from them, Senior Sergeant Stephanie Phelp's immediate family sat in several rows of white chairs, the rest of her relatives gathered behind, their contingent almost as large as that of the New South Wales Police.

As the priest began the service, Jack stood at parade rest, as did the police officers around him. The quiet reverence and solidarity of so many proudly worn uniforms was as palpable as the grief. It was a comfort to Jack, a reassuring weight that held his other, more personal feelings down. Here, he was part of a larger whole, not an individual. It gave him the strength to get through this funeral better than he had the last one.

Towards the end, Stephanie's family stood and slowly moved past the lowered coffin, letting handfuls of dirt cascade over the polished surface as they said a teary goodbye. At the end of the line, Adam Quinn waited patiently, and when it was his turn, Jack saw tears falling freely down his pale cheeks. The last of the sod crumbling from his fingers, Adam looked up and met Jack's gaze.

Adam paused, then shook his head, brushed the dirt off his hands and stepped back into the crowd of Stephanie's family.

Afterwards, as the two separate groups gradually mixed in swirls of blue and black, Jack found Adam already heading out of the cemetery.

"I have a plane to catch," Adam muttered as an excuse for not lingering.

"Do you need a ride to the airport?"

"I have an Uber coming." But now that he wasn't moving, Adam couldn't seem to get going again.

Even more so than at any other time, Adam looked defeated. Shoulders slumped, hands listless, eyes bloodshot and shadowed, and he wouldn't meet Jack's gaze. The bold, confident man Jack had come to know, to like, had retreated.

It hurt to see Adam's brightness dulled, to know it was Jack's fault for not working faster. Two had fucked with Adam's head, much as he'd done to Ethan in their childhood—and over the past several weeks. Ethan hadn't spoken directly about it, but Jack could guess at some of what he'd been dealing with behind Jack's back. As much a victim as Adam, Ethan couldn't be blamed for Two's actions and Jack felt sick when he remembered how angry he'd been with his lover. He needed to make up for that, and he needed to make sure Adam was okay, too.

"Adam," Jack started, his throat tight with guilt and sadness.

"Don't," Adam said quickly. "It's not your fault."

Before Jack could get a protest out, Adam shoved his hands in his pockets, focused on a weeping angel bowed over a grave beside them and continued.

"I should have seen it, and I didn't. It's all there now, plain as fucking day and yet, I was blind to it all. The interest, the eagerness to be helpful . . . the manipulation. I was too obsessed—" He cut the words off with a sharp shake of his head. "Too focused on my own selfish wants to see that the devil was right beside me, whispering in my ear the entire time. That's why I said no."

The sudden non-sequitur threw Jack. "What? You said no to what?"

Finally, Adam looked at him, eyebrows raised, a hint of his old, wry self in the expression. "Isn't that why you followed me? To try to talk me into taking the job?"

"What job?"

"The job your boss offered me after subjecting me to two days of *debriefs* and *counselling*," Adam spat. "I might be useless at spotting psychopaths when they're right in front of me, but I'm not stupid, Nishant. Ms. McIntosh wasn't making sure I was okay, or that I wasn't going to spill precious government secrets. She was fucking interviewing me for a job with your . . . your *agency* or whatever the hell you call it."

"ISO," Jack muttered, reeling. McIntosh had offered Adam a job?

Adam rolled his eyes and found strength in anger or frustration to keep walking. "I don't know exactly what department you two work for, but I know it isn't ISO. Don't worry, I won't tell anyone. I just want to forget about it and everything that happened, and you. Don't . . . don't try get to in touch with me. Please."

Stung, Jack watched Adam stalk away. He'd known right from the start there was no chance at a real friendship with Adam, and yet it cut deep to hear it spoken so plainly.

Jack would honour Adam's request, but that didn't mean he wouldn't do whatever he could to make sure the man wasn't hurt further. Which made him wonder about the mysterious job offer. Jack turned and searched for McIntosh in the crowd and found her chatting with Superintendent Julia Dumay. Neither woman looked angry or upset with the other. In fact, they appeared downright chummy. Good relations with domestic law enforcement was vital to the Office's operations, so undoubtedly McIntosh was working to smooth things over with the superintendent. Yet Jack had to wonder if that was all it was. Likewise, the Office already had a contingent of mental health professionals on hand, so why was McIntosh after another psychiatrist?

Or had she been after Adam's profiling skills?

Leaving McIntosh to her politicking, Jack trailed Adam out of the cemetery. He'd hoped for a more positive farewell with the man but making sure he was safe, even from a distance, seemed to be all Jack would be allowed to do.

Moments after Adam got into the back of a silver Commodore, Victoria eased into the space the other car vacated and Jack carefully slid into the passenger seat.

"We're following that car?" Ethan asked even as he palmed the steering wheel into a turn after the Uber.

"Please. Just have to make sure he's okay."

Ethan's hand landed briefly on Jack's thigh, then it was back on the gearstick as they trailed Adam's ride to the airport. They watched from the car as Adam walked into the domestic terminal.

"Do you think he'll be all right?" Ethan asked softly.

"I hope so. He didn't deserve anything that happened to him."

"No one does."

The uneasy memories of how Jack had blamed Ethan for Two's actions surfaced again as he lost sight of Adam. God. He would spend the rest of his life making sure Ethan knew how sorry he was. Which he would start on right now.

"Let's go. It'll be sunset by the time we get there." Jack smiled at Ethan. "It'll be perfect."

Jack was right and by the time they'd reached Middle Head, the sun was going down behind the city, throwing gold and silver rays into the burnt-orange sky. Over the water, clouds reflected hues of purple and pink, giving the ruins of the fortifications a soft sheen of colour as they walked to the very end of the point. Ethan carried a white urn, its edges trimmed with burnished copper. Jack carried another one, white with black trim. He stopped a couple of meters back from the edge, letting Ethan move ahead alone.

In his black on black clothes, his lover cut a stark shape against the blue water and brilliant sky, his head bowed over the ashes of the woman he called Nine. His sister in all but blood.

The Office had offered burial for Nine, but Ethan had refused. Partly because a body meant evidence, but mostly, Jack suspected, because Ethan needed this exact moment. His grief and his guilt needed to set his sister free.

After a long, silent communion with the dead, Ethan gently removed the lid off the urn and tenderly tipped it up. An evening breeze swirled in and caught the falling ashes. The fine grey cloud drifted out over the water of the bay, rising and falling, almost in time with the waves of the ocean, or with the beat of a heart. Then, in an instant, it was gone, scattered by a sudden gust.

Ethan closed the urn and cradled it in his arms. Jack ached for him. He wasn't sure he knew exactly how Ethan felt about Nine, or Two, or any of his 'associates,' but emotions were never clear cut. Nothing was ever pure hate or love, guilt didn't always come from doing the wrong thing, and grief was a pain unique to everyone, understandable, but ultimately fathomless to others. All Jack prayed for was that Ethan got the time he needed, and that Jack could be there for him.

Wordlessly, Ethan held out his hand and Jack went to him, ready to exchange urns. Instead, Ethan wrapped his arm around Jack's neck and pulled him close. Slipping both urns out from between them, Jack returned the one-armed embrace as tight as he could. Ethan shivered, whether from sorrow, or the cool evening breeze, Jack wasn't sure, but he chose to believe it was because Ethan felt his support and devotion—and love.

"Whatever you need," Jack whispered.

Ethan shook and his hand pressed tighter to Jack's back, then he pulled away. Silently, he gave Jack the empty urn and took the full one. About to step away again, Jack was stopped by Ethan's hand on his arm.

"Stay with me."

"Of course." Jack moved behind him, one arm over Ethan's shoulder, hand covering his heart, as if he could protect it from the world.

Leaning back against him, Ethan opened the second urn and, as another breeze eddied by, turned it over. Two's ashes rushed away on the wind, scattering and vanishing almost immediately.

Ethan watched them go, his heart rate speeding up even as his body sagged. "I shouldn't . . . Not after everything he did."

"It's okay," Jack said firmly. "You don't need to excuse your feelings."

After a moment, Ethan held out Two's empty urn and let it drop. The ceramic shattered as it hit rocks far below them. He took Nine's urn back and consigned it to the same fate.

Jack wrapped both arms around Ethan and held him while he trembled.

All the colour had bled out of the sky and water, leaving the world dark grey and silver, by the time Ethan stilled. It was the same predatory mien that had once scared Jack, but he knew it for what it was now—Ethan battling for control over potentially crippling emotions, be it anger, doubt, grief, or even confusion. Jack held on until Ethan won through, slowly relaxing against him.

"What do we do now, Jack?" he asked a while later.

"Anything you want."

Ethan turned around in Jack's arms, studied him for a moment, then removed his sunglasses. His eyes were a little red and shiny, but his smile was soft and warm as he wound his arms around Jack's neck.

"Anything?" There was a teasing hint to Ethan's tone.

Jack tried to keep a straight face, but it was hard when Ethan smiled at him like that. The exploding grenade under his ribs almost went unnoticed amongst the heat and weight of Ethan pressing against him. When Ethan slipped the chin strap for his slouch hat down and tipped it off Jack's head so it hung down his back, he lost the fight and grinned. He knew what was coming, or hoped he did, and there was no fear, no doubt, just a building anticipation that was heady and sweet and little nerve wracking.

"Hmm, but there is so much I want . . ." Ethan's sly words trailed off as Jack ran his fingers through Ethan's hair. His eyes drifted shut and his head tipped back into Jack's hand.

Perfect.

Here, in the same place Ethan had kissed him, Jack finally let go of all the stupid excuses that had held him back and kissed Ethan.

The lips and tongue that shaped Jack's name met his. They moved against his and spoke silently of everything Ethan's mind and heart and soul put into his name. Into every word he used to seduce and enchant and lie. The words he used to tell Jack about his cars and the joy and release of mad speeds. His mouth moved against Jack's and tasted of the way he would purse his lips or grin like an excited kid, and how he would fight the smile but that rogue corner would always win, quirking upwards. Their mouths opened, tongues touched, and breath was shared. Breath that sounded of Ethan's gasps when he asked, begged, pleaded for Jack. That sounded like the warm, comforting presence of him next to Jack in the night, content and secure. Sounds that had come to mean Jack wasn't alone. And by the way Ethan pressed even closer and moaned into Jack's mouth, he felt the same.

Christ. Jack lost himself in the kiss. He teased Ethan's tongue with his own, caught his upper lip for one breath, then two, before diving back in to taste more, to explore and touch and devour and offer himself in any way Ethan wanted, needed, demanded.

Ethan was tentative, letting Jack drive the kiss, his spine arching under the pressure, head tilted back, throat exposed, lips pliable and soft. But at the first hint of Jack pulling back, at the barest lightening of the connection, Ethan surged after him. He clamped one hand to the back of Jack's head and the other closed around the shoulder strap of his Sam Browne Belt where it angled across his chest. Suitably held, Jack was kissed back, hard and thoroughly. Lips, tongue, and teeth opened him up and breath, sounds, and taste left him raw even as he was filled with rushing heat and comforting peace.

Slowly, the passion settled into gentleness, lips sliding soft and sweet over each other, the tips of tongues touching between little, smacking kisses. Ethan's mouth stretched into a smile against Jack's.

"What?" Jack asked, loath to lose contact so the word was muffled by Ethan's lips.

Ethan pressed another lingering kiss to Jack's mouth and then leaned back far enough to focus on him. He blinked almost sleepily, his smile going from smirk to soft. "You taste like coffee."

"Sorry." Jack licked his lips self-consciously, loving the way they still tingled and felt puffy and wet from kissing.

Arms going around Jack's neck again, Ethan whispered, "Don't be. I find that suddenly I don't mind the flavour."

Jack snorted and tightened his arms around his lover. "Crazy bastard."

"Half right, Ja—"

The last of the word was lost inside another kiss.

CODA

When Jack finally released my mouth, I sighed and rested against him, cheek to cheek, chest to chest. His heart was thumping hard, but that was all right, because it matched my own. Two frantic beats, arrhythmic but somehow perfectly metered.

My lips felt bruised and swollen, tenderised by the first, sharp edges of Jack's stubble, and my ribs ached a little from the strength of his hold. For a moment, I felt detached from the sensations, that old defensive mindset I'd learned over the years. If it wasn't my body these things were happening to, then it wasn't me experiencing it. But I didn't even have to struggle back to myself this time. All it took was Jack turning his head and pressing his lips to my neck to solidify me in his arms. There was still a faint quiver in my nerves, perhaps from the thrill of the kisses, or perhaps from letting myself be vulnerable. Either way, I thought I could live with it if it meant all the other sensations—the good ones—stayed as well.

"God," he murmured against my skin. "Why did it take me so long to do that?"

The slowing rate of his heart gave an abrupt kick at his words, and mine followed suit. I had suspected why Jack wouldn't kiss me but it had taken hearing it from someone else to drive it home. It had hurt to accept Jack didn't feel the same way about me as I felt about him, but it had galvanised me into action. I'd ceased trying to convince Two to leave the country and started doing what I could to stop his vendetta. Too late I'd realised just what his overall aim had been.

"I had to earn it." I half hoped Jack wouldn't hear my whisper.

Jack lurched back like I'd stabbed him. "What the fuck?"

He didn't let go, though, hands gripping my waist, fingers digging in like grappling hooks. I slid my hands down from around his neck and rested them on his chest, medals under my right hand. His heart rate had kicked up again.

"Ethan, you didn't have to earn anything. I'm the one who held back. It's all my fault for shoving my head so far up my own arse I couldn't see just how I felt about you."

I shook my head. "I should have told you about Two from the beginning. So much of what happened could have been avoided."

Jack tried to reel me back in, but I pressed against his chest, keeping this small distance from him. I needed a clear head.

"Yeah," he conceded when he worked out I wasn't going to give in. "A lot of stuff wouldn't have happened if you had, but you never know. It could have been worse. We can't know what might have been had you made a different decision. Isn't that what you told me six months ago in Vietnam? You spending time with that sick— with Two might have been the best possible scenario."

My shoulders shook with an involuntary reaction to recalling those times. Two's sweet joy at seeing me, his promises to not hurt me . . . his flares of anger when I tried to convince him to leave, to not go after Jack. To let me be free.

With a soft moan, Jack cupped his hands around my face and leaned in to kiss me. Soft, short touches of compassion and sorrow. "Not for you, though. Jesus, I'm so sorry I got angry about that. It wasn't your fault."

I clutched at his hands. "It was. I made the choice to not tell you."

"Sometimes, there isn't a—"

"There's always a—"

Jack pressed a finger to my lips. "Sometimes, there *isn't* a choice." He drew his finger over my mouth, up my cheek, under my eye and then into my hair. Beautiful brown eyes going soft, he repeated, "I am so sorry you had to deal with him, as a kid and now. Anything you need, just ask me, okay, baby?"

Despite the twisting guilt and flowing doubts, I had to laugh. "Baby?"

Grimacing, Jack muttered, "I was trying something. Clearly it didn't work."

My laughter subsided into a smile as I closed the space between us. "Don't sell yourself short. It may have worked more than you thought it did."

"Yeah?" Jack tried to keep the grin off his face but didn't entirely succeed.

"Yes."

And it was true. The weight of Two and Nine still tugged at my shoulders, like a faint gravity patiently waiting to draw me over the cliff with their ashes. The lap of the water below was Nine's laughter and the sigh of the wind was Two's whispered lies of comfort. Yet, just knowing Jack was here for me, forgiving and willing to help, quietened my doubts and worries.

"Yes." I moved closer until we were almost kissing. "You give me so much, Jack. Warmth and comfort and a secure place to be myself. You give me acceptance and understanding. You've given me the life I always wanted but never thought I could have."

Jack closed his eyes and let out a little sigh, then when he seemed in control again, smirked and said, "You forgot orgasms."

My arms tightened around his neck and I muffled very undignified snorts of laughter in his dress uniform. "And you give me so many chances to laugh."

"At me?"

I soothed Jack's faux-wounded frown with kisses to his brow, cheeks and lips. "At us both."

"That's okay then." His frown turned into a naughty grin and his hands slid down to grasp my arse. "So, about those orgasms . . ."

"You might get to kiss me senseless out here, but I draw the line at public nakedness. Take me home, Jack."

A growling kiss and then Jack was hauling me back through the ruins and to the carpark. I didn't even care that he got behind the wheel and held his hand out for the keys, or that he rarely used two hands to steer because one seemed permanently fixed to my thigh. He did keep his hands to himself in the garage, until we were in the private lift. We kissed and groped frantically all the way to the penthouse. I was breathless, hard and unable to stop touching him by the time we reached the front door. Jack crowded me against the cool steel as I unlocked it, grinding his cock into my buttocks, nipping at the back of my neck. For a very brief moment I cursed my need for so much security, wanting to already be inside so Jack could make me forget everything. But Jack didn't grumble at the few extra seconds it took to open the door. His impatient rutting was an entirely different matter, one I was incredibly sympathetic about.

Then we were inside, the door was locked and it was my turn to shove Jack up against it. He landed with a slight *ouf* and a cute scramble to discard his slouch hat before I pressed him back into the hard surface. Our teeth clacked as we both lunged into the kiss, chuckles mingling and muffled as we tried to correct it, both going one way, then the other, bothersome noses in the way. Jack laughed and, hands on my head, titled me the way he wanted and we managed a long, deep kiss that weakened my knees and had my nerves sparking.

When need for air and sanity made me pull back, Jack shifted his lips to my cheek, jaw, temple, that awful spot behind my ear that made me whimper and claw at him, wanting more, less, anything and everything.

"Jack." I hated sounding whiney but it made Jack growl against my skin, his fingers digging in harder. Wrenching away from his hypnotic mouth, I gave my own threatening rumble. "Bedroom, now." I broke out of his hold and, grabbing the shoulder strap of his belt, hauled him off the door and towards the bedroom.

"Yes, sir," Jack snapped in his best parade ground voice. Then softer, "And now I have a uniform fetish."

"Don't worry, Jack. It won't last long."

"God, I hope not. Popping wood at an ANZAC Day ceremony would *not* be respectful."

Which reminded me. I stopped so fast, Jack bumped into me. Turning, I steadied him, then carefully removed his medals. I had visions of ripping him out of his uniform but that didn't include damaging something so precious to him. Jack stopped breathing as I worked, his chest still under my fingers. Once they were free, he pulled in a deep breath and watched as I put them back into the velvet box he'd brought them back from the Office in. I set it in the middle of the sideboard.

"So we don't forget to return them to your work." Our work, now, but I couldn't quite say it so casually.

Jack reached around me and opened a drawer. "I won't be taking them back there. They live here now." He set the box in the drawer and closed it firmly.

Breath caught in my throat and heart skipping beats, I opened the drawer and carefully removed the box.

"Don't you want them here?" Jack's tone was carefully neutral, his presence at my back going wary.

"I do," I whispered. "Very much, but I want them as secure as they can be."

Our lusty dash became a quick walk, Jack at my side, one hand on my lower back. In the back corner of the bedroom, I crouched and opened the hidden floor safe. Inside it were my Desert Eagles, Jack's preferred H&K USP, a packet of my fake passports and IDs and nearly $100,000 in various currencies. I nestled the velvet box into a corner, closed the safe and stood.

Jack kissed my cheek. "Thank you."

I caught him in a fierce, desperate hold. "Thank you for trusting me."

"Always," he murmured. "Always."

Not that either of us had softened in the meantime, but the urgency of minutes ago was back and suddenly the handy straps of Jack's belt weren't so enticing as I struggled to get him undressed. He laughed and knocked my trembling hands aside to undo the buckles himself. I settled for buttons and zips, then down to my knees to unlace his shoes and wrestle them off. Above, Jack shucked belt, jacket and shirt in one move, then pushed his pants down, lifting one leg at time to let me haul off his shoes and step out of the last of his uniform.

Which left him only in a pair of white, sinfully tight boxer briefs. The material almost glowed against his brown skin, and seemingly made it a deeper, richer shade. I couldn't take my gaze off him, tall and lean and so beautiful as he stood over me, locks of black curls tumbling around his face as he looked down, the prominent bulge of his erection straining at the material of his underwear. Tenderly, he touched my upturned face, fingertips brushing hair back from my forehead, then drifting over my cheekbones, along my jaw, over my slightly parted lips.

The world fell away. I'd never knelt for Jack before and my pulse kicked wildly. I wanted him, so badly, like this, but at the same time, I was in another room, in another time and my instinct was to push him away.

Phantom pain shot through the scars on my back. Flashes of my first target putting me on my knees and opening my mouth . . . The cognac and Sugar hadn't distracted me from the job. The touching and kissing hadn't waivered my conviction to prove I could do this. But that loss—*surrendering*—of control made me forget why I was there, what I had to do. Every instinct they'd whipped into me warred with a natural drive to escape.

"Ethan?"

The word wrenched me out of the past, caught me and held me. It wasn't my name, but I wanted it to be. Wanted to be the person Jack saw when he said the name.

He cupped my cheek and I leaned into it, taking the comfort and support he offered.

"Don't."

That was all he said, but I saw so much more in his eyes, felt it in his hand. Don't worry about it. Don't be scared. Don't let them win. Don't do anything you don't want to.

Carefully, I lowered Jack's briefs, freeing his hard cock and balls. He caught his breath as I curled my fingers around him and stroked gently. This was easy. I enjoyed giving Jack this pleasure, thrilled at the way he bit his lip and groaned. The hair on his thighs tickled my lips as I kissed and tasted him there. The scent of his body, a hint of soap, touch of sweat and rising aroma of arousal, incited a hunger that still startled me upon occasion. No one else had ever had that effect on me. Neither of the women I'd been with, and certainly none of the men. Which may have had more to do with the nature of the person and situation than anything else.

Seduction had never been part of my plan in the desert. All I'd been after was a slight lowering of Jack's guard, enough to let me work out if he was a traitor to the Meta-State or not. My response, physically and emotionally, to his touches and kisses had surprised me. Not even when bedding a target *was* part of my plan did I ever react so viscerally to a male—to anyone. But somehow Jack got past my shields and disinterest in sex. He'd made me feel alive and excited, and aroused just to be in his presence—before he'd even touched me seductively.

Jack was different in so many ways. He always had been, always would be. So it wasn't hard to move my mouth to his cock. I'd very much enjoyed fellating him previously, but I'd relied on my rules to keep me safe, even though I knew Jack wouldn't hurt me. This time, though, I didn't need them as much. Hopefully not at all. I let his heavy shaft rest on my tongue as I sucked, getting familiar with the width and length of him, gently pumping my fist along the rest of his cock. Jack's hands clenched at his sides, twitching like he needed to do something else with them. He'd bit his lips together, eyes scrunched up in frustration. I loved that he was respecting my rules even though I hadn't specified them this time.

Not quite ready to give in completely, I popped my lips off the end of his cock and said, "You can talk, Jack."

He let out an explosive breath. "Oh fuck. Don't stop, but do stop if you want. Jesus!"

I chuckled and nuzzled into his groin. "I don't want to stop. I'll let you know if I don't like anything you do, though."

"Good, good." He looked like he wanted to touch me but still wasn't sure about it.

Not sure either, I took him in my mouth again and teased him with my tongue. His thigh trembled under my hand as I stroked it in time with the pumps of my other fist around his cock. I flicked that sensitive spot under his glans with my tongue and was rewarded with a wordless cry and rush of pre-cum.

"Ethan, God, fuck, yes," Jack gasped when I went back to simple sucking.

After a moment, his hand found my head, soft and tentative. I pushed back into it, letting him know it was all right, as well as needing that familiar touch as a reassurance. He gave it to me, carding his fingers through my hair. I let go of his shaft and cupped his balls as I sank down further on him, closed my lips and sucked back hard. Jack jerked with the action, fingers clenching against my head and letting lose a string of nonsensical sounds that nevertheless felt like the highest praise.

This was me doing these things to Jack. Things that Jack had done to me so many times. I had wondered if everyone felt as wild and silly as I did when Jack sent me crazy with passion. I still wasn't certain I was giving Jack everything he gave me, but I was desperately overjoyed to know I was at least giving some small measure back to him this way. And wanted to give him even more.

Tentatively, I damped a finger with saliva and traced it around Jack's entrance. The response was instantaneous. The cock on my tongue pulsed and the thigh under my hand twitch violently. Thrilled beyond reason, I kept it up until, without thought, my finger was inside him.

"Christ." Jack's back arched sharply and his body simply drew me in ever further. "Shit, Ethan. I'm going to fall over if you keep that up."

I stopped everything and stood. Jack gathered me close and kissed me deeply, sweetly.

"Bed?" I managed between kisses.

"Hell yes. But first . . ." Swiftly but lovingly, Jack stripped me from my suit. When he got to my socks, he looked up questioningly.

I was used to keeping them on now, but that shame had been revealed, so I nodded and he pulled them off. Jack guided me to the bed and lowered himself on top. Bodies aligned and touching, we kissed and I could have been entirely satisfied with that. I hadn't felt anything lacking in our previous physical relationship, but now that we had this, I felt so much more. It was easy to understand Jack's reasons now. The simple pleasure of sharing breath, of trusting someone else with your air and soul, was powerful in a way I'd never recognised before. A little more stimulation and I could come like this.

Jack travelled down my body and returned the blow job enthusiastically. I was a writhing, gibbering mess within moments. I could definitely come like this.

Except that Jack stopped and slithered his way back up to kiss again. I thrust my tongue into his mouth, lapping at the new flavour.

Jack laughed. "Better than the coffee taste?"

"Much." I grabbed his head and kissed him again.

"Ethan," he murmured against my lips some time later.

"Hmm?"

"It's my birthday tomorrow."

"I hadn't forgotten." I was rather looking forward to it, as I had a present I truly hoped he loved.

Jack sat up, straddling my hips and ground his arse down on me. "Well, I was sort of hoping you would give me a present now."

Synapses short circuiting under the intoxicating sensations happening at groin level, I wondered for a moment how I would get the present delivered a day early. Then he moved my hand from his hip to his arse, pressing my fingers into his crack.

"Oh."

Grinning, Jack leaned down and rubbed his nose over mine. "Oh indeed, old chap. What say you?"

My cock was certainly eager but some reticence must have shown on my face. Jack put a soft kiss on my lips and said, "It's okay if you don't want to, but I'd love it and I'll do whatever you want."

"Are you sure?"

"Certain." Jack's smile went wicked. "I'll guide you through it."

My cheeks flamed, which was surprising because I was certain every drop of blood had departed for points south. "I meant, are you well enough?" The last thing I wanted to do was exacerbate the injury he'd suffered because of me.

Jack slid off me and lay prone, head pillowed on his crossed arms. He smiled at me. "I'm fine. I want this so much. Don't want to wait."

I rolled over and rubbed my cock against his hip, one leg sliding across the back of his thighs. Jack humped against the mattress and moaned. The action drew my eye to the white dressing over his wound. It was stark against his brown skin, a pointed reminder of how close I'd come to losing him.

"Jack." I traced my fingers around the edge of the bandage.

"It's okay. Not your fault."

Unable to agree, I distracted myself with his tattoo. I loved it. The black outline and silver shadings that created a simple but effective image of a Saint Thomas Cross. It was such an integral part of Jack, a voluntary scar he'd etched into his skin as a punishment, but one that had become a sign of survival. So like my own scars. Touching his tattoo, kissing his warm skin, soothed me. Wounds healed and the scars they left were testaments of life.

My hand drifted down to his firm, rounded arse.

It reminded me so much of that first time, in the cave. Except this time Jack was giving me dirty, sweet kisses, and our positions were reversed. It was me reaching for the lube and coating my fingers. It was me marvelling at how I pressed a finger into his willing body.

I sat up and watched what I was doing. Up to my last knuckle and still Jack was trying for more. Was this what Jack felt when it was me on the receiving end? This amazing sensation of heat and tightness and, more intoxicating, trust. Jack was letting me into his body, wanting me inside. It was a powerful realisation.

"Jack." I was dizzy with desire.

Hips shifting, Jack demanded, "Another."

I complied, quickly following it with a third finger. Amused by Jack's increasingly desperate sounds, I slicked up my cock and prepared to sink into my lover.

"Wait," Jack gasped.

"Did I do something wrong?"

He pushed up under me. "Get off."

Worried, I did so and Jack flipped over.

He settled back down with a sigh, then hauled me back on top. "Much better. Need to be able to kiss you."

My flagging cock surged with refreshed lust and moments later, with Jack's left calf resting on my shoulder and his right leg bent to keep pressure off his wound, I pressed into him.

Jack may have made a sound, but I lost it in my own moan of exquisite pleasure. It was like nothing I had experienced before. It wasn't just the firm heat bearing down on me, or the strength of the body pushing back against me. It was the lack of artifice between us. Jack *knew* me. Knew everything that mattered about me and to me. I had willingly removed the armour for Jack and in return, he didn't blame me for stripping him of his. I'd never had this sort of openness with anyone, ever.

"Jack," I groaned out around all these revelations.

He hooked a hand around the back of my neck and drew me down for a kiss. A kiss so wet and hungry I forgot everything else and pressed my body to Jack's. I lost control of my actions, letting primal urges drive me. All I knew was a powerful need to be close to Jack, to feel this deep connection forever.

Jack's hands roamed everywhere, from my shoulders down to my arse, fingers digging in, pulling me closer. He traced my ribs and brushed over my nipples, cupped my cheeks and ran his fingers through my hair. The hard line of his cock was a delicious friction between us, smearing our bellies with pre-cum.

Clamping his knees to my sides, Jack wound his legs around me. The shift let my cock plunge deeper and faster and made his spine arch. Jack threw his head back and I lunged for his throat, kissing and nipping, quickly becoming overwhelmed with all the sensations. It was easier when Jack was in charge, but this . . . this was glorious, too. Especially when, at the end of each thrust, Jack started making soft, breathless grunts, sounds that I had to taste, licking them off his lips. I moaned Jack's name over and over because that was the only word I knew right then. It was enough to convey my every feeling though because Jack kissed me each time.

Then it all became too much to comprehend. The world was a fuzzy blur, as if I was in one of my cars, driving so fast everything else just vanished. I balanced on a knife edge, the thinnest margin between control and chaos. One tiny misstep and I'd crash.

"Jack. I can't . . . it's too much . . ." I buried my face in his chest. "I'm going to . . . ngh!" With my last measure of will, I held my orgasm back. I didn't want this to end. Wanted to be here forever.

Ever contrary, Jack said, "Do it." His hands moved down my back and squeezed my arse, pulling me in harder. "Let go for me."

I toppled over and came in a frantic rush, hips totally out of control, pounding hard and deep. Jack held me tight throughout. Sounds echoed around me, maybe they came from Jack, maybe from me. I didn't know, didn't care. All that mattered was the way Jack caught me before I could fly completely apart.

When awareness returned, I was cradled on Jack's chest, familiar, cherished hands gentling down my spine and back again to brush through my sweat-tangled hair.

All the movement was over, the sex complete, and yet I still felt wild and disordered. My limbs trembled and my heart was shaky.

I wasn't sure what was swirling through my mind, be it flying thoughts I couldn't capture or just lingering fireworks. Normally, such chaos sent me into lockdown, a desperate fight to regain control, but right now, I was too wrung out to follow hard won instincts. Too mellow and startled and too much in love.

"Ethan."

Something shifted inside me. Something different to the pound of blood or the way my body heat seemed concentrated in my chest, leaving my limbs weak and my head light. It almost felt like a definite *clink*, like a particularly stubborn lock suddenly giving way to the picks and tumbling open.

Ethan.

Jack had been calling me "Ethan" long enough I had come to feel comfortable hearing it from him. Ethan Blade was never meant to be used as a name. It had simply been how Two, Four and myself had picked up targets. A single "assassin" covering the three of us, to throw off those who compiled information for the John Smith List. I had used it openly on the Valadian job to inspire a reaction in my main target I could use—Valadian trying to control me. Which had hindered my task to get the second target to trust me. I'd managed it, though. To a certain extent.

And here I was, with a target-turner-lover, my entire life shifted ninety degrees off course. No longer an assassin operating outside of the law, but a member of a legitimate, if secret, government agency—which still gave me serious pause when I thought about it. No longer alone but in a real relationship—much more acceptable than the previous fact but still rather startling.

I wanted to be the Ethan Jack saw when he used the name, the Ethan he smiled at and touched softly and kissed. And in the moment Jack said "Ethan" in *that* tone, with *those* feelings behind it, I *was* Ethan.

"Yes," I said, then firmer, "Yes."

"Um, Ethan?"

The name made me feel as warm and content as the arms still around me. "Mm, yes." Then Jack's tone registered through the fog in my head. Pushing myself up I blinked him into focus, suddenly unsure. "Was it all right?"

Jack was beautifully tousled, black curls delightfully disarrayed, lips wet and well-kissed, the brown skin of his neck and shoulders darkened in places by my attentions. Just looking at him made all my worries slink away and hide. Even when Jack furrowed his dark brows and said seriously, "No." Even when he paused for the tiniest, longest, second before adding, "It was perfect."

I gave him a moment to clarify with a "but," and when it didn't happen, my heart soared. "I'm a quick learner."

"Yeah, you are."

A slight shift from Jack alerted me to the fact I was still inside him. Personally, I didn't mind when Jack lingered, but he might not like it as much. I pushed up and sat back on my knees. Jack's legs, locked firmly around my waist, kept us intimately joined. Wondering how to go about extracting myself while appearing suave and experienced, I looked down and the blunt visual of how we were connected sent all the blood that wasn't keeping me semi-hard to my cheeks and neck. It was . . . surprising and intensely arousing. Before I could suggest we start all over, I noticed something else.

"Jack, you didn't come." Clearly I hadn't been good enough.

Jack's teasing "Make me" eased the sudden burst of anxiety before it really got hold and surprised a little laugh out of me.

I was about to move when Jack tightened his hold and kept me exactly where I was. "Stay put and make me come."

Oh. Oh. *Oh.*

Certain I was blushing right down to my sillily elated heart, I boldly took hold of Jack and started stroking him. This was something I knew I could do, had very much enjoyed in the past, but this time, with my cock still buried inside him . . . My gaze found Jack's and was caught by his dark eyes, the way they locked onto me and didn't waver, even when he bit his lip and writhed in that peculiar mix of frustration and pleasure that meant I was doing something right. I could almost believe I was doing everything right when Jack's whole body went rigid and he came.

Feeling Jack tighten around me and pulse with the force of his orgasm nearly made me come a second time, but the stimulation was over too fast. Jack melted into the mattress, a lazily smug smirk curling his lips. I leaned down and kissed him, soft and tender because Jack was mostly unresponsive. The motion let my cock slide out of him, both of us acutely sensitive to the movement.

Prepared, much to Jack's amusement, I cleaned us up with some wet wipes and we snuggled down together.

"I've been thinking," Jack said, tracing patterns on my hip.

"Congratulations. I think you burned out all my synapses."

Jack smiled. "I hope not. I need some answers."

I opened one, wary eye. "Yes?"

"You and Two grew up together, and you trained and worked together. He followed me around Bangkok and took photos with a neural implant. You have a neural implant, don't you."

Oh. We were having *this* conversation right now. Some of the warmth pooling in my chest cooled but I managed a nod.

"When I call you, is that what you use?"

"Yes."

"Okay. And that's how you got the spyware into the Office last year."

"Yes."

Jack absorbed that. "You were never part of a traditional military organisation?"

"No."

"It was all this Cabal."

"Yes."

"And since you're not really Ethan Blade, what do I call you? Paul?"

"Paul St. Clair died a very long time ago. I can't be him any more than I can be Ethan Blade." I rolled over and pushed against Jack's chest, needing to warm up again. "But I know who I want to be. I want to be the Ethan you see. The one whose name you said during sex. I want to be him so badly."

"You are." Jack wrapped his arms around me. "You already are."

I nodded, relieved he believed that. "Happy birthday, Jack."

We fell asleep like that, wound around and through each other. Until something woke me up.

Ping.

ACKNOWLEDGEMENTS

Short and sweet . . . Many, many thanks to Dorothy, Rose and You'll-always-be-Blanche-even-if-you-can't-answer-the-Which-Golden-Girls-Character-Are-You-quiz-right. You know who you are.

~ Sophia

ALSO BY L.J. HAYWARD

M/M Romantic Suspense

Death and the Devil Series
Where Death Meets the Devil, #1
Where Death Meets the Devil: Coda, #1.2
Bargaining with the Devil, #1.4
When the Devil Drives, #1.6
Devil in the Details, #1.8

Urban Fantasy

Night Call Series
Blood Work, #1
Demon Dei, #2
Here Be Dragons, #2.5
Rock Paper Sorcery, #3

ABOUT THE AUTHOR

L.J. Hayward has been telling stories for most of her life. Granted, a good deal of them have been of the tall variety, but who's counting? Parents and teachers notwithstanding, of course. These days, the vast majority of her storytelling has been in an honest attempt to create fun and exciting ways of entertaining others (and making money).

As such, she is still a mad (always provoked!) scientist in a dungeon laboratory (it has no windows—seriously, the zombie apocalypse could be going on outside and she'd have nary a clue) who, on the rare occasions she emerges into the light, does so under extreme protest and with the potential hazard of bursting into flames under the southeast Queensland sun.

Visit L.J. at her website, ljhayward.com; on Twitter, @ljhayward; or on Goodreads, goodreads.com/L.J.Hayward.